Rise of The Witnesses

By Elias Fenic

2nd Edition 2026

ISBN - 979-8-9996103-3-1

Published by Elias Fenic LLC

Austin Texas

All rights reserved. No part of this publication may be reproduced, stored or transmitted in any form or by any means, electronic, mechanical, photocopying, recording, scanning, or otherwise, without written permission from the publisher. It is illegal to copy this book, post it to a website, or distribute it by any other means without permission.

Using this book in whole or in part it to train artificial intelligence is strictly prohibited unless rights to do so are obtained in writing prior to said use. Unauthorized use of this work for the purpose of training Artificial Intelligence will be subject to legal action.

This novel is entirely a work of fiction. The names, characters and incidents portrayed in it are the work of the author's imagination. Any resemblance to actual persons, living or dead, events or localities is entirely coincidental.

DEDICATION

To my wife, Rebecca; without whom, I may never have reached the end of this journey. Your love, support, and influence shaped every page. To my friends and the players of Blight of Divinity, the Dungeons & Dragons game that inspired this story. Your generosity in granting me permission to base this book on your characters and choices made this journey possible. While the book has taken on a life of its own, I am eternally grateful for your contributions. To god and my faith, the source of my strength and talent.

"...Through steel and spell, through blood and flame, the mortal legions took their stand. Still, fire fell, and the dragons wept, as darkness swept across the land..."

—Mahtsarian Hymnal: #101 Edrage's Fall

Table Of Contents

1. The Forbidden Hunt 19
2. Betrayal 33
3. Lillia 57
4. Unveiled Temptation 67
5. The Councilor 81
6. Judgement 93
7. A Chance Encounter 105
8. Dreams 121
9. Reunion 131
10. The Headless Snake 149
11. Prodott's Caravan 167
12. Providence 185
13. Murder and Fortune 203
14. Healing Hope 225
15. Life Seeker 237
16. Shadow Magic 259
17. Fallout 273
18. Moving Forward 281
19. Whispering Shadows 299
20. King of Crows 309
21. Death 319
22. Glossary of The Divine Language 331

Language of The Divine

THE THIRTEEN DOMAINS

 Nehfesh

(Soul)

Ore

(Light)

Loshek

(Shadow)

Tavek

(Desire)

 Mavet

(Death)

Mayeem

(Water)

Muhava

(Nature)

Mishmat

(Dicipline)

 Ebra

(Wrath)

Aish

(Fire)

 Zedecl

(Justice)

Seraah

(Justice)

 Ahava

(Love)

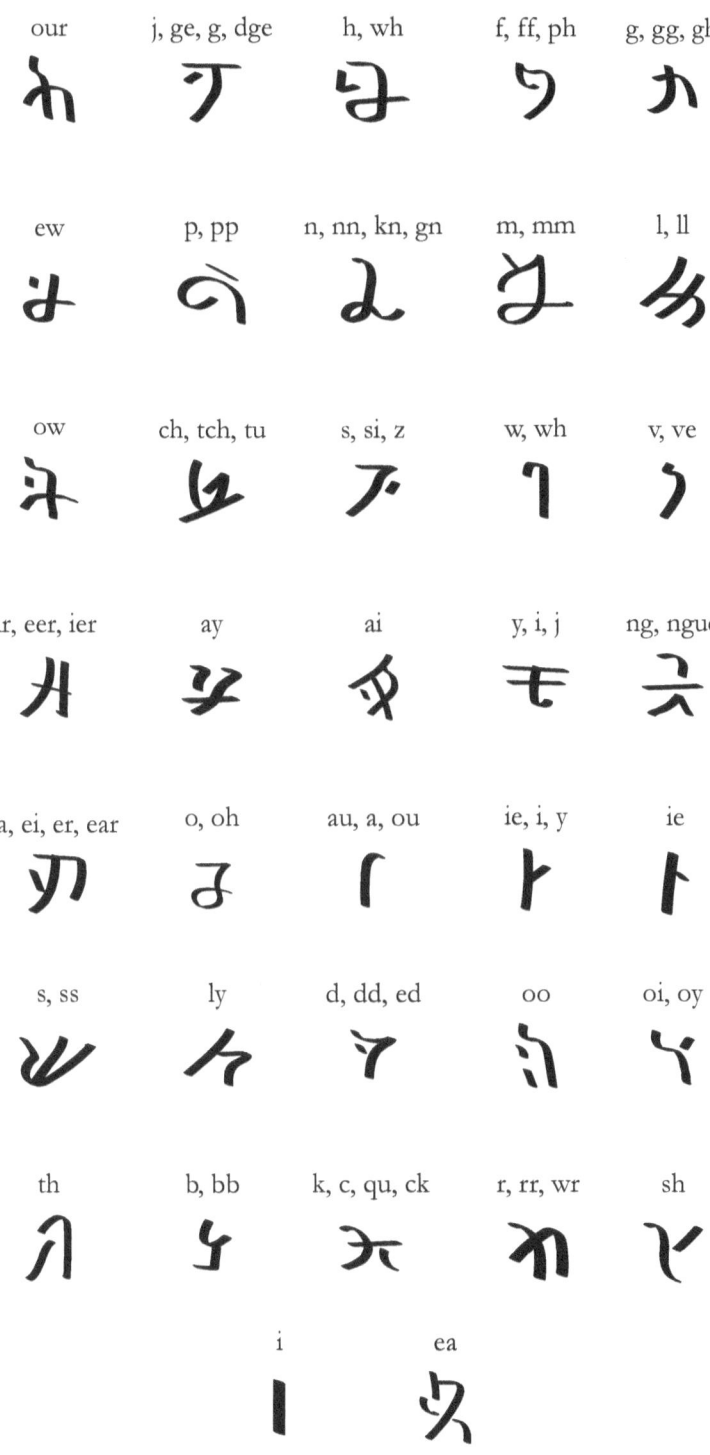

Preface

This book is the culmination of my life's work. The first in a saga set in the world of Albrene, a world I have been building since 2010. Every bit of my passion and dedication went into crafting this story and it holds deep personal meaning for me. The struggles that the characters face reflect some struggles I have been through in my life. They are an exploration of the battles we fight within ourselves and the choices that define us.

This book originates from a home brew Dungeons and Dragons game I wrote, which unfolded in the world of Albrene, a world which lore I have been crafting since 2010. The players of that game were kind enough to grant me permission to use their characters and choices as inspiration for my novel. Since that game, the novel has evolved and taken on a life of its own. Though many of the events of that game are no longer recognizable, I will forever be grateful for their contributions.

I hope this book will immerse you in its world as deeply as it did my players.

"…Beware the whispers in the night, the gilded gifts, the hollow dreams. Erithia's touch is as cold as ice, His promises, but poisoned schemes…"

—Mahtsarian Hymnal: #101 Edrage's Fall

1

The Forbidden Hunt

Warm morning light scattered through the dense tree canopy, dominated by a harmony of red and gold. A crisp fall breeze swept through fallen leaves, permeated with the refreshing aroma of pine.

Ayela leaned against the trunk of a tree, shrouded by a nearby shrub. Gusting wind tossed two dark brown, messy braids over the girl's shoulders. Bruises painted the sides of her neck in contrast to the rosy flush beneath her tawny skin.

Ayela's breath caught at the sound of rustling leaves.

She halted, glancing down. A relieved breath escaped her lips. She gently plucked the corner of her burlap shirt from a dying twig, careful not to snag the threadbare fabric or snap the branch.

She pressed a crudely carved wooden longbow to her chest. Frail leather strips wound around the grip of the bow. They matched the hand-stitched quiver dangling at her hip. A distinctly carved diamond-shaped spiral adorned the top arm of the bow.

Ayela peered around a tree. The trunk easily obscured her thin frame as she squinted to make out the fauna of the forest.

Amidst the sparse undergrowth stood a family of deer of varying size. The spotless fawn being the closest would be the easiest to hit. But it was too small to feed the others. The buck in the center was too large. Ayela admired the many branches on the stag's antlers. Too much of that majestic beast would go to waste. Then, a doe stepped out from behind him. The perfect size.

Ayela balled her empty fist and recoiled from the tree. She released a shaky breath and peeked around the trunk once more. The color drained from her freckled cheeks. The reality of her intended deed plagued her mind. She naively imagined the widowed buck raising his child, encouraged that he would survive.

Ayela took a deep breath and drew back the empty bowstring. Cursing her inexperience, she slipped an arrow from her quiver and crept back out from behind the tree. Methodically, she checked her stance, adjusted foot placement, and stretched chilled fingers along the string. Ayela fired, hissing when the bowstring bit into her skin. The deer scattered. The rustling of bushes and grass drowned out any noise created by the arrow's impact. She lowered her arm and held a hand over her raw wrist.

Ayela listened with bated breath. Her shoulders slumped after minutes of relative silence. She groaned and began a search through the leaf-littered underbrush. Her spirits diminished with each step further into the growth.

Round, deep-brown eyes welled with hopeful glee at the glimpse of blood. "Yes!" Ayela pumped her fist.

She imagined the others would be proud when she returned. Eema, the housemaster, would overlook her sneaking out that morning; the gluttonous witch would take the largest portion after all. Adina would rejoice at the chance to cook with fresh meat.

Her chest burned with anticipation when she discovered more blood, a trail leading through the forest.

Her studies cautioned against approaching prey too soon, since it could bolt away. She needed to wait to be sure it was dead. The search began, though it took only minutes of tracking to locate her kill lying by a tree. If not for the arrow and blood, the doe's dispassionate remains could have embodied a peaceful slumber.

"Not bad." Ayela admired the arrow lodged just behind the deer's shoulder. "Could have been better."

Ayela drew a knife from her belt before turning to the tree towering above her kill. She carved a diamond-shaped spiral, like the one adorning her bow, into the tree. This marked the spot of her first kill. Ayela closed her eyes and stepped back before looking at the carcass, her smile lessened at a twinge of guilt that shadowed the edges of her mind. She'd won the hunt, at the cost of this innocent soul.

She kneeled, pressing her hands together. "Oh, great Musar," Ayela reverently whispered. "I recognize thy dominion over the land and over the animals that feed upon it. I thank thee for thy gift, that it may feed my brothers and sisters and bring them great joy."

Ayela cleaned her kill in silence. She cut the edible portions into steaks, wrapping them in salted skins and storing what she could in pouches by her sides.

"Amen." Ayela nodded when she was done.

"Amen." A rich baritone voice followed, startling Ayela.

She leapt to her feet, knuckles paled by the tightened grip on her knife. Frantic eyes searched through the surrounding trees. "Who's there?" She yelled.

"Apologies. I didn't mean to startle you. I am Bahn." A young man, a few years older than herself, walked out from behind a thick bush. The stranger stopped some distance from her before leaning against a tree. A pillar of rising sunlight haloed his bronze-enriched hazelnut skin and gleamed off his polished, clean-shaven head.

Ayela faltered, her breath caught. "Why are you here?" she remained poised with her bloody knife between them. "Are you following me?"

"I am a sentry for the druid clan that protects this forest."

If that was true, had she wandered into their territory? If she were poaching, he was likely to arrest her. Or worse.

"Don't worry, you have shown respect to Musar in your kill. Though I am no threat to you, these forests aren't safe. I can walk you out, if you'd like."

"I think I'll be okay." Ayela examined Bahn; no visible weapons. He was tall and toned, a thick tanned-leather shirt rested over his chest. Lighter sleeves, frayed at the edge, exposed firm arms folded over his chest. Bahn's skin was rough, blemished by three thin scars aligned under his left eye. Rings of emerald, vine-like markings wound around his neck and arms. The markings of a druid.

"Your pouches seem full. Mind if I take what you can't carry?" Bahn seemed quite respectful, unwilling to approach without Ayela inviting him.

Ayela looked away, fumbling with the ties on one of the cumbersome pouches by her side. "Uh, yeah." She stepped aside, paying close attention to the curious man now walking toward the deer. She pushed past a bush toward the path she'd taken into the forest.

Just before Ayela was out of sight, Bahn called, "Won't you at least tell me your name?"

"Ayela," Ayela uttered, unsure if her timid voice reached him.

"A pleasure to meet you, Ayela." Bahn stood, holding his fist over his chest with a subtle bow. "May the forest protect you on your journey." Still bowed, he looked up with enchanting forest green eyes. "I do hope we meet again."

Ayela spun away from Bahn and hastily retraced her steps taken before dawn. The journey back would be easier with the sun in full bloom. Soon enough, she'd be within the security of the city walls.

Ayela emerged from the forest's edge into the vast fields leading to Hatave. The massive city stretched from below her into the horizon. From her vantage point atop one of the many foothills that hosted Lapid's forest, she could see over the outer walls and into the disorganized Southtown. A haphazardly assembled collection of homes and buildings of varying age and style. Most featured walls of wood and thatch roofs. The Citadel jutted into the sky near the horizon, an anomaly in the city's design. The Citadel was a narrowing, inconceivably tall, cathedral-like tower of gothic design that dominated the city center. Behind her, the twin-peaked Mount Lapid stood. A proud symbol of Hatave.

She began her trek toward the city's entrance. A large gatehouse flanked by two of the many towers that dotted the rain-weathered stone wall. Guards walked at predictable intervals atop the battlements. One level below their route, shadowed by a significant overhang, were small, vertical windows recessed into the wall at strategic intervals. Ayela imagined the archers surely lurking within the shadows of the windows. Each keeping a dutiful watch on the crowd below.

All walks of life waded their way through the crowded city gates, eager to go about their tedious affairs.

"Great," Ayela said, recognizing the long, sandy blonde hair of one of the male guards. She approached the gate, pulling her hood low to conceal her face.

Ayela slunk in with the crowd, careful not to look at the guard. She had almost passed the gate when an armored fist caught her hand.

"Hey." Ayela turned to the taller man's grasp, allowing him to spin her around.

"Sneaking out again?" he said with a chuckle. "You just love pissing Eema off."

Ayela gazed through his open visor, tracing the stubble peppering his sharp jawline and studying the intensity of his gaze. The orange hues of his eyes danced like flames around his elongated pupils. A long red cloak draped over his shoulders and wrapped around his waist. A break-away clasp held it in place. The outline of his well-concealed wings was only just visible beneath its crimson folds and added to his broad silhouette.

"Kiyle," Ayela said, composing herself. "I didn't think your shift started until later." She dropped his hand when she noticed the other guards taking interest.

"One of the gate guards is sick. They assigned me instead. Double shift, lucky me. You successfully pissed the bitch off, by the way. Eema's out for blood this time," he said, "and she has a right to be. You're too young to be wandering the streets before dawn, much less out in the forests."

"And how many times did you sneak out again?" Ayela said in a huff, following Kiyle down the street. "Just cause you don't have to live with her anymore doesn't give you a right to lecture me."

"Yes, but I am trained to defend myself. And you're a…" Kiyle caught himself at Ayela's glare. "I wish you'd let me come with you, at least. Could've helped you bring back more."

"And what would people say then?" Ayela laughed. "I'm sure you get enough grief for befriending a peasant. Not to mention your upbringing. Wouldn't want them thinking we're…" Ayela laughed, cut off by Kiyle's gentle push. She scrunched her burning nose, adjusting to the familiar stench of waste that wafted from the open sewers on either side of the street.

They turned, crossed a rickety bridge spanning a canal, and fished between two wooden buildings. The street they emerged on hosted buildings in poor states of repair, even by Southdown standards. Many had roofs plagued by rot and mold. Some with walls clearly inadequate against the coming winter's chill.

"You know, manage to survive Eema and the Southtown guard isn't too picky. They'd likely accept you once you come of age. What with your archery skills and all. Just promise you'll be careful of Eema."

Ayela pulled away, stepping ahead of him. "You worry too much."

"And you don't worry enough," Kiyle said, trailing after her.

"Any progress with Eema?" Ayela asked, her voice now low, as though afraid the crone would somehow overhear her despite being nowhere in sight.

"No, unfortunately. She's too well…" Kiyle stopped. His eyes narrowed, turning cold as he looked past her.

A poised woman appeared from a large wooden building ahead of them. Her older, porcelain skin contrasted against obsidian-onyx hair. Tattooed amidst her forehead was a single crescent-shape covering the keloid scar of a brand. Her striking eyes fretfully surveyed the masses before pinpointing Ayela.

The young girl stiffened when the woman pointed a harsh finger at her and stormed in their direction.

Kiyle moved past her, hand resting on his sword. "Gods, Kiyle, it's only Adina." Ayela caught his arm and pulled him off balance before pressing her arm into his chest. "She raised us for Mahtsar's sake." Ayela yanked on his arm to emphasize, "What's wrong with you?" She held firm, even as the sides of his cloak ballooned with his partially expanding wings.

"Sorry," Kiyle hissed, arching his back and relaxing his form. Despite the Drakyn's tone, the corners of his mouth lifted slightly. His hand fell from his sword, and the hate in his eyes subsided. "You know how I feel about Moonborns. How my kind feels," Kiyle whispered against her ear.

"Wasn't so long ago that you believed differently." Ayela pulled away, holding her elbow.

"Ayela!" Adina barely stopped her charge before clutching Ayela in an unyielding embrace. "We have been worried sick! Eema's furious," Adina scolded.

Ayela blew a strand of Adina's silky hair out of her mouth. "I've only been gone a few hours. It's not like I went far," Ayela mumbled over the woman's shoulder. She watched Kiyle's red cape ripple in his rush to escape Adina through a wall of merchants without so much as a glance back.

"A few hours!" Adina lurched Ayela back to arm's length. "Young lady, it's been eight hours. You went to the forest, didn't you?" Ayela lowered her gaze at Adina's pointed accusation.

"At least you have something to cook this time."

"Don't change the subject, little doe. You could have been killed."

"How?" Ayela scoffed at the Moonborn, gesturing to the surrounding streets. "Like Eema always says, we're worthless, dirty orphans. Doubt anyone would bother me. And I was careful in the forest!"

Adina shook her head, "you know that's not true." Adina paused, looking at the meat soaking through the pouches.

"Quickly, then. I suppose we should cook that venison before Eema comes back from the markets."

Someone, rather something, caught Ayela's attention. It appeared ill-defined and ghastly gray; a complexion like a decrepit corpse. She squinted through seemingly stagnant pedestrians as a nauseating chill shot through her. Drowned in an icy lake of fear, her throat tightened and her insides stirred. The creature's grisly, sunken, endless black eyes watched her. It floated backward, following ahead of them as a murky apparition. It couldn't be a trick of the eyes; it was too real. A jagged, fanged grin ripped cheek to cheek. She was paralyzed; unable to scream, unable to move

A nameless body of the crowd passed her vision, and it was gone.

"Did you…" Ayela's mind blanked. The moment hidden away, no more than a forgotten nightmare.

"Hm?" Adina hummed.

"Nothing, I," Ayela said, her face scrunched in frustration as she rubbed her temples, "can't remember." She looked back with a blank stare. But shrugged, seeing a pair of children playing. "Guess it wasn't important."

A diminished door marked the entrance to the once majestic home turned orphanage. Now a husk of decayed framework and weathered stone. Years of neglect and weathering storms had devoured the clay walls. A sight all too common in Southtown. Even against the bleak sight, joyous laughter emanated from beyond the soggy mortar. Still, compared to the condition of many a home in Southtown, this was far from the worst shelter.

The door creaked on stubborn hinges when Ayela entered. The piercing noise quelled the cheerful spirit within.

Inside, a flood of musty warmth met Ayela. Various tapestries and furs hung on the raised walls. Several rooms connected to the foyer with low-hanging arches. The faint pattering of children's feet echoed from the next room.

"Aya! You're back!" A little one happily called when they rounded a corner. Two toddling children reached for Ayela with a bouncing hug. Their adorably innocent faces drew an endearing grin from Ayela.

"Did you do it? Actually, do it this time?" said an older child, nudging the first two aside.

"I did," Ayela laughed, tousling the child's hair. He looked up at her with hopeful eyes, "but Adina and I have to cook it first." A wave of gleeful bellowing filtered through the children. The horde hurried down the hall into their one shared room to play before dinner.

Soon, the delectable aroma of freshly chopped herbs and ground spices filled the kitchen. Ayela smiled at the fresh series of playful screams and laughter that pierced the thin walls.

"How does Eema hate listening to them so much?" Ayela chopped the chunks into smaller bits.

"Eema is," Adina started, "Eema. But she has a point about your sneaking out. Southtown is too dangerous for you to be alone, especially late at night."

"Early morning." Ayela said with a forceful chop of the last of the meat before carrying them to Adina to drop in the large pot of broth now boiling over the fire.

Adina comedically scowled. "You assume you're old enough. That people won't bother you. But you're only sixteen." She side-eyed the young girl pointedly. "Anything could have happened to you." Her movements to snatch the venison became more erratic, punctuating her words, "Horrid people, vile, monstrous. You could've been hurt!" The poor woman swiped the spoon from the soup, pointing it at Ayela. "Or worse! It's dark!"

"You're right!" Ayela reactively held up the emptied cutting board. "I'm sorry. I was only thinking about the others."

Adina's stern eyes softened as she lowered the spoon back into the stew.

"I just wanted a special dinner for Kings' Day. She's never, I just, I'm sorry, okay?"

Teeming silence fell between them while the meal continued to boil. Eventually, the succulent scent of home-brewed, hearty stew permeated the air. An influx of the children's laughter deafened when the front door creaked open. The children scurried to hide their toys. All stood out of sight from the front door.

A stout elvish woman entered the kitchen. She carried a basket of fresh vegetables and potatoes. "My, my, Miss Adina. That smells delicious." Her raspy voice mocked sincerity. Ayela shrunk under the elf's sharp glare. She popped her gluttonous lips at the cauldron's contents. "Wherever did you acquire such exquisite ingredients for such a meal on King's Day?" the woman spoke meticulously. She pushed her bangs behind a pointed ear and leaned over the stew with a poorly feigned mask of contempt.

Adina curtsied. "Lady Eema, I stole nothing, if that's what you're implying."

"The nerve. How else if not raided from my storage?" Eema said.

"It's from me," Ayela butted in. "I killed a doe and brought…"

"I forbade you from hunting, little wretch!" The unbound warden blazed through a chink in Eema's façade. "You deliberately disobeyed me!" Her squawks reverberated off the kitchen walls.

Ayela's head hung. She shrank. Her fists clenched at her sides.

"Please, I've already spoken with her..." Adina attempted to intercede.

"Interrupt me again, death witch, and I'll have you on a pyre." Eema threw Adina a silencing palm, her eyes unmoving from the subject of her rage.

Ayela reluctantly met the soul-sucking stare of Eema's frigid eyes. "I wanted us to have an actual meal for King's Day!" Ayela simmered. The old crone had left for the markets that morning and returned with nothing special. Not even the melon she had promised the week prior. "Every kid with a family gets a feast, or a cake, or something special to commemorate the founding of The Union. Why're we always forgotten? We get nothing! If you won't get it for us, why can't we get it for ourselves?"

Braids flung about when she reeled away. Eema's cruel grasp caught Ayela's face. Tapered nails threatened her skin, one digging in under her eye. The side of her head whacked against the wall. A compound of agony and alarm rushed across Ayela's features as she clung desperately to the older woman's arm. "You will not talk to me that way!" spit flew from Eema's pitching lips.

"I just..." Ayela yelped, cut short by Eema's backhand smacking her against the wall. Adina flinched at the crack of knuckles on skin. Her head sank into her shoulders as she withdrew into her cooking.

"I loathe the day your parents abandoned you on my doorstep. You were unwanted then, and you're unwanted now!" Ayela winced, further readying herself for the second blow from Eema's raised hand.

"The stew's ready!" Adina hastily implored.

Eema proudly watched Ayela crumple to the floor. "Adina, your only job is to watch the children. You can't even do that. Disappointing." Eema swiped the spoon from Adina's hands.

Adina stepped back, reassuring Ayela with a concerned glance.

Eema fished around for a good-sized chunk of meat to sample. She savored the rich venison. Her hard eyes softened with a prolonged sigh. "Gamy, but you've made worse." Eema shoved the spoon back to Adina.

"Children! Set the table!" Eema barked. She stormed toward the door, stopping beside Ayela. Eema's gaze searched for something that Ayela refused to give. Ayela never let Eema see her cry. Not because it didn't hurt, but because that's what she wanted, and it was one thing Ayela could deny her. "You are confined to your room till I say otherwise. Except for our requisite trips to the library. Further disobedience will cost you meals." Eema left with a huff, footsteps thundering up the stairs to her suite.

"Are you okay?" Adina kneeled beside Ayela.

Ayela vainly kneaded her aching jaw. She released a trembling breath of relief when Eema's door finally slammed shut above them.

"Let me see," Adina's affectionate whisper nurtured a spark of hope near extinguished.

Memories of her mother's caring grasp siphoned yet more tears. The vague remembrance of fierce copper eyes melted by kindness. The wistful scent of mint-washed, tightly wound dreadlocks that fell over her shoulders. All eclipsed by the night that ended at Eema's doorstep and the stranger that left her there.

Gentle fingers lifted Ayela's chin.

"Nothing's broken at least, but there'll be no hiding this one." Adina smiled. "I'll never understand why you continue to spark her anger."

"Better me than the others," Ayela said before continuing under her breath. "I'll be free of her soon enough."

"Maybe sooner than you think," Adina whispered.

"What do you mean?" Ayela looked at Adina with concern. "I already…"

"I'm working on something. Don't get your hopes up yet, though." Adina stood with an outstretched hand.

Eema's footsteps thudded down the stairs. "You'd best get to your room. Wouldn't want to push Eema further. I'll bring a nice bowl up to you soon."

Though Adina's plans remained a mystery, the hope she gave, however small, was more than she'd had yesterday. And that, she could hold onto.

2

Betrayal

Etch by etch, Ayela painstakingly carved vague floral patterns into the central support beam of her attic. She'd done so each passing night before bed, except this morning; so near to completion, she yearned to finish.

"Hm." Ayela eyed the finishing touches with shadows strewn by swaying candlelight. The clumsy masterpiece was a depiction of various flowers that wound around the beam. Better than any carving she'd done to date. She smiled pridefully, resolving to show Adina when they returned from the library. Ayela considered for a moment that perhaps she could make small trinkets and sell them, as so many do in the markets.

She yawned as the faint rays of pre-dawn light painted the walls from a small window, placed uncomfortably low on the far wall.

"Finally." Ayela lifted a floorboard, tucking her knife into a small cubby alongside her bow and arrows.

Though not a room, and poorly insulated, the attic was at least a private place to herself, even if her bed was half-rotten and buried by Eema's forgotten hoard. She cautiously stood, bending low to keep from hitting her head on the low-hanging ceiling and supporting beams impeding her living space.

She carried the now stub of a candle to a small desk with a broken mirror, and a two-legged splintered stool propped against the wall.

Ayela balanced on the chair and pressed her hand against the splotchy, yellow-black bruise. Just the newest of Eema's marks. "At least it's healing. Just wish it were just three inches to the left." Then she could cover the mark with her hair. Ayela watched herself scowl through the broken mirror, wishing Eema had taken more care with the placing of the bruise. She combed her fingers through her hair, tugging the dense curls over the left side of her head and some to cover her face. "No braids for a while, then."

A soft rap echoed through the room, followed by three more. A signature knock of Adina.

"Morning, Adina, almost ready!"

Eema would simply have barged in like the bull she was.

"Good, I was just coming to get you. The others are downstairs. I believe it'd be wise for you to be there before Eema comes down.

"Of course." Ayela opened the door and headed downstairs.

Ayela grimaced and evaded eye contact with the colorful portrait of the Lady Eema playing nobility with the Chief Judge of The Union. "I'll destroy that awful painting one day."

Adina sighed and urged Ayela forward. "And when you do, Eema will have your head displayed on a pike outside. Right after she makes me punish you."

"Yea." Ayela trailed off, imagining the painting being defaced and burned.

"Cheer up," Adina chimed. "I bet you're looking forward to seeing Lillia."

Ayela smiled, picking up her pace at the thought of the spirited friend that awaited her at the King's Library.

They entered the common room, passing under the well enough maintained stairs leading to Eema's room. The other children sat on a rug settled near the corpse of a fireplace. Several were playing games with one another, though they fell silent when Adina entered.

Adina nodded to the children. Ayela couldn't help but snicker at the grins the five children gave Adina.

Eema huffed, side-scuttling down the stairs with brittle bones and a busty, inordinate ball gown of an obnoxious gold faux silk. "If only they would listen to me so readily." She side-eyed the children's lessened smiles. "Everyone ready to go?" Several hanging chains of jewelry tipped with counterfeit precious gems dangled from her neck and sagging earlobes.

Ayela turned away and stifled a grin. She imagined Eema in a panicked waddle as she fled a thug in broken heels. All for her fake jewels.

"Yes, Lady Eema." Adina bowed.

"Good." Eema approached Ayela, who startled at her outstretched hand. "Remember, you made me do it." Eema lifted Ayela's jaw to examine her eye with a conceited smirk. "Maybe you'll heal before testing me this time. Shall we behave today?"

Ayela pulled away, teeth grinding down any sort of retort that would warrant her staying behind. "Yes, Lady Eema." At least she could re-imagine Eema at the mercy of some crook with a dagger to her throat.

"Good, come then." Eema strutted toward the door. "Single file, Adina, Ayela, you're on foot. No one gets out of the cart."

They dragged beside Eema's wagon. Eema's prized horse parting the sea of commoners with its noble insignia embroidered on a violet throw crafted from a heavy wool.

Many gathered supplies to last the early winter. Others hurried purposefully towards some unknown aim.

An approaching stranger caught Ayela's eye. He subtly nudged Adina before continuing on. Adina opened her hand to find a small, folded square of parchment.

"Adina?" Ayela said, seeing Adina slow, losing pace with the group.

Gray eyes darted across the unfolded paper, reading and rereading what it said. Her breaths were shallow with fear. Or was it panic?

"Adina?" Ayela said again, closer now, with her hand on Adina's shoulder.

"It's nothing." A lie betrayed by the concern written across her brow. Adina thoroughly shredded the paper and allowed the wind to carry the remnants. "We're falling behind." Adina stiffened but urged Ayela forward, taking deep breaths.

Adina fixated on Eema. Solemn contemplation replaced her usual nurturing smile. Her shoulders drooped. What could the note have said to upset her?

Time passed in silence before they reached the oppressing inner wall of Hatave. Dense barbs and spikes riddled the wall around sharp overhangs and arrow slits. The construction proudly displayed the wall's purpose of reminding the lesser Southtowners of their place at the nobility's feet.

Six fully armored guards stood on either side of the arched entrance to Midtown. Two soldiers barred the entrance, questioning everyone who attempted to pass through. Each held halberds adorned with the king's banner. Their group slowed, allowing the guards to inspect them on their way through the gate. Ayela distracted herself by admiring the even brick beneath her feet, striving to appear unsuspicious despite having nothing to hide.

The streets of Midtown, thanks to the wealth and welfare of the upper class, were cleaner and more organized. The farther from the wall, the bigger the houses got. Even the air grew devoid of the ever-present stench of sewer water. And the guard's eyes followed them everywhere. They were anomalies, threats that didn't belong.

"When I leave the orphanage, I'll live in Midtown." Ayela smiled at the idea.

"Creatures of your station will never make it into Midtown. You are simply not of noble blood." Eema jabbed loudly, glancing down at them with a disparaging grin and a dismissive gesture. "You are not wealthy, you have no marketable talents, and you never will. Best to squash those dreams now before they take root." Fire built behind Ayela's eyes.

She turned to Adina, expecting her usual soothing remark, but Adina's gaze was transfixed on the ground. Surely her mood would improve once Eema left them at the library, like it always did. Still, Ayela couldn't shake the anxiety brought on by Adina's peculiar demeanor and the mysterious note.

The Citadel Tower reigned over them, ascending into the clouds. Jagged buttresses and decorative tiers unified the varying shapes of its many levels, with some hanging out over the city in seemingly unsupported architecture. Its black stone and pristine finish marked its anomalous nature. Not much was known of The Citadel's origin, except that Hatave was built around it. A structure that predated even the largest city in The Union.

Maji dueled on its lowest battlements, practicing the magic they learned at The Citadel School. It was a hard life, being conscripted to The Union as a mage in the United Militia. Forced into gladiatorial matches for the entertainment of the masses.

"Things could be worse. At least I don't have magic." Ayela mumbled.

Her friend, Lillia, had shared many horror stories regarding that wretched place over the years. Stories passed to her by her father, whom she owed for protecting her from that life, and from the fate that had taken Lillia's mother.

Soon, they turned off the main street into a courtyard overlooked by The King's Library. A large stone-walled building with colorful windows lining the third floor. Two long blue banners were draped beneath windows, each adorned with a gold starburst around a merchant's balance.

Webs of dead and decaying vines replaced the beautiful flowers that once adorned the library's walls. Ayela imagined the summer birds happily chirping in the fountain marking the courtyard center. Now it was a barren stage set for the harsh winter to come.

Eema strutted ahead of the group, banging the star-shaped knocker on the door and stepping back.

"It will be better." Adina eventually reassured.

"What!" Ayela startled. "You're not about to confront her now?"

"No, not that." Adina motioned for Ayela to get in line with the others. "Don't worry."

Ayela wanted to push for more than just Adina's vague words, but the lock clicked open.

The heavy door groaned, swinging inward to reveal a tall man wearing a long white robe. Streaks of gray disrupted his dark blond hair, matching his short, peppered beard. Standing beside him was a short woman with evenly cut brown hair and a simple white dress. She stood with hands clasped in front of her, the perfect image of patience. "Lady Eema, welcome. Will you be staying with us today?" The man's measured words held steady, hiding any emotion he carried.

"Master Kote." Eema curtsied. "Leaving, I'm afraid I have business with the Chief Judge." Kote's shoulders relaxed momentarily at the news before swiftly returning to a proper stance. "Mary." Kote turned to the woman beside him. "Have the others get the reading room ready. And see that Lillia knows they've arrived."

"Of course." The woman bowed before striding back into the library.

"One thing before I go. That one." Eema pointed a fat, gnarled finger at Ayela. "Is to study bestiaries today. Can't seem to keep her away from the forests. She needs to know their dangers. Maybe throw in a book of crime reports while you're at it too. Rat's been sneaking out at night again."

"If that's what you wish," Master Kote said.

A girl hurried through the foyer. Her hair flowed in golden curls like honey, matching the sweetness of her beaming smile. "Ayela!" Lillia's youthful, elated voice called. She held the skirt of an elaborately decorated dress, swept past her father and Eema, and leapt for Ayela. "Finally, you're here!" Her arms enveloped her friend.

"You just saw me last week." Ayela laughed and returned the hug, only to shove her back after Lillia tickled her side. "Stop it," she spoke firmly, unable to fight the subtle smile at seeing the hint of her mischievous glee.

Lillia caught the dimming of her own smile. The black eye and healing abrasions on Ayela's cheek were all too common and unwarranted. Her eyes flashed back to her friend, determined not to acknowledge the injuries. "That bitch."

"What was that?" Eema sneered.

"Oh, I'm sorry, Ms. Eema." She curtsied. "You must have misheard me. One as magnanimous as yourself surely could never stoop so low as to warrant such a remark." She grinned and tilted her head, fluttering her long lashes. "I was only referring to whoever would harm those so much smaller than themselves. Surely that isn't you."

Eema glared through a downturned gaze as she forced a smile with shoulders drooped. "Just darling, as ever." Her defeated voice betrayed her cracking facade as she turned and left.

"Ahem." Lillia's father cleared his throat.

Lillia started at the sound, noticing him looking down at her from the corner of his eye. Though a tad amused, he still raised a brow expectantly. Reminded of her place in society, Lillia curtsied to Adina. "Lady Adina, it's nice to see you."

The woman looked alarmingly subdued and unlike herself, "It's nice to see you again, as well. Though I can't stay for lessons today." Adina gave Master Kote a farewell nod.

"Why?" Ayela asked, stepping after her.

"I have business at the markets." Adina faltered in her reply. A terrible liar.

"Whatever you need to do," Master Kote said and stepped beside Ayela, holding her in place. "I will take care of the children."

Ayela fiddled her fingers; her chest burned with anxiety. A dozen questions begged to be answered, but Ayela held her tongue.

"Where's she going?" Lillia questioned, daunted by Adina's unsettling demeanor.

Ayela rubbed at the trepidation that climbed up her neck but shook it off. "I wish I knew."

"She'll likely be back before the day's out." Kote motioned for them to follow into the library. "Don't you two be running off after her? I am sure everything is alright."

Ayela watched Adina meld into the crowded street before conceding to follow the others into the library. "What was that book you wanted me to study today?" Ayela asked Lillia, determined to put Adina out of her mind.

"Legends of Mahtsar and Her Lost Verse." Lillia comically blanched, unimpressed. "Why is that so hard to remember?"

Ayela shrugged, barely uttering an, "I don't know?"

"It's one of the Mahtsarian's most revered tomes!" Lillia cried, throwing her hands in the air above her.

"I'm not Mahtsarian!" Ayela echoed her tone of desperation. They soon reached the large door that marked the entrance to the library's atrium. "If the goddess exists, she can't be as powerful as they believe."

"You believe in Musar, Father Earth, don't you? Is it too far-fetched to believe in other gods as well?" Master Kote smiled, pushing open a towering door and guiding the children through and into the library's atrium.

"Mahtsar and Naqam are supposed to stop people like Eema. But no prayer has ever done any good against the likes of them." Ayela muttered under her breath, half-hoping the defiant phrase hadn't been heard.

Once, she had been entranced by the enormity of the library. An array of colors burst from the stained-glass dome window three balconied stories above. They cast patterns on the floor and tables in the center of the cylindrical atrium. The winding wrought-iron staircase at the far side of the room pierced through each floor.

The other children scampered ahead, their voices resonating through the otherwise vacant library. It was strange; The Union's policy for educating the misfortunate. So little attention was given to their daily care, yet the largest library in the city was always emptied for their benefit.

"Eema again?" Master Kote's kind voice kindled a fleeting hope that something would change. Yet, Ayela averted from his scrutinizing gaze. Choosing to rush past him, toward the shelves containing bestiaries. Master Kote's gentle hand caught her shoulder, stopping her flight.

Still, Ayela hung her head. Another report would be little more than an exercise in vanity. "No, Master Kote. I fell." Ayela lamented. None cared to investigate such claims. Not against Eema.

"There's no need to lie, child."

"But there's nothing you can do about it. Nothing anyone can," Ayela's voice quivered. "You've tried. That's more than most. I just need to wait it out. I'll be free of her, eventually."

Kote sighed at her reply before embracing Ayela. "I wish I could do more, if only she weren't so close to the chief judge. I wish I could adopt you."

"I know." Ayela pried herself away with a thankful smile. They'd had this conversation before. He meant every word, but nothing would come of it. Nothing could come of it. "I just don't understand why she keeps us."

"I won't pretend to understand. Some people are just…" Kote sighed. "Perhaps there is no rational explanation for it."

"I thought we were reading Legends of Mahtsar; why the bestiaries?" Lillia sat across from Ayela at a small reading table, looking over the stack of books piled before Ayela.

"Eema's trying to scare me from the forest," Ayela mumbled with a wave of her hand, her gaze unmoving from the text. "Eh. It's not working."

Ayela recited freshly read passages, describing the monstrosities that haunted the forests, some unsightly and malformed; the gods clearly had a sick sense of humor. But with each description, Ayela's grin grew. "Shoot, this just makes me wanna explore it more."

Lillia laughed. "Hey, speaking of adventuring." Her voice dropped to a grave whisper. "When're we going to run away together? "

"Soon, I just…" Ayela started.

"He's already set the wedding, literally a month from now." Lillia's hopeless tone drew Ayela from her reading. "And the sooner you're away from bitchface, the better."

"Just tell your dad you don't wanna get married. Simple."

"I can't! Sweet Ahava!" Lillia rested her chin in her hands. "I just can't."

"Then tell me! Why not?"

Lillia's eyes screamed with words unspoken. Yet her mouth held tight. "Look! I learned a new spell. For our adventure. Tested it and everything." Her voice was small, preoccupied with the blatant desire to change the subject.

"Don't change the subj–" Ayela jumped at the desperate grasp of a hand on her arm.

"We need to leave! Now!" came the hushed, urgent voice of Adina, painful and ragged.

"Wha–?" Ayela looked up over her shoulder and reached for the woman's hand. "What's going on?"

Adina glanced far off to Master Kote, breaking up a fight between two of the younger kids. "We must go." She grabbed Ayela's wrist. "Now!"

Ayela searched Adina's panicked eyes and stubbornly remained seated. "But why? What's wrong?"

"Eema's dead. No doubt they'll blame me." Adina again attempted to tug Ayela to her feet.

"Huh?" Ayela's heart pounded, her eyes darted to Master Kote, who now looked toward them. "Why would they think it was you?" Ayela struggled to keep her voice low. "You'd never…"

"Because whoever did it used dark magic. I'm a Moonborn. They won't ask questions; they'll just kill me. I have to run."

"Are you coming or not? We can start our own orphanage, like we always wanted."

"No, that's, uh, that's not," Ayela's indecisive gaze finally caught Lillia, rigid with silent shock. She couldn't imagine leaving her friend, the children. "That's not right! You've been distant, you're hiding something!"

"We don't have time!" Adina begged, then finally dragged Ayela to her feet.

"No!" Lillia lunged over the tabletop and grabbed Ayela's other hand. Unconcerned about being quiet or disruptive. "Innocent people don't run!"

Adina yanked on Ayela, glaring at Lillia. "You don't get it, you privileged, ignorant child! Moonborn, my brother was ten when the guard executed him, with only an accusation!" Her voice carried emotions long buried. "For me, they would not think twice."

"You never told me that." Ayela studied Adina's mannerisms. Afraid, that was clear. Everything in Ayela urged her to believe Adina.

Master Kote watched the distressed exchange with a concerned expression and approached them.

Adina's frantic eyes darted between Ayela and the intimidating form of the man.

"I worry they'll come for you, too. We must make haste." But Ayela pulled from her grasp. She looked at Lillia, squeezing her friend's hand. She had to decide.

"Please," Lillia whispered, "Something isn't right. Don't go."

Ayela looked between the two most important people in her life. She had known each for about as long as she could remember. But now, caught in such a difficult dilemma…

She felt obligated to see Adina safe. But with Lillia, she had time. The guard wouldn't look for Adina long, especially if they escaped undetected. They'd lose interest in just another Southtown murder. Even if it was a nobleman's jester. She'd avoided the guards often enough, sneaking to and from The King's Library and the southern gates of the city after curfew.

Ayela walked around the table and wrapped her arms around Lillia. "I'll come back for you. I promise."

Lillia's tearful eyes widened, then narrowed. She clenched her hands on Ayela's shoulders and pushed her back. "What? No! Think about this." Lillia tightened her grip, glancing toward Adina, who waited anxiously behind them. "Don't trust her. Something's not right."

"But I trust her." Ayela stopped, choked by a rebellious breath that refused to budge. "I'll be back before the wedding."

Ayela cupped Lillia's cheek, wiping away a tear while holding her own in. Ayela smiled, her gaze lingering on Lillia for a moment. "I'll come back for you."

Ayela reluctantly backed away from Lillia, seeing her friend sorrowfully watching her broke something inside her. Still, she followed Adina's beckons out of the library.

"Ayela! Adina!" Master Kote reached Lillia, only to watch them rush out the door. He loomed over Lillia, stern expression demanding, "What is going on?"

Adina broke into a brisk walk across the courtyard and onto the city street. She darted around pedestrians and surveyed the distant crowds for any threats. Adina stopped when a contingent of guards rounded a corner onto the main street ahead of them. She searched nervously for a way around, pulling Ayela with her into a narrow alley.

"I know about the note." Ayela stopped, pulling her hand away from her as the guards passed the alley. "What did it say?"

Adina's expression soured. "Does it matter?" She paused, taking a deep breath. "Gods, it said someone was going to kill Eema." She turned away to check the streets, "I found her at the markets, dammit; but I didn't stop them, couldn't stop them."

Ayela couldn't catch Adina's eyes, but she heard the defeat in her voice.

"I hadn't even decided if I wanted to."

Ayela's eyes widened at the iniquity implied by Adina's words. Sure, she herself wouldn't have blinked twice at Eema's demise, but it was still surprising to hear the malice in Adina's voice. "How did she die?"

"I went to the markets to find her. She saw me and she was angry; gods know why! Suddenly, she was screaming, then fell. She…died at my feet." Adina grabbed Ayela's wrist, pulling her out into the street. "That's why we have to run."

"But why did someone kill her?" Adina didn't answer as they snaked through the crowds in silence.

"It was a Moonborn." One pedestrian uttered as they passed. "Necromancer, more likely." Another whispered.

Adina picked up the pace before darting into another alley ahead of another group of guards. She stopped, pulling Ayela against the wall as a guard turned, looking down the dark alleyway.

"Gerald! come on. We have to reinforce the south gate." Called another guard as he was about to walk farther into the alley.

"Fuck," Adina breathed when the guard moved on. "Since when do they do their job so well?" They cautiously exited the alley and continued their way toward the gates. A few streets later, they froze at the sound of a trumpet.

"All citizens are to return to their homes." A man on a horse cried after lowering the trumpet. Two guards stood on either side of him, and the crowd halted to listen to the crier's message. "Be on the lookout for a female Moonborn necromancer. Report any sightings to the guards immediately. Do not engage with her, she is to be considered highly dangerous."

"Dammit." Adina pulled the hood of her cloak over her head as they dispersed with the crowd toward the southern gates of Midtown.

"No, no!" Adina slowed when they approached the gate into Southtown. Two rows of guards stood under the arch as they carefully eyed everyone who passed through.

"Why can't I catch a break? They'll no doubt have the other gates locked down too." Adina released a shaky breath and ducked behind a wall near the gate.

Ayela watched Adina peer nervously through the crowd at the gate guards. She closed her eyes and bounced before banging her head against the wall. "No choice. Kakh'tavak, Takhet." Ayela shivered as Adina uttered a spell in shadow speech.

Adina held her hand over her face. "Tathar anee'rek." The air grew stale.

Ayela's hair stood on end. Adina's pupils widened vastly, her irises obscured by inky blackness. To Ayela, her features shifted, her appearance was unknowable. The woman felt down her flushed neck. Her chest heaved, lips parted in a voiceless moan. "Fuck… that feels…" Adina coughed, catching herself stumbling forward. She shook her head before returning her gaze to Ayela.

Adina stared dumbfounded at Ayela for a moment, then hastened through the guarded gate.

Ayela jumped, "Wha–Hey? Hey!" She quickly caught up to Adina and scowled. "What the heck was that?"

"Nothing!" she flustered, composing herself and clearing her throat. "Just a spell, Illusory Disguise. Keep moving." Adina's hands trembled while they returned to a casual stride.

"Daht." Adina ducked into an alley past the gate.

Ayela pulled her hand away from Adina as black mist dripped from her face and her eyes slowly returned to normal.

"Please tell me that wasn't dark magic."

"Only a minor spell, Little Doe." Adina smiled reassuringly, walking further down the alley. "It's just this once, like a tool. There is nothing wrong with using it when you must. I'm still in control, am I not?"

Ayela looked down, conflicted by the stark shift in Adina. "No." She shot back up, "You said; you told me you didn't use dark magic!" Ayela stopped behind Adina, yanking her sleeve. "You lied!"

"I had no choice." Adina sighed.

"You taught me it is never worth the cost!"

"Ayela!" Adina's authoritative tone broke Ayela's grip. "You trust me, don't you? I would never put you in danger. Now come, we're almost there."

The two turned onto the road that led to Adina's front door, though they stalled in pace. Leaned up against the door, waiting expectantly, stood Kiyle. His wings twitched, unfurled behind him in an intimidating display of mottled red and black. His hand rested on the hilt of his sheathed sword.

"You!" He advanced aggressively towards them. "Foul, murderous bitch! I knew it. I always fucking knew it!" pointing an accusatory finger at Adina. "Not even Eema deserved that death. No one should die like that!"

"She didn't do it." Ayela blocked his rampage.

Kiyle halted, stunned by her comment. "What?"

"You know what a monster Eema was. Maybe she didn't deserve it. Still, you can't seriously believe it was Adina." Ayela's voice faltered, questioning the validity of her last statement. "We both know it, right? She would never. This is Adina, our Adina, remember?"

"Ayela, you're confused. She's the only one capable of dark magic, she killed Eema." He took Ayela's wrist, "I need to get you outta here. She's too dangerous."

"Don't touch me!" She yanked her arm out of his protective grasp. "Are you really that power-drunk? That you would forget all she did for us?"

"Ayela!" Kiyle begged.

"No! You can't see past her race! Ever since you let the fools in the city guard get to you, you stopped trusting her. You don't listen to me! You've changed." Ayela shoved his shoulders as she raved, "I've had it! She is barely strong enough to cast a disguise spell, idiot, let alone brutally murder someone!"

"You're blind." Kiyle calmed, his hand reaching for his sword. "Come with me. Now, Ayela."

"I didn't kill her," Adina sounded oddly calm. "That kind of magic requires a pact with Erithia, a pact I'm not foolish enough to make. Please, you could help us. See reason."

"I do see reason." Kiyle's stance deepened. His grip tightened around his sword.

"Don't," Ayela pleaded.

"Think about this, kid." Adina's voice adopted a frigid tone. "If I were a necromancer, do you really think it wise to attack me?" Her head tilted downward, a deathly gaze curtained behind her long dark hair.

Kiyle stepped back, his brows narrowed.

"Please believe me, she didn't do it," Ayela's words verged on empty. She knew Kiyle, knew he wouldn't listen.

And he didn't. Her words fell on deaf ears. In his mind, the only way to save Ayela now was to get help. With a powerful swipe of his wings, Kyle bound down the street. Away from the two of them.

"Great. Of course! Bloody coward, now they'll know where we are." Adina muttered, unlocking the door to her home. "The fuck did I do to deserve this?"

Inside was dark, musty, and cluttered. It was a strong contrast to the clean, well-kept orphanage.

"He won't turn us in," Ayela lied to herself.

"Yes, he will. He's a Draken. It's all his kind know to do."

A spark caught Ayela's attention, jumping from Adina's hand to a nearby lantern. Light flooded the room, casting menacing shadows from the sparse furniture and strewed living space. Ayela stayed by the door to avoid Adina's panicked search for items they would need. She threw a large backpack onto the straw bed along the back wall, then another smaller bag. "This one's for you. I packed it with some of your clothes last week."

"Why did you?" Ayela stopped when Adina glared at her.

"I've been planning to adopt you. I just wasn't old enough." Adina continued packing clothes and food into the bags. "My birthday is next week. I'll be twenty-five. I planned on surprising you."

Ayela's eyes widened. Her mind stopped, staring at the only woman she saw as a mother figure. Her use of dark magic forgotten, Ayela's chest swelled. Had Adina really cared that much? Did she even have the means to care for the two of them? She looked over the run-down apartment.

"Don't look so surprised, little doe." Adina stopped to embrace Ayela. "I've always considered you family. Just wasn't able to make it official. Not until next week. Gods! Why today? Couldn't he have waited just one more fucking week?" She hastened her packing.

"I don't know what to say." Ayela smiled, unfallen tears moistening her eyes. She'd given up hope, resigned to wait out the remaining two years of Eema's hell.

"You don't need to say anything." Adina smiled. "But you could help me pack. If we don't get out fast, it will all have been for naught."

"Sounds like there's..." Ayela startled, turning toward the door where she heard armored footsteps.

Bright light beamed through the cracks in the doorway, and the door shattered in a blinding flash. Ayela fell to her knees at the explosion, covering her head. Sunlight and soldiers filtered into the small basement apartment. The men's hollers were scarcely audible through the ringing in Ayela's ears. Last stood Kiyle in the doorway, his sword drawn.

She didn't even have a chance to feel the betrayal.

One guard lifted a glowing hand toward Adina, but stopped dead, frozen in place. All the guards were still in mid-action.

Ayela's stomach knotted as an ominous shadow filmed over Adina's eyes. Blackness smoldered behind her. The smoke seeped into cracks, forming up her neck towards her face. "Adina?" Ayela stumbled backward, vision flashing between her and Kiyle, who beckoned from the doorway. She stepped back, hitting a wall.

A dark chuckle echoed behind Adina. "The bargain is struck. Seek what is desired," sneered an eager, seductive voice resonating from the smoke before fading distantly. "Always a pleasure."

The pendant around one soldier's neck emitted a flash of white light, then crumbled to the floor in ashes. He stumbled forward, drawing a dagger, and charged Adina.

Adina's pitching shrill sent tremors through the air that threw the guard back. She staggered; her hand wrapped around the guard's dagger buried in her side. Blood dripped from the knife as she pulled it free, grunting aggressively and hurling the icy blade against the floor. Black cinders pulled the wound closed, leaving only a hint of a scar.

Weapons clanked against the floor, and Ayela's spine crawled with worsening dread. A chorus of choked, harsh, piercing cries filled the room. Instinct commanded Ayela to flee, but fear paralyzed her, forced her to watch. Ayela's insides heaved at the smell of rot invading her senses. Her back pressed against the wall as her nails dug into the wooden floor.

The guards clutched and tore at their shriveling, graying skin. The chorus of cracking bones and squelching of muscles tearing fell to a hush.

"What the fuck…" Kiyle stumbled and dropped his sword.

Wisps of white drained from the soldiers' mouths, conjoining into a swirling ball in the center of the room. The corpses' skin bubbled and swelled, sizzling, before bursting in a deluge of black, corrupted viscera.

Ayela finally screamed at the mist of blood that rained at her feet.

A cursed laugh emerged from Adina's dark form. She circled her hands before her, the swirl of white energy mimicking the movement, before darkening into a nearly invisible black cloud.

Kiyle thrust his hand at Ayela, burning eyes pleading for her to grab hold. But leaden tendrils crept around him.

"Run!" He managed before shadows drug him toward the center of the room. They lifted him off the floor and into the ball of dark magic.

Ayela threw herself forward futilely to catch his hand, falling into a gob of molten flesh.

Kiyle's face twisted in agony, mouth gaped by a silent scream, etching itself into her mind. Her eyes welled, vision blurred as she watched his head contort farther than it was ever meant to. In the room's silence, the crack of his snapping neck stabbed through her ears, as clear as clacking swords. His wings fell limp at his sides. It… She dropped his body with a haunting, heavy thud.

His face fell in her direction, morphed by anguish, stuck in terror, and with a stony stare. Dead.

In further torment, her friend's shoulders lurched. An inky mist plunged into his gaping mouth with the sound of a dozen whispers.

Kiyle's bones quivered and creaked, his movements jerked, slowly lifting himself off the ground. His neck crackled gruesomely. Head wrenched this way and that, snapping up till his lifeless eyes found Adina.

Kiyle's revived corpse emitted a deep, rattling groan.

Ayela's breath became fast and shallow. Mentally, she waited for herself to jolt awake from this nightmare. Her wide, bloodshot stare looked down at her bloodied, shaking hands. She looked past her hands at the guards' corrupted remains, and reluctantly back up to Adina and the husk of her lost friend.

"Outside, stand guard. Let no one else in." Adina commanded.

Obediently, as a mindless servant, Kiyel's corpse walked past Ayela without a glance.

"Ayela," Adina's all too calm voice alarmed her.

The dark magic filling the room retreated into the shadows.

Ayela seethed. The reality of deceit and betrayal shown in Adina's gaze; the pure-black eyes of a necromancer.

Ayela leered up at her and panted, "You killed… all of them."

"I had no choice." Adina hung her head, her voice soft and mournful, "Kiyle will get us through the guards."

"That's not Kiyle!" Ayela raged. Her friend was gone.

Adina stepped toward Ayela. Ayela closed her eyes, swiftly forced herself up onto unsteady feet, and stepped back.

"Little Doe, please. You know I could never hurt you."

Ayela opened her eyes but gasped at how abruptly close Adina had gotten. She felt her back hit the wall, avoiding Adina's reaching hand and smacking it away.

Adina recoiled, her hand settling against her chest. She turned, surveying the carnage of the room. "Dammit."

Adina had already planned their escape, and so she remained adamant. It was too late to turn back now. Roughly, she grabbed at the frightened girl's shoulders.

"No!" Ayela thrashed and kicked Adina's shin, making the woman hiss, "Don't touch me!"

Ayela ducked and rushed for the door, but it swung shut, a squirming blackness coating its surface.

Ayela yelped, then quickly pivoted to back away from Adina, keeping her distance. She braced herself as Adina stopped at the door.

Adina roared before punching the door, splintering several pieces of wood. She sighed; a tear fell from her featureless eye. "I trust you'll reconsider. I'll get the others and wait for you." She opened the door, looking at Ayela one last time, "Don't make me come find you." And left, leaving the door ajar behind her.

Ayela waited a moment before sinking to the ground. Her mind attempted to recuperate. Able to recall every scream, every contorted expression, every gruesome sound. She was so convinced Ayela would go with her. The old Adina would have known better. Would have recognized the monster she'd become. What changed? When did it change? Was the old Adina ever even real?

She didn't know how long had passed till, "I'll get the others and wait for you," echoed in her ears.

"Shit!" She shot up and stood, her red, welled-up eyes widened. "Lillia! The kids!"

Ayela stumbled and ran through the door, streets and alleys, ignoring odd looks from strangers.

The horizon burned with the golden glow of sunset. As she trudged against icy gusts and a trickle of snow that ushered in the waning glow of twilight. The blood on her clothes hadn't fully dried. Adina's lies still stung. But she ran anyway. Because Lillia and the children were still hers to protect.

3

Lillia

Lillia glanced at the walls, where shadows of her father's guards lurked. Each guard wore chainmail with hoods that blocked their faces from view. Their firm hands locked on the hilts of their weapons, ready to draw at a moment's notice. They were there to protect her and the children, but try as she might, she couldn't ignore their suffocating presence. She preferred it when they kept out of sight.

Lillia sighed and returned to her book, trying to shake the weight of their watchful, unwavering gaze as she lulled the children to sleep.

As she read, the last child at her side yawned and closed their eyes. Innocently ignorant of the news of Eema and Adina. All nestled in blankets, cushions, and pillows, improvised bedding packed tightly onto the third floor of the library.

With the children asleep, her task was complete. But now the unease lingering in the air only grew. With Ayela missing, and Adina posing a threat, Lillia couldn't quell the knots festering in her gut. Intrusive thoughts and images of the worst-case scenarios for Ayela, possibly dead in a ditch or enslaved by Adina, plagued her mind.

No. Adina wouldn't do that. Lillia had to believe that there was still some semblance of the Adina she'd known left in the necromancer they said she'd become.

Her ears perked at the sound of her father's distant, urgent voice echoing from the floors below. His muddled tone only added to the sense of dread that permeated the air.

Lillia slipped away from the children, carefully closing the gate that blocked the stairs behind her. She took a moment to double check that all the children were still sound asleep before releasing a sigh of relief.

Lillia lifted her dress and hurried down the stairs. If her father had returned, he'd have news of Ayela.

"I wish you would reconsider." Lillia overheard a thickly accented stranger's voice. "Dari—" The man, who was slender and well-dressed, stopped speaking when he noticed Lillia standing at the top of the stairwell.

"Lady Kote, I presume," the man said, bowing to her. "Delighted to make your acquaintance."

Lillia curtsied in reply, bowing to hide her cringe at the man's apathetically feigned greeting. Mistrust played across her face, more so than she would have liked.

The stranger's stiff stance, lavish purple cloak, and ornately polished steel armor signified his position of nobility, yet his deathly white skin and gray irises betrayed him as a Moonborn.

A thick plume of black feathers adorned his collar, blending with his pressed, oily black hair. In place of the cruel Mahstarian brands that dominated Adina's features, were two black crow's feet tattoos under his eyes.

"With all due respect. Reconsider my offer." The man returned his attention to her father. "The children would be much safer under my care."

"My militia is more than enough." Master Kote's poised hand gestured around them. "As well, we have two of the finest citadel magi. With all due respect, your lordship, we have this handled. We have no need of your assassins." He ultimately motioned to the door where two armored guards stood at attention.

"Very well." The Moonborn turned, his cloak gliding behind him as he left. "Have it your way, Ethan."

"A pleasure, as always, Lord Azvrey."

The large entry door creaked closed.

"Dad?" Lillia stepped toward her father.

"Hm?"

"Who was that? I didn't think there were any Moonborn nobles."

"Zethrid Azvrey. A powerful man; not to be trusted." No hint of hesitation, only a vague warning. He turned to her, quick to change subjects. "Are the children asleep?"

She nodded, and he hummed again. They stood silently beside each other. Her gaze searched the floor. "Any word about Ayela?"

"No." Rattled anxiety underlined his soft voice. "But we're sure she's alright."

Lillia's breath stopped, hanging on her father's words.

"We already knew she was following Adina. Guards raided her home, but Adina… She, she only left with one guard. Without Ayela." He placed a gentle hand on her head, stroking her bangs back. "They found a trail of footprints separate from Adina's leading away from the house, but they ran cold. They're looking for Ayela. We will find her." Master Kote smiled. "What worries me is the guard she left with hasn't checked in anywhere. Meaning he's dead or helping her."

"Do you think Adina will come here?"

"No doubt. That's why I've called in all the guards. But she could've been here hours ago. Problem is…" Kote stopped, his gaze fixed on the door. A ruckus came from outside, and the two soldiers standing watch drew their weapons.

"Lillia." Master Kote's authoritative voice called to her, laced with an underlying urgency she had rarely heard. He reached for the sheathed dagger strapped to his hip and moved to place it in his daughter's hand, drawing a rapier from his other side. "Remember your lessons?"

"Huh? Oh, yes, but..." Lillia started.

He stemmed any objections with a soft kiss laid along her hairline. "Go upstairs." He smiled knowingly, something unreadable darkened his expression, yet she understood all the same.

Advancing awareness dawned on them by nothing. Not a sound, but remote stillness. Quiet. The suffocating blanket of suspense weighed on her every nerve. A crashing thud of something heaved against the door, knocking dust from the stone frame above it. The lack of clashing swords denoted they'd gotten through the guard, but how so soon?

Kote scowled at the door as his daughter recoiled at another crashing thud. "Run!" He yelled before joining the guards standing heedful of the door.

Lillia knew not to hesitate, though her heart wished to remain. She ran, crossing the atrium and leaping two steps at a time up the sole winding staircase.

Her father's guard had taken position around the children; swords drawn and shields ready. The children huddled in the center, the eldest was on his knees with arms frantically holding back the youngest of the children. His terror-filled eyes searched Lillia for any explanation. She feigned a reassuring smile, fighting to suppress her own fear for their sake.

"Milady," a guard whispered to Lillia, beckoning her to enter their protective formation. "Quiet now."

Something seeped from the ceiling; darker, blacker, melting down the walls and snuffing out the torchlights with a hissing chorus. The darkness consumed every bookshelf, every column, her world bathed in inky sludge that ran as molten wax.

Lillia's knuckles strained, clutching the hilt of her father's dagger. Still, the darkness crept closer, and whispers enshrouded them.

"Heh, yeah, nope." Lillia tittered, closing her eyes.

Whether her frightened mind was responsible, or it was an effect of the spell, they were illusions. Had to be.

The undulating clamor of battle rang from below. Sounds distorted, muffled by the black viscous barrier. She reached forward, breathing a heavy sigh when she felt the cool metal of the guard's armor beyond her sight.

"Don't move." The guard ordered in a hushed breath.

Her heart stopped when she heard the clang of a sword hitting the tile floor. Then the thud of an armored body. Something wet, dripping.

Lillia forced her mind into silence, sifting through her library of thoughts for the words she needed. She held her hand out in a fist. Her father would forgive her, she had no choice but to defend herself and the children. "Mamana shehl'ore." Lillia cringed at the familiar spasms caused by magic flowing through her. A faint orange glow ignited through her fingers. Lillia sighed, chest quivering in near panic at seeing the slug-like deformations coating her arm race away from the light.

"Living darkness, then." Lillia smiled at the small bubble of light she'd created around her fist. "This is necromancy."

"Liiillia." Adina's drawn-out whisper hissed around her, casting from all directions. "I see you and the children." Lillia's jaw set. Thoughts too numerous to read flooded her mind. "I will leave here with them. Do not fight me. Let me take you to her." Her voice was confident, seductive even, with sinister tones dripping from every note.

Lillia hesitated. Did Adina have Ayela? Had Ayela known? No. No, Ayela wouldn't have gone if she'd known. And the only way Ayela would be with her now. Gods, she couldn't think of that. "No." Lillia breathed when the crash of a guard's armor hitting tile thundered around her. She reached forward again, finding nothing.

Lillia ground her teeth, straining to hold concentration on the spell she'd started.

"Come with me. Ayela will join us later."

Lillia didn't answer. She focused on her hearing, listening for footsteps. Then something tall stepped in front of a waning torchlight just ahead of her.

"Laruthah!" She opened her fist, filling the room with blinding white light. Adina's spell broke as the living darkness retreated into the shadows. The guards lay sleeping in a circle around the children.

Adina screeched, stumbling back with one hand shielding her turned-away face. Steam rose from every surface of her exposed skin. The sickeningly sweet smell of burning meat thickened the air as her flesh reddened, her open hand taking the worst of it.

Lillia held the spell, supporting her arm, already burning with fatigue. She pushed closer, away from the children.

"Dai," Lillia breathed when her fingers fell numb. She stumbled forward, momentarily overcome by the spell's cost.

Adina screamed, charging for Lillia. Her skin blistered, disfiguring her appearance into that of a howling banshee.

Lillia sidestepped, nearly falling. Adina turned, swinging at Lillia. But she ducked under the blow, slicing under Adina's arm with her father's dagger.

"You know magic?" Adina chuckled, an injured arm limp by her side. Inky arterial blood spurted from under her arm. Adina turned, her face cast in shadow. The worst of her burns now leaked black sludge that formed a film over her charred skin. For a moment, her countenance changed, almost back to how Lillia remembered her.

"You don't have to be like them." Adina gestured to the atrium floor, where the clash of swords resumed.

Lillia didn't listen, couldn't listen. She charged again, but Adina vanished in a wisp of smoke.

Adina stood at a distance, the bleeding on her limp arm having slowed. She glared at Lillia. "You were supposed to understand!"

She muttered something under her breath before holding out her burned hand.

Lillia shouted, "Mageen!" And summoned a flash of hot white light, deflecting Adina's spell. Lillia fell to one knee. The surrounding library spun, and her vision blurred. Soot coated the library floor in a perfect arc between them.

A stinging numbness spread up her arms. The strain of excess magic had exacted its toll. As her ability to control the surging power within her waned, she feared being overwhelmed and consumed by Mahtsar's divine energy.

"What's wrong?" Adina mocked in a cooing voice. "Hit your limit already?"

Lillia charged again, but Adina was faster. She grabbed Lillia's arm, wrenching it away and forcing Lillia to drop the knife. Lillia screamed as Adina twisted her arm further, causing a distinct crack, and the rending of flesh as jagged bone pierced her skin.

Adina's swift kick to her stomach cut Lillia's cries short. She doubled over, knees buckling beneath her. Shadows of unconsciousness loomed at the edges of Lillia's vision as Adina held her upright with an iron grip on her broken arm.

Adina's face, already marred by burns, twisted with hatred as her bony fingers closed around Lillia's throat.

"You should give my master a try." She sneered. "His is limitless power." With a fierce grip, she forced Lillia's surrendering form to the ground. Lillia imagined death as a welcome release from the terror and pain she was experiencing. Her thoughts wandered to which of the gods she'd follow in the end. Tears welled at the thought of never again seeing Ayela's smile.

As Lillia's vision faded, she fixed her gaze on Adina, who bore a fleeting expression of remorse. Adina's grip loosened, her mouth twitched and eyes flickered with an inner turmoil, conflict etched across her features. The old Adina once again surfacing, if only for a moment.

A screech of unrestrained frustration echoed through the air as Adina hurled Lillia's head against the ground. "It didn't have to end this way… I'm sorry! Whore brat!!"

A sharp pain shot through her skull as she lay there, disoriented and confused. Dizziness clouded Lillia's vision. Her head pounded, the throbbing obscured the guards who rushed up the stairs and surrounded Adina.

As she lay on the ground, Lillia heard the muffled voices of those around her through the loud ringing in her ears. Despite the disorientation and pain, she struggled to roll onto her side. She watched blearily as Adina stood and glanced from guard to guard.

Adina moved through the encroaching circle. Her raven hair swayed with each turn and weave of her figure. The guards gave chase, their steps quickening as they tried to keep up with her agile movements.

Lillia lay there for a moment, trying to gather her wits, then a firm hand lifted her shoulders, gently sitting her up. Her eyes widened as Adina threw herself backwards through an ornate, colorful stained-glass window. She gasped; her numb, broken arm held tightly to her stomach, pain subdued by the rush of adrenaline.

Lillia lunged free of the man supporting her.

"Milady!"

She ignored the voice, stumbling through the remaining guards crowding the window. Shakily, she followed their horrified gazes down.

Lillia's heart pounded. Her breath grew shallow as she strained to comprehend the unfolding events. Despite the overwhelming fear and panic that threatened to consume her, she couldn't bring herself to look away, compelled by a morbid curiosity that she couldn't shake.

Adina's body of contorted limbs and mangled flesh, laid in a crumpled heap on the street below, settled on the other side of the wall. The snow beneath her stained black with her blood.

Lillia closed her eyes and couldn't help but breathe a sigh of relief as she tried to compose herself. "It's over. It's over, thank the gods," Lillia said in a whisper.

Several sentries rushed and swarmed her corpse with weapons drawn.

Lillia leaned in and peered closer, puzzled by their abrupt alarm.

Her stomach lurched as the corpse's arm twitched. Then moved, dragging through the snow and toward the body. Every bone and joint crinkled and snapped against flesh as they popped into place with each subtle movement. Her maimed form reassembled and rose to its feet in an unnaturally fluid manner.

One guard charged forward, then froze. All the guards around Adina halted mid-action. One by one, they dropped their weapons, shrilling in terror as their skin turned white. Swelling and sloughing off their bones before they fell in a heap of black sludge.

Adina left the carnage behind, limping at first before breaking into a sprint southward, away from the library.

She watched Adina's form disappear into the flurry of white beyond the lanterns' reach. Lillia stepped back from the window, hand over her mouth.

As Lillia closed her eyes, her mind swirled, and her ears rang. She bumped into someone solid. Lillia looked up, relieved to see her father's familiar face. She leaned into him, cradling her throbbing arm.

He embraced her, kissing the top of her head. Lines of blood from an unseen injury stained his sleeve. Still, the comforting firmness of her father's grip returned a stolen sense of security.

A mage in a white robe kneeled before Lillia. His gentle hand glowed with healing magic and moved over her arm as he asked her questions. But she barely registered his words, her mind engrossed with the fear of the necromancer, reaping innocent souls, loose in the city and Ayela, alone in the cold. Her toes curled not from the physical pain, but from the cracks of despair that spread over her very soul. She wasn't broken. Not yet, but she would be if Ayela didn't return.

"Mahtsar, I beg you." Lillia whispered. "Bring her back to me."

4

Unveiled Temptation

Ayela stumbled over the ice-covered cobblestones of the now desolate Southtown streets. Her arms tightly gripped shivering shoulders in a futile fight for warmth. The wind stabbed at her lungs and cut her lips like frozen daggers. Her ears ached, growing numb from the unrelenting wind. The dying light of twilight cast an eerie glow through the storm clouds, blistering snowfall, and once-homespun buildings. Ayela's eyes darted from shadow to shadow, alert for any signs of movement. Her breath came in brief gasps of misty clouds, trying to outrun the encroaching darkness of the bitter winter night.

Numb fingers dug into her arms as Adina's unforgettable, hateful expression burned into Ayela's mind. Master Kote would have caught wind of Adina by now, and would have guards posted in every nook and cranny of the library. Still, Ayela's throat clenched at the thought of Adina seeking revenge on Kote, the children, and Lillia. Lillia knew magic. Would she even pose a chance against Adina, or would Adina kill her just as she had the guards?

Ayela reached to wipe away a falling tear, but stopped and stared at the inky, corrupted blood soaking the sleeves of her dress. She lowered her hand and pressed forward, toward the city center, toward Lillia.

Though, a realization struck her. No matter how much she wanted to, she'd never be let into Midtown, not covered in blood and filth, and in tattered clothing. She'd be arrested just for approaching the gates.

"Oh, Ayela," she complained to herself. "What am I doing?"

Owing to the risk of encountering Adina, getting clothes or washing off at the orphanage was ruled out. That left only using the public bathhouses, but she had no money to afford such a luxury. She sniffled, drawing in a painful breath. It was getting colder. With the year's first snow in full force, she needed shelter more than anything.

Ayela recalled the past weeks with Adina, searching for any sign that she'd changed. But she seemed to find nothing. Not before the note passed to her. What if she had been honest? What if something else killed Eema? She'd mentioned a man, "I should have stopped him," she'd said. But it didn't matter now, now she'd made a pact with Erithia. The Adina she knew was gone. A tear fell from Ayela's eye at picturing Adina's hurt expression. Did she honestly think Ayela would go with her? After witnessing her transformation.

Ayela approached an empty, decrepit building with a half caved-in entrance. The walls, plagued by rot, reeked with the miasma of mold.

Despite its condition, it provided a reprieve from the stiff wind.

Ayela's gaze lingered on the far staircase that led to a pile of snow-covered rubble. She crossed the perilous threshold, brushing away cobwebs from her face and hair.

"Better than nothing," she said, with hands clasped tightly over her shivering shoulders.

She sat against a soggy wall, her eyes falling to scarcely cracked slits. Her freezing arms ached, pressed against her chest.

"Maybe I should have," she groaned and pulled her legs in to trap what little heat she could. She yawned, a false warmth creeping into her extremities. Her head drooped into her knees. "Mahtsar, is there any hope for me?"

Ayela studied the ceiling, hoping that the goddess of light would extend her aid, as in the stories so often preached by the Mahtsarian church.

But that hope was in vain. If Mahtsar existed, the goddess wouldn't care for a nobody like her, who had never uttered a single prayer in her name.

"So, this is how it ends," Ayela huffed, surrendering to the cold.

A biting breeze pierced the threadbare leggings beneath Ayela's dress, jolting her from a shallow slumber. Faint moonlight filtered in through the holes in the ceiling, spreading sinister shadows along the floor.

Ayela groaned, prying open her frozen eyelashes with a faint sigh of wonder. "I'm not dead?" she whispered, and felt at her frosted clothing and chilled skin. Ayela groaned, frost sloughing off her shoulders as she stretched. Her arms were stiff, but somehow not frozen. Perhaps some deity had protected her from the cold after all.

Sighing, she stepped out into the frosty night. The indifferent stars gazed down through a now cloudless sky, as if in silent tribute to the magical transformation below. Freshly fallen snow shimmered in the starlight, layering the city in a blanket of sparkling powder that seemed almost too wondrous to be real.

"Makes almost freezing to death worth it." She whispered with a faint hint of a smile. Another cool breeze stung Ayela's windburned cheeks. She rubbed her shoulders vainly for warmth before hurriedly retreating into her shelter. "Never mind."

A homely radiance slowly grew inside the old structure, as though an unseen fire burned somewhere within. In the center of the room sat a neatly folded, simple wool blanket.

She glanced around once more. "Hello?" Ayela called out, but found no one.

Ayela approached the blanket with a sense of intrigue, nudging it with her foot before picking it up. Her fingers felt the soft and plush material, as though crafted from the finest, most otherworldly fabrics. It was warm, as though it had been sitting by a fire. Ayela adorned herself in the ample, endless folds of the blanket and audibly sighed into it. Ethereal warmth washed over her as she slumped against the wall, soothed to sleep by this newfound comfort.

Ayela jolted awake, drenched in a chilling sweat, when a deafening creak pierced the silence. Still encased in the mysterious blanket, she searched the dimly lit room.

Her heart stuttered, breath catching in her throat as she noticed something that surely didn't belong. A lithe, monolithic figure lurked in the shadowed corner of the room. It leered at her, languidly drifting closer.

Adrenaline rushed through her. She fumbled onto her feet and readied herself. Her hand rested on her hip, where she typically stored a small dagger; a dagger she'd left at the orphanage.

"Now, Ayela, my dear, no need for that," the figure purred enigmatically. Sinister sweetness underlined their voice, causing the hairs on her neck to stand on end. She winced, recognizing the voice. The same that had emerged from the dark mist that lurked behind Adina.

"Erithia," Ayela choked out.

Her dreary surroundings misted into a lush spring garden. The damp wall against her back bloomed into the trunk of a regal tree. Above her, a cluster of vibrant red pomegranates dangled tantalizingly, just out of reach.

Erithia removed the hood of their silky black cloak. Complex gold floral designs of indiscernible depth adorned its glossy folds. Intricate, thin markings aligned with their smooth cheekbones and chiseled jawline. Delicate yet resolute, their sharp features were akin more to finely sculpted art than human.

Ayela stood before the deific being. Her confidence waned, and a peculiar sense of meekness weighed upon her as she took a step back. The haunting black eyes of the deity, shimmering with silver irises, bore into her with a mocking gaze. A foreboding strain tightened inside her chest and muscles, sealing her in place.

"Oh, no, darling. Surprised?" They cooed tunefully, a sly grin spreading at observing Ayela's unease. "You should feel privileged. I'm rarely one to stroll these earthly realms, let alone lend a hand. Especially to someone like yourself, even with it being part of another's pact. You really should thank dear Adina. But charmed, really, to see you again, Ayela."

"I don't want your help." She pulled the blanket tighter around her.

"Is that so?" Erithia inquired. He made a soft tutting sound, gracefully sauntering along a dense strawberry bush tangled over a white garden fence. The fabric of their clothes swayed behind them like wisps of smoke. With a gentle touch, black manicured nails caressed the lush leaves. Strawberries grew and ripened, following in response to the elegant gesture. "Though you find solace in my gift?" They plucked one of the brightest fruits, scrutinizing it meticulously, only to watch it decay and crumble in their fingers. "So impetuous. Of course, you're welcome, by the way."

"I…" Ayela faltered, the implications of accepting such a gift dawning on her. Her grip on the quilt reluctantly loosened, fighting her instinct to shield herself from the cold.

"Where'd you think it came from?" Erithia purred, tilting their head. "I know you too well, Ayela. You'd never stoop so low as to strike such a trivial deal with someone like me." A sinister cackle echoed. "Oh no, you always need a little more… persuasion."

Cherished memories of listening to Adina's cautionary tales of Erithia's temptations surfaced. Ayela glowered at him in disgust, taking another tense step back.

"Up yours! Like I'd ever…" Ayela's voice trailed off at the sound of youthful laughter.

A child from Eema's orphanage zoomed between them. Behind the running toddler trailed a pathway of gold. Ayela traced the path that wound through a luscious landscape and up to a grand orphanage.

In awe, Ayela trailed toward the mystical white stone structure adorned with intricate columns and abundant windows. Before her stood a pair of majestic mahogany doors. Her heart brimmed with anticipation as she knocked. Ayela smiled when the doors swung open on balanced hinges, welcoming her in.

Tall ceilings of gothic grandeur ascended to dizzying heights. Obsidian chandeliers hung from the ceiling. Each was garnished with twinkling candles that mirrored on the marble floor beneath, illuminating the room in an illustrious glow.

Amidst a throng of gleeful children, stood Adina. Her face filled with radiant joy. The black eyes of a necromancer were barely visible through her genuine smile.

"Just utter the word and all of this…" They gestured to the grand room filled with laughter, "…can be your reality." Erithia's eloquent voice whispered hypnotically into her ear. "A sanctuary for the forsaken, unloved children of your world." The God of

Death and Desire circled Ayela, hand conducting the symphonic intricacies of the luxurious interior. "An architectural marvel! All sprung from your imagination. A haven, where you and dear Adina can offer the nurturing care they yearn for, the affection Eema so cruelly denied you." Erithia prowled closer to Ayela as a predator closing on its prey.

"I... I can't," she murmured, more to herself than to the deity before her.

"Perhaps," they began, their words adopting a darker tone, their charming facade waning. "You prefer the cold winter's chill to the warmth of your heart's desire?" Faced with silence, a scowl carved into their expression. "Ayela, do you think you can make it without my help? You would've frozen if not for my charity, just now. The other gods don't bother with those as small as you." Erithia exhaled a resigned sigh, their visage once again softening.

"I admit, your dreams stand out against..." they flicked their wrist dismissively, "the humdrum pursuits of most mortals." They smiled, devoid of any warmth, "It's commendable to see such kindness, oh, so, genuine selflessness, from someone in your unfortunate station."

Ayela bit her lip, failing to look away; to resist the tempting illusion before her: Adina. Ayela knew she should be angry, yet a fog of pleasant memories blotted out any excuse as to why.

"Little doe!" Adina called out.

Ayela faltered, "Adina?" Admonishing words escaped her grasp.

"I prayed he'd bring you back to me," Adina muttered as she made her way over and cupped the girl's face.

Ayela stared at her wide-eyed, surprised when she felt the woman's touch. The soft sensation of her palms cradling Ayela's face gave question as to the reality of the vision before her. She watched Adina's eyes water when she didn't pull away.

"I was so worried, but you're safe now, here with us." Adina took Ayela's hand and led her further into the building.

"A'la!" a child yelled, waving along with a few others to catch her attention. Then they all ran off to play and laugh with the rest of their lot. She recognized a few of the children's faces from Eema's orphanage.

"This isn't... this can't be real?" Ayela stammered. Her eyes flickered to Erithia, who lingered behind Adina. Their grin served as an enigmatic veil that concealed any emotions they might harbor.

Drawn by the jubilant children at play, such innocence unscathed by Eema's abuse; Ayela couldn't contain her tears.

"Oh, Ayela." They tutted behind her and gently grasped her shoulder. Their hand subtly motioned toward Adina as they leaned down. "Adina is real. All of this can be real. I promise." Erithia's gaze bore into Ayela's, an inscrutable smile playing on their lips. "All you ever dreamed is within reach. All I need, is one whispered word."

Ayela froze, shaded memories dancing at the edge of her consciousness. Adina couldn't be here, could she? Ayela had escaped. But why? Why had she escaped? Why was she running from Adina? "And the cost?" Ayela's heart teetered, and she glanced wearily between the two.

"Hardly a toll," Erithia purred. "I only need your assistance tending to these children, alongside Adina, naturally. Just for as long as I desire."

Ayela's lips parted, ready to relent, but she noticed Erithia's brows knit. Their composed expression disrupted with widened eyes, bewildered and incredulous.

She followed their gaze with a glance and saw her. A girl in a flowing blue dress moved gracefully across the room, a vision of a free spirit guiding the children through a dance. The cascade of familiar gold curls hid her face, capturing Ayela's gaze in an unexpected trance.

In that fleeting moment, Ayela's outstretched hand conjured a flash, a memory of the girl's authentic smile. A sudden wave of icy uncertainty coursed through her. Hastily, she withdrew her hand as the ghostly form turned to face her. Ayela clenched her eyes, crouched down, and clutched her head. She refused to witness the deceiving visage of her friend cast by this illusion.

"No." She rose from her crouched position; eyes fixated on the ground, and backed away from the god before her. An imperceptible shackle lifted, freeing Ayela's soul from its unseen burdening weight.

"No! I will never join you!"

Recollections of the day's tumultuous events crashed through her consciousness like an unrelenting tide. The haunting image of Adina, mastering sinister arcana, replayed a tormented tapestry of shadows and lives ensnared by Adina's excruciating curse.

Twisted manifestations darkened the dreamscape, disintegrating like sand into smoke, unraveling the orchestrated display of cunning manipulation.

Erithia's eyes dilated, and their carefully crafted mask crumbled. "What?" They whispered in disbelief.

Ayela let out a shaky breath, looked at Adina teary-eyed, and tentatively backed away. A webbed scar warped her face as though burned by searing flames.

"Ayela, please!" She stepped, stumbling, on the brink of collapsing to her knees. Her eyes were wide with panic as she reached for Ayela's wrist. "I can't do this on my own. I need you by my side!"

"No!" Ayela's uncensored screech tore through the air. She hastily gripped her hair, then swung her arms at her sides in an aggressive display. "You've become the one thing you always warned us against. I trusted you; I loved you, but there's no undoing what you've done. What you've lost."

Adina wilted. She reached out, fumbling for the right words. Her gaze, heavy with anguish, dwelled on Ayela.

Erithia's knitted brows deepened into a furrow. Their wide eyes shifted into a piercing gaze, and a harsh frown formed on their lips. Their initial incredulity morphed into outright ire.

They whispered to themselves, "It was never like this, you've…" The god clenched their jaw but composed themselves. Forcefully, they adjusted their sleeve cuffs with a controlled yet sharply executed yank.

"That's enough. Leave. Now," Erithia commanded.

Ayela gritted her teeth.

Adina attempted to voice her protest, but Erithia strolled through her, dispersing the woman into a cloud of smoke. The remnants of her presence whisked away in the frosted wind.

Ayela staggered backward into the dilapidated house, pressing herself against the damp wall.

Erithia stalked closer and regarded her with a dry stare. "How disappointing," they began in a tense, low tone as they turned away, looking distantly. "Your desires, it seems, lie elsewhere."

They snapped their gaze toward her, looking down from the corner of their eye, their irises flashed with an iridescent silver hue. "I, who have traversed countless epochs, have observed the intricate ravels of your soul's odyssey time and time again. The echo of your presence induces seismic shifts in the world, just like it always has and always will."

"Heh?" Ayela's lip curled up awkwardly.

Erithia inhaled sharply with wide, flared eyes, nose scrunched indignantly. Slowly, they exhaled.

"Tonight, my Ayela, I grant you this gift; through winter's chill, you will see dawn." They stepped back, a smile creeping across their lips. "And a promise; there will come a day when desperation will consume you. When that day comes, you will beg of me, and I'll be there."

Erithia vanished, leaving behind a twinkling violet flame that emitted a faint warmth, just enough to ward off, yet not entirely dispel, the chill. The room remained unpleasantly cold.

Ayela didn't know how long she stood there, or when she fell to her knees. Lost in time, gazing at the flame until her eyes drifted to the quilt she had abandoned earlier. Longing for its warmth, she sighed and wrapped it around herself as the snow drifted in through the open door.

Every ounce of her felt drained and exhausted. Lying down and hugging her knees with her last bit of effort, Ayela watched the flame till her mind drifted back to her earliest memories. She smiled faintly, recalling the comforting smell of her mother's roast cooking over the fire and the warmth of their home. She pictured her mother's stern face that softened on occasion and her father's playful dances as he entered the room before asking Ayela to return to her chores. But... a memory... or was it a fantasy?

Adina's plea intruded back into Ayela's mind and confronted her current reality. Tears filled Ayela's eyes as she hiccupped, releasing a plume of misty breath. Once-shared memories took on a bitter tinge. Each warm moment, even the aroma of Adina's meals, became a haunting reminder of what Erithia's corruption had stolen from her.

She tightened her grip on her knees. What more could she have done? Been faster to have believed Adina? stepped between her and the guards? Perhaps if she'd done more, trusted more, Adina wouldn't have resorted to necromancy. She'd seen Adina with Erithia. And the other children had seemed to be illusions. Did that mean Adina hadn't gotten the children? Could it mean Lillia and Master Kote were safe?

"Mahtsar, if you can hear me. Please see to their safety. Protect the children. Protect Lillia." Her shoulders trembled as an emptiness grew within her. Doubts rose in her mind, echoes of words she'd said so often before. The times she'd denied or argued the goddess of life didn't exist. Why was she wasting her time praying to such an apathetic goddess?

She urged her mind to quiet with clenched eyes. Desperate to find sleep, clutching onto the faintest hope, yearning to see the other orphaned children, Master Kote, and her only friend that meant the world to her, Lillia.

Ayela stirred, hearing distant muffled yelling throughout her unpleasant sleep, gradually growing louder and clearer.

"—tinguish it!" The brusque command wrenched Ayela awake. "Wake up! Extinguish the flame! Now!"

Ayela gasped and shot up, her frantic eyes scanning her surroundings. She froze at the sight of four sword-bearing guards. Their snow-dusted crimson cloaks swept the floor. The flame behind them faded to nothing, leaving only the dancing light of the guard's torches. But she didn't notice.

"Get up! Drop the blanket!"

Ayela's heart trembled. She released the blanket and cautiously rose to her feet. Her voice hurt, but hoarsely she spoke hoarsely, "What did I do?" She rubbed her hands over her freezing shoulders.

They didn't answer, only charged. She screamed as one pushed her against the wall with the flat of his sword. She felt the sharp edge pull at her dress.

Frightfully, she complied, hands bracing against the wall.

Armored hands roughly patted her sides in search of weapons before cold shackles closed around her wrists.

"Don't bother with magic, witch. These'll sever any ties to the gods or magic," a guard stated, his tone authoritative and matter of fact. After a final check of her restraints, the guard pulled her up. Ayela's arm ached under the awkward force. "No sudden movements, understand?"

Ayela nodded.

"What is your name?"

"Ayela," she replied, her voice barely a whisper against the wind outside.

"Speak up!" he demanded.

"Ayela, my name is Ayela," she repeated, her voice trembling.

Silence followed for a moment as one of the guards whispered to the other.

"Come with us. The watch commander will want to speak with you." Another guard grabbed her shoulder tight and dragged her toward the door.

"Am I under arrest?" Ayela questioned, fear tinging her words.

They didn't answer, only drug her toward the snow-coated streets.

Reluctantly, Ayela glanced at the blanket before she ultimately yielded to the guards, knowing she had no other option. With a grimace, she stepped out into the frosty night air. Wherever they were taking her, hopefully, it would at least be warm.

5

The Councilor

The relentless drip of water echoed through Ayela's forlorn holding cell. She sat, back against the sodden stone walls, in the corner opposite a solid steel door. Her damp, soiled, bloodstained dress clung to her skin as she gripped her empty stomach.

Flickering light fell into her cell from a feeble window by the door. The light caressed a cracked wooden plate that lay beside Ayela's knee. Her stomach growled, echoing the memory of fragrant bread and hearty stew from days past.

Ayela ambled toward the room's center, careful not to scuff her ankle, already raw from the hefty chains anchoring her to the back wall. Her chains pulled near taut; she kneeled beneath a persistent droplet that danced from a corroded culvert in the ceiling and cupped her hands. The icy water sparked cool relief against her cracked lips. Yet, she retched at its iron-rich, gritty taste before forcing herself to take another drink.

Memories of Erithia's tempting vision danced over her mind. An enticing reprieve from her current circumstance. She bit her lip and shook off the visions. Each passing hour had strengthened the nagging urge to accept Erithia's offer. To call on their aid, as Adina had. Unlike the deafening silence of the other gods, Erithia would answer.

She startled, thoughts interrupted by a distant door crashing open, "…a child! For Mahtsar's sake, you can't neglect her. No matter what she's done." A male voice admonished, slamming the door again. Purposeful footsteps advanced toward Ayela's cell, heralding the alluring aroma of freshly baked bread. She rose on unsteady legs, tentatively stepping toward the door, nearly tripping when the chain pulled tight.

Keys rattled against the steel before the door slowly swung open. The man bore the visage of an elf. An appearance not dissimilar to Eema, if not for his contrasting lithe build. His robe was pure as freshly fallen snow and embroidered with gold symbols. Taking center stage was the predominant sigil on his chest: a brilliant sunburst encircled by an oddly bewitching set of wavy rings. It was the insignia of the Mahtsarian church.

He presented a plate to Ayela. "Go on then." The elf's voice dripped with feigned compassion. "Eat. I hear they've not been feeding you." The plate hosted the sparse feast of a freshly buttered bread roll, a slice of steaming ham, and a lone stalk of celery. "My name is Jonah, your council."

"Thank you," Ayela managed. Struggling to contain herself as she accepted the plate and sank back into her corner. Chains rattled behind her while she ravenously consumed the meager offering. "I'm Ayela," she said between bites. "I've asked the guards, but has anyone told Master Kote I am here? I am sure he would…" Ayela started.

"You were caught using dark magic." The man's harsh, hasty reply cut Ayela off. "There's nothing he could do." Jonah stepped into the hall and drug in a wooden stool, which he placed near the center of the room. He shook his head as a drop fell into his hair, then moved the chair just to the left. He sat, studying Ayela as she ate, but his eyes were fixated on the wall behind her, studying something out of sight. Ayela looked behind herself in confusion, seeing only the wall and her shadow.

"Alool," the priest spoke in a commanding tone as he held his hand in a peculiar gesture. A bright, steady, cold-blue light floated above his open palm. He moved it side to side, continuing to look behind Ayela.

"They tell me you've been unwilling to cooperate." His tone had changed, no longer feigning compassion, but measured.

"I have been cooperating." Ayela said between bites. "I've done everything they asked. But It's my right to refuse to talk without a counselor present."

Jonah sighed, "Ayela," he leaned forward. "You would save everyone a lot of time if you just confessed." Still, his gaze never left hers.

"But I didn't," Ayela choked. "I did nothing wrong." Ayela's voice was timid; her breaths were uneven as she paused her feast. Blocking the growing light with her hand. She'd hoped to at least get a neutral arbiter. Someone not already convinced of her guilt. If this was her only defense, she may as well call on Erithia now.

"If you confessed, at worst you'd see a few more days in jail, followed by some time as a Mahtsarian acolyte.

"For what! What did I do!"

"The guards witnessed you conjuring a dark flame."

"I don't even know magic! I didn't conjure anything!"

"The dark fire they had you extinguish, you saying it summoned itself?" Jonah closed his palm, extinguishing the offensive blue light.

"No, they," Ayela paused, realizing the absurdity of the truth. "It was Erithia."

"Right, Erithia, the source of dark magic." He rolled his eyes, the disingenuous, empathetic tone returning. "You used his power to cast the flame. I get it, really, I do. A cold night, and you had nowhere to go. Had to survive somehow. But dark magic is forbidden. They know you fled Midtown with Adina. You were seen entering her house, where several guards were found dead. Killed by dark magic. They found you sleeping by a dark flame. We know Adina was a necromancer, and it looks as though you were her apprentice."

"I know how it looks!" Tears filled Ayela's eyes, and her throat constricted with a surge of hopelessness. "But that's not what happened! I don't know magic!"

"And that confirms it." Jonah stood before taking the nearly finished plate from Ayela. "If we're gonna do this, I'm gonna have to cleanse you first."

"What do you mean?" Ayela mumbled, her spiraling emotions derailed in confusion.

"You're infected by a shade. Saw it almost immediately."

Ayela thought back to her interaction with Erithia, shuddering with a lingering desire to accept his offer. "A shade?" Ayela's voice dripped with concern. Her imagination ran wild with horrors. She'd never heard or read of such a creature.

"Yes, a shade. A spectral parasite created by Erithia. It finds and attaches itself to vulnerable individuals. You likely empowered yours when you used dark magic."

"I didn't use dark magic," Ayela growled. "You said parasite. What is it doing to me?" Ayela asked, rising to her feet.

"Besides reporting everything you do or say to Erithia? it feeds off potent emotions. Shades seek to influence their host's actions so they may feed from the emotional consequences."

Jonah pulled a glass bottle from under his robe. A quaint wooden cork plugged the miniscule mouth of the bottle. Far too narrow for efficient drinking.

"Step over here." He pointed toward the ground midway between the wall and the door. A raised section, untouched by the dampness of the leaking ceiling.

The bottle squeaked with the gentle effort of Jonah removing the cork. "This will not hurt you. However, the shade is going to fight back. Do only what I tell you. Do not trust your own ideas during the ritual."

"Can shades make us do things?" Ayela wondered, thinking back to how different Adina had been before she'd given in.

"No. So long as you aren't a necromancer, you still have free will. The shade just muddies the waters by giving you bad ideas and clouding your judgement." She watched as Jonah moved around her. He formed a near-perfect circle with the water before re-corking the bottle. "When I finish the incantation, the water will glow bright white. When that happens, and only when that happens, get out of the circle. You will feel a strong desire to stay. That is the shade's influence."

"How did you see it, what does it look like?" Ayela asked.

"It's hard to describe, an odd shadow, I guess. That doesn't quite match you. I studied it under the light spell I cast, eventually seeing its face. The distinct toothy grin. Impossible to spot unless you're emotionally distressed. Remember, don't move while I do the incantation."

"Mahtsar e tephilla el at, mi'titeen pe'el Ayela shelo Erithia keshef." Ayela's heart rate increased with every syllable of Jonah's incantation. True to his word, the water on the floor ignited with brilliant white light.

Warmth flooded through Ayela's body. She smiled at the memory of a time she and Adina had snuck out of Eema's orphanage. They visited a heated bathhouse in midtown. She closed her eyes for a moment, basking in the pleasant, palpable memory of warm water. She sighed, allowing her mind to lull into a peaceful quiet. Her knees weakened with the urge to sit on the damp stone floor.

"Ayela!" Jonah's harsh scream pulled Ayela from her memory. The glow in the water dimmed. "Move!"

Ayela obeyed, stepping out of the circle. She grimaced as sharp tendrils clung to her skin, pulling at her hair like thick wax. The welcome warmth from before turned ice cold as she stumbled out of the glowing water, falling to the ground.

Discordant wails flooded the room with dreadful echoes that threatened to dissolve Ayela's will. A gnawing void of longing and regret grew within her, begging her to return to the circle. Trapped behind the arcane barrier was the grotesque figure of her shade, an abyss of malevolence, an abstraction of humanity. A row of glistening teeth dominated the shade's face, each cruelly distorted. Floating orbs of blood-red light hung in sunken sockets too far apart.

The creature convulsed, thrashing against the barrier. Each attempt, growing in desperation, sent ripples of shadow and dread through the air. It pressed against the light, looking for a moment as though it might break free. With a screech, it was hurtled back to the center of the circle. Ayela froze, limbs unwilling to move. She shrank before the creature's unbridled hatred screeching through the barrier. She jumped as the horror crashed against the barrier again.

Ayela remembered this creature. A hazy memory from some time past. How long had it been feeding off her?

"Bawkah de hamma." Hot light filled the room with a blazing roar. A legion of pained screams erupted from the now pillar of solid white light. The stench of sulfur and burning wood flooded the cell as smoke collected on the ceiling.

The light faded, leaving them in dark silence. All that remained of the shade was a perfect circle of soot on the floor.

The priest massaged his hands and flexed his fingers. He looked at Ayela with a warm smile. "How do you feel?"

"Like I just ran a mile. Is it gone?" Ayela rose to a sitting position.

"Yes." Jonah offered a hand to hoist Ayela to her feet.

He studied her, dragging the silence on. "Ayela, the guards believe you are a necromancer's apprentice and an accomplice to Adina. By your passing through the light, I know you aren't too far gone. Not yet anyway. I assume you know what's become of Eema and The Orphanage?"

"Adina said Eema was killed. How did she die?"

"You really want to know?"

Ayela hesitated. "Did the bitch get what she deserved?"

"Not sure anyone deserves what Adina did." He sighed. "I won't recount the reported details. It was slow and painful." He studied Ayela's indifferent reaction.

"What about The Orphanage?"

"Your caretaker is dead, and you want to know about the home?" Jonah leaned back disapprovingly.

"Eema was an abusive bitch. Anything she got, I'm sure she deserved worse."

"It was destroyed. Some sort of dark magic explosion. They're still…" Ayela's ears rang as she imagined Adina destroying the orphanage. She pictured her attic room and the murals she'd carved. Her secret stash of hunting supplies and the small pouch of gold that had been all she had. Her vision blurred with tears as she realized Adina must have gotten past Master Kote's guards and Lillia and taken the children.

"Hey." Jonah shook Ayela's shoulder.

"Did Adina," she hesitated to ask. "Is Lillia…"

"Lillia?"

"Master Kote's daughter. At the library. Adina said she was going there when I refused to go with her. Is she," Ayela stopped, her voice refusing to finish.

"Both she and Master Kote are fine and well. They fought Adina off."

Ayela fell back against the wall. Tears of relief streamed from her closed eyes. "Thank the gods."

"We need to focus on you. I am your counsel; my job is to discern the facts of what happened and represent you to the guards and judges. I won't lie to you. The deck is stacked against you. Depending on what you tell me, I will either clear you of any wrongdoing or lessen the severity of the crime you will be accused of. For me to do my duty, you need to be perfectly honest with me. Tell me everything you can remember as accurately as you can. Hide nothing, and do not twist any facts for your betterment. Understand?" Jonah's voice rang with sincerity. "Start where you believe the events that led you here began."

"Are you willing to believe what I say? Or have you already decided about me?" Ayela considered his request.

"Look," Jonah sighed, rubbing the side of his neck. He looked down at Ayela. "I got nothing against you, kid, but I've counseled countless dark magic users. In this city, nine times out of ten, it doesn't matter what I tell the guards. They saw you using dark magic. You lived with Eema, and she's dead. Witnesses saw you leave with Adina, and we found guards killed by dark magic at her house. With Adina either escaped or killed in the explosion at the orphanage. At best, the guards believe you're an accomplice. At worst, they're out for retribution for their fallen comrades, and you're their scapegoat. I doubt there's much I can do to sway them. I hope to pardon you of lengthy imprisonment or execution."

"But I didn't do any of that!" Ayela cried, burying her head in her hands.

"Just…" Jonah lowered his gaze, pinching the bridge of his nose. "Start at the beginning."

"Okay, I suppose this all started on our way to The King's Library. The other orphans and I were on our weekly trip. Someone passed Adina, Eema's aid, a note when we were in the street. That's when her demeanor changed. When we got there, Kote gave us a free day. Adina left after we arrived, which was unusual. She's always stayed by the children, caring for them more than herself."

"Okay, continue."

"While I was studying at The Library, Adina came back. She was nervous about something and told me that Eema had been killed and she would be blamed for it because she was Moonborn. She asked me to leave the city with her."

"Why did you go?"

"I…" Ayela fought to remember her reasoning.

"Likely, the shade influenced that decision. Why did she only take you? Why not the other children?"

"She said she'd planned to adopt me. I trusted her." Ayela wiped a tear from her eye. "She was basically my mother. She was Eema's assistant for most of my life."

"I followed her through the city, back to her house. Guards broke in while she was trying to pack supplies. They tried to attack her. That's when she…" Ayela's voice left her. She struggled to find the words to describe the horrible scene. Her tongue swelled. She fought back the image of Adina's hate-filled expression.

"It's okay. Come back to me. What did Adina do?"

"Adina made a deal with Erithia, I think… She killed the guards and Kiyle. She was protecting herself. She…"

"Just tell me the facts. I don't want to know the motivations or speculations."

"After Adina killed the soldiers, she killed Kiyle and reanimated his corpse. She said he would get her past the gates. She offered to take me with her, but I refused. Then left to get the other children." Ayela stopped, studying the priest's reactions.

"What happened next?"

"I left her house. I wanted to go to the library to warn Master Kote and Lillia, but I knew the city guard wouldn't have let me into Midtown. I needed shelter, so I found an abandoned building. I curled up in a corner and was going to wait out the night. That's when Erithia visited me."

"Erithia?" Jonah narrowed his eyes in disbelief when Ayela nodded in confirmation. "A god visited you, in person? Not just any god, but him. Why would he visit you?" Jonah's voice dripped with a mixture of jealousy and disgust. He shook his head, studying Ayela's mannerisms. "If you're gonna lie, that's…"

"I'm not. They said Adina made a deal with them to ensure that I would be cared for that night. They wanted to tempt me, tried to get me to make a deal, but I refused."

"Right. You resisted the god of desire. In person?" Jonah nodded, turning away from Ayela. "While infected by a shade, no doubt."

"You have to believe me! That's what happened."

"Child, no one is going to believe this fable! The gods don't visit people in person. Even the tempter. He works through agents or through apparitions, even they are difficult to resist. You're either lying or mistaken. Even if I believed he visited you in person, there's no way you'd be able to stand against him." Jonah sneered. "You can't seriously expect me to believe that story."

"It's the truth," Ayela muttered, allowing her eyes to trail away from Jonah. She imagined the spacious building she had seen Adina in.

"Even if I believed you, there's no way a judge would." Jonah repositioned himself on the chair. "First, where did the corrupt blood on your dress come from?" He gestured to the black stains littering the sleeves and hem of her dress.

"The spell Adina used to kill the guards. It melted them, turned their blood black. It was… messy." Ayela cringed as she recalled the sickening squelch of Adina's shoes dredging through the black soup that had coated the floor of her house.

"Just like Eema," he muttered. "Okay. And what about the dark fire the guards found in the building?"

"Erithia said it was a gift. Something to get me through the night. Maybe it was part of Adina's deal. But I swear, I made no deals with him, and I didn't use his magic."

"Even harder to believe, he never gives freely." Jonah looked towards the prison door. "Another lost cause," he mumbled. "There's no chance we get a judge or the guards to believe this story. Gods, I don't even believe it. I'll just tell them you confessed to conjuring the dark flame."

"No! I never confessed to anything."

"Girl, I don't know what you want from me. I tell your outlandish story and they'll burn you as a necromancer. We must work with them. Give them something, or they won't believe a word you say."

"Fine, have a Paladin of Naqam judge me then." Ayela spat, heart racing from the stories she'd read of a Paladin's harsh version of justice.

Jonah's face went white at the mention. He closed his eyes, taking a deep breath. "You have a death wish? You reek of guilt and lies. That alone is enough to warrant execution by their hand. I'm trying to help you here."

"But they also know when you aren't lying. It's the only way I get out of this."

"I won't let another…"

"You can't refuse me!" Ayela stood. "It's Union Law. I have the right to request a paladin's judgement."

"I suppose it's better than facing the pyre." Jonah rubbed the back of his neck. "Look, I'm sorry, kid. It's just," He trailed off. "The last time I called on a paladin, it was a twelve-year-old kid who'd been caught stealing food. I had to watch a paladin slaughter a child who would only have gotten a slap on the wrist. You sure you want this? Once I tell the guards, there's no going back."

"The only thing I feel guilty about is that I did not defend my friend. Maybe if I had believed her and defended her, she wouldn't have made a deal with Erithia. But I have broken no laws and done nothing wrong. I don't fear the judgment of a paladin of the goddess of justice."

"We'll get this over with then." Jonah hesitated before leaving the cell. His tone shifted to one of remorse. "I'll have the guards send for a Paladin of Naqam. Make your peace, Ayela, it may be a few days before I can get one here. I'll see that the guards take care of you. You deserve fresh water and a full belly when you…" He stared at Ayela, unable to finish. "It's the least I can do."

Jonah shut the door behind him, leaving Ayela to contemplate the decision she'd made in silence. With him gone, Ayela curled into the corner, the rhythmic drip her only company. Let the paladin judge her. At least this time, someone would listen.

6

Judgement

A metallic murmur sliced through the silence of Ayela's dreamless sleep. A serenade of sliding steel plates and armored steel boots echoed from beyond her cell door; the foreboding executioner's prelude.

Ayela stood on shaking legs and rubbed the lack of sleep from her eyes. Her heart raced with the wild imaginings of the paladin she was soon to face.

Ghoulish light flooded the room as Ayela's cell door swung open. She stumbled back, tripping over her chains at the sight of the paladin. The armored knight ducked under the doorframe before rising to a menacing height. The paladin's right hand cradled a ball of arcane light that cast a cerulean hue over her mirror-like silver plate armor. Her left rested on the pommel of a longsword at her hip.

The paladin floated the orb of light to the center of the cell, where it hovered. She stared at Ayela in silence, with only the sound of her gentle breath echoing through her helm.

Her statuesque form finally broken, the Paladin lifted her helmet, revealing a fierce woman's face with translucent skin. Ayela could make out the silhouette of the woman's skull beneath her nose and around her shocking purple eyes. Occasional flashes of violet energy webbed through her flesh, shedding pale light over her armor. A Stormborn.

"You are Ayela?" The paladin asked. "My name is Tam. I am a Paladin of Naqam. I understand you wish to be judged by me rather than undergo a union trial." Ayela's racing heart calmed at the sound of The Paladin's soothing voice.

"Yes," Ayela stammered. "Thank you for coming."

"As is my duty. No thanks needed. Have they treated you well? Ensured you were well fed? Provided plenty of water? Fresh clothes?" She looked over the semi-fresh burlap shirt and pants the guard had provided Ayela.

Ayela hesitated. "Yes."

The paladin sighed, shaking her head. "I see through your lies, child. I will see they face justice.

"No." Ayela begged. "They…"

Tam cut Ayela off with a raised hand. "Your concern for them speaks well of you. But laws have been broken. Now, should you agree to be judged, I'll place you under an honest mind spell. It will enhance your memory, allowing you to recall details you may otherwise have missed or forgotten to disclose. It will also make it more difficult for you to recall or recite false information. I will also channel the goddess Naqam during our interview. She will discern any amount of guilt you feel for what has happened. She will also see through any deception or lies. Lying during our interview will cause an automatic judgment of guilty. If she detects guilt within you, I will attempt to discern the source of the guilt. If you have broken any laws or acted with malice, I will return a guilty verdict. If I judge you to be guilty, I will execute you. If I judge you to be innocent, you will be released and cleared of all wrongdoing. Do you understand?"

"Yes."

"Okay." The paladin stepped toward Ayela and unlocked her shackles before turning around and motioning for Ayela to follow. "I will take you somewhere more private for the interview."

Ayela followed Tam through the door and down the short hallway. Sunlight beamed through the guardhouse entrance to their right. Patches of melting snow permeated the street beyond the threshold. Jonah and several guards sat around a table. Their faces were painted with distress at the Paladin's glare.

Ayela's thoughts wandered to what might come after the interrogation. She set her jaw, resolving to never step foot in another orphanage, no matter what. Ayela was free of Eema, and though she despised Adina's actions, she was grateful to be free of her. She wouldn't squander this freedom.

Tam opened a simple wooden door before motioning for Ayela to enter. Inside was a cylindrical room with a single chair in the center. Dried bloodstains soaked the floor beneath the chair. Two candle fixtures hung beside the door. Each filled the room with a faint light and welcoming scent.

"Sit there, Ayela, and we will begin." She closed the door. "Okay, I want to be sure you have indeed chosen to be judged. I cannot judge you unwillingly. You must freely accept my judgment and acknowledge the finality of it. There are no appeals, no reversing my decision. Are you choosing to be judged by me, a Paladin of Naqam, freely of your own will?"

"Yes."

"And do you understand and accept the terms of our interview and the judgment to follow?"

"Yes."

"Very well." As Tam finished, she held her hands out toward Ayela. "Grasp my hands."

"Mamana shehl'zedecl," Tam began as Ayela grasped both her hands. "Ayela, shafat shehl'ehmehm ve'mideh-tova shehl'Naqam." Tam opened her eyes, revealing two orbs of writhing electricity that pierced Ayela. Her gaze invaded Ayela's mind as fierce white pupils opened in the center of Tam's eyes.

"Ayela." Tam's disembodied voice enwrapped her, entrapping Ayela's gaze and full attention. Its every note was a booming resonance that bristled Ayela's nerves. Her heart thrummed wildly as her gaze locked onto the paladin's electrified eyes. Crackling arcs of electricity cascaded over Tam's face, leaving luminous trails that lingered in her translucent skin.

"There is no need for fear. What you see is a glimpse of Naqam's essence as she observes our interview through my eyes. We will start with a simple question. Do you feel any measure of guilt for the events that led you to this interview?"

"Yes."

"Please elaborate. Why do you feel guilty?"

"I was not supportive of my friend. If I was more supportive, maybe she wouldn't have become a necromancer."

"Is that all you feel guilty for?"

"Yes."

A silence drug between them, one far too long for comfort. "There is no reason for you to carry this guilt. Release it, for you cannot control and so are not responsible for the choices of others. Now, I want you to recite everything you remember about the events. Start where you believe you should start and leave nothing out."

Ayela thought for a moment, clarity and calm reaching every corner of her consciousness. "Weeks ago, I was returning from hunting in the forests. Ayela's voice was even and slow as she stared into the paladin's eyes. There was a creature, the shade. I saw it following us, Adina and I. Days passed like normal. Then, the day it happened, when we were on the way to The King's

Library, someone passed Adina a note. A male Moonborn. No markings. That's when she changed, became nervous, quiet."

She continued to recall the events to Tam, just as she had done with Jonah. She ended with her denying Erithia's offer. As she finished, Tam stood before her in silence for some time. Her piercing eyes searched Ayela as though studying her every mannerism.

"Qets," Tam whispered after a lengthy silence. Her eyes returned to their purple hue. "Naqam has found you innocent of all wrongdoing. Your councilor will see to your release." Tam opened the door where Jonah and the guard captain waited outside. "She is cleared of all wrongdoing. Naqam finds her innocent. You will now bring all guards responsible for her care to this room unarmed for judgement."

"But..." the guard captain began a hasty defense.

"Laws of Hatave prohibit the neglect of prisoners. You will not impede my investigation."

"Yes, paladin." The guard captain conceded.

"Lady Tam," Ayela began, eliciting a raised eyebrow.

"Please show them mercy. They..."

Tam interrupted Ayela with a hand on her shoulder. "Your heart will take you far. But only if you temper it. Sometimes a heavy hand is needed to correct the wrong in this world. Rest assured, they will not be killed. But you are likely not the first neglected. Measures must be taken to see that you are the last." She returned her attention to the guards and Jonah, who were gathered outside the room. "Jonah, the method of her release is left to you. See to it now." She nudged Ayela toward the councilor.

"You told her what you told me?" Johan's jaw slacked when Ayela nodded.

"Councilor." The paladin's tone lowered, rumbling through the room. "Know your place. Naqam finds her innocent. There will be no further questions as to her past."

"But the gods don't talk to mortals. You must be mist—"

"Are you questioning Naqam's judgement?" Tam's words cut through the air like lightning. The room fell silent. Electricity arced over the armor on her arms. "I would think those following Mahtsar would see her strength and celebrate it. Or perhaps it is your faith that falters."

Jonah bowed his head and stepped back. "It is as you say. I did not believe a god would have visited her."

Tam's eyes softened.

Ayela took a step toward Johan and the guard who'd just moments ago imprisoned her. "You had no reason to believe it." Each of the guards stood breathless at hearing Jonah's admission.

"A god actually visited you? In person?" A guard asked. His voice and demeanor bled disdain, or was it jealousy?

"As unbelievable as it sounds. Yes. And I denied them." Ayela lifted her chin. "So, what happens now?"

"We figure out what to do with you." Jonah rubbed the back of his neck, then motioned for Ayela to follow. "We can't send you back to the orphanage. Adina and Kiyle fled into the building moments before a dark magic explosion that damaged the structure beyond repair. and Citadel Maji are currently working to contain the corruption. They report that Adina and Kiyle's bodies were inside. I'm sorry, they're gone."

"But I saw her…"

"I'm sorry." Jonah placed a hand on her shoulder, squeezing slightly. "Do you have anyone? Friends, maybe that would take you in?"

"No," Ayela whispered between strained breaths. "The only friends I have left are Master Kote and Lillia at The King's Library."

"I wouldn't consider them friends, Ayela." Jonah sighed. "Kote is an advisor to the chief judge and king. He holds more influence than almost any other member of the nobility. You don't reach that level of power without blood on your hands. Even so, he never took steps to stop what Eema was doing. No one did. You'd be safer in Southtown's slums than with the nobility."

"That's not true. He made several reports. It's not his fault."

"If he made reports, something would have been done about it. I'm sorry."

Ayela didn't answer, unwilling to believe him. Master Kote had told her on several occasions that he wished he could do more. No. If Master Kote was as powerful as he said, more likely Jonah was afraid of what Kote would do if they learned she'd been kept here. Regardless, he would not let her go to Lillia.

"I can place you in the orphanage where some of the other children are," Jonah offered. "I can promise their housemasters are nothing like Eema. A kind and caring couple."

"No," Ayela whispered, heart aching at refusing to return to the children who cared for her so much. They were safe. At least she had to believe so. But she wouldn't step foot in another orphanage.

"Please, it really is best. And you'd be with the children you know."

"I don't care." Ayela lied. "No, no more orphanages. I want to be on my own," she demanded, holding back tears as she looked Jonah in the eye. "I won't stay in another orphanage."

"Listen, these are good people. Most housemasters are. Let us…"

"No, I would rather stay on the streets."

"I'm not sure you know what you're saying," said a guard standing in the doorway behind Jonah.

"What about a shelter?" Jonah suggested. "There is a women's shelter near the southern gates. They may have an opening for you. We would just need to find you a job within the next few days."

"Maybe, though, the shelters have been full since the fire in Southtown last month." The guard said.

"Ayela, please. Stay at an orphanage. It isn't safe on the streets." Jonah insisted.

"No."

"Ayela, we can't just let you be homeless."

"Yes, you can. I'll go to the shelter you mentioned. Even if they don't have room for me, they'll have warm clothes and food. There are plenty of abandoned buildings in Southtown. I'll stay in one of those until I find a job and can afford a long-stay room at an inn."

"Erithia may tempt you again," Jonah warned.

"I said no once. I can do it again." Ayela rose to her feet, feigning determination as she began thinking of jobs she could do.

"What jobs will you try to get?" The guard asked.

"I'll try apprenticing under someone, maybe a tailor or a baker. I have woodworking skills, maybe a carpenter. Or maybe I could," She stopped herself before volunteering for the guard. She'd witnessed how harsh they could be. Did she really want a part of that?

"There's no point in taking you to an orphanage, is there?" Jonah smiled. "You'll just leave the first chance you get."

"That's right." Ayela returned his smile.

"Thought so," Jonah said. "You got a strong will, kid. You might just survive out there. I'll arrange for a guard to escort you to the shelter. Hopefully, they'll have room for you."

Having led her out, the guards and Jonah vanished back into the guardhouse. The door shut with a resounding thud, echoing the finality of her isolation. She released a trembling breath as her fragile frame fell against the cold, stone guardhouse wall. A solitary tear sank down her cheek.

Ayela's lungs seized, refusing to take another breath. Echoes of the children's laughter played in her mind like fleeting shadows. Children she would never again see. She imagined them helpless at the hands of another Eema. No older sister to protect them. Her once dream of owning an orphanage of her own seemed so far beyond her. The phantom fragrance of Adina's stew wafted over Ayela, renewing the pain of hunger. Adina's smile haunted her, whisked away by the black eyes of a necromancer. No, Jonah said the children were safe. Would be cared for.

Tears streamed between sporadic breaths. Burdened by the weight of her new reality, Ayela's limbs failed her. She slid down the wall.

Ayela looked up, studying the menacing architecture of the guardhouse. A clear symbol to all in the area, and a formidable structure should the city fall under siege.

She had turned down her only offer for help. Now she was on her own. Past the guardhouse, sinister, uncaring clouds drifted by. Evening was approaching, and another winter storm was soon to begin. Now, even Master Kote was out. Hate it as she did. Jonah's words spread doubt. Kote was well-connected. Moreso than Eema. How else would he have had such a position as king's librarian? He had to know by now where she was, and he'd done nothing. But Lillia, she needed…

"Ayela?" a young man's voice called from above her. He was a guard, clad in a gleaming chainmail uniform and flowing crimson cape. His youthful exterior belied the contradictory aura of power and authority that accompanied one seasoned in years. "I'm to take you to a shelter. Please, allow me to help you." The guard commanded with an outstretched hand.

Ayela wiped her eyes, wrestling to her feet. Warm solace bloomed through her as she grasped the guard's helping hand. An unbidden smile lit Ayela's face, unraveling the previous uncertainty.

"You're going to be fine." The guard's honeyed reassurance replayed in Ayela's ears as they approached a large building with a line of homeless people standing outside. "You will survive." A flood of confidence surged in Ayela's heart as the guard's hand squeezed her shoulder. His caring eyes twinkled with uncanny wisdom.

Ayela's breath startled. The guard's gaze flashed molten gold with distinctly slit pupils. He smiled; his eyes having returned to their ordinary brown. The guard bowed his head to Ayela before ducking into the passing crowd and disappearing down the busy street.

"Those eyes," Ayela mumbled as she searched the crowd for the guard. Forgotten memories of gold eyes played before her from long ago. She was young, looking into a stranger's face. The mysterious gold eyes stared back at her before leaving her on Eema's doorstep.

Surely her stressed mind had conjured the vision of a dragon's eyes. There was no other explanation. Ayela took a deep breath of wintry air. The shelter was behind her. Its walls, a patchwork of varying materials, left one to wonder as to its stability. A line of vagrants wrapped around the building. Each looked equally disheveled as

JUDGEMENT

Ayela. "Here's to new beginnings," she whispered before starting for the line's end.

7

A Chance Encounter

Ayela nestled against the shelter wall, spine stiff from the numbing cold. The chaotic street before her was peppered with patches of melting snow. In futility, she fought to pull her woolen cloak closer to her body. Ayela grinned as she pictured the genuine smile of the tall elf who had given it to her.

Eyes closed, head leaned back against the wall, Ayela's mouth watered at the dulled recollection of Adina's venison stew, or the scent of freshly baked bread from the library kitchens. Anything to purge the bitter taste of potato soup; the only meal the shelter had served all week.

Three gold coins clattered into the freshly emptied soup bowl by her side. "Thank you!" Ayela leapt to her feet, eyes wide. Her chest burned with gratitude, but her benefactor had vanished into the crowd. Her shoulders sagged as she looked on. She'd hoped to thank one so generous in person, but there was no one there. Only the crowded street and another homeless man eyeing her bowl. He was old and frail, with splotchy cheeks sunken to his skull from years of malnourishment. Ayela leaned forward to grab the coins. They were heavy, circular coins, with a square stamped on either side.

"Gold marks?" Ayela marveled at the rare sight before looking through the crowd toward the group of people that had passed her. They weren't wealthy, just average people. "Who in Southtown could afford to just give away three gold marks?"

The homeless man's attention was now on a wood carving in his hands. Despite missing several fingers, he held it steady and was busy carving intricate details into the totem. She counted the numerous meals she could eat on the abundance of coin she now carried.

She sighed. It was more than she needed. Far more. All she needed was to get to Midtown.

Ayela approached the man, clearing her throat of the stench that surrounded him. She hesitated, nearly stepping back as he looked at her with one eye open, the other sewn shut, with a grizzly scar reaching from his forehead to his nose. His hide jacket was riddled with holes and weathered thin by years of use.

Ayela separated two of the gold coins and held them toward the man. "Here. You need these more than me."

Tears welled in the old man's eye as his wrinkled face lit into a wide, near toothless grin. "Thank you, dear girl." He rasped. "But this is more than an old veteran like me needs. One mark'll get me a warm meal and new clothes. Maybe a night in a proper bed if I play it right." He handed a coin back to Ayela. "Got the sense you'll put it to better use. But be quick about it, and don't let folk around here know you got money."

"Gods bless you." Ayela knelt, hugging the man.

"Now, get out of here," the old man chuckled.

Ayela slipped the two gold coins into one of the inside pockets of her thick coat before turning around. She froze. A man had caught her eye from across the street. She recognized his bald head and vine tattoos. A smile crossed the man's stern face. Bahn's dark green eyes glistened in the sunlight.

A CHANCE ENCOUNTER

"Ayela? It's good to see a familiar face." Bahn smiled, stepping to her.

"Yes," Ayela whispered as she studied the black speckles dotting his irises.

Ayela screeched. Her vision flashed white. Bahn stood before her. He was older, his expression filled with hate, his eyes shrouded in shadow, just as Adina's had been. Ayela stumbled backward, her eyes clamped shut. Her feet tangled beneath her and she fell back. Ayela's breath came in quick bursts; her mind drew back to the piles of flesh and black blood she had dredged through.

"What! What's wrong?" Bahn asked, having caught her mid-fall. His concerned expression was now free of shadows.

"Nothing," Ayela breathed.

"What happened? Do you need help?"

"No." Ayela stepped away from Bahn

"Surely there's something," Bahn started.

"What are you doing in the city?" She half-smiled, rubbing her shoulder and looking through the crowd for other druids. "I thought druids never left the forest."

Bahn looked down as a shadow of grief crossed his eyes. "It's… I uh… I was banished." He recoiled in a shameful whisper.

Ayela studied his expression as questions about his intentions sprouted in her mind. "Doesn't it take a lot to be banished from the druids? What did you do?"

"I'd rather not talk about it," Bahn said.

"It wasn't me?"

"No, not at all. Just…" Bahn hesitated. "What about you? What are you doing on the streets?"

"No." Ayela stepped back from Bahn, "I meet you once in the forest, then you happen to find me in this monster of a city? Do you think I'm stupid?"

"It really is a coincidence. I swear. I was just following…"

"Why were you banished?" Ayela's eyes narrowed. She wouldn't be taken for a fool. She knew little about the druid's culture. But she did know they didn't tolerate dark magic. And she wasn't going to let another Adina into her life.

"I'm not going to answer that right now." Bahn's voice carried a hint of irritation amid sadness. His gaze left Ayela's "I stole something. Okay. I was just trying to help an old woman."

Bahn's voice shifted as he spoke. It was subtle, but Ayela noticed it. His pose shifted in the silence. He still wasn't looking her in the eye. He was lying.

"Look, we can help each other." Bahn stepped forward. "Surviving together is bound to be better than being alone. I could…"

"Thanks, but no," Ayela grimaced. The image of him as a necromancer resurfaced in her mind. "I'd rather be alone. You should go." Ayela left before Bahn protested, hurrying through the crowds. Hatave was too large a city for a random druid she'd met in the forests to find her by accident. Something wasn't right.

Ayela eyed every alleyway on her path to the markets, examining the surrounding pedestrians. Her knuckles ached, clinging to the coins in her pocket. She locked eyes with a group of people in an alleyway she crossed, and her breath caught in her chest. They were rough individuals wearing tattered leather armor and armed with short swords or daggers. One had a rather ornate longbow along with a short sword and dagger in his belt.

"Shit," Ayela cursed under her breath and bolted. The bowman's face split into a rotten grin as he motioned for the others to follow. They entered the crowded street and gave chase.

Panic flushed her heart as she dashed forward, weaving through the crowd in search of a guard. Her breath hastened. She was near the market; there would be guards at the market.

Ayela screamed when a gruff hand seized her matted hair. It pulled her off her feet where another hooked under her shoulder and dragged her backward into an alley. Several in the crowd turned to face her, seeing the armed individuals dragging her into an alley. All hurried away, feigning ignorance. A guard in full plate rounded the corner, Ayela's eyes lit with hope.

The bowman turned and tossed a silver mark toward the guard. Ayela's jaw dropped as the guard stooped down and picked up the coin. He bit it a few times, then turned to the crowd.

"Run along. This doesn't concern you!" The guard's grave intention enshrouded Ayela as the armored officer nodded in understanding to the hoodlums.

"Let go of me," Ayela yelled. She struggled to free her restrained arms.

"Aw, this one's got fight in her," one thief sneered. They turned a corner out of view of the street.

"Look, little girl." The bowman knelt in front of Ayela. "We got nothin' against you, but you got the look of someone with a heavy pocket. Hand your coin over without a fight, and we promise you'll walk away from this unharmed."

"Yeah, we promise." The thieves holding Ayela laughed as she struggled to break their grasp.

The bowman reached dangerously close to Ayela's chest, his eyes filled with hunger. "Tell me, girl, is there an inside pocket in that coat of yours? I bet you keep your coin there."

Determination born of desperation surged within Ayela. She twisted a wrist free from the man holding her and balled it into a clumsy fist. Ayela winced as the bowman's nose cracked under the force of her strike.

"You bitch," the bowman screamed. Those behind Ayela grabbed her free wrist and pulled her back to the ground. The bowman stumbled backward while holding his bleeding nose.

"Let me go!" Ayela rolled to her side, breaking free from one thief before kicking the other's crotch with all her strength.

"Fu—" He breathlessly fell to his knees, clutching himself. The bowman drew his dagger.

"You'll regret that."

Ayela crawled backward. Her clamoring hand landed on a brick, which she hurled without hesitation. A stroke of luck saw the brick knock the dagger from the bowman's hand. He held his fingers and spewed a string of expletives. She followed the dagger until a boot stopped it from sliding. She followed the leg to see Bahn standing behind the bowman, and relief surged new life into her muscles at seeing the familiar face.

Bahn spun the surprised man around before unleashing a flurry of punches to his chest and head. The bowman fell like a crashing timber at the final blow to his chin.

Another screamed and charged Bahn with a drawn short sword. Bahn stepped to the side, grappled the man's hand, and twisted it behind his back. He grabbed the blade from the thief's broken grip and slammed the pommel into his nose, visibly breaking it. The thief gasped, stumbling forward a few steps before Bahn spun, landing a lightning-fast kick to the man's temple. The thief smashed to the ground, head bouncing on the cobblestone.

Bahn faced away from the last thief who, having recovered from Ayela's strike, lifted his sword. Ayela kicked outward, her foot catching his ankle. The man fell, his face banging against the rough cobblestone. The thief's sword slid across the ground, away from his hand and into Bahn's grasp.

Bahn held the man's sword to his neck. "Leave."

The thief scrambled to his feet, running out of the alley without so much as a backward look to his unconscious companions.

"You okay?" Bahn asked through winded breaths. He held his hand out to Ayela.

Ayela examined the thieves that lay near motionless, collecting snow. Her heart raced. Bahn just held his hand out to her as though nothing had happened.

"Come, we should leave before they wake up." Bahn said.

Ayela's gaze fell to the bow, still strapped to the bowman's back. It was simple, yet elegant. She couldn't remove her gaze from the subtle carvings in its handle. Gingerly, she lifted it from the unconscious bowman's back. It was light, well-balanced.

"Ayela?" Bahn waved a hand before her. "You alright? We need to leave."

"You fought well, Druid," the smooth stranger's voice broke Ayela's trance.

Two armored figures stood at the entrance to the alley. One was tall with broad shoulders. He wore a steel breastplate over a thick white padded shirt. The whites of his eyes were starkly visible against his ash-gray skin. His short hair was ink-black and neatly groomed, matching his pencil-thin beard. A large round shield was strapped to his back, and a long sword sheathed at his hip.

A pair of unfurled mottled red and flesh-colored dragon-like wings dominated the other's figure. They rested like a cloak around his shoulders. He was tall and buff, with narrow shoulders. He wore a breastplate of identical make to the first, with a steel pauldron covering his left shoulder and leather braces on his wrist. His hand rested on a sword sheathed at his waist. His fair skin blended into his long, flowing bleach-blond hair and fiery orange eyes on an otherwise human face. He was a Draken, the near spitting image of Kiyle but with wings confidently on display instead of hidden, as Kiyle always preferred.

Bahn adopted a defensive posture between the two armed men and Ayela.

"Relax, we do not wish to fight you." The ash-skinned man's voice held a thick accent, an imperial.

"We're mercenaries," the Draken added. "Got a tip someone was in trouble back here. My name is Logane, this is Zaktan." The Draken walked toward Bahn and Ayela. Bahn kept his guard, studying the approaching mercenaries. Ayela gripped the bow with a white-knuckled fist. The mercenaries stopped a short distance from them, their postures relaxing somewhat.

"You handle yourself well," Logane said more softly now that they were closer. "We're in the market for new swords in our band. You interested?"

Bahn's guard relaxed. He glanced at Ayela with a thoughtful expression. "Only if she joins as well," Bahn said, turning to the two mercenaries.

"What?" Ayela scowled at Bahn.

"The girl?" Zaktan scoffed, examining Ayela. Disgust dominated his face. "No, she's too…"

"Zaktan," Logane muttered, turning to his friend.

"You can't." Zaktan swung his arm in Logane's direction, displaying his disapproval.

"Kid, we saw Bahn fight, but what could you offer our group?" Logane asked, turning his attention to Ayela.

"Not so fast." Ayela shook her head. "Who are you with? What mercenary band? And why are you so eager for recruits that you would just hire someone off the street?"

"A sharp one, huh," Logane muttered.

A CHANCE ENCOUNTER

"Yeah, boss. Why we resulting to the bottom of the barrel?" Zaktan's question felt more like a dig at Logane than a genuine inquiry.

"You wanna join or not?" Logane dodged the question. "As King's Guild Mercs, you have my word. An honest, even cut of every bounty. Now, what can you offer the guild?"

Ayela's heart pounded in her chest, unsure of what to say. The King's guild, if he was being honest, was one of the most powerful guilds in The Union. It'd be a life of adventure, for sure. One not unlike she and Lillia had dreamed of. And it would promise a better life than that of the street urchin she was becoming. "I'm a decent shot with a bow." Ayela gestured with the bow she'd taken from the thief.

"We do need an archer," Logane said, scratching his shaved chin.

"Logane," Zaktan groaned.

"Tell you what, meet us at The Headless Snake tomorrow evening. We'll test her skills then and discuss this further." Logane nodded, turning from Bahn and guiding Zaktan away from the alley.

"Are you insane!" Ayela breathed once the mercenaries were out of earshot. "I barely know you. What were you thinking?"

"A way of surviving, maybe." Bahn shrugged. "Forgive me for assuming, but we both need money, food, and shelter. We're alone in this city with no way of finding work. And what is The King's Guild?"

"One of the most powerful guilds in the nation. They're a collective of mercenary groups that operate independently under some common code. I don't know more than that." Ayela rubbed the bridge of her nose. "For now, I'd like to get some warmer clothes and some actual food." Ayela walked away from Bahn, stepping over the archer. She stopped when she saw a small coin purse at his side. He was to rob her, maybe worse.

It was only right she return the favor. She chuckled at seeing his swollen, purple jaw that was slightly askew, clearly broken. "Serves you right, asshole." She untied the coin purse from his belt, fighting the biting chill that crept under her coat before unbuckling the bow's holster and strapping it to herself.

"So," Bahn asked, standing behind her. "What do you say?"

"Thank you for the help, but…"

"Give me a chance to earn your trust."

"Why?" Ayela asked pointedly. "You've already lied to me. And you won't tell me what you did."

"Because I think we were meant to find each other. How else would I have run into you in this gargantuan city? The gods have put us together. May as well make the most of it."

"You have got to give me more. Thank you for saving me. But, if you want me to trust you, I need to know why you were banished. I refuse to put blind trust in another person."

Bahns shoulders sagged. "Someone got hurt because of a mistake I made." Bahn looked away again, setting his jaw. But not in deception this time. She could hear the restraint in his voice. He was in pain. "It wasn't my fault. It was an accident. But it didn't matter. You won't get more out of me right now. It's just… too fresh of a wound."

"Thank you." Ayela, at least, could sympathize with the pain she saw in him. A similar pain to what she felt. He'd lost someone, someone close. A knot formed in her throat at the remembrance of Kiyle's face moments before Adina killed him. She heard him whisper to run. Felt his neck snap and bend. Lifeless.

"Ayela?" Bahn asked, shaking Ayela from her stupor.

"Look, I appreciate you saving me. But I…" Ayela tapped her foot, struggling to put her words together. "Being a mercenary doesn't sound awful. Kind of like the idea of a life of adventure. And I know someone who would drop everything to join."

"So, you're in?" Bahn sounded far too excited, his earlier tone shifting dramatically.

"Let's just get somewhere warm and get some food." Ayela sighed, allowing herself to imagine a life as a mercenary. She had plenty of questions, and she still didn't fully trust this druid. But his arrival in the street couldn't have been coincidence.

All that fell aside with the renewed decision to find Lillia. An idea that hadn't crossed her mind till now except in occasional flights of fancy. She recalled the promise she shared with Lillia, to run off on some adventure before her arranged wedding. Maybe the gods were helping her after all. The timing was just about as perfect as it could be. Maybe this is what she was supposed to do. Maybe this druid was right and Musar was intervening in her life. She smiled at the thought of regaling Lillia with stories over a remote fire.

Or maybe she was getting ahead of herself. "Let me think about it." She would go to Lillia, that much she knew, but Bahn she still wasn't sure of. He wasn't telling her everything, but Ayela wasn't sharing either.

"Should we tell someone about the guard?" Bahn whispered before they stepped out of the alley and onto the semi-populated city street.

"No," Ayela muttered. "No guard will care about us, and we don't know what connections those people had. In this city, reporting things like this is a good way to get killed or arrested. Best to forget. They surely will."

Bahn sighed, shaking his head. "That's not right."

"Maybe not, but saying something won't do anything for us. I'd rather know exactly how you found me. This city is way too big for it to be an accident. If you want to earn my trust, spill."

"I was following an old man who guided me to the shelter. Pure coincidence you were there."

"Sure," Ayela mumbled, recalling the gold eyes of the guard who had brought her there more than a week ago.

"There was something strange about him, though. Could have sworn I saw gold eyes."

"What did you say?" Ayela stopped, spinning into Bahn.

"Gold eyes. He had gold eyes. But only for a moment."

"You read minds or something?"

"No."

"Forget it," she continued, not wanting to admit her encounter with the guards. Divine intervention wasn't something that just happened. And he didn't need more reason to believe they were destined to travel together. "We have a problem, though. I don't know the first thing about being a mercenary." Ayela led Bahn into another alley some distance from the scene they'd fled.

"You have good instincts. I can train you. It'll be fun, an adventure. We'd make enough money to have shelter and food. You said you want to get out of the city."

"How would you train me?" she asked.

"I was a guard for the druid clan in Lapid's forest. You've seen me fight. I could teach you a few basics. And you already know how to shoot a bow. Saw you in the forest."

"You didn't see the many days of missed shots," Ayela mumbled.

Ayela examined the bow's structure. Its arms were crafted from a polished hardwood. Smooth curves ran the length of the bow's fine craftsmanship. She ran her fingers over the engraved handle, where the wood was glued to an ivory spine. A series of strange runes ran its length, forming words in some foreign language. Ayela held the bow out in front of her. She adopted an archer's stance, with the string pulled to her cheek for a time, before relaxing her arm.

"It's heavier than I'm used to, but not overwhelming. I'll need to practice with it before we meet Logane and Zaktan. Do you think they would mind if we brought someone else with us," Ayela asked.

"For your friend? I don't know. Maybe." Bahn shrugged. "For now, I'd say we've been in the cold too long, and the wind is picking up. It's getting late, and we need to find shelter."

"Food first. We'll hit the markets, then head to the building I've been staying at in Southtown." Ayela led Bahn toward the market. "That's how I've survived so far."

"Yes, essentials tonight, then we can get some supplies tomorrow, train a bit, and you can get your friend." Bahn smiled. "This'll be fun. You'll see."

"There." Ayela pointed toward a small building nestled between two houses. "That's where I've been sleeping."

"It isn't much, but I can keep us warm here." Bahn stepped through the broken doorway.

An unnatural chill breathed over Ayela's neck when she crossed the familiar building's threshold. The paint on the walls had peeled since she was last here, and a musty stench hung heavy in the air. Ayela looked to the corner where she'd met Erithia, cursing the longing she felt for the pleasant warmth he'd provided.

"Something's not," Ayela began, wishing she'd been able to find a better home. But it was the best she'd found.

"Mamana shehl'aish, lohm malom." The palm of Bahn's hand emitted a faint orange light. He pressed it against the wall next to the door. Lines of glowing embers etched themselves into the wood around his hand. The building's temperature rose to a comfortable warmth near instantly. Bahn stumbled to the side, pulling his hand away from the wall.

"Strange, that spell doesn't usually take that much energy." Bahn leaned against the wall, looking toward Ayela. "I suppose magic on an empty stomach was a bad idea." He smiled. "Ready to eat?"

"You know magic?" Ayela sat next to Bahn, before misgivings lifted at the pleasant warmth filling the room. She broke the small loaf of bread they had bought before the markets closed and passed half to Bahn.

"A little, mostly just utility spells. Good for wilderness survival. It's too bad we didn't have time to get more supplies."

"We'll go to the market tomorrow for more food and warmer clothes. The guards won't let us into Midtown looking and smelling like this." Ayela pulled at her wet, torn clothes. "I'll try to save some money for a bath as well." Ayela sat against the wall opposite Bahn, watching the last rays of sunlight disappear behind the buildings.

She yawned while the room's temperature stabilized. "Thank you, for before." Ayela closed her eyes. She worked to massage her aching knuckles. Her fingers still trembled at the brazen hunger that'd been in the bowman's eyes. She shuddered to think what would have happened if Bahn hadn't come. "Tell me about the old man who led you to the shelter," Ayela prodded.

"He was peculiar, old and frail, but he held a sense of authority about him. He found me wandering the road outside the city and asked for my help to deliver goods to the shelter. Then I saw you and I just had a bad feeling," Bahn admitted. "So, I followed you. Just in case. I'd have left you alone if nothing had happened."

Ayela rested her head, believing his story. "I'm glad you did then." She smiled. "About the druids. I can tell it hurts. If you need someone to talk to, I've lost people too."

"No." Bahn looked away from Ayela. "I didn't lose anyone. Not like that. No one died. I..." Bahn hung his head. "I was defending some of our sacred land and made a mistake. Someone got hurt, and I desecrated something sacred in a reckless attempt to prevent outsiders from entering. I would have been executed for it, but my father bartered for my banishment instead."

"And that was worth execution? Desecration of a religious site?" It didn't make sense. She knew druid law was harsh, but that didn't sound right.

Bahn didn't answer, only turned over and pulled one of the thin blankets they'd purchased over his head.

Resigned for now that she wouldn't get more information, Ayela closed her eyes and pulled a blanket over her shoulders. Unwelcome tears welled in the longing remembrance of the blanket Erithia had given. She opened her eyes again, scanning the room in a vain wish that it was still there. Sinking back to the wall in disappointment, Ayela welcomed sleep.

8

Dreams

Milky pillars of polished granite rose as monoliths around Ayela, a radiance tamed by the polished red and black marble beneath her feet. The air was light with the scent of lavender incense. Beautiful patterns of light streamed throughout the circular room from stained-glass windows lining the walls that reached to an unruly height.

Ayela swayed to the distorted, distant melody that permeated the air. Her pillowy white dress flowed with her every move. A gentle hand grasped hers. Lillia stood beside Ayela, dressed in a dark blue dress with a black belt and faint gold embroidery around the seams. She was only a few years older than Ayela remembered, yet Lillia's hair was a shimmering white. Their eyes locked for a moment, and everything around them stood still.

"Will you dance with me," Lillia asked.

Ayela blushed with excitement. Lillia smiled, and they sprang to the dancefloor. But as they waltzed, the world grew darker. Light stopped shining from beyond the windows that twisted into grotesque displays of blood and violence.

Ayela's chest surged with panic. The music became deeper, heralding chills that rushed through her body. An impenetrable shadow lingered in the far corner of the room, slowly growing toward them. A large, inky hand gripped Lillia's neck. Panic bled from the woman's eyes. Ayela reached out, fighting to keep hold of Lillia. But she was ripped away, choked to unconsciousness by the hand as inky tendrils spread over her body. The entity dragged her lifeless form into the darkness. Ayela fell to her knees, numb. Then, all was silent.

A growl resonated from somewhere in the distance. Finally obeying, Ayela tripped over her feet in her haste to flee. Her arms flailed, struggling to maintain balance. The room transformed into city streets; the sky was a dark, blood-red. She looked behind her only to trip and fall onto the cobblestone road, allowing darkness to overtake her.

Ayela stood before a mirror where a hate-distorted reflection of her as a necromancer mimicked her every move. Erithia's wicked grin loomed in the mirror. His hand held a chain that bound Ayela's wrists.

Heavy air threatened to suffocate Ayela, pressing on her as though she were submerged in wet sand. Darkness again swallowed every aspect of her vision. She could no longer feel the ground beneath her. She could not hear herself scream. There was only the void. Then there was one word.

"Ayela." Someone was calling her.

Ayela thrashed in the darkness, screaming in surprise when her fist collided with something tangible. She opened her eyes, finding herself sitting against the dilapidated building's wall. Bahn sat on the ground next to her, massaging his chest. The white glow of moonlight shone through the windows of their shelter. The occasional cool breeze from the open windows accented the pleasant warmth of Bahn's spell.

"What, what happened," Ayela asked, breathing deeply and struggling to calm herself. Her breath quickened, scarred by the sight of herself as a necromancer.

DREAMS

"I'm not sure. You were sleeping, yet you seemed scared. I've only ever seen that in the forest." Bahn stopped for a moment as worry flashed across his face. "What did you see?"

"I was engulfed by darkness coming from the corner of the second floor of some elaborate building. Then I," She caught herself, "I've experienced nothing like it."

"If you were one of the elemental races, I'd say it was a nightmare, but humans can't dream unless they have powerful magic. You don't have magic, do you?"

"No. It couldn't be that. I was tested as a child. No magic, not even the slightest connection to the gods."

"Hmm," Bahn looked thoughtfully at the stairs. "You've stayed here before. Was any powerful dark magic cast here?"

"Uh…" Ayela hesitated. "I mean, not by me."

"Hey, no judgement here." Bahn threw up his hands. "Since there was dark magic here, I'd say it's probably a blight. As far as I know, they only live in corrupted trees. But if the wood in this house…" Bahn smiled at Ayela, "If there has been strong dark magic here, a blight could have been created. I will cast it out. Don't worry. I've banished them more times than I can count."

"What is a blight?"

"A blight is a creature created in the aftermath of powerful dark magic. It feeds off the life force of those that enter its territory, eventually growing strong enough to kill, creating another blight. Once they become powerful enough, blights cause strange dreams in the minds of those whom they seek to drain. It is the creature trying to establish a connection to your soul." Bahn paused, examining Ayela's worried expression before continuing. "But don't worry, I will not let it harm you." He smiled warmly and tugged at the collar of his new jacket, adopting a confident pose.

Ayela snickered.

"I've killed many creatures like it when I was with the druids. Sleep now. I'll have you drill a few basic defense techniques in the morning before we go get your friend. Then we will meet Logane and Zaktan at The Headless Snake. Hopefully, they'll have some low-risk jobs for us."

"Good," Ayela muttered. She imagined what sort of tasks qualified as low risk for a mercenary. "Where is The Headless Snake, anyway?"

"I passed it on my way into the city. I can get us there. Come to think of it. The old man took me on a longer route to reach the shelter than necessary. Almost like he wanted to show me the bar."

"Look, I wasn't straight with you before." Ayela yawned. "The gold eyes. I saw someone like that too. The guard who led me to the shelter a few weeks ago. What if he's the one who tipped off Logane and Zaktan? What if it's the same person, or thing, pulling us together?"

"Don't think the gods intervene like that. At least I've never heard of it." Bahn shrugged.

"Except Erithia." Ayela rubbed at her eyes. "But this didn't feel like him."

"Agreed. It felt warm, good. Like, genuinely," Bahn affirmed.

"And so far as I can remember, there's only one god with any connection to dragons. And Lapid is dead, his corpse entombed in Mount Hatave. At least, that's what the texts say."

"Somehow, I doubt the god of war, anger, and hate would feel so welcoming and reassuring," Bahn laughed.

"That's what I was thinking. I can picture the eyes perfectly, though. When we go get my friend at The King's Library, I want to do some research. We won't have too much time, but with Lillia's dragon obsession, I bet she could point us to the right book."

DREAMS

"So long as we can still get to The Headless Snake at a reasonable time." Bahn yawned. "Anyway, I'd better see to that blight. You get some rest."

"Alright, well, goodnight, Bahn," Ayela yawned. She smiled at the familiar sensation of floating to sleep. Ayela pictured the pleasant dance with Lillia. Her eyes watered and breath quickened at the remembrance of the darkness taking Lillia away.

Ayela opened her eyes, struck by the realization that she hadn't marked her way lately. She stood and grabbed a small, sharp stone from the surrounding rubble before kneeling by the wall. "As good a place as any." She pressed the stone into the wood, dragging it back and forth over the surface in a tired display. A single tear escaped her closed eyes when she finished carving the familiar diamond spiral. She leaned back, admiring her work.

"What's that," Bahn asked while he watched her.

"It was part of my family crest. A symbol of good fortune." Ayela smiled, hoping to relieve her fears and burning eyes. She leaned her head against the wall. "My mom taught it to me, said it would bring luck if ever we were separated. No one left to carry it but me now." She turned away from Bahn, unwilling to allow more prying questions.

Ayela wiped a tear from her cheek as she emptied her mind and strove for sleep.

The blinding light of the noon sun greeted Ayela when she opened her eyes. A pleasant spring breeze graced her face. She was lying in the middle of a wagon trail, winding between the rolling hills of the grasslands west of Hatave.

The unmistakable Mount Lapid towered over Ayela. Its twin crimson, snow-capped peaks rocketed through the sky. Ayela gazed longingly at the mountain. She imagined the fierce dragons that made their home in the red cliffs near the heights of the fire god's grave.

Time moved around Ayela. The hills shifted. Grass grew rapidly beneath her feet. The crumbling, overgrown remains of a stone structure erected itself surrounding her. She stood in awe of the sun. It grew into a massive body, emitting a brilliant orange light that illuminated the world with comfortable warmth. Vines bolted from the ground, embracing the newly erected walls and growing bulb-like structures that erupted at various points. The bulbs hastily grew toward the engorged sun, undulating in ways reminiscent of a snake. The bulbs bloomed into a luminous collection of colors that encircled Ayela.

Ayela jumped at the trickle of water behind her. A fountain stood tall in the center of the ruin. Its flawless stone seemingly unaffected by time. Ayela blinked, her mouth falling open in admiration of the flawless woman before her. It was only a statue, but carved in perfect detail. The statue's loose dress flowed as fabric, taken by the wind, outlining her curvaceous form. Calm waters gently flowed over the edges of a bowl held above the woman's head. Curious patterns of broken sunlight danced on the ruined walls, reflected off the rippling surface of the water in the fountain's base.

Thunder rolled over the grassland, heralding a warm breeze and the scent of rain. A layer of clouds obscured the sun, illuminated by flashes of lightning. A section of clouds parted, spreading around the sun as though it had descended below the clouds in all its glory.

"Ayela," a powerful male voice called to Ayela.

Ayela turned toward the voice, lifting her gaze to Mount Lapid. Her eyes widened, breath caught in her chest. The mountain's twin peaks were now ablaze with fire, spewing smoke into the sky.

"Ayela," called the voice again. This time closer, as though from someone standing beside her.

Ayela yelped, stumbling backward and falling to the ground. A massive wolf towered over her. Its long coat was a mixture of gray and brown that flowed as though weightless in the faint winter breeze. Ayela's heart slowed. Her gaze shifted between the wolf's emerald and sapphire eye, unable to decide where she should rest her sight. She recognized this wolf from illustrations within tomes she'd read in The King's Library.

"Musar." Ayela's jaw slacked. Her mind wiped clean of all thought. She stood, or rather, sat, before Musar, God of Earth. Ayela scrambled to her knees before his magnificent form.

"There is no need for fear," the wolf spoke, his lips forming words unnatural to a beast's form. Ayela's mind fell silent. The creature before her sat peacefully on the ground. Two large tails swayed gently behind the wolves near eight-foot seated form. "We have been watching you. One with the capability to shape the future, to herald an age of light, or an age of darkness. We grow hopeful of your strength in denying the temptations of Erithia."

"Erithia said the same thing," Ayela said. "Why me?"

"Whether because of chance or the Nali, you stand in the position to influence great change in the world. I am forbidden from saying more."

"The Nali?"

"You will learn in time. As you must. We have faith in you. The others forbid me from saying more."

"Others?"

The wolf stood, walking to the fountain. "The other gods are here with us in spirit, but I speak with you in body. Lapid in his mountain prison, Mahtsar in the sun's light, Naqam in the storm and wind surrounding us, and Ahava in the water of this fountain." The wolf looked longingly at the statue before taking a seat. His serene eyes locked with Ayela's. "Come, sit with me."

"Am I dreaming?" Ayela asked.

"Are you?" Musar replied, a hint of amusement in his voice. "It can be difficult for one to distinguish a dream from a vision, or if you aren't careful, from reality itself. Seldom, a rare few, are lucky enough to find them one and the same."

Thunder rolled in the distance at Musar's last comment. Musar sunk his head in a slight chuckle.

"You said Lapid's prison. I thought he was killed." Ayela glanced towards the flaming peaks that surged with a red glow.

"Yes, prison. But not..."

Ayela ducked, nearly falling forward as lightning exploded behind them, obliterating a stone wall. Thunder rolled in varied pitches for what seemed forever, piercing even through the ringing in Ayela's ears.

Musar looked to the sky with a snarl before returning his gaze to Ayela.

"Not allowed to say more?" Ayela asked through heavy breaths.

"It would seem not." Musar breathed.

"Why am I here? Where are we?"

"You have not left your place of rest. We visit you because we found it necessary to speak with you. Many have taken the path you're soon to embark upon in times long forgotten. Many have strayed, failed, or fallen away; yet others have turned away, neglecting the choices to be made either out of fear, lust, or shame. None before have we seen who denied the tempter in person. You are the first."

"I am the first what?"

"We have given you a gift. Something we hope will prepare you for the trials ahead. A gift we have only bestowed once before." Musar continued in a whisper. "We hope your path will prove more fruitful than hers."

Ayela lurched as lightning struck the ground next to Musar's tail. Thunder echoed words Ayela didn't recognize.

"I know what cannot be said!" Musar growled to the heavens. "There is no need for your tantrums."

A sudden gust of wind nearly blew Ayela off her feet before the clouds dispersed in a wave of light that emanated from the burgeoning sun.

"Thank you." Musar bowed to the sun. "Remember, Ayela, you will witness great things, and terrible things. Hard choices and sacrifices lie ahead of you, and the choices you make will change the world. For better or worse, remains to be seen."

"And if I want no part of this, whatever this is?"

"Choosing not to choose is a choice in and of itself. One many in your place have made. We believe you will make the choice that is right for you, right for the world."

With those words, Ayela's vision faded to black, and she felt herself once again drifting into the void of sleep.

9

Reunion

Ayela's heart raced as she startled awake to Bahn's scream, "Time to train!" Bahn swung a thick wooden branch toward Ayela.

"Wait!" Ayela ducked as the stick slammed against the stone wall above her head. "What are you doing?" She shot to her feet.

"Defend yourself. Show me what you can do." Bahn circled around her, holding the stave toward her with one hand braced stiffly against his chest.

Ayela's mind flashed to Eema, thrashing her as Bahn tapped her shoulder and chest with the stick.

"Good." Bahn grinned as Ayela stepped away, narrowly dodging his third attack.

"Stop!" Ayela's harsh voice boomed through the house as though spoken by some otherworldly entity. Bahn halted mid-swing as a flicker of fear passed over his face. Ayela held her hand up between them as the room spun ever so slightly. "I'm... not ready for that."

Bahn smiled. "Yes, you were. You dodged my attack, then warded me off with magic."

"What?" Ayela said in near-panicked breaths. Her eyes were tightly closed as she strove to block painful memories.

"You're more capable than you know. My trainer once told me that every fighter has his or her own way. The lesson was always to find his student's strengths by forcing them to act on instinct. I planned on attacking you further, but your words stopped me. For a moment, I couldn't move."

"You're wrong," Ayela laughed, stepping away from Bahn. "You have to be. I don't have magic. I'd have killed myself with it by now if I did. I was tested. People don't just get magic. Unless…" Ayela thought back to her dream of Musar and his mentioning of a gift. She smirked, dismissing the preposterous idea with a wave of her hand. That dream couldn't have been more than… Could it?

"The blight, did you ever find a blight here?" Ayela said.

"No, actually. I didn't."

"That doesn't… I can't have magic. I don't know how to control it. It's too dangerous!" Ayela paced, hands fidgeting with the hem of her shirt.

"I know I felt something." Bahn dropped his hands before tossing the stick back into the corner of the room.

"But that's just it!" Ayela said, flustered. "If I somehow have magic now, I need to learn to control it before I overcharge and kill myself. How do I even access it? Much less prevent myself from using it." Ayela paced away from Bahn, clutching her hair in frustration. "You know magic, teach me to control it."

"I'm sorry. Druids' control of magic is innate. It's not something I can teach because I never had to learn myself. Regardless, you will need to learn self-defense. We can start there. You mentioned a friend who knows magic. Maybe she could teach you. For now, hold out a fist."

Ayela extended her hand in a tentative fist. "I'm still not convinced it was magic. It couldn't have been." Who was she kidding? Erithia had visited her in person, and now the other gods in a dream. They said they'd given her a gift. Magic was certainly a possibility.

"When you're throwing a punch, it is important to keep your wrist flat, fist tight, and thumb down." He let go of her wrist and held his hands up in demonstration. "Stand like this. Elbows tucked in, one hand in front of the chest, one in front of your face, feet slightly apart. This is a ready stance, for both offence and defense."

"Why are you doing this? Helping me, I mean." Curiosity broke Ayela's concentration as she mimicked Bahn.

"I don't quite know," Bahn whispered as he stared into her eyes.

Ayela coughed, breaking the silence between them. "What's next?"

"Now we throw a punch. Follow me."

Ayela followed Bahn, punching with her right hand.

"Keep your elbows in and be sure to punch through your target. Here." Bahn instructed before holding his hand flat in front of her. "Imagine you are hitting something behind me and punch my hand." A smile broke over Bahn's face when Ayela struck the palm of his hand. "This time, imagine that you are a rock tumbling down a mountain at an unstoppable speed. Imagine something or someone you would like to hit, then strike. Just be sure to keep your wrist flat, fist tight, thumb down, and elbow in."

Ayela thought back to the last time Eema had hit her and threw her body into the punch.

"Damn," Bahn said as he recoiled his hand. "Nicely done. Again." Bahn stepped aside to let her strike an imaginary target in front of her. Ayela couldn't help but smirk at Bahn subtly massaging his hand.

"Drill punching for a while. Switch hands with each punch. I'll watch."

Ayela's heartbeat increased with every punch. She had to learn control. More importantly, she had to know if she had magic. It needed to be one of the first things she told Lillia. There hadn't been a blight, so there was no other explanation.

Ayela dropped her burning arms, relaxing her stance. "Markets then?"

"Yes, then we'll go to Midtown for your friend. We don't want to keep Logane and Zaktan waiting too long."

She massaged her aching arms before leaving the musty structure ahead of Bahn. A twinge of regret played over her mind. She'd been on the street for weeks. *Why didn't I try harder to get to Lillia?* It didn't matter now, and perhaps it was for the best. A flicker of hope twinkled in her eye at the imagined scene of Lillia and her sitting by a fire on the way back from their first job. Surely, things were looking up from here.

Ayela clasped her hand over the two gold marks and a minuscule handful of smaller silver and copper coins in her jacket pocket. She pressed through the crowded Southtown Market. The ice from the day before was slowly melting under the sunlight that shone through the partly cloudy sky.

"Do you know where a good clothing stall is?" Bahn walked beside Ayela.

"No, we'll find one, though." They wound through the maze of stalls in search of something resembling food or clothing.

Ayela pressed through the sea of people toward a bread stand at the end of the street. "Want some breakfast?"

Ayela stopped just short of the stall. Someone in a brown hooded cloak stood by the counter. Silky strands of black hair fell from under the hood. She handed the stall owner a silver coin. "Adina?" Ayela muttered. She retreated at the sight of the woman's ghostly white skin and slightly pointed chin. Sweat beaded on her forehead. Her vision narrowed, ears rang, blocking out all except the haunting figure before her. Blood stained the sleeve of the woman's cloak. Fresh blood.

Bahn stepped part-way between them, fists by his side at sensing Ayela's tension.

Ayela sighed when the woman turned toward them. Sharp eyes dashed between Bahn and Ayela. Three distinct red tattoos, painted over harsh brand scars, framed her face. This woman was older than Adina. Her features, well-defined and sharp, were almost elf-like. But her black irises, ghostly skin, and Mahtsarian brands betrayed her true nature as a Moonborn.

"I'm sorry, I thought you were…"

"Eema's murderer?" The Moonborn cut Ayela off. "Entire city heard. Doesn't mean you gotta treat us like we're all monsters to be feared. Not all of us are necromancers."

"I wasn't…" Ayela started. Her eyes widened as they locked on a sword scabbard by her side, its hilt revealed by her taking the baker's money. Next to the hilt, barely visible in her belt, was a small chain holding a pendant featuring a crow's foot holding two feathers. The symbol of the Nighthawk Assassins. Ayela stepped back, her voice caught in her throat.

The woman glanced behind Ayela toward the soft chinks of a guardsman's armor echoing from further down the street. A glare on the woman's chest caught Ayela's eye. She was wearing a small white pendant on a heavy silver chain. Warm air brushed over Ayela's face when she gazed at the gem in the center. A faint yellow glow gleamed from within the crystal's translucent surface. The nighthawk turned in silence, walking away from Ayela and Bahn. Ayela watched the woman dart into an alley, deftly evading a guard patrol.

"Who was that," Bahn asked when they moved on.

"A Nighthawk, a member of the assassin's guild," Ayela muttered. "We should move on." Ayela eyed the passing crowds. They continued to another bread stand some distance away.

"Nighthawks," Bahn asked when they approached the next stand.

"While The Kings Guild runs most above-board contracts. The Nighthawks are just as powerful. The biggest players in Hatave's criminal underground. Most of the city guard won't dare cross them."

"And Adina? You knew a necromancer?"

"No, she wasn't always one." Ayela bought a loaf of bread from the baker. "She turned herself into a necromancer. Made a deal with Erithia to save her own skin, and mine." Ayela muttered, handing a piece of bread to Bahn. "All of it's my fault."

"You shouldn't blame yourself for another's actions," Bahn remarked while they fished their way through the market. "Was she the source of dark magic in that home?"

"No, and why shouldn't I blame myself? She made the deal because of me!" Ayela's voice grew in frustration at the resurfacing tears. "I was the reason she didn't get away. Now she's dead or worse, all because I didn't trust her."

"You didn't trust a necromancer. That's good, isn't it?"

"Let's just... I can't right now." Ayela set her jaw. "We need fresh clothes. Then we can go to Midtown."

REUNION

One silver mark for boots, three silver for our baths, Ayela moaned as she clasped her hand around her lonely silver mark. Tinges of regret at having given away the third gold mark played at the edges of her mind, only to be driven out. "I'll make it," she whispered to herself, enjoying the sensation of freedom from the dirt and grime of nearly a month on the street.

"I really hope we can afford food for the three of us tomorrow."

Ayela straightened the sleeves of her woolen shirt. She scratched at the roughly stitched seam, thankful at least that it was warm. She stopped before the Midtown gate. Memories flooded Ayela of the many times Adina had led her and the other orphans through the gate. Somehow, despite everything, she missed those simpler times.

"State your name and business in midtown." The guard's graveling voice ground away the memory. He was an older man whose brown eyes betrayed a battle-scarred soul. His plate armor gleamed in the sun under his crimson red shoulder cape.

Ayela braced herself for the harsh admonishing of the guards that so often stopped and questioned her on her solo trips to the library. "I'm Ayela, this is Bahn; I'm visiting a friend at the library. Her name is Lillia," Ayela replied innocently, striving to ignore the memory of Kiyle's death as it writhed at the fringes of her mind.

The guard's stern eyes softened at the sound of Lillia's name. "Ayela? Really..." The guard looked Ayela head to toe. "She will be thrilled to see you. Last we were told, you were dead. Killed by Adina. I will take you to her."

"Killed!" Anger flushed Ayela. Had the guards that held her truly told Kote and Lillia she was dead? Is that why Master Kote hadn't come to find her? "That's okay." Ayela growled. "I know the way."

"Please, I insist. I can't let you wander midtown alone. The other guards can cover my post here while I take you to The King's Library." The guard in front of Ayela and Bahn motioned to the other guards at the gate, forming several quick signs with his hand before returning his gaze to Ayela. "I am Captain Zan. I'll escort you to the library."

"Wait, Zan, as in Uncle Zan?" Ayela asked. "Lillia's uncle?"

"Not by blood," Zan laughed. "But yea. A close friend of Master Kote."

"But you're a guard captain. If you don't mind my asking, why were you posted at the Midtown Gate? Isn't that a recruit's job?" Ayela asked as they walked.

"We're short-handed. And I may be old, but Mahtsar help me, I won't sit around while my men need help. Besides, it's been too long since I hit the streets."

"Is that why you insisted on accompanying us?" Bahn asked.

"No, Kote is an old friend. I haven't seen him in several months. That, and a new law ratified by the chief judge. Because of the protest, we can't allow Southtowners to roam the Midtown streets without an escort. Personally, I think it is ridiculous and impractical."

"Protest? For Adina?" Ayela asked as they stopped to allow a small boy in a bright red tunic to run past them. She hadn't thought Eema and Adina's events would have such an impact.

"The guard has been cracking down on Moonborn more than usual after what happened to Eema. It's been the worst in Southtown. They always get the rotten end, no matter how many policies and laws are enacted. This time, other races are coming to their defense, which is encouraging. But it's the people that need to change, not the law." Ayela bit her lip at Zan's last statement.

"Don't misunderstand," started the guard when they fell silent. "I mean, all people need to change, not just one race or class. To most, Moonborns are manifestations of Erithia's influence and, thus, are inherently evil. I don't buy that, though."

"How come?" Bahn asked.

"The gods either never existed or are dead. It's been five thousand years since a recorded sign, and Erithia's Empire hasn't pushed our borders since the last war almost two thousand years ago. I think they realized the truth, no reason to continue the god's eternal war if they're dead. Needless to say, that belief is frowned upon by many of my comrades."

"And if I told you I've seen a god?"

"I'd say you were drinking the same crazy soup as the guards from the Southtown Barracks. They spread some crazy rumor that a Southtowner claimed to have spoken with Erithia in person. Even said a paladin proved she was telling the truth and let her live. It makes little sense. If I am wrong, and the gods aren't dead, the only reason Erithia would talk to someone is if they were their puppet. If they were their puppet, there is no way a Paladin would let them live!"

Ayela considered correcting him, exposing herself as the subject of the rumors, but thought better of it, as he would expect a full recounting of events. Something she didn't want to do.

"If the gods are dead, where does magic come from?" Ayela challenged instead, choosing to move on from the rumors about her. "Regardless, it's not that Moonborn are innately evil. Just that society's expectations mold them." Ayela's voice grew soft as she thought back to her last moments with Adina.

"Wise words from one so young." Captain Zan laughed. "An age-old debate. Are we born who we are, or are we shaped by our environment? Is it fate, or is it circumstance?"

"Which do you think it is? Fate or circumstance?" Bahn asked.

"I'd say it's a bit of both. I believe we are born with certain tendencies, but it is our circumstances that shape who we grow into. That, and the decisions of the individual." The captain smiled as they turned off the street into the familiar courtyard of The King's Library.

"You're not what I expected," Ayela said as they approached the library door. "When I first saw you, I thought you were some battle-hardened veteran who would treat me like a filthy Southtowner. But you didn't. I wish more guards were like you."

"Thank you, Ayela. I'm glad I didn't offend you with my radical views." He laughed. "If I may, one last thing. I don't know what you two have been through, but I can tell something's hurt you. I know the look. The world may seem dark and vicious, but it's not all bad. Remember that and look for light in the darkness. Find it, hold on with all of your might. Because, given time, the darkness will pass." Ayela closed her eyes for a moment as a small knot formed in her throat. "It is those without hope that become lost." Zan smiled before turning to knock on the door.

Ayela imagined the anger Lillia would surely feel at her having taken so long to return. And how Kote would react upon learning the guard had lied to him.

Almost a minute passed before Ayela heard the door lock lift. There, framed in the doorway, backlit by the library's warm sunlight filtering through the stained-glass windows, was Lillia. She wasn't wearing her usual formal dress. Instead, she wore comfortable-looking travel-trousers and a white tunic with long baggy sleeves.

Lillia swayed in silence. Her mouth was slightly ajar as her eyes looked Ayela head to toe. She held a single hand over her chest while the other hid behind her hip in a guarded pose.

Ayela shifted her feet. Her eyes locked with Lillia, sharing in her friend's uncertainty. "Hey," Ayela managed only a whisper, her planned reintroduction vanishing from her mind.

"Ayela?" Lillia's voice shook, teetering on the border of unbelief and hope.

"Yeah, it's me." Ayela stepped up the stairs toward Lillia, moving to embrace her.

Lillia stepped back, her face turning to anger. "Hey?" Lillia yelled, tears welling in her eyes. "That's all you say, hey?!"

"I thought… They told me Adina killed you!" Tears fell down Lillia's cheeks. "Do you have any idea what I've…" Her hands clenched into fists by her side. "What took you so long?"

"I couldn't. They held me in jail for days. When they finally let me out, I had nothing. No way of getting past the midtown gates, no money for food or to bathe. Nothing. I had to focus on surviving." Ayela stepped forward.

"You left me here, alone." Lillia's demeanor shifted from anger to relief. Her shoulders slackened as she looked longingly at Ayela. "I mourned you!"

"I'm sorry," Ayela cried. "I never meant to hurt you. I…"

Lillia breathed deeply in a vain attempt to regain her composure. "I was so scared without you. Scared I'd have to…" Her hands trembled. "Just give me a second." She turned back into the library. Motioning for them to enter behind her.

"I'm here now, and I'm not going anywhere." Ayela stepped forward, turning Lillia around and cupping her cheek in her hand. Lillia leaned into her and closed her eyes, allowing Ayela to wipe away another falling tear. "I'm so sorry."

"Is Master Kote home?" Zan interrupted, smiling with a tear in his eye as he watched their reunion.

"No, Uncle, sorry. He's at the palace, a meeting with several of the judges and other nobility. I don't think he'll be back tonight," Lillia said. She let Ayela go and straightened her shirt, as though suddenly aware there were others present. "You staying for a while? My father put me on house arrest after…

well... You know. It is awfully boring here. Who's with you?" Lillia said as she looked to Bahn.

"This is Bahn. Bahn, this is Lillia. And, yeah, I was hoping to stay for a bit."

"I must get back to my post. Tell your father I stopped by and that I'd like to catch up sometime. It was good talking with you, Ayela." Zan turned away, leaving Lillia, Bahn, and Ayela standing in the doorway. He stopped, turning toward the two. "If you're planning what I think you are, please be careful. And do an old man a favor. Leave a note." The captain smiled and left the group, disappearing around a corner. "Be sure to tell your father Ayela is alive. He will want to know."

"Will do, sir." Lillia bowed to Zan and shut the door behind him.

Inside was exactly as Ayela remembered, except for a traveler's pack some distance from the door. There was also a distinct lack of servants doing their routine cleanings or re-shelving of books.

"Lillia, what's going on? Where is everyone," Ayela asked.

"I convinced father to give everyone the day off. Said I wanted time alone before the wedding tomorrow." Lillia brushed hair away from her face. "In reality, I was planning to leave, to Korvania, like we planned."

"By yourself?"

"Well, you were dead. Who else was I gonna go with?" Her tone bordered on irritation. "A day before the wedding. Any later and I'd... We'd..."

Ayela hesitated as silence drug between them. "I have..."

"What happened?" Lillia demanded. "The guards told us they found your corpse in the orphanage, buried under the rubble about a week after everything happened." Lillia stood uncomfortably in the otherwise silent foyer.

"No, they held me for several days. I had to request a paladin's judgement to get out."

Lillia closed her eyes and shook her head. "Why would they lie to us? The only reason my dad stopped looking for you was that they told us you died."

"Probably trying to cover up how they treated me." Ayela said. "No food, barely any water, and chained to a stone wall for days on end."

Candles along the wall flared with Lillia's enraged breath. She caught herself, closing her eyes and calming her breath. "I knew the guard was corrupt, but. Why?"

"It doesn't matter. Things seem to be working out now. We've got a plan." Ayela gestured to Bahn. "If you're interested."

"Bahn is it," Lillia asked. "How do you two know each other?"

"Bahn saved my life," Ayela interceded.

"What do you mean, saved your life? From Adina?"

"No, after. Some people tried to rob me. He stopped them," Ayela said, nodding at Bahn. "I'd met him before that, anyway. He's a druid from Lapid Forest."

"What's a druid doing in Hatave," Lillia asked, looking between Bahn and Ayela.

"It's complicated." Bahn rubbed the back of his neck as he spoke. Clearly uncomfortable watching the two reunited friends.

"We're becoming mercenaries together. I was wondering. You said you wanted to go on an adventure," Ayela asked. "Surely joining us is a more exciting adventure than starting over in the mountains?"

"I don't know." Lillia grinned as she looked at the floor. "I had all these plans."

"You'll join then?" Ayela smirked. "Come on, I know you can't pass an opportunity like this. We want you as our healer, since you know healing magic."

"Well, I wouldn't say I know healing magic. More like I've used healing magic, only the Light-based, not the dark stuff." Lillia said as she brushed a curl of hair off her face. "Come, we should gather some supplies. Bahn, you mind waiting here?" Lillia grabbed Ayela's hand, pulling her down the hall.

"I still can't believe you're here." Lillia murmured as they walked toward her and Kote's living quarters and the kitchen. "I can't imagine how hard it's been for you."

"Could be worse, honestly. I've been staying at this old, abandoned house and begging at the shelter for food. I tried starting as an apprentice with several carpenters or bakery stalls, but none would have me."

"What about a letter? Postage is cheap." Lillia turned to Ayela with a disbelieving look in her eyes.

"I never had enough to do more than eat. Until now."

"I'm just glad you're here, and that you made it before I left. Now!" Lillia pointed sharply at Ayela. "How long have you and Bahn been seeing each other?" Lillia asked. "Is that the real reason you kept sneaking out?"

"No, no. It's not like that. He's just helping me get back on my feet." Ayela laughed before moving through the open archway toward the kitchen, rubbing her chilled hands. "He caught me poaching in the forest last time and let me go. He found me in the city after I got out of jail. It was his idea to become mercenaries together, and I like the thought of it. He's training me in self-defense."

"Uh huh." Lillia rolled her eyes unbelievingly. "He just found you… in this city."

"Yeah, about that. I don't think it was coincidence. Both of us saw something. I don't have time to explain much. But do you know of books that would describe creatures with dragon eyes that can take the form of a human?"

"What are you saying?" Lillia's face bore disbelief at Ayela's words.

"This person with dragon eyes. They guided Bahn and I together. Brought me to the shelter and a few days later, brought Bahn."

"You think a dragon is meddling in your life? You know how unlikely that is. Only the High-Dragons of ancient legend could take human forms. And they stopped interfering in mortal lives when Lapid was killed."

"Not sure, but both of us saw a flash of golden dragon eyes."

"I think there is a book upstairs with illustrations of what high dragons are supposed to look like. Maybe. But if I remember right, dad has it locked in a cabinet. It's too valuable a tome. No way I can get into it without his keys." Lillia bit her lip.

"Okay, say you saw what you think you saw, and a high dragon really is pushing you into mercenary work with Bahn. Why?"

"Can high dragons cause dreams?" Ayela asked.

"Dreams? Not that I know. Why? You're not having dreams. Because that would mean you had magic."

"I am."

"That's a big problem! Veil's shroud, how in the god's name do you have magic! That's not possible. You were tested." Lillia furiously grabbed a second pack from the closet before harshly closing the door.

"I know. But I've had two dreams since Adina lost it."

"Felt anything? got dizzy when you were upset, or done something magical by accident?"

"Once, when Bahn first tried to train me."

"Gods, Ayela. And you're going on a mercenary mission."

"Was hoping you could help me."

"It's not that simple. Control takes time to master."

"I know. It took you months."

"And I still don't have it entirely mastered." Lillia looked Ayela over. "Be very careful. Monitor your emotions. That's the primary thing. Uncontrolled magic is tied to emotions. It's why we're tested as infants. Powerful emotions open the door to magic. But if you don't know how to close the door, it'll overwhelm you. We don't have time to teach you to close it. So, stay calm."

"I think I can do that."

"You better hope so."

"Here." Lillia opened a thin white wood door, exposing the clean marble-floored room that was their kitchen. Inside, there was a partially packed satchel of dried food sitting on the counter. "Danger of magic aside. I'm glad you made it here today. Before I ran off." Lillia's lip quivered as her gaze lingered on Ayela. "Really didn't want to go alone. You better not fucking blow yourself up. I couldn't—"

"I won't." Ayela closed her eyes, taking a moment to enjoy the familiar smell of fresh bread and spices.

"I packed provisions to last myself a few days. Give me a bit to pack a little more. Although I only have two tents. I like the new outfit, by the way, it suits you." Lillia smiled before quickly turning away.

"Please, it's just what was available." Ayela smiled as she helped Lillia gather supplies. "Do you know how to use that?" Ayela asked as she saw Lillia tuck a small dagger in her belt.

"Of course, I convinced father to let Uncle Zan train me. It came in handy when Adina attacked."

"So, she did attack! What happened?"

"She and Kiyle attacked the library. Father's guards killed Kiyle outside, but he kept coming back. Adina broke through the skylight. I fended her off for a while. At least until she broke my arm." Lillia flexed her previously broken arm. "Honestly, I think she'd have killed me if the guards hadn't shown up when they did. That's when she ran, fled the library without the children."

"Broke your arm!" Ayela rushed forward, pulling up Lillia's sleeve. All that remained of the injury was a fresh red scar and nasty yellow bruising. "Yeah, my dad had a healer from The Citadel treating it over a couple of days. Just a little sore now."

"How'd she get away?"

"Jumped out of the top-floor window. Splatted against the ground, then healed herself with dark magic. Killed several city guards on her way back to Southtown."

"Jumped out a three-story window onto stone and just walked away? How is anyone supposed to stop a necromancer?" Ayela marveled.

"Light magic. It's the only reliable way to deal damage to them, aside from decapitation or destroying their heart. Anyway, ready to go?" Lillia hoisted a large travel pack over her shoulders and handed one to Ayela. "Oh, and I brought a bit of money I've been setting aside." She jostled a coin purse under her shirt.

"I wasn't going to ask."

"But we need it. So, you ready?"

"Yes, we'll head back to the building we've been staying at. We have some things to pick up before we meet the others."

"Others?" Lillia asked as they reached the front of the library, where Bahn was waiting.

"Yes, two other mercenaries who we'll be joining," Ayela said as Bahn stood from the bench he had been waiting on. "Logane and Zaktan."

Lillia handed a heavy satchel and spare tent to Bahn before shouldering her bag and tent.

"Where will we be meeting the mercenaries," Lillia asked.

"Some place called The Headless Snake," Ayela replied.

"Oh! The note. Dad will want to know you're alive. He deserves to know where I've gone." Lillia took off her pack and pulled out a small parchment and a stick of graphite. She wrote her father a note before scratching a series of symbols onto the page and rolling it up. She placed the note on a table in the entryway. Ayela recognized the symbols as a code that she and Lillia had created years ago.

"Don't want him finding us too fast." Lillia shrugged in response to Ayela's questioning look. "Sorry, Dad." Lillia hung her head before following Ayela out of the library.

10

The Headless Snake

"There it is." Bahn pointed toward a large, two-story building, "The Headless Snake." He gestured to a hanging sign above the door that featured a carving of a snake with its head cut off.

"This place is a wreck." Lillia slowed her pace. Her face twisted in revulsion at seeing the decrepit tavern.

"Even for Southtown, this is…interesting." Ayela eyed the collapsing second story and clear wood rot plaguing the half-fallen structure. The building was larger than all the surrounding establishments, making it feel even farther out of place.

"It could do with a remodel, sure. But I've heard this is the best place for budding mercenaries to get a start."

"This looks like a hangout for criminals." Lillia's eyes shifted between Ayela and The Headless Snake as she fidgeted with her sleeve. Fear-born reservations showed in her narrowed eyes. She was out of her element, farther into the slums than she'd ever been.

"I don't know about criminals. There were some rough individuals in there when I visited, but I didn't see any criminal activity. They have a job board with plenty of work for mercenaries." Bahn smiled.

"When did you visit this place?" Ayela inquired, furrowing her brow at Bahn. "Didn't you just get into the city? How would you know so much about it?"

"The old man. He brought me here on the way. It was out of the way of our destination. But he claimed there was someone he had to talk to. We didn't stay long, but he told me about the place." Bahn paused. "Come to think of it, we didn't actually talk to anyone here. He just nodded to someone before telling me about the place."

"Are we sure we should be trusting this man? It feels like we're being set up for something." Ayela spoke, her suspicion growing.

"He didn't ring any warning bells for me." Bahn shrugged. "Aside from the eyes, and I'm not even sure I saw that."

"You did." Ayela stopped ahead of the group, "I saw them too. The guard who brought me to the shelter. And before you say it's the gods bringing us together, I'm not so sure."

"Why didn't you say earlier?" Bahn scowled. "And what makes you say it's not the gods?" Bahn took a few more steps toward The Headless Snake before turning back. "The druids teach that the dragons are agents of the gods. I know it wasn't a dragon. But we saw Dragon Eyes. So, it must be their influence. What else could it be?"

"A trap." Lillia folded her arms over her chest. "Seriously, you two just going to walk right into the place this person wanted you to go?"

"Aren't dragons supposed to be good?" Ayela asked

"No, that's not what I'm saying. I don't think it was a high dragon. The chances of it are, well, impossible." Lillia said. "It's far more likely someone or something else is using magic to make you see and feel certain things."

"That's a lot of trouble to go through." Bahn shook his head. "Why would someone go through all that just for us? Far more likely an answer to our prayers."

"The gods don't work like that," Lillia muttered.

"But what if they do?" Ayela said meekly.

Lillia looked her over, shocked by her friend's sudden shift in view. "Thought you didn't believe in the other gods. And Musar has no connection to dragons."

"All I know is someone with ill intent would just attack or kidnap us. They wouldn't lead us into a trap. Gods or no gods, someone is playing a larger game. And I feel like we're just pieces on their board." Ayela looked toward The Headless Snake. "I think we should play along. At least for now, with caution."

"I feel like this is a bad idea," Lillia breathed.

"Look. I can't explain it. But I have a feeling we should follow," Ayela said.

"I trust you, Ayela." Lillia relented after a long pause. She stepped toward Ayela. "But this stranger pulling strings... it makes me nervous."

"Do you remember Maximara," Ayela asked Lillia.

"The old hero Maximara? The dragon princess? You mean from Dragon Lands?"

"She was a dragon that could take the form of a human. Maybe that's what we're dealing with," Ayela suggested.

"Maximara is a fairy tale," Lillia's tone dripped with disappointment at the notion.

"But don't some fairy tales have an origin in truth?"

"Yeah, some. But Dragon Lands is old. Like, before written history old. Passed by word of mouth for generations." Lillia discounted the theory with a wave of her hand. "And there are no other accounts like it. Just the illustrations in the mythology codex I told you about at The Library."

"But the legend specifically mentions eyes of gold."

"Yea, and the legend also has four-armed giants, merfolk, and floating cities. Not exactly the most credible source," Lillia said.

"You think he was an actual dragon," Bahn asked.

"The guard who took me to the shelter. He had the same eyes you describe. And I," Ayela hesitated, unwilling to revisit the events that landed her at Eema's doorstep. "I've seen them before. The eyes, I mean."

Bahn scratched his chin. "As I said, I've felt that the gods brought us together. Maybe I was right?"

"Come on," Lillia chuckled. "I'm religious enough, but the gods haven't directly influenced the world like that since the last great war five thousand years ago." Lillia looked between Ayela and Bahn before again turning to the tavern. "Gods, I hope you're wrong, though. Maximara's story doesn't exactly end well; none of the legends do. Any time the gods get hands on it doesn't work out for the mortals."

"Guided here or not, mercenary work seems our best chance at survival." Ayela strode toward the door of the tavern.

"Will they even let us in," Lillia asked. "We aren't quite of age to be in a tavern."

"Southtown pub owners don't care. If you have money, they'll serve you," Ayela said.

"But that's against the law," Lillia mumbled as she walked behind Ayela, her arms crossed over her chest.

Warm music filled the air as Ayela, Bahn, and Lillia entered The Headless Snake. Ayela stifled a cough at the stench of ale that assaulted her nostrils. The tavern's patrons were a mix of people, from the typical impoverished Southtowner to the experienced, well-armed mercenary with polished armor.

"Her music is lovely." Lillia bounced, pointing to a woman sitting on a small pedestal in the center of the tavern. Several men and women surrounded her. All intently watched the gentle movement of her hand playing the red-wood violin. The musician's smooth skin was translucent and shimmered in the candlelight. Her vibrant red hair accented her skin, drawing attention to her fierce facial features. Her dark blouse floated on her shoulders. She rested her cheek against her instrument. Her movements were graceful yet swift and full of energy, synchronizing with the warm, fast-paced melody she drew from the violin.

Ayela couldn't help but stare into her striking purple eyes and the storm that seemed to rest behind them. "Who is the Stormling?" Ayela's eyes widened, locked with the woman's movement when the melody broke into a peculiar rhythm. The Stormling's movements evolved into an enthralling display of sensuality. Ayela traced arcs of electricity that flowed over her toned body, moving with contagious energy.

"No idea. She wasn't here last time; her music is wonderful, though." Bahn broke his stare with the elemental and approached the bar, followed by Lillia and Ayela.

"Who's this?" A stern male voice called from behind Ayela. "I'm Logane." Logane reached to Lillia with an open hand expectantly.

"A pleasure, my lord." Lillia shook his hand elegantly with a bow of her head. "I am Lillia."

Zaktan snorted from behind Logane, chuckling under his breath while he sat at the bar.

"No lords here," Logane laughed. "Just Logane. This is my charge, Zaktan." Logane pointed to the man next to him. A deep sadness betrayed Zaktan's bitter exterior. His slick black hair fell loosely to the sides, a stark contrast to how it had been fixed in the alley. He searched Lillia and Ayela, judging their capabilities, before turning back toward the bar. "Don't mind him; he'll warm up to you."

"I thought we could use a mage on our side." Ayela smiled, patting Lillia on the shoulder.

"Another child?" Zaktan growled. "Logane, can we talk about this?"

Logane glared at Zaktan, who rolled his eyes, turning back to the bar. "We already talked to the blacksmith." Zaktan's harsh accent grated on Ayela's ears. He motioned for the bartender. "Nickul, how about a round?" Zaktan called to the bartender. He placed a single piece of silver on the counter.

"What he means is, we figured it would be easier to negotiate payment if we talked to the blacksmith ourselves. We have more experience and a reputation as mercenaries." Logane sighed, sitting down next to Zaktan. "He agreed to pay everyone with a piece of armor from his stock in addition to the bounty. He doesn't know the rest of you are new to merc work. Though the pay will have to be split differently with the addition of your friend."

"That was kind of you," Bahn replied. "What's the contract?"

"Guarding a caravan." Logane replied. "It shouldn't be too hard. Apparently, this blacksmith's shipments are being attacked upon return to Hatave. No one has been seriously injured in the raids. It's the lowest risk contract that was posted. We will meet the caravan at the west-most gate of Hatave tomorrow morning. Tonight, we'll talk about your skills and what you can and cannot do. Then we'll discuss strategy for the caravan." Logane nodded toward the man who approached them with two drinks. He wore a dusty cream-colored shirt beneath a black apron. His face was oddly unremarkable. Aside from his warm smile, short hair and brown eyes, he held no features Ayela could easily use to distinguish him from another person.

"Good to see you again, Logane. New friends?" The man held a warm smile. "I'm Nikul, owner of this fine establishment. If there's anything you need, just give me a shout." Nikul stood there for a moment, as though expecting an order.

"I'll take water for now," Bahn said.

"Sure thing." Nikul turned toward the other end of the bar before reaching for a glass and dunking it into a large barrel. He handed it to Bahn before moving on to the other patrons.

"Who is the woman playing the violin," Lillia asked, still enamored with her music.

"The storm elemental? I don't remember her name, but I know she plays here a lot," Logane stated before taking a small sip of mead. "She used to use her magic in the shows. The crowd loved seeing her sheathed in lightning. The new laws against destructive magic have really taken a toll on her performance."

"So, kid." Zaktan turned to Ayela. His hostile tone dripped with mistrust. "You'll forgive my candidness, but aren't you a little young for merc work? People die in this profession; we kill people in this profession. Are you ready for that?"

Ayela smiled, confidently setting her shoulders. "We're ready for it. Wouldn't be here otherwise. I'm an archer, and Lillia's a healer. From the looks of it, you need us." Her feigned confidence waned at the thought of taking a life. She hadn't considered the need to kill. Maybe it wouldn't come to that just yet.

"Hmm." Zaktan paused for a moment, lost in thought.

"Zaktan, those are two roles we're missing. The more support we have, the less dangerous the mission will be for all involved." Logane placed his calloused hand on Zaktan's shoulder.

Zaktan groaned disapprovingly.

Logane sighed, with sagging shoulders. "You are inexperienced. Means you should avoid getting close to any attackers. Simply for the sake of putting Zaktan's mind at ease. Could you show us how well you can use that bow?" He gestured to the bow slung over Ayela's shoulder. The one she'd stolen from the thug who'd attempted to rob her. "There is a target in the alley behind the tavern."

"Yea, gotta know if we can trust your shot before we let you cover us in battle," Zaktan growled.

"Not a problem." Ayela slid the bow off her shoulder and followed the others out the back door.

Ayela grimaced when her foot sloshed through a thin layer of gray icy muck on the stone floor of the narrow alley behind the tavern. She gulped, hoping the slop was only mud.

Even with the door closed, the Elemental's music still softly rang through the air. A painted hay target stood against a stone wall at the back of the alley. The target was closer than the deer in the forest had been.

"You've got this," Lillia whispered with a knowing smile. This was going to be easy.

Ayela smirked and drew an arrow from the quiver fastened around her waist. Ayela raised the bow and pulled the string back with three fingers. She pictured the stance and position the archery books in the library had taught her. The position she'd practiced time and time again. The bow hardly made a sound as Ayela released the string.

"Yea!" Lillia squealed when the arrow struck the target with a satisfying thud. Ayela nodded, her grin spread. The arrow was embedded in the target dead center on the coin-sized bullseye.

"Nice shot," Bahn exclaimed.

"Okay, let's see if you can do it again," Zaktan muttered. "Prove it isn't beginners' luck."

Without hesitation, she drew the bow, following the same motions as before. The arrow again struck the target with a resounding thud, causing several strands of straw to fly off the top. The arrow had struck the left edge of the bullseye.

"Again." Logane said.

Ayela drew the bow again and fired quicker than the previous two shots. The arrow flew true, scraping the side of the first arrow and hitting the target near dead center.

"A'ight, I admit. You ain't as bad as I feared," Zaktan sighed, dropping his cloak to reveal his polished breastplate and padded armor. He opened a crate behind him and pulled out a small bundle of blunted practice arrows.

"Zaktan," Logane started.

"You promised," Zaktan growled. "I have to know I can trust her nerve." He threw the arrows down at Ayela's feet and walked toward the target. Once there, he drew his sword. Its perfectly shined and polished blade glinted amber hues in the setting sunlight. The sword was clearly a piece he took pride in. His eyes adopted a hunger reminiscent of the thugs in the alleyway. "Stop me before I get to you or feel my blade against your skin."

"Zaktan!" Logane protested.

"Relax, her friend's a healer. I won't do too much damage. Just make her hurt." He smiled widely at the last bit.

Ayela's heart raced in her chest; her eyes locked with Zaktan's. His sinister demeanor left no doubt in Ayela's mind. This was no hollow threat. He meant every word.

"Ayela, no." Lillia stepped forward.

"What, no faith in her?" Zaktan huffed. "Or do you think yourself not capable of saving her?"

"I'll do it." Ayela's fist tightened around her bow as she lifted the bundle of arrows and dropped them into her quiver. She imagined his smug face battered by the practice arrow. How humbling it would be for him to be bested by a novice.

"Mahtsar's sake, no!" Lillia protested, grabbing Ayela's wrist.

"Trust me." Ayela smirked with perhaps unfounded confidence. "Going to knock this prick down a few notches.

"You think so?" Zaktan backed toward the target, arms raised and sword in the air. "Little girls don't belong in our world. Someone's got to show you that. Might as well be me." Her blood boiled at his dismissive tone.

Zaktan stopped in front of the target. "Take aim, girl, 'cuz here I come." He lifted his sword threateningly at Ayela.

She aimed, arms trembling, nerves shaken by the approaching villain, despite her earlier confidence. She fired, color draining from her face when the arrow went wide, missing Zaktan entirely.

"Where's all that bravado now?" Zaktan taunted, taking small steps forward.

She notched another arrow, taking aim. Zaktan picked up the pace. She fired.

"Shit!" Zaktan cursed, stumbling to the side when the arrow deflected off his breastplate, narrowly missing his neck.

He broke into a jog as Ayela notched another arrow. Her ears rang, blood boiled. The world seemed to slow as she took aim. She saw only Zaktan charging her with murderous intent. He stepped to the side, now only a few steps from her. He lifted his sword to strike. Her aim adjusted as if on instinct when Zaktan lunged. She fired.

The world spun slightly as the arrow struck Zaktan. Zaktan stumbled backward. His sword clattered to the ground at Ayela's feet. "Fuck!" He garbled while stumbling into the wall and clutching his face. The arrow clattered to the ground behind Zaktan as he slid down against the alley wall. Blood flowed freely from between his fingers.

Lillia dashed past Ayela without a word, pulling at Zaktan's frantic grasp. "Let me help you, dumbass," Lillia commanded.

He relented, allowing Lillia to pry his hand away.

All of them stepped back at seeing Zaktan's mutilated face. The arrow had struck his nostril, tearing it from his skull along with a large flap of skin that ran under his eye, exposing bone.

Lillia stepped in, struggling to compose herself. He screamed as she lifted the flap of skin into place and closed her eyes.

"Mamana shehl'lahee, bawsar e'nilud lehtahlen." Warm light radiated from beneath Lillia's hand as she held her palms over Zaktan's face. He screamed in pain, tears flowing from his eyes as the sweet smell of burned flesh rose between them.

"Dai" Lillia fell back from Zaktan, eyes closed and breathing heavily. "That's all I can do for now." She gasped.

Zaktan felt his mended face. The bleeding had stopped, and the flap of flesh had reconnected. Yet a clear, cauterized gash was present. It spread from his deformed nostril to under his eye. A clear path where the arrow had traveled. He rested his head against the brick wall in silence.

"You asked for it," Lillia grumbled while Ayela helped her up.

"You idiot." Logane lifted Zaktan to his feet. "How'd you think that was gonna go?"

Zaktan only grunted in response. He broke from Logane's grip and stormed back into The Headless Snake.

"Guess all that reading pays off," Lillia laughed.

"Reading? You mean you learned how to shoot like that from books," Logane asked, a look of astonishment flashing across his face. "No one taught you?"

"I suppose, though I have practice hunting in the forest." Ayela shrugged. "I've hit a running target before."

"I told you she was good," Bahn boasted.

"Yea." Logane smirked. "Might should've mentioned that to Zaktan first. Come, we should discuss the strategy for tomorrow." Logane motioned for Ayela and the others to follow.

Applause roared through the bar when they reentered. The Stormling musician had finished her song. She stood, bowing her head in gratitude. "Thank you all for your kind praise. I only wish I could have provided the light show I am known for." The woman strapped her instrument onto her back and began walking toward the bar to collect her tips. The patrons of the bar returned to their tables and the food and drink that awaited them. It was only a moment before a myriad of voices and clanking cups echoed through the building.

"Lillia, you proved you know some healing magic. What can you do exactly?" Logane asked as they walked toward the table Zaktan had claimed.

"I know the control words for basic light-based healing and have studied anatomy well enough to use it for first aid on most races and many creatures. I can prevent infection, slow bleeding, neutralize most poisons and speed up the healing of minor injuries. So long as no one gets too badly injured, we should be fine." Lillia responded with a confident smile. Her expression soured when they sat across from Zaktan. He held a wet cloth to his face.

"Oh, fuck off," he growled. "I wouldn't actually have done it." He leaned back and closed his eyes.

"This is the first time I've been able to test my limits." Lillia continued. "Can't do more than what I showed you. Not all at once. I can keep it from scarring, though. I'll have to try again in a while."

"So, the burning question. Are you registered? Were you trained at the Citadel?" Logane sat next to Zaktan.

"No," Lillia muttered. "My father paid for a private tutor. We've kept my abilities somewhat secret."

"A costly feat. Your father is a noble," Logane asked. Shrugging when Lillia didn't answer. "Thought as much. Adds

THE HEADLESS SNAKE

another layer of risk." Logane puzzled. "I'm guessing he doesn't know you are here."

"I left a note. He knows I intend to become a mercenary."

Logane shook his head. "And I'm sure he will let his daughter go with no trouble at all. If he comes for you, we will not stop him. We'll turn you over to him. We can't afford to make enemies of a noble house. For now, we're just going to pretend we didn't know. We'll have to be careful when you use magic for now. But you'll need to be registered eventually if you're to continue with us. We could probably pull enough strings to keep you out of The Citadel, though."

"What about offence? Know any destructive spells?" Zaktan asked.

"Only one," Lillia said with a scowl. "But it only works against Moonborn and necromancers."

"Figures," Zaktan huffed.

"Do you want me to not finish healing you?" Lillia asked. "Because I don't mind leaving you all disfigured. It'd be an improvement, anyway."

Zaktan simply grunted in response with a half-smile.

"Down to business," Logane exclaimed, clearing his throat. "There'll be three wagons in the caravan. There are five of us. On the way to the mine, the wagons will be empty. Our employer has already paid for the materials, so we probably won't be attacked on the way to our destination. That in mind, we should split into groups, with two in the front and three in the back cart."

"Yes, that makes sense. Who should go in what wagon?" Bahn asked.

"It doesn't much matter until we pick up the goods." Zaktan answered, pulling the slightly blood-stained cloth from his face. "We won't be attacked until we are headed back. At that point, we should be more strategic. A fighter in each wagon and you two in the middle." He pointed to Lillia and Ayela.

"Agreed, and I believe we should remain in the wagons with the supplies. The aim is to capture or kill whoever is responsible for the thefts. If the bandits see us, they will either bring larger forces or not attack at all." Logane downed the rest of his foul-smelling mead. "Any objections?"

"Do you have a place to stay tonight," Logane asked when no one objected.

"Not exactly," Ayela admitted quietly.

"Why don't you stay with us at the Blood Rose Inn? It won't be much more for a few extra beds, and something tells me you could use a good night's sleep before we hit the road." Logane stood, motioning for the others to follow. "I've got a feeling things will go well for everyone." Logane tossed several coins onto the bar as he spoke.

"Thank you." Ayela's heart fluttered at the idea of a soft bed with warm blankets to snuggle into.

"See you soon, Nikul!" Zaktan called to the bartender.

"Y'all be safe out there," Nikul happily replied.

The inn was only a few blocks from The Headless Snake. A humble abode with far less flair than Ayela imagined from a name like The Blood Rose. But inside was warm and quiet, with a quaint fireplace. There were no rooms, only beds lining the walls with a trunk at the foot of each bed. Sleeping patrons already filled several of the beds.

Lavender incense burned on the counter, eliciting a yawn from Ayela as it slowed her thoughts. She already felt herself drifting off at just the sight of an actual bed.

Logane handed a few coins to the innkeeper, who nodded without a word before returning to reading a book on the counter.

"We've already bought supplies for you lot. So, no worries there." Logane whispered. "A padded coat for each of you, though they'll be big, and a supply pack. Get some rest. The innkeeper will wake us at dawn. Lillia, you'll have to wear one of Raesra's old coats. It'll be big on you."

"Raesra?" Lillia asked.

"Our old mage. She's... look, our last mission didn't go well. Lost a friend, and another isn't doing too well. Our small band was down to half. To be honest, it's one reason we're bringing you three along."

"But you're in The King's Guild. Not to look a gift horse in the mouth, but why hire us? Why not ask your guild for help?"

"We did. Our request was denied. So, we basically had three options. Merge into a larger party, take on contracts with the two of us and no support, or find new hires. We can discuss this more another time. For now, you all need sleep."

Ayela chose a bed beside Lillia, who sat with the covers pulled back. Zaktan kneeled before her as she again worked to heal his nose. Her shoulders slouched when she finished. His injury was now little more than a subtle scar.

He felt it for a moment, then grunted in approval before heading to the back of the inn to sleep beside Logane. He stopped partway there and turned back to Ayela. A new look was present in his slightly softer eyes. Perhaps a hint of acceptance.

"You've been practicing, haven't you?" Ayela whispered to Lillia.

"Don't tell father." Lillia's face darkened. "If I ever go back."

"You miss him?"

"This is what I've always wanted," Lillia trailed off, dodging the question. "To follow in mum's footsteps. Become an adventurer." She shrugged and turned toward Ayela. "He'd never have listened. Besides, I couldn't well let you run off by yourself." She brushed the thought of her father off with a grin. "Nowhere I'd rather be," Lillia yawned and fell into her bed beside Ayela's.

"Do you think you'll go back? Once this is done?" Ayela hated to ask, selfishly hoping Lillia would stay, afraid her longing for home would outgrow their bond.

"No." Lillia's reply was faint, barely audible as she lay back on the bed. She mumbled something else, but Ayela couldn't hear.

She started to ask but thought better when Lillia turned to her with watery eyes and a smile. Guilt chewed at Ayela's gut when she lay down facing Lillia. First, she'd caused Adina's downfall, or at least been the reason Erithia could dig their claws into her. Now, she'd drug her friend into a life of danger, just so she wouldn't be alone. They'd planned to become adventurers. But mercenary work. How could she have thought this would be better? It certainly would pay better. "How selfish am I?" Ayela breathed, too quiet for anyone to hear. She broke eye contact with Lillia and turned onto her back, pulling the covers close.

"Sorry," Ayela breathed.

"For what?" Lillia's tear-strained voice peaked.

"I've pulled you away from your cozy life. Pulled you into danger you hadn't wanted."

"Ayela, I was going to leave anyway. I'm just happy to be with you instead of on my own. By the veil, Ayela. Yesterday, I thought you were dead. Now." She smiled, "I have hope."

Ayela returned Lillia's smile, warmed by the idea of tomorrow's adventure with a friend by her side.

THE HEADLESS SNAKE

"That night," Ayela asked after a moment of silence passed between them. "What happened at The Library? Adina said she was going to take the children."

"She tried." Lillia breathed, turning onto her back once more and massaging her wrist. "I managed to fight her off. With the help of my father's guards."

"Like, you actually fought her. But she…"

"Was a necromancer, yea. I got lucky. She nearly killed me." Lillia's voice saddened. "For a moment toward the end. It looked like there was a part of the old Adina trying to break free. Like maybe she was still inside somewhere. Beneath the hate and corruption."

"What happened to Adina?"

"She escaped. The city guard chased her back to the orphanage, where there was a dark magic explosion. They say she overcast. But you can't overcast dark magic, I think it was something else."

"What about the other children?"

"They stayed with us for a few days until Kote found them all good places to go. Homes he personally knew were suitable. There was no way to keep them all together, unfortunately. So, they're dispersed throughout various homes in the city."

"They're safe then." Ayela bit her lip. She prayed the gods wouldn't allow any of the children to fall into the grasp of another Eema.

"Ayela," Lillia's voice cracked again.

"Yes?"

"Thank you," Lillia breathed. "Thank you for coming back to me. And for bringing me with you. I just…"

"I know." Ayela smiled, allowing Lillia's words to fade as a tear fell down the side of her face.

Lillia's chest fell, as though holding back words she'd half-intended to speak.

"Goodnight." Ayela reached over, grasping Lillia's hand.

"Goodnight," Lillia replied, returning the grip before turning away from Ayela.

Ayela closed her eyes, forcing her mind still as she awaited sleep. Her limbs ached, feeling miles away as she sank into the comfortable bedding. She wandered back to the dream she'd had. Being in the presence of the gods. Foolish as it might be, she imagined it had been real. Bahn's comment about magic surfaced in her memory. If the gods had given her magic, she needed to know. She exhaled sharply, vowing to ask Lillia about it tomorrow. For now, they needed sleep.

11

Prodott's Caravan

Ayela found herself engulfed in an endless expanse of swirling fog and shadows. Whispers echoed around her like the tortured souls of the damned. Frigid air pierced her aching lungs. The clang of clashing swords reverberated through the ethereal fog, accompanying pairs of figures too amorphous to identify. Each was engaged in what she could only imagine was heated combat. Anguished, garbled screams roared from below, the familiar, yet indescribable howl of a dying friend. She choked on every breath, as though suffocated by the essence of dread itself.

Ayela tensed at the twang of a bowstring. She ducked, hair standing on end at the whistling of an arrow, narrowly dodging. Its path sliced through the fog, momentarily revealing a man with a raven's head holding a bow. Her fist tightened around her own bow as she took aim and fired. Then, all was dark, blanketed in a silence so palpable that it weighed Ayela down. She fell to one knee, exhausted.

Searing pain shot through Ayela's skull. She slumped to the ground. The darkness lifted to returning fog. Ayela closed her eyes, groaning as she rolled over. The piercing sting of frozen grass pricked at her back. Through the spreading ache of her bleeding head, she sensed the malevolent gaze of an entity unknown. Unwilling to open her eyes, she clamped them shut, awaiting whatever terrible blow should follow. The sensation remained.

Fear, overcome by morbid curiosity as to the identity of the malicious presence, drove her to open her eyes. All at once, two piercing blue orbs confronted her. Ancient fury tinged by hate radiated deep within their dilated pupils.

Though Lillia's voice called to her from beyond the distant fog, she could not tear her gaze from the unblinking eyes. Each detail burned into her mind with vivid clarity. The eyes had a purpose, a mission of dire importance that drove her to…

"Ayela!" Lillia's scream and concerned slap jolted Ayela awake. Her bed was drenched in sweat. Her heart raced, her breaths ragged. The others stood around Ayela, clothed for the day in armor and winter coats. Lillia squeezed Ayela's shoulder. Concern bled from her intense gaze.

Ayela flushed at seeing Zaktan's disapproving snarl. She opened her mouth to speak but found her throat too parched to utter a sound. Only able to cough, Ayela sat up with aching muscles. She felt the back of her head, thankfully devoid of any wound.

"What happened?" Lillia's question was almost a whisper, as though she didn't want the others to hear just how worried she was.

"Thank you," Ayela croaked between gasping breaths as she accepted a glass of water the innkeeper offered.

"I'm fine." Ayela lied once she'd had enough to drink. Too tired to explain the dream she'd had or the dreadful eyes that still haunted her. "Nothing to…"

"Liar," Zaktan said.

Lillia glared at Zaktan, who, surprisingly, stepped back.

"Just a dream." Ayela fought to convince herself. Though this was unlike the others she'd had.

"How's that possible? You don't have magic." Lillia sat back on her knees beside Ayela's bed.

"Not entirely true." Bahn admitted.

"You're telling me you've got magic, but no training with it?" Logane placed his hands on his hips.

"I don't know!" Ayela buried her face in her palms. "Never used magic, Bahn says he thinks I did, once. But I've never used it before. And people don't just get magic. Besides, mage dreams are pleasant. This was a nightmare."

"And you were tested." Lillia said. "I was there. A very clear result, if I recall."

"Yeah, no connection to the gods. No magic at all." Ayela said.

"But you have dreams?" Logane asked. "You don't have dreams without magic of some kind. The test must have been wrong."

"As I told Bahn, if I had magic, I'd have killed myself with it by now."

"There has to be some other explanation," Lillia said.

"Some people develop magic after encounters with powerful magical beings. Seen anything mystical lately?" Zaktan suggested.

"That is so incredibly rare. And she hasn't," Lillia started.

"Let her answer," Zaktan said.

"I…" Ayela stopped herself before mentioning Erithia or the shade. She considered her dream with the gods, but that was surely no more real that her other dreams.

"Well?" Zaktan ordered.

"No, I've had no encounters." Ayela spied the glow of morning outside the windows. "Enough fuss over me. Shouldn't we be leaving?"

"We were actually about to wake you when you started screaming," Bahn said.

"Yeah, wailing like you were about to be killed or something." Zaktan smirked. "Was kinda funny to see."

"What did you see? In your dreams, I mean," Lillia asked.

"I don't know. Just a general sense of," Ayela trailed off. "Fear? I guess. There was a battle, but the only thing I saw for sure was a pair of bright blue eyes. Everything else was foggy."

"Strange, but then again, mage dreams never make much sense." Logane shrugged. He held a hand up to silence Ayela's resumed protest of the notion. "Regardless, there's no denying there's a chance you have magic. You're gonna stay far outside of battle. Heightened emotions don't mix well with untrained magic. You'll need to get tested again. In the meantime, Lillia will teach you what she can." Logane insisted. "For now, it's time to go. Gather your things and put on that armor." He motioned to the padded coat at the foot of her bed. "We're heading out."

Clothed and on the way to the southern gates, Ayela gazed into the eyes of every man they passed. Nearer to the city's entrance, she'd relaxed somewhat, growing confident it was mere paranoia that led to her search for the hateful blue eyes. Still, she couldn't help but glance at every passerby with trepidation.

The stench of uncleaned stables greeted Ayela as she, Bahn, and Lillia followed some distance behind Logane and Zaktan. Barely sunrise, and the gates were already getting crowded. Though, no caravans or wagons in sight.

"Looks like we made it here first," Logane said. "Good." He gazed around the city entrance, quickly scanning the crowds. The gates were already open for the day, with guards monitoring the comings and goings. They'd stop the occasional person to check for illicit goods or weapons. But simply nodded to the heavily armored Logane and Zaktan as they passed.

"Wait past the drawbridge, out of the crowds," Zaktan suggested.

"Yea," Logane nodded before motioning for the others to follow.

They situated themselves to the left of the drawbridge and waited.

"Why did the guards let us pass," Ayela asked.

"They know me. Know I'm not a safety risk," Logane said.

"Shut up and don't move," Zaktan said when three covered wagons rounded the corner past the gates and approached the guards. "Let us handle it."

Logane shook his head. "Could be more pleasant about it." Logane elbowed Zaktan's side. "But yea. Let us do the talking. Just observe for now." Logane grinned at Ayela.

"You the Mercenaries Dowage sent?" Asked a heavyset man with a long, peppered black beard. He pulled the reins on the wagon and hopped off, visibly shaking the vehicle as he did so.

Ayela's face drained of color at seeing the man. His eyes, though filled more with indifference than anger, were identical to the pair she'd seen in her dream. So similar as to leave no doubt in her mind that they were the same.

"Don't look like much." He sniffled, wiping his nose with his hand before reaching to greet Logane.

"Prodott, I assume. A pleas—." All sound deafened to a ringing in Ayela's ears. Unwittingly shuffling backward, she recalled every detail of her nightmare while looking into his striking eyes.

Logane held his fist to his chest, giving a slight bow to Prodott as they continued talking, but their words were lost to Ayela.

Prodott returned Ayela's gaze first with confusion, then disappointment.

Lillia broke Ayela out of her stupor with a subtle tug on her arm.

"…our apprentices. We take full responsibility for their actions." Logane drew Prodott's attention away from Ayela and Lillia.

"They let children into the mercenary guild now?" Prodott sneered, scanning the group, making no attempt to hide his judgment of their gear and apparent ability or lack thereof.

"As a second-rank hunter of the mercenary guild, I vouch for my wards," Logane exclaimed.

"Good enough for me. Hop in back and we'll be off. We're already behind schedule." Prodott remounted the wagon. "We will head west toward Mt. Lapid for a couple of hours. Then, south toward the mining village resting in the foothills. The journey will take more than a day one way, so we'll need to make camp on the plains southwest of here. You can meet the other drivers then. It is winter, I hope all of you brought proper equipment. It may get cold tonight. Jimm, the second driver's our cook. He'll be providing you meals."

Ayela stepped into the back of the wagon behind Bahn and Lillia before settling as comfortably as she could against the tarp, monitoring Prodott as he checked the carts and horses one last time before heading to the front as their driver.

Ayela started to tell the others when Prodott was out of earshot but stopped. Unwilling to admit the absurdity of her concerns. Mage dreams didn't come true. And any notion they prophesied the future was foolish. Still, she'd keep her eye on Prodott.

Ayela yawned, watching Bahn, who sat near the edge of the covered wagon. He searched the partially thawed plains for any sign of trouble as a dutiful guard. Wind howled outside, thankfully blocked by the wagon's tarp.

"Four hours in, two days to go," Ayela sighed, resting her head on the tarp of the wagon. The wall of Hatave was hardly a line on the horizon behind them, with the Citadel Tower a silhouetted needle jutting into the sky.

"I don't know what it is," Bahn's soft voice pierced the silence. He looked toward the back of the wagon, where Lillia lay sleeping. "But there's something special about you, Ayela."

"I…" Ayela's cheeks burned. She struggled to speak. "You mean the nightmare?"

"I don't know. But no matter what happens. Know I will protect you. There's a reason I was led to you. So, you have my vow, no harm will come to you while I am here."

Ayela watched Bahn return his gaze to the road behind them. He continued his search as though nothing had been said. She huffed a frustrated breath, puzzled by the druid's comment. Her mind wandered back to their first meeting in the woods. And the guard that'd brought her to the shelter. The same shelter the old man had led Bahn to, and their dragon eyes.

Lillia's whisper derailed her line of thought. "He's handsome, isn't he?" Ayela's heart lurched in embarrassment. Lillia, from her feigned sleep, had heard Bahn's comment. Ayela set her jaw, shrinking into the tarp behind her.

"Stop. I told you. It's nothing like that. He is helping me, that's all." Ayela struggled to keep her whisper below the ambiance of the wagon wheels. She crossed her arms, glaring at Lillia.

"If you say so." Lillia's signature grin dominated her face; the one that meant she held some juicy secret.

"Spit it out," Ayela demanded.

"Nope." Lillia smirked. "You said to stop."

Ayela let her head fall forward in defeat before turning her head toward Bahn and the retreating road.

"What if this is a mistake? What if Eema was right," Ayela asked. "What if I'm better off staying a nobody Southtowner?"

"You were never a nobody Southtowner." Lillia muttered. "You're so much more than that."

"I learned a hard lesson recently." Bahn's eyes never left the road as he jutted into their conversation. "You can't always live your life by the expectations or rules of others. Sometimes there are forces we cannot control that push us away from everything we have ever known. We must forge our own path, without the limitations placed upon us by family, friends, or society."

"But what if those limits are necessary," Ayela asked.

"If you believe them, and want to be limited by them, sure," Bahn said. "But I prefer to test the waters and learn what works for myself. I'll follow my moral judgment before relying on some elder or judge to teach me right from wrong." Bahn's words pierced through the stale air within the wagon as silence fell between them.

"You're not about to go anarchist on us, are you, Bahn." Lillia sat up, studying Bahn.

"No, I didn't mean it like that. I just think some laws are outdated or just flat out wrong, like in the tavern; the new laws seriously hindered the Stormling's performance. She shouldn't need to change who she is or hold back just because some man with a fancy house told her to."

"But the laws are there for a reason," Ayela said. "Lillia, you remember the lecture Kote gave us when they passed the law? Damage was being caused by people misusing magic or from their inexperience. They were starting fires or accidentally hurting livestock and people or themselves."

"Yes, I think regulation is important," Lillia agreed. "But I don't agree with the blanket ban, either."

"Many of man's laws are unjust," Bahn said. "Sometimes, I think a life of freedom in the countryside would be the best way to live."

"Not a life for me." Ayela said. "I like the wilderness; for visiting, hunting, adventuring. But not to live. I prefer the comforts of the city."

Periodic idle conversation broke the silence for the remaining hours of the day. All the while, Bahn never left his post at the wagon's edge. Ayela struggled to relax against the tarp. Tired as she was, every time she closed her eyes, the phantom of Prodott's vengeful stare plagued her. Lillia lay stretched out on the floor, smiling at the ceiling with closed eyes. Surely daydreaming of the adventures of the future.

Ayela jumped at Prodott's sharp voice, yelling over the wagon. "We're turning off to set camp." Sunset's crimson hue burned across the cloud-covered sky, illuminating the inside of the wagon with ominous reds and oranges. "Hold on, it'll get rough."

"Finally," Ayela yawned, eager to stretch her legs after nearly a day of travel.

"We should help set camp," Bahn stated when the wagons came to a stop over a small level part of the ground.

"Do you two need help with your tent?" Bahn stepped out of the wagon and reached in to help Ayela and Lillia out.

"I think we can manage," Lillia chimed, stepping down and rejecting Bahn's offer for help. "Thanks, though."

"We'll have dinner ready momentarily." Prodott stood in the center of the circle of wagons. Next to him was a pile of metal rods and a cooking pot. "Just need to start a cooking fire."

"Should we train while dinner is cooking," Ayela asked Lillia after they'd finished setting up their tent. "With magic, I mean."

"Not sure how good a teacher I'll be, but sure. We'll train behind the wagons," Lillia whispered. "I don't want any distractions."

"So, how do we start?" Ayela said once they were out of sight from the others.

"Honestly, I'm not sure." Lillia rubbed her temple. "It was so long ago for me."

"I guess," Ayela started. "What does it feel like to use magic," Ayela asked.

"Like energy flowing through you," Lillia said. "Descriptive, I know." She sighed. "You feel your muscles twitching in response. Honestly, it is quite uncomfortable, anxiety-producing. And if you use too much, your fingers go numb, you get dizzy. Go farther and you go boom."

Ayela gulped, imagining herself overcome by magic and everything ending in a spectacularly painful explosion. "So, the most important thing should be how to stop, right?"

"Okay... think of it like there is a door inside you. One that you have to learn to close. It naturally opens when you are angry or afraid. You've probably felt that before. A burst of energy. Your face gets hot, and you want to hit something."

"Um." Ayela started.

"Basically, when you have magic and you reach that state, your door will swing open on its own and you will start channeling elemental magic. Like the wind of a blizzard when a shutter flies open. Without control words, the magic is shaped by your subconscious, and if you channel too much, you burn out. Right now, because you have never used magic before, the amount you can use before burning out is tiny. But the more you stretch your limits, the more you can cast. Like any muscle, you can build endurance."

"How do I close the door?"

"First, learn to control the door. And you have to keep a cool head to keep it closed. The problem is the magic. The wind blowing in the window makes it harder to close. When you channel magic, it amplifies your emotions."

"So, just deep breaths and calming thoughts?" Ayela asked.

"Actually, my tutor had me meditate to get the hang of it. She put a lot of effort into having me entirely empty my mind. So that when I want to stop magic, I just empty my thoughts. And practice has gotten me used to using magic without it impacting my emotions. Usually."

"Like the meditation Master Kote had us do from time to time?"

"Kind of, but he would have you meditate on questions he'd asked or the work you were doing. Here, just follow me." Lillia sat with her back against the wagon, folded her legs, and rested her hands on her knees.

Ayela followed suit, doing exactly as her friend.

"Now, close your eyes and focus on your heartbeat. Try to hear it, feel it in every inch of your being."

Ayela took deep breaths, listening to her body.

"Now, focus your attention on your core. Eventually, a heat sensation will build where you are focusing."

The two of them sat for a time in silence. Ayela felt every heartbeat in the tips of her chilled fingers and toes. Her muscles relaxed, the tension she didn't know she held fell away. A momentary shiver ran down her spine as she felt as though something menacing and unknown rested at the fringes of her consciousness. She forced her mind still, ignoring the sensation. Subtle heat, near imperceptible to the environment, built in her chest. Her heart pulsed slower still. Ayela felt she might float away.

"Do you feel it," Lillia asked, noticing the change in Ayela's breathing.

"Yes," Ayela answered, nearly losing concentration on the spot of warmth.

"Try making it move. Slowly shift your focus to another part of your body. The warmth should follow. Try to keep your mind clear of all thoughts."

Ayela grinned at the ease with which it moved.

"Once you can move it a bit, try making it bigger or smaller." She continued after several minutes of silence. "What you are feeling is your door. It's called your anchor. The amount of magic you channel is based on its size. And where you are focusing is where the magic will flow through. Before you can even think of casting a spell, master controlling this, even when not meditating. Right now, with you focusing on it with a clear mind, you are holding the door closed. But that is easy to do while meditating. It is entirely different when you are channeling magic, or when you are angry or afraid."

"Makes sense." Ayela muttered, still struggling to control the spot's size.

"We'll practice this for a bit. Just stay calm and keep it in your chest. Don't worry about changing its size yet if that's giving you problems. Eventually, controlling this will be second nature to you."

Ayela opened her eyes, focus broken by footsteps approaching. She gasped in surprise at seeing the sun nearly below the horizon. She questioned how so much time could have passed so quickly.

"Ayela," Bahn said, stepping around the corner. "Still wanting to do some physical training?"

"I think we've meditated enough for now, anyway. We can do some more on the way to the mine tomorrow." Lillia offered a hand to help Ayela up. "You two have fun. I'm gonna go check on dinner." She trotted off without waiting for Ayela's exasperated reply.

"Now, let's run a few drills before dinner gets ready. Just like you drilled yesterday."

Resigned, Ayela entered a ready stance and punched the air. "Like this?"

"Exactly. Now, I want you to hit my hand a few times." Bahn held his hands out in front of him. "I want you to focus on form, keeping your wrist flat and fist tight."

Bahn moved each hand every time Ayela landed a hit, placing his hand over his chest, stomach, and side several times. "These are the areas you want to aim for when you're punching. When you hit, you want to rotate your hips into the attack to give it more weight. Drawing a bow for hunting has given you much of the strength you need. But you need good technique as well. We'll practice that more another time. For now, I'm going to show you how to not get hit. "

"Many people try to stop the attack by blocking either with their hand or whatever weapon they are carrying. But the most effective way to not get hit is to dodge and counter. Since you are an archer, you will want to keep as much distance between you and the enemy as you can. Ideally, you will never get into hand-to-hand combat. If you get into a fight, you need to learn to move away from your attacker. Hit me, I'll show you."

"Okay." Ayela threw a punch toward Bahn.

Bahn stepped to the side at the last moment, his fist stopping just shy of hitting her in the chest. "When someone attacks, they almost always leave an opening for you to counter. If you can dodge that first attack, strike at them while they recover unless they are carrying a weapon. If your opponent is carrying a weapon, I want you to run toward me. At least for the time being."

"Got it." Ayela smiled

"Let's drill this a few times. We'll go slow at first. I'll be the attacker." Bahn returned to a ready stance before slowly punching toward her. Ayela mimicked the movements he had shown her, matching his speed. She stepped aside and struck toward Bahn, stopping just shy of his chest.

"How will going slow like this help me in an actual fight?" Ayela asked before completing another drill. "And where should I strike if my opponent is wearing armor?"

"Your body has a way of remembering movements you've made over and over. Going slow like this will help you make those movements when you need to," Bahn replied. "If you are fighting an armored opponent, aim for unarmored parts or try to knock them off their feet."

"Now, I want you to step to the other side, pushing my fist out of the way while punching my side here." Bahn held his hand over his side, just below his ribs. "Once we do this a few times, we'll speed it up."

"Dinner is ready," called the gruff voice of one of the caravan drivers after they had finished several more drills.

"It's getting too dark anyway. We'll practice some more tomorrow," Bahn said, motioning for her to follow.

"Enjoy your training," Lillia asked when the two of them returned to the campfire just as the last glow of sunset fell below the peak of Mount Lapid, her blond hair gleaming off the firelight.

"Yeah, got some more self-defense drills down."

"Sounds productive," Zaktan remarked, his voice dripping with sarcasm. He dipped a spoon into the large pot standing over the fire and poured the chunky stew into a bowl. "Curious how useful it'll actually be."

"Any progress in controlling your magic," Logane asked.

"As much as could be done," Ayela answered.

"Here." Prodott handed Ayela and Lillia a bowl of stew. "It's my specialty, vegetable and jerky stew." His voice was dry and even. Devoid of any readable emotion.

"Thank you," Ayela said, remembering how excited Adina had been when she cooked the stew with fresh venison.

"Just wait until you try it," mumbled another caravan driver, walking past them toward the fire.

Ayela looked worried for a moment, thoughts trailing to her vision. She smelled of the stew, reading only the bland scents of vegetables and unseasoned meat. Logane caught her attention with a nod as he downed a spoonful of the soup. The other drivers were all eating from similar bowls, and she'd watched him scoop hers out of the cauldron. Ayela sighed, cursing her delusional worry before cautiously sampling a spoonful of the broth.

Despite its lack of added seasoning, the warm broth and hearty vegetables soothed Ayela's cold-chapped lips. There was no strange, bitter, or strong taste in the soup. She sighed, relaxing as she went for another bite. No way these drivers could spring for a poison rare enough to not have a smell or taste.

"It's not horrible," Lillia mumbled, struggling to chew the rehydrated meat floating in the stew.

"It's better food than I've had in days." Ayela eagerly scooped up a vegetable with her spoon.

"Here." Lillia handed a chunk of bread to Ayela out of the supplies she'd brought. "Anyone else want some?"

Prodott thanked Lillia, taking the roll and dividing it between the group.

"Do you know what happened to the other caravans," Ayela asked Prodott.

"I doubt I know any more than you do," he replied. "They all returned to Hatave, beaten and without the shipment. Though no one has been killed."

"Is this your first time on this route? Do you know of any bandit strongholds," Logane asked.

"I traveled this way once before on a job for another merchant." Prodott's voice faltered slightly as he answered. "And bandit strongholds don't last long this close to the capital."

"That makes sense," Ayela stated. "Too many mercenaries and Union soldiers to track them down. Though you know this place well enough to not need a map."

"I know the area, yeah. Been runnin' caravans round these parts for most'a my life. Just only traveled to this village from Hatave once before."

"Right." Zaktan gulped down the last of his bowl. "Anyway, we should set up a watch and get some rest. Won't be much on the way back."

"I'll take first shift," Bahn volunteered as he finished his stew.

"I'll take second," Logane added. "Four-hour shifts."

Sleep evaded Ayela, whose closed eyes revisited the horrid fog and shadows of battle that had been her dream. Any effort to dismiss her suspicions as mere fancy was met with an equally ferocious resurgence of the visions. It was as though some otherworldly entity had latched onto Ayela, forcing her to live through it time and time again. Eventually she gave up, opening her eyes.

There, she was again confronted by the domineering orbs of hate that were Prodott's eyes. She could not scream, unable to move, and yet assuredly awake. She heard Lillia's pleasantly soft snore beside her. Heard the howling wind outside. Felt the warmth from Bahn's enchantment on their tent. But just as surely as reality, she saw the floating eyes above her. Each bore into her soul with an increasing hatred that eclipsed even what they'd presented before. Her mind raced with puzzling possibilities. The eyes were surely a figment of her imagination, yet she yearned to assign a meaning to them. Why was she seeing Prodott's eyes filled with the hatred that wouldn't leave her? He'd only ever been kind to them.

It wasn't until dawn broke that the vision faded and Ayela could again move.

Sluggish and deprived of sleep, she donned her quiver and arrows. Without a word, she left the tent, dragging herself into action as they packed up camp.

She climbed back into the cart behind Lillia and Bahn, her back barely hitting the tarp before she fell asleep.

12

Providence

Ayela fluttered awake when the wagons came to a stop. Her heavy eyes gazed out of the wagon, where she saw several small buildings and shops. The sky was laden with storm clouds yet to spill their deluge. The air bit into Ayela's ears with every gust. Leafless trees swayed slightly alongside yellowed grass, there was no mistaking the approach of a winter storm.

"Are we finally here," Lillia asked.

"No dreams then," Bahn asked.

"Thankfully, no," Ayela laughed. Happy to be rid of the haunting eyes. Even the sight of Prodott tending to the horses no longer filled her with dread. She stepped out of the wagon, her feet slipping slightly in the dark, icy mud coating the ground beneath the wagons. "Oh, that feels good." Ayela stretched her arms and legs, pulling at her cramping muscles.

Mount Lapid loomed high over their heads, a marvel of the natural world. Low clouds shrouded the twin crimson peaks, threatening to flood the town with fog or snow in equal measure.

"Don't get too comfortable. Once they load the shipments, we'll be returning to Hatave," Zaktan sighed. He held a lump of fabric and fur out toward Lillia, Bahn, and Ayela. "The temperature is dropping, and a storm's rolling in. That coat won't protect you enough. You'll catch a chill." Zaktan now wore a different, much heavier black fabric, with white fur lining the inside of his coat.

"Thank you." Ayela blinked, shocked at the sudden change in his usual prickly attitude. She wondered if her shock at the kind gesture went unnoticed while she donned the thick fur coat. Adjusting her quiver to fit snugly at her hip.

"Don't thank me. It wasn't my idea. Prodott and Logane insisted you not freeze to death."

"That's not a bad look for you, Lillia." Ayela smiled, watching Lillia tie the black bear fur cloak at her waist.

"It's too big." Lillia muffled a complaint to Ayela. She lifted several inches of the cloak out of the sludge at her feet. "And it stinks."

"At least it's warm." Ayela eagerly rubbed her hands together. A bitter wind rushed past them, brushing the long gray and white fur on her cloak against her neck. She pulled the collar up to form a guard over her ears. "I want to check with the supplier here, make sure his books match what we know about the shipments," Ayela called to Logane. "How many times did you say the shipment was stolen?"

"That's actually a great idea." Logane stopped next to them, as though about to protest. "When we talked to Dowage, he said he had ordered five shipments from this mine. The first shipment did not get stolen, and one other shipment did not get stolen because it had a city guard escort."

"Everyone else is dressing for the cold and the storm that's blowing in; why not you," Lillia asked.

"I'm a Draken, I don't get cold," Logane stated. "Inner fire and all that. Come, let's find the person in charge of the mine." He flexed his massive wings as if to impress before leading the way into the settlement.

"If he's guilty, do you really think he'll just hand over the documents," Bahn asked.

"He will to me," Logane said.

"Bahn, and I will wait here." Lillia smiled. "We'll keep an eye out for trouble with Zaktan."

Prodott was busy talking to a tall man wearing an elegant fur-lined red vest. He stood near the largest building in the quaint village. "My guess is he's the one in charge." Ayela pointed toward the tall man.

Logane cleared his throat. "Who oversees this mine's bookkeeping? I need to inspect your logs." Ayela recoiled at Logane's commanding tone. Prodott and the other man quickly turned to Logane, their faces blank, stunned by the sharpness of the demand.

"I oversee the books. My name is Owen. Might I ask on whose authority you are acting," asked the tall, vested man.

"I am a Paladin of Lapid and a Second-Class Hunter of The King's Mercenary Guild. I operate under the authority of Lapid, The Draken Council of Elders, and The Kings Mercenary Guild via a contract with Dowage, your customer."

"That is an impressive bunch of titles." Owen paused, weighing his options on the matter. "Very well, my lord," Owen's tone carried a daring hint of mockery. "I have nothing to hide. I will fetch the books for you while my men load the wagons."

"Ayela," Logane stated, breaking her trance. "The Quartermaster'll bring the ledger to us in a moment. Keep your eyes peeled; I get the sense that he is hiding something from us." Logane looked over the workers carrying out tasks around them. "We should regroup with the others while we wait. What gave you the idea of checking the books?"

"I know a bit about Union Business Standards. Studied them at The King's Library. I figure a mine this large has to keep track of their sales for taxes, and the logs would need to be accurate."

"You studied business standards?" Logane furrowed his eyebrows, scrutinizing Ayela's claim.

"Yes, a friend and I had toyed with the idea of starting a business. A shelter for children. I had free access to the library."

"Still think you'll start that business?"

"No. Don't think that's in the cards now." Ayela held one hand over her shoulder, looking away from Logane.

"Sorry to hear that."

"Does anyone else think those people look suspicious," Bahn asked, gesturing toward a group of people on horseback near the houses across the street from their caravan. Each of the riders wore dark cloaks with red accents along the sleeves and collar. Some were talking with one another while the one in the center held a steady stare toward their caravan.

"Yea," Zaktan mumbled. "Those are Nighthawk assassins in their ceremonial garb. Keep an eye on 'em for now. Chances are they aren't here for us. The Nighthawks and King's guild don't interfere with one another's business."

"Fat chance. We're meant to see them," Logane muttered. "I saw them when we arrived. They wouldn't make themselves visible for no reason."

"What should we do then?" Zaktan turned to Logane with his hand resting on his sword pommel.

"Continue the contract," Logane sighed. "Nothing else we can do. Dowage said nothing about their involvement. And they'd have let us know before leaving Hatave if we were treading on their toes. Maybe it's a message to someone else. Besides, killing us would violate guild treaties. They wouldn't risk it."

Ayela watched the Nighthawks, eyeing their swords and the hoods covering their faces. It was a power move to show themselves like that. Ayela took a shaky breath, recalling her first encounter with a Nighthawk Assassin.

She was young, small, and weak. Her mother was screaming over her father's body. Robes of black and red whirled overhead. Raven feathers dangled from a sword sheath. Blood mixed with water on the brick, flowing in the rain. Metal clashed overhead, a clap of thunder and a white flash. The assassin fell, with smoke rising from his robes. More leapt from the shadows. Ayela's mother screamed for her to run before they tackled her. Her mother's garbled attempts at breath echoed in Ayela's ears. The assassins stood, blood on their daggers. Her mother lay motionless at their feet. Air rushed by as her feet carried her. Then, all was black. The musty smell of potatoes dominated her senses. Scratchy burlap brushed against her cheeks. Someone lifted her over their shoulder.

"Ayela?" Logane snapped in front of Ayela's eyes, drawing her back. "Ayela, this was your idea; why don't you look through it with me," Logane asked. "We'll check the ledger while the others keep a lookout."

Logane gently placed the thick, haphazardly bound book on top of a large, neatly constructed crate near their wagons.

"Uh, yeah," Ayela's voice quivered. She swallowed, studying the books. It was a welcome distraction from the vivid recollection of events she thought were long buried. "It looks like they formatted this ledger by Union standards." Ayela cleared her throat, discreetly wiping a tear from her eye before gesturing to the neatly organized tables covering the ragged, dirt-coated pages. "This shouldn't take too long."

"Well, I'm impressed. You know more about business standards than I expected." Logane looked up from the ledger, scanning their surroundings before returning his attention to Ayela.

"Here, this is the first time this mine filled an order for Dowage." Ayela pointed to an entry with Dowage's name written next to the shipment's description.

"It is dated almost exactly a month before the first stolen shipment," Logane added.

"A month later, the next shipment, and just a few days after, we have a shipment with Prodott as the lead driver. But he wasn't driving for Dowage." Ayela continued skimming the records in search of the other stolen shipments.

"Look for any received shipments of similar size or value to the stolen shipments," Logane instructed.

"The next shipment to our client was the guarded shipment. You can see the official Hatave seal here. Then, the two stolen shipments afterward. There are hardly any received shipments except for noted payments that correspond with caravans a few days later."

"The assassins left. They headed south," Zaktan said as he walked up next to Logane.

Ayela closed her fist to conceal her trembling fingers.

"That's a relief," Logane sighed.

"All loaded. Ready to depart," Prodott called shakily as he fumbled with the ties on one of the wagon coverings.

"He seems on edge," Bahn stated.

"Everything okay?" Logane looked up from the ledgers.

"Let's get out of here. We don't want to be late," Prodott responded.

"Ayela, does everything look in order with the ledger?" Logane asked.

"I see nothing that would suggest the supplier is behind the attacks. Though they could be forged, it is hard to say."

"It was worth investigating." Logane closed the leather-bound book before motioning to the others. "You go ahead. I need to return this to the quartermaster and ask him a few questions." Logane gently closed the ledger and began heading toward the large house near the front of the village.

"Where's your friend going? We need to leave," Prodott asked when Ayela and Lillia passed him to enter the now cramped wagons.

"Are you sure everything's okay? You seem nervous." Ayela eyed his quivering hands and shifting eyes. "Logane is returning the ledger; he'll be right back."

Prodott's sudden shift in mood called back her paranoia. She looked over the other drivers, all seeming equally on edge.

"We have the goods now… This is the half of the journey that the past caravans have never gotten through. And I know you saw them too. Makes a guy nervous."

"You said yourself; no one has ever died. Things will be fine." Bahn said, briefly placing his hand on Prodott's shoulder, garnishing a forced smile. "Assassins don't leave people alive."

They loaded into the wagons, sandwiching themselves between the crates of metal and smithing supplies and the wagon tarp. There was scarcely enough space to move, much less sit comfortably. Ayela found herself stuffed on one side of the cart, half sitting on the edge of a crate with her knees crammed against the wagon tarp. Her back was bent awkwardly to keep from hitting the overhanging crate above her. Lillia climbed to the top of the pile. Lying between the wagon and the top of the crates.

Tense silence dominated the interior of the carts while the hours dragged on. Ayela studied her bow, fighting to distract herself from the racing possibilities of what might come in the following days.

"Is it absolutely vital for us to stay under the tarps?" Lillia struggled to find a comfortable position in the narrow gap between the top of the heavy crates and the rough steel supports of the wagon's ceiling.

"Logane and Zaktan said it was." Bahn's voice was barely audible from the side of the pile of wood and metal filling the center of the cart. "Especially with the temperature dropping outside."

"I can only imagine how Zaktan and Logane feel right now, covered in armor and stuck in the same position we are." Ayela rested her head against a large crate. "If we are attacked, how will we get out of the wagons in time to do anything? It took us at least a couple minutes to get settled in here. I don't think we could get out of here as quickly. Especially with this bulky coat."

"I…" Bahn shuffled uneasily, jostling the contents of a crate. A heavy thud rattled the floor of the wagon. "We should try to get into a position that minimizes the time it will take for us to get out."

"Probably a good idea." Ayela crawled closer to the canopy entrance.

Winter storm clouds raged in the sky above, bringing virulent winds that pierced the wagon's tarp. The dense overcast sky blotted out the sun, leaving the landscape shrouded in a drab gray that darkened as the hours crawled on.

Ayela stretched her aching back. She ran her fingers over the etchings covering her bow, tracing the ornate textures. "You know, there are etchings on this bow." Ayela examined the small series of runes etched into the wood. "I think they're in Divine or Elemental. I can't tell. I wonder…"

"Let me see! I can read Divine," Lillia squealed, stretching down from the top of the crates to grab the bow.

"Here," Ayela laughed, passing the bow up to Lillia.

"The symbols read Khi-bawkash. It translates to Life Seeker, or Guide to Life, or something like that. I can't tell whether it is magical or not. It could just be that someone named the bow. If it were magical, it would need a power source or focus, but I don't see one."

"So… no way to tell if it's magical or not," Ayela asked.

"Not without knowing how to activate it. I noticed some other, smaller runes on the side of the handle, but I didn't recognize the language." Ayela smiled at Lillia's eager shift in tone. "My dad might know more about it. Not that we can ask him. I don't think he would welcome seeing me after sneaking away. Today was the wedding day," Lillia muttered, her voice trailing into silence. "I hate to think what punishment he has planned for me," Lillia moaned. "I wonder if it would be better for me to never go back." She handed the bow back to Ayela before retreating to her position on the crates, out of Ayela's sight.

"Do you really want to cut all ties with him?" Ayela's heart sank at Lillia's wounded tone. "He cares for you a lot."

"I don't know," Lillia admitted, her voice growing quieter. A faint sniffle echoed over the crates.

"Does he even know you didn't want to marry?"

"No, I never had the heart to tell him. He seemed so proud that he'd secured a future for me."

"You should find a time to at least talk with him. Maybe get him to meet you somewhere in the city." Ayela paused, waiting for a response from Lillia. "I would go with you. You wouldn't have to do it alone." Ayela craned her neck, attempting to see Lillia. But she had crept further back in the wagon.

Ayela glanced at Bahn, who was only just visible on the other side of the crates. His gaze was focused on the road, shifting occasionally from side to side. Ayela sighed, resting her head against the crates behind her back. They were hours till sunset, yet already every bump shot through her aching back. Folding her legs as best she could, Ayela placed her hands on her knees and began an attempt at meditation. But worries about Lillia and Master Kote's relationship, accompanied by the bumps of the road and her aching spine, made focus impossible. Grunting after what seemed like forever, Ayela relented and gruffly pressed her head against the crate with a thud. She would practice more that night. She just had to wait until they pulled off the road.

Ayela looked out over the retreating land, the furious clouds above seemed to rest only inches from the top of the wagon, and the icy air nipped at every inch of exposed skin. Ayela pulled the cloak tight over her shoulders and closed her eyes. Maybe she could at least get some sleep. Gods willing, she'd finally get a peaceful night's sleep.

"Everything hurts!" Ayela cried. The three of them struggled to remove themselves from the packed wagons. "Did we really have to go all day without stopping?"

"Stop complaining and pay attention," Zaktan growled. "Does this place seem familiar?" He walked up behind Ayela. The frozen grass beneath them crunched like fresh snow. "I think this is the same place we stopped on the way to pick up the shipment."

"We're in the planes. Everything looks more or less the same. How can you tell?" Ayela stretched with a forceful yawn.

"That grove of trees on the hill. Their relation to the road and Hatave in the distance." Logane replied. "I was wondering the same. It is peculiar, though not an impossible coincidence."

"I've had a rotten feeling about Prodott from the beginning. This doesn't help," Ayela admitted.

"Pay attention to instincts like that. Can save your life," Logane said. "Alright, we go off our own provisions tonight. Don't eat or drink anything they give us. We'll keep two-hour watches. Everyone else, sleep in your armor. Weapons close. But don't let them know we suspect anything."

Ayela stood around the campfire with the others, picking at their dried meat and bread rations. All were silent, save for a few unsuccessful attempts to drum up conversation. Each of the drivers looked pale as they scarcely attended to the evening's conversation. It was as though they were bogged down in thought.

"Zaktan," Bahn started after a particularly long silence. "If you don't mind me asking. Are you from The Erithian Empire or did you grow up in The Union?"

"I do mind you asking," Zaktan groaned. "But if you must know, I defected from the Erithian military."

"How did you turn away from The Empire, from Erithia," Bahn asked.

"Look, tree boy," Zaktan groaned. "The Hatave guard already grilled me when I defected years ago. I have no intention of reliving that now."

Logane threw a look of warning to Bahn, but he persisted.

"I'm sorry, I'm just curious. I heard those that join them never want to leave."

"I never joined them. In the empire, there's no choice. If you're fit, you're in the military. You never even think of doing anything else because there's no freedom of thought. Only reason I'm here is I got lucky and broke away."

"But it has to go deeper than that. You were part of The Empire, you were addicted to Erithia's magic, and you walked away."

"I was under their control! I was not addicted to their magic. There is a difference," Zaktan's voice deepened. His face contorted, darkened with frustration. "I was one of a few soldiers that would occasionally show individuality. Whenever this happened, I would be brought to a general for re-education.

In The Empire, there is no individuality, no emotion, no choice, no thought. There is only an overwhelming desire to follow orders and an ever-present need to be stronger, to have more power. No loyalty, no friendship, no camaraderie. There is only ambition to surpass your peers and obey Erithia's generals. At any cost."

"I didn't," he faltered, taking a breath to calm himself. "I didn't turn away from dark magic because I was never addicted to it; I have no connection to his magic and never will," Zaktan softly added. "What I cannot understand is people who willingly turn to their magic, knowing that they risk enslaving themselves."

"I don't think I could ever understand it either," Ayela whispered.

"Necromancy is for cowards," Logane exclaimed as he added another log to the fire.

"Moonborn are…" Zaktan began.

"I'm going to check the perimeter," Bahn exclaimed, storming away from camp.

"What's his problem?" One driver asked, having leaned in to observe the conversation.

"Who knows? Maybe it's a druid thing," Logane muttered.

"As I was saying, Moonborn are the worst of them all. They use their race as an excuse to give into dark magic when, in reality, they're just too weak-willed to resist. They have no one to blame but themselves."

"They're not all like that," Ayela muttered.

"You're right. There are few exceptions. But I've given members of their race many chances and been burned every time. Except for one. Anyone with ties to Erithia is too dangerous to be allowed any degree of freedom. I just wish The Union Judges would see that truth as the Mahtsarian Republic has," Zaktan growled. "They're either already under his control or they soon will be. There's a reason their worshiped as demi-gods in The Empire. They have far too much power that is far too easily controlled by the enemy."

Ayela stood, quietly slipping away from the others. Zaktan continued raving, but Ayela couldn't listen. Finaly out of earshot, Ayela sat on the back of their wagon.

"You okay?" Lillia lifted herself onto the wagon to sit next to Ayela.

Ayela focused on the ground, treasured memories of her time growing up with Adina played in her mind. How kind of a soul she'd been before Ayela let her down. "Oh look," she muttered, "it's finally snowing." Snow began falling at an increasing rate. She held out a hand to catch a few of the light flakes. "Why do people make judgments about others so hastily?" Ayela's chest ached as she thought of her last conversation with Adina. "You know as well as I the good Moonborn are capable of."

"This isn't about Zaktan, is it," Lillia asked, placing her delicate arm around Ayela.

"Why could I not have simply trusted Adina instead of falling for the Moonborn stereotype? If I had trusted her, maybe she wouldn't have given in." Ayela let the now-melted snow fall from her hand. "I could have defended her. Maybe Kiyle would have given her a chance. Maybe she would have resisted Erithia." Knots formed in Ayela's throat. She fought in vain to hold back the torrents of guilt and sorrow that threatened to overcome her. Ayela buried her head in her knees when tears began breaking free. She knew it was irrational. She shouldn't be blaming herself, but the thoughts came anyway. "Maybe Kiyle would still be alive."

"Listen to me carefully," Lillia started, jumping down and placing herself in front of Ayela. "Look at me," she said, gripping Ayela's chin gruffly and pulling her to eye level. She wiped away Ayela's tears with her free hand. "It is not your fault! So what if you didn't trust her? No one would have. She was accused of murder, and she was running from the law. No matter the circumstances, no matter her race, she used dark magic. She made a deal with Erithia. Everything that happened was her fault. It doesn't matter if she killed Eema or not. She killed the guards, she killed Kiyle, and she would have killed me. It is not your fault. If you keep blaming yourself, you will never get over it."

"I know." Ayela's chest throbbed as she blinked yet more tears free. "Maybe the worst is behind me." She smiled. "So far, mercenary work isn't as bad as I feared. I think my parents would have approved of what we are doing."

"You've never talked about your parents. What were they like," Lillia asked softly. releasing Ayela's chin and grasping her hands.

"Well, I was young when they... so I remember little. My mother was in the military or something like it. She was always going out on missions. She was strong, always the one to do the discipline. I remember when she taught me to braid my hair. I remember her smile when I finally finished on my own. My father was, well, I don't really know what he was. But I know he was kind. Too kind. He was the one I would always go to if I wanted something."

"They sound wonderful." Lillia smiled.

"They were." Ayela wiped away what remained of her tears with a smile. "My number one favorite memory from before the orphanage was my mother reading to me. She would read in silly voices for each of the characters." Ayela giggled when she recalled her mother's vigorous mannerisms.

"Ready to do some training?"

Lillia rolled her eyes, dropping Ayela's hands as Bahn rounded the corner of their wagon. "We were..."

"Let's go for a walk. We can get some target practice in before the bulk of the storm hits." Bahn motioned toward a lonely tree a short distance from the camp.

"But." Ayela looked to Lillia, loathing to end their conversation.

"Go... get some training in. I'll make sure our tent is set."

"Thanks, Lillia." Ayela jumped from the cart, hugging Lillia and blinking away the last of her tears. "For the talk, I needed it." She backed away, lingering for a moment before following Bahn past the wagons toward the tree.

"What happened after I left," Bahn asked as they waded through the waist-high grass on their way to the tree.

"Nothing," Ayela stuttered.

"Something happened. If you want to talk, I'm here." Bahn smiled before pointing toward the tree. "In the Druid clans, they teach us to control our emotions, to keep from displaying weakness to those around us. Instead, we channel our emotions into our conditioning and combat. I want you to try channeling whatever powerful emotions you feel into every arrow you put into that tree. Aim for that knot."

"That can't be healthy," Ayela scoffed as she drew the bow, notching an arrow. "And it doesn't sound like a good idea given that I might have magic."

"Fair enough. But I find the contrary," Bahn laughed. "I find releasing your emotions on the battlefield or into some training dummy gives you clarity and strength beyond that which you would typically have. At least as long as you have discipline and don't lose control. Besides, it provides a way to release the tension caused by bottling everything up."

"Kibackash." Ayela released the arrow, struggling to recall the phrase Lillia had read from her bow.

"We'll never get that arrow back," she moaned when her arrow flew past the tree into the tallgrass of the plains. "And not so much as a spark."

"Try again."

"So, you just fight with your feelings?" Ayela notched another arrow.

"Not quite. We train and master techniques, then learn to control our emotions and unleash them at the right moment. It takes practice, though. If you get too angry, you lose control, and that's dangerous."

"Yes!" Ayela whispered. Her arrows struck the tree just below the knot she was aiming for.

"Good, again."

"Bahn, can I ask you something?" Ayela notched another arrow, exhaling carefully before taking aim at the tree once more.

"Sure."

"When you said there was something special about me, what did you mean?"

"Well," Bahn started. "When I saw you in the forest, my first instinct was to arrest you, as our laws dictate for poachers. But when you killed the doe, you knelt in prayer. At that moment, I felt as though Musar was telling me there was something different about you. That I needed to let you go."

"That's it?"

"No, when I... left the druids, I was wandering aimlessly. We both met the dragon who brought us together. And I told you I felt the gods were behind him. Out of all the people I could have run into on the road, it was him. Then, when I saw you at the shelter, I couldn't help but feel it was providence guiding me. Musar wants us to survive together."

"What will you do after this mission," Ayela asked.

"If you'll allow, I want to do more contracts with you. I would protect and train you for whatever great destiny awaits us. That won't stop after this mission."

"So, you think the gods guided you to me? That's the only reason." Ayela hardly noticed her fingers release the bowstring. Her arm instinctively drew and notched another arrow just moments after it struck the tree.

"That's the fifth hit in a row. Looks like two of them were almost dead center." Bahn gently rested his hand on Ayela's shoulder. "A few more shots, then we should get back to the others while there's still a little light."

"It's barely even sunset!" Ayela protested. "Listen, if you expect more from me…" Ayela fired another arrow. "Damn," she muttered when it scraped the side of the tree-trunk.

"Storm's picking up," Bahn chimed before turning toward the camp. "Grab your arrows and come back to camp. Weather permitting, we can train more in the morning."

"Seriously?" Ayela groaned, staring at Bahn as he strutted back to camp. She balled her fist, groaning before gathering her arrows from the tree and surrounding dirt before returning to camp.

13

Murder and Fortune

Ayela stood suspended in a pool of viscous, coagulating red liquid that had no discernible beginning nor end. It pulsed rhythmically as to the beat of some great, unheard drum. Waves surfaced periodically, as though driven by moving entities unseen beneath the surface. Each movement churned the plasma with sloshes reminiscent of the viscera left behind in the aftermath of Adina's spell. Ayela halted, nearly fainting at the curiously sweet, unwelcome stench of rotting meat that wafted into her face.

The horrid stench of death hovered before her, no matter how hard she fought to brush it away. Tired from the effort, she accepted her inability to rid herself of the smell and pressed on toward the unreachable horizon; driven by an unknown aim.

Ayela walked as if in a trance, knowing that what she saw couldn't possibly be reality. She recalled lying down in her tent beside Lillia. She was in her armor, with her bow and quiver beside her. Bahn and Zaktan were on watch. Lillia and Logane were to wake in a few hours to replace them. Then it would be her and Zaktan.

Despite this knowledge, the scene before her was crafted in such vivid detail that it couldn't be a mere fancy of the mind. She had control of her thoughts, could reason, but her body refused to obey her commands, dredging on.

Something hard brushed against her submerged foot, then sloshed below. Finally, her feet halted. Ayela closed her eyes, sure that whatever horror had just surfaced from the depths of this lake of blood was something she had no desire to see. Still, her insufferable curiosity overpowered her. With a deep breath, Ayela looked down. She screamed, stumbling back at seeing a body vaguely resembling a woman. Its form was mutilated almost beyond recognition, with gashes and cuts over nearly every part. The skin was fat and tight, bloated by decomposition, yet the lips were blue. Frost, uncolored by the bloody lake, gathered on her blond hair and pale skin. Disfigured as she was, the realization as to the corpse's identity slowly dawned. She wore Lillia's clothes, bore Lillia's face.

Ayela opened her mouth to scream once more, but no sound emerged. She turned, running from the body. Renewed desire to escape this hellish trap surged through her. She ran one direction after another. But all led to the endless, featureless expanse. She stopped, falling to her knees some distance further and screamed into the void. The black sky swallowed her voice with no reverberation or echoes to be heard. All was silent save for the rhythm of the blood pulsing against her legs and her heartbeat in her ears.

Her chest ached with the horrid possibility that this was her new reality. Trapped forever in this endless sea of blood, to be tortured by some malevolent creature. Or punished by some unknown god.

Another slosh some distance from her interrupted Ayela's thoughts. She looked to see a trio of corpses floating in her direction. One, a winged man wearing plate armor. Surely

Logane, the other, though disfigured, had a skin of an ashy gray. Zaktan. That left Bahn as the third bloated and freezing corpse.

This was another nightmare, of that she was sure. She had to wake up. Had to be free of it. She slapped herself. No effect. She tried again, then stopped as a shadow overtook her. Blocking out some unseen light.

She felt the familiar, dreadful presence before she saw it. The eyes bored into the back of her skull. Prodott. She spun, seeing his massive form looming over her. He swayed as in a stupor. Unnaturally proportioned arms gripped a blood-covered dagger in one hand. Two raven feathers hung from its hilt.

He lifted the knife in disjointed, jerky movements unnatural to the human form. The blade was sharp and glistened with fresh blood as it hovered over Ayela's chest. She tried to run, but again found her faculties beyond her control. The world spun around Ayela. She was on her back, Prodott over her, knife ready to plunge.

Ayela lurched out of her bed, covered in sweat and shivering violently from the chilled air. She was back in her tent. Lillia slept peacefully next to her. The wind blew gently against the outside, lifting the flap of their tent to reveal a budding layer of snow. Yet, she still heard the pulsing slosh of the blood. She still felt its revolting warmth against her skin. Her blood still rushed with Prodott's malevolent gaze.

Something drove Ayela to rise. She donned her fur coat and quiver and picked up her bow, leaving the tent. She rounded the corner. There, she saw Zaktan warming his hands by the fire. Prodott stood behind him, knife in hand, about to lunge at Zaktan.

She didn't think, didn't hesitate. Limbs moving almost of their own accord, she notched an arrow, drew and fired. All at once, the sensation and sound of the blood ceased. Prodott fell back, an arrow in his chest, piercing his heart.

"What the fuck!" Zaktan jumped up, drawing his sword. He looked first at Ayela, then at Prodott. "ALARM!" He screamed louder than she imagined he could. "ALARM!"

Logane rushed toward the fire from the camp's edge, sword drawn. Lillia walked up behind Ayela, who still hadn't moved. Her arms trembled, and her sight locked with the now dead Prodott. A single wisp of black smoke rose from the arrow. Her mind was numb.

"Ayela?" Lillia shook Ayela's shoulder, pushing the arm holding her bow down to a more relaxed stance. "What happened?"

"Prodott, he…" Ayela paused. "He had a knife."

Logane checked Prodott's body, picking up the blade before he and Zaktan walked toward Ayela. That's when Ayela saw the other two drivers leave their tents. They walked toward the fire, then stopped when they saw Prodott. They looked at one another, understanding evident on their faces. Both bolted in opposite directions upon seeing Logane approach. He didn't bother giving chase as they disappeared beyond the veil of snow and darkness at the camp's edge.

"Ayela, you good," Logane asked, sheathing his sword as he approached.

Ayela nodded.

"Finally," Zaktan grunted when Bahn emerged from his thick leather tent. Wearing the coat Zaktan had given him. "If we had been under attack, you would be dead."

"Ignore him." Logane's typical crimson cape was missing, allowing the polished steel of his breastplate to gleam in the firelight.

Ayela marveled at the snow melting almost instantaneously after contacting Logane's armor. Subtle clouds of condensation rolled off his shoulders. Waves of heat distorted the air around his body.

"Given the Nighthawks we saw in the village and the knife Prodott tried to use on Zaktan, it's a good bet the other drivers will return with backup." He held the knife up to the group. Two crow feathers dangled from the hilt.

Ayela cupped her hands and blew into them. She stared at the knife; slow realization dawned on her. It was the knife from her dream. Thick snowfall nearly obscured the road beyond their camp. Ayela's thoughts trailed to the sight of Prodott being struck by the arrow, smoke rising from his corpse as though from some magically enhanced shot. She smirked, suppressing the urge to giggle. Ayela shook her head, disgusted at herself for giggling at the thought of a man's death.

"But didn't you say all the past drivers returned badly beaten? And this was the first time Prodott had driven for Dowage," Lillia asked.

"Prodott's been acting strange since we left the mining village." Logane folded his arms over his breastplate, brushing his gauntlets against the polished steel.

"Sure, he was nervous, but this was the half of the mission that was to be most dangerous," Bahn said. "We sure he was about to attack Zaktan?"

Ayela glared at him, "I'm sure."

"How did you know? I watched you walk out of your tent and shoot him without missing a beat. I didn't even hear him behind me."

"Another dream." Ayela admitted. "I saw Prodott with a knife, about to stab me, and all of you were dead." Ayela stopped, shrinking before the disbelieving gazes of all around. "I left the tent just wanting to get the sights out of my head. That's when I saw Prodott creeping up on you with a drawn knife. I just reacted."

"But that means…" Lillia stepped back from Ayela.

"No time to discuss that now. We have a problem. With the storm picking up, it would be the perfect time for an ambush." Ayela tugged at the sleeves of her coat. She stared into the tall grass, yet to be filled with snow. "Logane's right. We have to assume they're returning with the assassins."

"Agreed," Zaktan nodded.

"What if we hide in the grass around the camp?" Ayela pointed to the grassy hill a short distance from camp. "It's tall enough that we could conceal ourselves completely while kneeling, especially on this dark of a night combined with the snow."

"You're full of ideas," Logane muttered. "The ground isn't covered enough yet for us to leave tracks. But we don't want to risk losing sight of each other if the weather gets worse."

"The wind is coming from the north; Ayela could perch on that hill, giving her a decent view of the camp without the worry of wind interference. We could wait until the drivers come back and see what they're up to." Lillia smiled. "If things go wrong, she can cover you guys."

"You ready for that?" Logane muttered.

"She's not ready to defend herself alone yet, but I can guard her and Lillia while they focus on ranged attack and defense." Bahn stretched his arms over his chest.

"Zaktan and I will remain at the edge of the camp. We'll give the signal to attack when the time is right." Logane rubbed at the stubble forming on his chin.

"'Bout what I said before." Zaktan approached Ayela. "I was wrong. There's a killer in you, after all." He nodded to Ayela.

Ayela's mind went numb at the compliment. She hadn't wanted to kill him. But what choice did she have?

"You though, sure you're ready to kill?" Zaktan gestured to Lillia.

"What do you mean?" Lillia asked.

"Zaktan is right. I get the impression you've never taken a life. These people are here to kill us. We have to be ready to stop them at any cost. It is the only way mercenaries survive. Like it or not." Logane stepped toward Lillia. "If you go into battle without the will to kill those who would kill you, you become a liability."

"She's not ready," Zaktan whispered.

"You underestimated me." Ayela said. "Don't make that mistake with her." Ayela slung her bow over her shoulder. Her limbs burned with adrenaline-fueled confidence.

"We'll see," Zaktan mumbled.

"They're gonna expect us to be packing up camp," Logane said with a faint edge in his voice. "If they have even half a brain, they will use the grass to get close and surround us." Logane turned to face the road once more. "Zaktan or I will attack first. Do not make a move until then."

"And for the love of the gods, don't fire arrows anywhere near us!" Zaktan growled.

"There! Someone's coming!" Lillia pointed toward the road, where the glow of torchlight peered over the hill to the south, shimmering through the snow.

"Go! And ignore Zaktan. You can do this," Logane yelled.

Ayela grabbed Lillia's hand and pulled her into the grass. They followed closely behind Bahn. Ayela's pulse roared in her ears as the icy darkness closed in around her.

Lillia stumbled forward, her foot snaring on some unseen obstacle.

"You alright? We need to keep moving." Ayela helped Lillia steady herself before pulling her up the hill through the gradually building snow.

"Ayela," Lillia panted. She turned back to look at the camp. "Your dream…"

Ayela knelt, drawing her bow before fishing an arrow from her quiver. "What about it?" She fumbled a bit in the dark, eventually notching the arrow and looking back toward camp.

"You know there's only…"

"Later." Bahn cut Lillia off. "Talk about that later."

Ayela closed her eyes. The sinister wind burned her lungs with each breath. "Okay, we've got this, right?" Ayela sighed. "Not much of a hill, but still. It'll make things easier."

"You got a clear shot?" Bahn asked.

"Maybe, hard to say at this distance, especially with the snow." Ayela shrugged. Her hands trembled as her heartbeat grew faster. "Nighthawks, for sure." Ayela's mind flashed to her first dream, and the raven-headed man firing an arrow at her. Had he been a nighthawk?

"What did we get ourselves into?" Ayela stretched her numb fingers over her bowstring. She released a breath through clenched teeth, fighting to calm herself. She welcomed the refreshing sting of the icy air and the wind howling around her. Ayela's heart refused to slow as she questioned the intelligence of her decision to become a mercenary.

"You've got this." Lillia's calming touch graced Ayela's trembling wrist. Her muscles finally relaxed. She raised her gaze to the camp when the five horsemen turned toward their fire and dismounted. Ayela imagined how high she might need to raise her aim to hit the camp. The lead rider of the five horsemen stopped and aimed a bow toward the camp. Moments later, sparks erupted from the campfire, and the tents huddled around it collapsed.

"Magic," Lillia whispered. "Something to do with that man's bow, or a spell he cast on the arrow, maybe."

Ayela clenched her teeth. "We'll have to take him out of the fight first. The last thing we need is another archer with magic." Ayela clenched her teeth, inwardly disgusted by the casual mention of ending this man's life. Did he have a family? No, he attacked them. It was her or him.

The mage's followers dismounted at the edge of the camp before drawing their swords. The second figure stalked into the camp, brandishing what looked like a long sword. His black, red-lined robe glistened in the firelight. The two caravan drivers followed shortly. One driver held a short sword while the other brandished what appeared to be a wooden club. The last of the figures ducked into the tall grass by the camp, his two small daggers glinting in the firelight before he disappeared into the shadows.

"When is he going to signal," Ayela asked, careful not to move. The enemy archer scanned the field around the camp.

"Ayela. When they give the signal, I want you to take out the archer. I think he is their leader. Take your time. A clean shot to take him down." Ayela's heart lurched at Bahn's hushed whisper in her ear. Her stomach knotted. She imagined the man's soon-to-be widow receiving news of his demise. Yet, her limbs itched to raise the bow and take aim, an urge drawn by some alien hunger.

"As soon as you see Logane and Zaktan, lose your arrow. Be ready, take aim, and do not hesitate. He wouldn't think twice before killing you."

Ayela drew back the arrow and took aim at the archer's leg. She squealed as the runes lining the bow's grip ignited with a soft sapphire light, reflecting off the falling snow and illuminating the hilltop where they hid. The bow had a mind of its own, pulling Ayela's aim to account for the wind and distance. Ayela released the bowstring in a panic. She ducked into the grass. "Why does it glow!" She cursed to herself. Ayela's breath caught in her throat. She saw a faint wisp of black mist run over the arm of the bow. She closed her eyes while a surge of tingling pleasure shot up her arm and through her body. Her heart slowed, her mind focused. She returned her gaze to the battlefield.

"Shit," Ayela gasped. The arrow had struck the ground between the archer's legs.

Ayela could hardly hear the battle cries of Logane and Zaktan. They rushed into the camp to fight the surprised intruders. Before Ayela could draw another arrow, the mage aimed his bow at their position.

A hot white flash illuminated the surrounding area. The smell of smoke filled the air. Tiny embers glowed on the ground in front of Ayela as the light dissipated. All the snow around her had melted in the flash of heat.

"What?" Ayela started as Lillia stumbled and fell to her knees, "Lillia!"

"Fire back," Lillia screamed.

Tears of anger and fear threatened to break free as she drew another arrow. The runes on the bow ignited, fighting Ayela to fine-tune her aim. She surrendered, trusting in the bow. Ayela's chest burned with a foreign warmth. Her fingers tingled, the cold forgotten. She strained against the pull of the bowstring. Her vision narrowed. She saw only the archer drawing another arrow; nothing else mattered. Ayela winced, feeling something shift within her. Her heartbeat increased, muscles tightened, her fingers twitched, nearly losing control of the bow. Wind whipped around Ayela, swirling snow alongside sparks of electricity along the arrow. She relaxed, allowing the bow's magic to work. Wisps of smoke gathered on the arms of the bow. Ayela yelled into the night, her voice carrying over the battlefield. A blast of air kicked up snow as Ayela fired.

Ayela's legs wavered. The arrow moved faster and flatter than any she'd ever shot. Her stomach churned. The world around her spun wildly. "What," Ayela breathed, falling to her knees. Black spots danced at the edges of her vision.

Eyes wide, she watched as the smoke that had gathered on the bow's arms flowed toward her hand. Ayela took a deep breath, invigorated by the magic. Her pupils dilated, sharpening every detail. She released a gasp as the tension of the battle released all at once, leaving a surreal calm. The arrow struck the archer's chest with an audible thud, knocking him off his feet in a cloud of pink mist, shortly followed by the low rumble of distant thunder.

"Lillia," Ayela groaned involuntarily, dropping her bow to brace herself against the rapidly refreezing grass beneath her. Ayela's vision blurred before fading to black. She released a soft groan when the frost-covered ground hit her cheek.

Her chest burned white-hot as her fingers tingled. Ice-laden air whipped around them as in a whirlwind.

"Focus Ayela! Calm?" Lillia's voice was barely audible, as though heard from a deep sleep.

Ayela released quickened breaths, fighting to empty her mind and slow the blizzard of emotions whirling within her. Had she killed the archer? Was Lillia hit? What was that flash? Her eyes shot open at a harsh sting on her cheek, and her head whipped to the side. Lillia sat on top of her, she'd slapped Ayela. Ayela's mind blanked, Lillia had hit her. Why?

"Close the door, make it smaller, hold it shut!" Lillia's voice dripped with scarcely contained fear.

Ayela closed her eyes, ignoring the stinging on her cheek and focusing on slow, steady breaths. Gradually, the spot of heat in Ayela's chest shrunk, and the surrounding wind died down. Ayela's arms tingled as though asleep, she felt as though she were flying in some maelstrom, but she focused. Contained the magic. Then, the heat in her chest was gone, but her fingers still stung.

"Fuck, Ayela. That was too close." Lillia breathed, her head sinking. Her hands trembled as she fell onto Ayela, hugging her tightly. "Don't. We shouldn't... Gods, you could have died."

Ayela returned the hug with barely functioning arms. "The others, what's happening?" Ayela turned over when Lillia rolled off her, she needed to see the battle.

"Shit," Bahn breathed before dashing toward the camp.

Ayela's vision cleared. She saw Logane swing a flaming sword toward a driver, cutting him in half from shoulder to hip. His wings erupted from his sides, lifting him off the ground as he leaped toward the assassin. Logane swung, a single slash across the man's neck. The man dropped his sword, clutching at his neck and falling to his knees. Logane pulled back and swung at the assassin again, cleaving his head from his shoulders. He then thrust his sword into the assassin's headless torso, setting it ablaze before removing his sword.

Zaktan was locked in combat with a driver wielding a long sword. While another assassin crept in behind him, brandishing daggers. Then the assassin turned, looking to the edge of the campfire light where Bahn stood.

The figure charged Bahn as though in a blind rage, recklessly swinging his dagger in the air. Bahn dodged the dagger before catching the attacker's arm. Ayela winced, seeing the man's arm snap before Bahn elbowed him in the face. He fell to the ground. Then there was silence. Zaktan stood over his opponent's body, panting. A pool of blood gathered under the driver.

"It's over," Lillia cried. "Thank the gods."

"Yea." Ayela clutched her stomach as she tried to stand. Lillia helped her to her feet.

"Ayela! That could have killed you!" Lillia screamed.

"I couldn't help it!"

"We shouldn't have had you fight. Gods, that was stupid." Lillia embraced Ayela again. "Damit Ayela, I can't lose you. Not again. Stop doing this."

"You think I meant to?" Ayela breathed. "Besides, the bow…"

"Activated by your storm magic, yeah." Lillia confirmed.

"Kind of hard to deny it now." Bahn approached them. "Test or no test. Come, we should get back to the others." Bahn gently guided her and Lillia back to camp.

"You! Why did you fire! I hadn't given the signal!" Logane screamed when they passed the wagons. Flames rose from his burning eyes. His lips twisted in a cruel snarl, like that of a rabid animal. Logane's wings were fully extended, their vibrant red and black pattern mesmerizing and intimidating. His eyes glowed as fierce orange embers. Brilliant flames ran the length of his sword, super-heating the cold air around his blade and distorting the surrounding light. His armor bled torrents of steam. Snow sizzled on his breastplate with every drop.

Logane charged toward Ayela when she opened her mouth to defend herself. His sword poised to strike.

"Enough!" Zaktan screamed, slamming into Logane's side to redirect his charge. Zaktan grappled Logane from behind, holding his neck with one arm and his sword arm with the other. "Battle's over, bird boy. Time to relax."

As Zaktan held Logane his expression softened. His eyes returned to normal. The flames died away from his sword, and his wings relaxed, if only a little

"Did you fire that arrow by yourself?" Zaktan asked through labored breaths from behind Logane, still grappling with him. "Or did Lillia cast a spell on it?"

"Never mind that. You could have gotten us killed!" Logane yelled, fighting to break free from Zaktan's locked grip.

"It wasn't me. When I aimed at the archer, the bow just lit up, I had to fire."

"So, what? You're saying that your bow is bound with an unknown enchantment, and you used it." Logane sneered, snaking free of Zaktan and stepping toward Ayela. "That's worse!" Ayela stumbled backward. The faint red glow of his eyes began to re-emerge. "You could have killed us all!"

"Logane! Remember Korvania." Zaktan said, stepping between Logane and Ayela once more. "The fight is over. Calm yourself. No one was injured. All is well."

The wind howled around the party for several minutes while Logane's heavy breathing subsided.

"I'm sorry," Logane muttered before turning away from the group. "Thank you, Zaktan. I... I think I need to lie down." Logane's speech grew soft. He stepped away, stumbling to the nearest body. He knelt and searched the corpse.

"What in Mahtsar's name was that?" Lillia asked. "Was he about to attack us?"

"Forgive Logane for his anger," Zaktan sighed. "He has difficulty controlling the dragon rage."

"Dragon Rage?" Ayela asked.

"He's a paladin of Lapid, God of Wrath and War. Damn near unstoppable in battle, but." He sighed. "It's hard to control afterward. Just lucky it was a quick fight. Back to my question. Was that you?"

"That was all her." Bahn smiled. "Confirmed, she's got magic."

"Dangerous and stupid. You could have killed yourself." Zaktan scoffed. "Doesn't matter now. Round up the horses." Zaktan sighed. "We need to move."

Ayela held her hand over her mouth when they walked through the camp. She recognized the caravan drivers. One lay with his torso cleaved in two, face down in a pool of his own blood. Ayela stifled a gag at the other driver, who was propped against a wagon wheel. His deathly white hand loosely grasped his slashed abdomen, failing to contain its contents. His eyes lazily followed Ayela. Still alive and scarcely breathing.

Zaktan stepped over the driver, drawing a small dagger to end his suffering. Ayela closed her eyes and shuddered when they passed the headless, smoldering body of the cloaked figure Logane had killed. A long streak of blood had splattered across Ayela's tent behind him.

Ayela's stomach grew weaker when they approached the archer, lying on the ground where Ayela had shot him. Her arrow had struck with such force that it tore a fearsome hole through his chest, burying itself in the snow behind the archer.

"You don't want to dwell on that." Zaktan's voice was low and unusually solemn as he pulled Ayela away. "At least his death was quick."

"We'll take Prodott back to Hatave and deliver the shipment. We should leave immediately." Logane said.

"Why leave immediately? The danger has passed, and we could use the rest," Ayela asked, looking longingly at the destroyed tent that held her makeshift bed.

"I think you know they're Nighthawks." Logane held a small, bloodstained parchment out towards Ayela. "They were behind the caravan attacks."

"Should we even return with the shipment," Bahn asked.

"What about them?" Lillia's voice quivered as she timidly gestured to the bodies strewn about the campsite. "Shouldn't we, I don't know…"

"What, bury them?" Zaktan scorned. "They tried to kill us in our sleep. What honor do we owe them? Let the scavengers at'em." Zaktan climbed into the driver's seat of a wagon. "Come on, don't want to be here when more show up.

"The nighthawks are honorable in their own way." Ayela muttered. "Maybe they'll understand. Besides, they'd want to honor their own dead."

"I think we'll be fine." Logane wiped his face with a red cloth, removing sweat and blood splatters from his cheeks. "There are treaties we must honor between The King's Guild and The Nighthawks. They attacked us, we defended ourselves. Retaliation would break those treaties, and there's nothing obligating us to deal with their dead. I already scavenged what is of use to us. And yes, we're still returning the shipment. Breaking a contract and stealing the shipment would be just as bad as having the nighthawks after us. We'd end up with bounties on our heads from The Kings Guild."

"If a Nighthawk approaches us, we can just tell them the blacksmith posted a contract with The Kings for us to defend a shipment. We didn't know about their involvement." Zaktan's voice carried confidence.

"Nothing to be nervous about, right?" Ayela's voice quivered as she spoke.

"More company," Bahn said, pointing toward the northern road, where several more horses and torches headed for the campsite.

"Lillia, Ayela, you two retreat into the grass like before. Just hide. No more fighting, understood?" Logane said. "If fighting starts, we'll end them quickly."

Ayela watched through the blades of grass while six more men on horseback stopped at the road's edge. Two broke away and rode into the camp. Ayela sighed in relief as the tension melted from her shoulders. She recognized the uniform plate armor and red capes of the Hatave city guard. The two horsemen stopped at the edge of camp, their horses prancing nervously before they yelled something to the guards on the road, who stormed into camp. One walked up to Logane, shaking his hand firmly while the others walked through the camp examining the bodies.

"What is the city guard doing all the way out here," Ayela asked.

"What do you bet my father sent them," Lillia sighed.

"How would they have found us? More likely it's a patrol," Ayela said.

"I left a note for Captain Zan. He knew we were headed to The Headless Snake."

"Lillia! Ayela!" Bahn screamed in their direction, motioning for them to return to camp.

"Thought so. That's Captain Zan." Lillia pointed to the man talking to Logane. "Father couldn't even bother to look for me himself."

"Well, you can always say no," Ayela muttered. "He'll listen to you," Ayela whispered as they stood and walked back toward the others.

"You really think we can convince six city guards to not take me back for the wedding? I am promised to a general's son, remember?" Lillia scowled as she approached the group. All of the guards were standard city guards, not even carrying the insignia of her father's private guard.

"You're gonna have to tell your father why, eventually."

Lillia groaned at the notion.

"You haven't told me either," Ayela said when they walked past the guards toward Logane, Bahn and Zaktan. "He seems nice enough, handsome, wealthy…" Ayela started.

"Drop it," Lillia muttered.

"Ayela, good to see you again. If I'd known what you were planning, I wouldn't have left you two alone." Captain Zan smiled through his open-faced helmet before turning to Lillia. "Put me on quite the hunt to find you. Your father wanted to come, but he is busy convincing General Aaron not to call for your execution." His gaze narrowed at that last statement, striving to drive home the severity of her situation.

"Execution!" Lillia cried out. "What lunatic…"

"You disgraced one of the most powerful noble houses. Your father is there right now, working to calm them."

"There is nothing to worry about." Logane stepped forward, determination in his gaze. "She is a recruit of The King's Guild, as such, she is under guild protection."

"Is this true? You've denounced your title and joined The King's Guild?" Captain Zan's eyes widened in disbelief. He looked as though torn between anger and bewilderment.

"Captain, you know what he wants. You know I won't go through with his plans. I would rather give up everything than do that." Lillia folded her arms across her chest, adopting a firm posture. "You're the one person I've told." Despite this, Ayela noticed the quivering in her lip as she glanced at Logane.

Logane had called them recruits, but had they really done anything so official?

"And you still haven't told your father," Captain Zan sighed. "Still, mercenary work isn't suited to someone as young as you are. And I have orders from the general and your father."

"Captain," Lillia warned. "My mother started at my age. Regardless, my answer is no."

"You heard the lady." Logane approached Captain Zan. "Besides, you wouldn't want a dispute between The General and The Kings. It wouldn't be good for anyone."

"Walk with me." Captain Zan held a hand out toward Lillia, motioning for her to head away from the others.

"Lillia," Ayela asked as Lillia glanced her way before stepping toward the captain.

"I'll be right back," Lillia said, following him to the edge of the camp.

Lillia and Zan whispered to one another, exchanging gestures as their conversation escalated.

"No! You, of all people, should know. I'll never love him!" Lillia yelled. "I couldn't love a man!" Lillia held her hand over her mouth. Her cheeks turned crimson. She hung her head, refusing to look the captain in the eye.

Logane and the others shifted uncomfortably, pretending they hadn't overheard their conversation. Lillia returned her gaze to the captain.

Captain Zan bent down, getting eye level with Lillia. He whispered something to her once more before wiping a tear from her eye. Lillia leaned in, embracing Zan, before he pulled away. She mouthed a thank you before turning back to Ayela with a weak smile. Captain Zan handed a piece of parchment on a board to Lillia, who withdrew behind a wagon.

"Men!" Captain Zan barked after a brief whistle. He and Lillia walked back to the center of the camp. "Mount up and return to Hatave. Get this message to Master Kote. Let no one else read it." He held up a rolled parchment in the air.

"Then bring this second letter to General Aaron. Again, both letters are confidential. No one else is to read them." The captain handed the two rolled and freshly sealed parchments to one of the other guards before turning toward the group. "I will accompany you for the rest of your journey back to Hatave. Master Kote gave me orders to ensure the safety of Lillia and Ayela; thus, I am staying with you. Sir Logane, I expect to be briefed on everything that has transpired to this point. And don't worry, I won't break any Guild laws by intervening in your mission. I act only as their bodyguard, and I won't be taking any of the proceeds from your contact. I am already being paid."

"Well, long story short, a blacksmith who was operating in Northtown hired us. The Nighthawks have been targeting his caravans. Tonight, the Nighthawks attacked with the caravan drivers.

Prodott, the lead driver, was a plant by The Nighthawks. We plan to turn his body over to the guard upon our return to Hatave."

"Leave it. I'll trust the word of a paladin over anything those witches'll get from the body. I'll still return to Hatave with you. When you're back behind the walls, I will have fulfilled my mission. Lillia, by then, your groom should know your denial and will have canceled the union." Captain Zan stated. "Gods willing, the General will be satisfied. I'll leave what you do after that to you. Though I'd hoped you would speak with your father. He will be more understanding of all this than you might think."

"Maybe," Lillia breathed as the other guards left the camp. "We'll see how things go."

"One hell of a coincidence you showing up right after the fight," Zaktan grumbled.

"Not sure what you're insinuating, but it is as you say. A coincidence. I've not slept since I heard Lillia was missing. Tracked her to The Headless Snake, found out you lot were on a mission to the mines. I only found your camp because your fire is in view of the main road."

"It doesn't matter." Logane waved away Zaktan's suspicion.

"Makes a little more sense now." Ayela nudged Lillia's shoulder before climbing into the wagon behind her.

"Yeah." Lillia smiled in reply, taking her position atop the goods. "Glad to have said it out loud finally," she whispered.

Ayela's smile faded when she retook her place beside the crates. Her sight rested on the bow. She recalled the intense sensations that had run through her when she had fired at the archer. It had been dark magic, that much was clear. She shouldn't have the bow; she shouldn't use the bow. But just now, it was the only weapon she had. She didn't have a choice. Right? Ayela closed her eyes, setting her jaw as the phantom sensation of dark magic played across her wrists.

Her grip tightened on the bow as she held it to her chest. She replayed every second of the night, savoring the twang of the bowstring as it took the lives of the devil, Prodott, and the assassin.

"Fuck," Ayela whispered, relinquishing the bow and allowing it to clatter to the wagon's floor. She huddled her legs in, repulsed by her actions.

"Ayela?" Lillia questioned.

She opened her mouth to tell Lillia, but stopped. Shame washed over her every thought. If she told Lillia, she'd have to admit she liked the feeling of Erithia's magic flowing through her.

"Ayela, about your dream," Lillia whispered as she leaned over the edge of the crates to see Ayela. "You realize the only source of divination magic is Erithia. Right."

Ayela hadn't considered that. Was it some cruel trick of Erithia to give her this bow, give her a connection to his magic so she could use it? Was he responsible for her terrible visions? But why would he help her?

"There's got to be another explanation." Ayela curled into a tighter ball. "No way I've used dark magic." She lied. Knowing full well the truth of the matter. She hadn't tried to cast his magic. But she'd be lying if she said she hadn't enjoyed it. She'd never even studied or imagined what dark magic would be like. Yet, she recalled the pleased look Adina had when she cast the disguise spell. Had this been what she felt?

"It can't be dark magic," Ayela muttered. "I never even said a control word. I never asked for their help." Ayela rested her head on her knees as tears formed in her eyes.

"We have to get you tested," Lillia said before returning to the top of the boxes. "Before you harm yourself. Or worse."

14

Healing Hope

The city streets were notably more normal than Ayela had feared. Given the winter storm the previous day and the early morning hour, few people wandered the street. She'd expected their caravan to be accosted by Nighthawk thugs the moment they entered the city. Shipments were no oddity in Southtown, but armored drivers led theirs and they had no city guard escort. To make matters worse, because of the size of their carts, they could only use the main roads. Their party was an anomaly, for sure.

The few pedestrians they had passed eyed them wearily. Any Nighthawk aware of the shipment would identify them immediately. They may as well have targets painted on their back.

"Relax," Logane said from the driver's seat beside Ayela. "Not likely we'll be attacked in the middle of the day on a main city road. Not with this many of us."

"And what about our destination? What's stopping them from laying a trap there," Ayela asked.

"If they were going to try something, yes. It would be there. But I doubt they will. They'll know by now that Dowage hired the mercenary guild. It's more likely they'll be after him. Not us."

Ayela breathed warmth through chapped lips into her numb hands as they entered the markets. More and more people were populating the streets now, with stalls having recently opened and customers beginning to arrive. Going was slow through the crowds, but most were eager to get out of their way when they saw or heard them approaching.

"There." Logane pointed to a newly remodeled shop at the end of the street. It was only slightly more put together than the shanty stalls and decaying clay buildings that occupied the surrounding blocks. The clay walls were near featureless, with pyramid-shaped blocky windows. A dense wooden shutter closed off each window. An ornately engraved sword and shield lay embedded in the mortar above the door.

Ayela shuffled uneasily in her seat atop the wagon. She groaned at the melted snow seeping through her clothes.

"Why is it closed," Ayela asked as they dismounted.

"Maybe he's out of supply?" Lillia shrugged. "They did say that he'd had several shipments stolen."

"The blacksmith'd better have a good explanation for not mentioning the Nighthawks," Zaktan grumbled.

They stood between the parked carts and the shop

"My money says he won't. As many times as they attacked, there's no way he didn't know," Ayela said.

"Probably right," Logane replied. "But I bet we won't find Dowage here at all. He hired us knowing the Nighthawks would attack his caravan." Logane pointed to Bahn, Ayela and Lillia. "You three stay with the wagons. Zaktan and I will go and check on Dowage."

Ayela drew her bow. Her fingers twitched with the remembered feeling of Erithia's magic flowing through the bow. "No," she whispered to herself, setting her shoulders and taking a breath. She relaxed her shoulders, forcing her hand free of the string. If they were attacked, she'd have to rely on Bahn. No way she would fire the bow again.

Logane approached the front door and pounded on it several times. Nothing. He tried again before stepping away. "No answer. Looks like we're going in the back. Zaktan, take the lead."

The two of them rounded the corner, disappearing from view. Minutes passed as hours while they waited, studying the locked door and closed shutter.

Ayela glanced at the street where curious pedestrians eyed their wagons. She ducked at the whiz of an arrow and the thud of it embedding in the cart behind her. Lillia screeched, and Bahn entered a ready stance. Fully on instinct, Ayela drew her bow and stood in front of Lillia as she scanned the rooftops. A mixture of fear and perverse longing itched in her fingers as she squeezed the arrow she'd notched. But there was nothing. No movement, no further arrows. No sign of the archer who had shot at them.

Still, all was uncomfortably calm, save for the oblivious crowd behind the carts. She glanced at the arrow, a black feather dangled from the rear, and a note was wrapped around the shaft. Cautiously, she approached and pulled off the parchment.

Ayela's eyes widened in disbelief as she read. "I don't think the Nighthawks appreciated him hiring mercenaries," she muttered.

Zaktan and Logane rounded the corner, returning from the blacksmith's shop empty-handed.

"What does it say," Bahn asked.

"To the mercenaries hired to defend the shipment."

"Well, go on," Logane ordered, seeing the arrow and the parchment.

"We understand you were ignorant of our involvement with Dowage. As a professional courtesy and in accordance with guild treaties, we have allowed you to live. We fulfilled our contract by orchestrating the attack on the caravan with the hope you would survive. We understand you are now in possession of the three carts of blacksmith supplies. Consider these supplies as payment, and encouragement to stay out of our affairs in the future."

"The entire shipment as payment," Zaktan wondered. "Are you sure? Let me see."

"You think they mean that," Zaktan asked, taking the parchment from Ayela and examining it for himself.

"What about the blacksmith," Ayela asked.

"Gone, Nighthawks took him out." Zaktan gestured to the building before returning to the shipment. "Logane, how much you think we could get for this?"

"About eight-thousand five-hundred gold marks," Ayela replied. "At least, that's what the ledger at the mine said."

"Shit." Bahn looked toward the shop, bewildered.

"But do we really want to take payment from The Nighthawks," Ayela asked after a concerned glance from the oddly silent Lillia.

"We aren't, in a way." Logane shrugged, rolling the paper up and tucking it into a pouch by his side.

"Dowage owes us for the job we performed. He can no longer pay." Logane's calculated tone betrayed his apathy toward Dowage. Or was it contempt? "Since Dowage can no longer honor his side of the agreement, we may extract whatever payment we deem necessary. There will be no problems with us taking the shipment."

"What about Dowage, should we report his death?" Lillia asked, fiddling with her hands.

"To who?" Zaktan scoffed.

"The Nighthawks killed him in Southtown. A place where they control about half the guards. We report it to the wrong person, and we'd be painting a target on our backs. We didn't kill him, and we left no trace of ourselves behind in there. There isn't even a body in there, just a lot of blood," Zaktan said.

"Let's move on from that grim business." Logane waved his hand before the party. "What's done is done. We are taking the shipment as payment. Bahn, Ayela, Lillia, how do you like mercenary work so far?" Logane climbed onto one of the wagon driver's seats. "Is it something you want to dedicate yourselves to?"

"I really like it," Ayela said without so much as a thought.

"Really," Zaktan asked. "Even the violence?"

Ayela's cheeks flushed. "Don't think I wanna go without that rush." She hated to admit it, but it was true. Disgusted as she was by it. Her fingers ached to draw the bowstring again. She hoped it wasn't the dark magic. That perhaps she'd just loved the thrill. But was that worse, that she'd enjoyed the fight?

"Ayela!" Lillia stepped back, concern painted on her face as she looked Ayela over.

"Oh, come on. You cannot tell me you did not enjoy yourself. Mostly at least," Ayela said.

"No! People died, and you…"

"I don't mean that I enjoyed that." Ayela hastened to correct herself. "But getting away from the city, going on an adventure like this. Even if it turned out violent. It's something I always dreamed of."

"Fine," Lillia conceded. "I didn't like the fight. But everything else. Yeah, I wouldn't mind making this my life. Traveling on the road with y—friends."

"Especially the payment," Bahn breathed.

"Don't get used to that. Most jobs don't pay anywhere near this. But yes, money is nice." Logane chuckled.

"But I think I need a little more experience before I can actually call myself a mercenary," Ayela laughed. "Namely, a magic tutor. I need to learn to control my magic before I kill myself,"

"Yes, you do." Lillia leveled her gaze at Ayela. "Before we go on another mission." She commanded. "Understood?"

Logane nodded. "That goes without saying. Our comrade, Raesra. She was injured recently, so she couldn't join us on this mission. But she would be delighted to tutor you, I'm sure. If not, we should easily be able to find you someone without sending you to The Citadel."

"Thank the gods." Ayela laughed, thankful at least that they weren't considering turning her over to Hatave's Magi. She didn't want to think what life as a conscripted mage would be like. She'd much rather have the freedom of mercenary work than forced military servitude. The damage she'd done to that archer would have been more than sufficient to warrant her service.

"I'm glad you all enjoyed it." Logane smiled at Ayela. "I plan to petition you for the guild. Make the three of you official members. It comes with several benefits, including higher respect and pay from clients, less chance of people double-crossing you, and you get some leeway with the guard."

"Logane." Ayela paused, brushing a stray hair out of her face as she caught a momentary smile from Zaktan that quickly vanished when he noticed her gaze. "Thank you for everything, really. I don't mean to be rude, but why are you so willing to help us? Don't get me wrong, I want to join the Guild. It's just… mercenaries aren't known for being trustful of others."

"The truth. At first, we were desperate. On our last contract, a couple of our squad members were injured; an archer and a mage. One of them didn't survive. We needed people to fill their roles, and you were the only ones to accept. As you say, mercenaries aren't quick to trust, and few would even consider working with an Erithian." Logane paused for a moment, looking toward Zaktan before returning his attention to Ayela. "On the mission, you three impressed us in more ways than one. Whether or not Zaktan wants to admit it, we are glad we recruited you. Now, let's go sell this shipment, then we'll celebrate at The Headless Snake."

"Sixteen-Hundred gold marks each," Ayela marveled, walking with the group toward The Headless Snake. "I knew it would be a lot, but still." She stared at the promissory note in her hand, rereading the number written on the parchment again and again.

"Nick, the bartender, has been wanting to repair the second floor of his tavern and turn it into an inn." Logane absently rolled his promissory note through his fingers. "I'd wager he would let us stay there indefinitely if we financed it. It could be our home. At least for a while."

"What about the Red Rose Inn? Couldn't we stay there?" Bahn asked.

"Gods no," Zaktan said. "It'll be much more cost-effective to have our own place. Besides, one of you snores like a sick dragon. We need walls separating us."

"Yeah," Logane laughed as they approached The Headless Snake.

The interior was quiet. The lull between mealtimes brought few patrons and no performers to liven the stale atmosphere.

"Nick!" Logane yelled for the bartender.

"What can I do y'all for?" Nikul placed a mug on the bar for Logane and Zaktan and filled it with a pitcher of amber-colored liquid. "The usual?"

"We're celebrating a job well done. A round for all of us." Logane grinned.

"And the kids' first mission at that." Zaktan smirked.

"Congrats." Nikul smiled as he began pouring drinks. He slid a small glass to Bahn, Lillia, and Ayela with a wink. A ruby-colored liquid filled the glasses. Nikul topped each with some sort of brown spice before sliding them closer.

"May we prosper, and our enemies fall," Logane shouted, holding his mug in the air. "To the King's Guild, and her soon-to-be newest members!"

"Hear, hear!" The few patrons of the tavern echoed with uplifted tankards.

Ayela and Lillia eyed their small glasses wearily.

"We're a little young to," Lillia started.

"Calm down," Nikul said. "You think I'd serve liquor to children?"

"They're Fire Shots. It's tradition. Gotta drink after your first mission." Zaktan's unusually smug grin only added to Ayela's suspicion.

"No alcohol. I promise," Nikul said.

"Bottoms up." Ayela raised her glass to Lillia. "Can't stop here, not after everything."

Lillia released a sigh of apprehension and picked up the glass.

The foul liquid burned Ayela's mouth and throat. Its fumes singed her sinuses and flushed her cheeks. It was as though she'd swallowed liquid fire that was slogging its way down her throat. Its cold heat surged through every inch of her being, burning her eyes and bringing her to the verge of sneezing.

Finally able to breathe, she and Lillia coughed and sputtered before cringing in disgust. Ayela slammed the small glass on the counter before resting her hands on the bar. Soon, the burning subsided to a bittersweet aftertaste that left Ayela's mouth sticky and parched.

Logane and Zaktan burst out laughing, as did several other patrons of the bar.

"You good there, princess?" Zaktan patted the two of them on the back.

"Another?" Nikul asked with a knowing smile.

"Fuck no!" Lillia waved Nikul off with a hasty response.

"Just water." Ayela managed. "Lots of water."

Bahn took a seat next to Lillia and Ayela, shaking his head as he placed his glass on the counter, motioning for Nikul to refill it.

"Bullshit," Lillia breathed. "No way you want more of that swill."

Bahn only smiled before downing the refilled glass. He was silent for a time, his eyes squinting before he released a bated breath and placed the glass on the counter.

"Well, color me impressed." Logane smiled. "Not seen anyone stand two glasses since Zaktan."

"It's not dissimilar to a drink my clan makes. Good for clearing up colds." Bahn smiled. "Used to love the stuff."

"Damn druids," Zaktan grumbled and stalked off to sit beside Logane.

"Anyway, how long have you owned this bar for now, five years," Logane asked Nikul.

"You know this, What's your angle this time?" Nikul draped a dishcloth over his shoulder

"And you've always wanted to turn the second floor into an inn?" Logane took a brief swig from his mug.

"Yea."

"We have a proposition for you." Logane slid his promissory note across the bar to him. "Sixteen-hundred gold marks to start, and more to come. We'll finance your renovations on the condition that we have a permanent residence here."

Nikul's eyes widened in disbelief. "Uh… As much as I'd love to, it would take over sixteen hundred to turn the second floor into an inn. Between wood rot and moisture damage, it's a miracle it hasn't caved in. Plus, with all of you staying here permanently, I'd need to add a third floor to keep a profit. Not to mention the permits to renovate and add a third floor."

"The swindler, as always. We've got more." Zaktan placed his note on the counter with a smug grin. "Another sixteen hundred."

"That should be enough to get you started. We will provide further funds as we are able. We'll need food and water with these arrangements, of course."

"I could," Ayela stopped when Logane glared at her.

"I think I could do that." Nikul smiled. "It'll be nice to see this place become what I always wanted it to be. Though, I can't recommend staying up there until I get it at least a little fixed up. You are welcome to sleep in the tavern in the meantime. We close up around midnight and don't open again until noon. I can get some bedding for you tomorrow. In the meantime, I can set up some modest accommodations in the storerooms. Would that work for a few weeks while I start the second-floor renovations?"

"Zaktan and I have a place to stay for another week. Does this work for you three?" Logane looked toward Ayela and the others, exchanging nods of approval. "It's settled then. We'll make this our home. And we'll help you get the inn you've always wanted."

"Nick! Can we get another round," screamed a patron from the opposite end of the bar.

"Duty calls. You know, another fellow posted a job on the bounty board. You should check it out." Nikul hid the banknotes in a safe under the counter before returning to the other patrons.

"I don't mind helping pay for the inn," Ayela said once Nikul was out of earshot. "I'd feel bad if I let you take on all the expenses."

"No." Logane smiled. "If you three are going to become mercenaries, you need your money for equipment and training."

"Consider it a loan. You can help us in the future." Zaktan smiled.

"We'll be heading out then. See you three here tomorrow night to look at contracts?" Logane asked.

"Sounds like a plan," Ayela said as she sat at the bar.

Nikul slid a plate of food before Ayela and Lillia. A thick slice of ham and several grilled vegetables. "Eat up if you want to finish before the dinner rush. Mira is playing here again tonight."

"So that's her name!" Lillia smiled.

"Yeah, thought everyone knew her." Nikul said before turning to the other patrons.

Ayela savored every bite of the rich meat and seasoned vegetables. Hope crept into her mind with a smile. She'd made it, or at least started to make it. No longer homeless, meals cared for, and more money than she could spend. Maybe it was all for the better. Her smile faded, wiped away by the nagging remembrance of the bow's dark magic.

Ayela looked over at Lillia, who was lost in the enjoyment of her meal. The only thing that mattered was that her best friend was here, embarking on this new life alongside her. The bow was tomorrow's problem. Right now, she could risk hope.

15

Life Seeker

"Strange to think that just a few days ago, I was on the verge of giving up." Ayela whispered, watching Nikul lock the front door behind the last of the drunkards. "Now, I dare to hope," Ayela yawned.

"What are you hoping for?" Lillia leaned back in her chair as she downed the last of the tea Nikul had brewed for them.

"That things will be better. That I can put the past behind me." Ayela smiled at Lillia before her expression grew grim. "That I won't have a connection to Erithia's magic."

"I don't think you have to worry about that," Lillia said. "Even if you did, you're strong enough to resist whatever temptations it would bring."

Ayela smiled, grateful for the attempt at reassurance. But it didn't change the fact that she'd used dark magic. It didn't change the fact that she'd liked it.

"There it is again." Lillia sighed as she moved closer to Ayela. "Something's been bothering you. And I think it's got to do with the lie you told everyone."

"Lie?" Ayela's eyes widened in panic. She wasn't ready to tell her about the bow. She didn't want to tell anyone.

"When you had your first dream, Zaktan asked you if you'd encountered anything that could've given you magic. I didn't want to press, but I know you lied. I can tell it's bothering you." Lillia rested her hand on Ayela's clenched fist. "Please, let me help you."

Ayela took a deep breath of relief at the out presented to her. "It was Erithia. I spoke with Erithia."

Lillia stopped. Speechless at hearing the admission.

"Yes, in person. Shortly after Adina turned, Erithia found me and tempted me. He showed me a vision of a grand mansion orphanage within The Empire. Adina and the other children were there. I almost," Ayela hesitated. "But then I remembered you and that you would be absent in that future. It is what allowed me to deny him."

"Oh." Lillia blushed and smiled. Hope gleamed in her eyes, not the judgement Ayela had expected. "I mean, if anything could give you magic. Speaking with a literal god would. I can see why you're worried about having a connection to dark magic." Lillia hung her head. "And I can see why you didn't tell the others."

Tension melted from Ayela's shoulders at Lillia's acceptance of her answer. She closed her eyes, cursing herself. Lillia was the closest friend she had. There is no reason she should hide this dark magic from her. If anyone could help, it would be her.

"But an actual god? You're sure." Lillia asked, pausing when Ayela nodded. "Even in the legends, they only ever communicate through agents or apparitions. They don't even talk in dreams."

"And that's just it. One of the first visions I had was of the other gods all meeting with me. It sounds crazy, I know. Musar was the one talking. He was an enormous wolf with multiple tails. The other gods were there in spirit, whatever that meant. Musar told me he gave me a gift. The more I think about it, the more I wonder, no, hope he gave me magic. I don't want my magic to have come from Erithia."

"We need to get you tested tomorrow." Lillia said. "Before anything. Most enchantment shops sell magic test kits. We'll pick one up when we get your bow identified."

"No!" Ayela covered her mouth. There was no logical reason to avoid identifying the bow. Lillia's plan was solid.

"Why?" Lillia scoffed. "It makes the most sense. We certainly aren't going back home for my father to test you. I'm not ready for that."

"I..." Ayela struggled to come up with a reason. It was hopeless. She either needed to tell Lillia about the weapon or say nothing. "It's... nothing. It's a good plan. Just us though, not Bahn." At least she could keep it from him. Maybe if only Lillia found out, things wouldn't be so bad.

"Okay." Lillia studied Ayela as though waiting for more of an explanation. "Just us then."

"Thank you," Ayela said. "You know, I always had Eema telling me what I couldn't do. Is it bad that a part of me is glad I don't have to deal with her anymore?" Ayela released a quick sigh when Lillia didn't respond. "I'm not saying I'm glad she's dead. I just..." A small tear swelled in Ayela's eye. Was it cruel of her to allow herself happiness or even hope? Did she even deserve it after having enjoyed the bow's dark magic? Had Kiyle died for nothing? "Gods, why did Kiyle have to die like that, why couldn't he have just let us go?"

"That you care enough to wonder says you're a better person than me. I, for one, am glad that Eema is dead. Bitch got what she deserved." Lillia said as she patted Ayela on the back. "I know you Ayela, have since I was four years old. You are kind and caring, and stronger than anyone I know. This guilt, it's normal. I know when my mom died, I felt the same for a long time. It gets easier."

Ayela turned away, slightly embarrassed by the compliments when Bahn looked over to them.

"Whatever's bothering you, I know you'll get through it. You always have, and you always will, and when you're ready to talk about it, I'll be here to help."

"We should," A yawn interrupted Ayela. "Get some sleep. Got an early day tomorrow."

"Yeah," Lillia agreed. "Nikul, did you get that bedding together yet?"

"Yeah, storeroom is all set for you. You can turn in whenever you like."

Ayela and Lillia headed for the storeroom, waving goodnight to Bahn, who was setting up in a booth along the wall nearby. The two of them entered the storeroom, where Nikul had laid out several blankets on the floor and a few burlap sacks of grain for bedding.

"Hardly the silk sheets I'm used to." Lillia complained. The storeroom was musty, and thick with the burning aroma of aging wines. "I never thought I'd say this, but I miss the library; my cotton bed and silk sheets, warm food every morning and night, scented candles augmenting the atmosphere. Never having to worry about my safety."

"You hated that life. Nothing ever happened. You were always complaining about how bored you were. And don't forget the duties of highborn women your father was always going on about. This is only temporary. Soon, we'll be in actual beds, not hay covered in fur. Just have to wait for the renovations to get finished."

"I didn't much like it there, did I?" Lillia said as she closed her eyes. "Goodnight, Ayela."

"Goodnight." Ayela lay there for some time as sleep evaded her. Visions of the battle played over in her mind; each ended with the bow and the dark magic she'd enjoyed. Ayela groaned, turning in her bed. She should tell Lillia now, before she fell asleep. Surely, she would want nothing more than to help her, right?

Ayela reached a hand out but stopped shy of Lillia's shoulder. Why was she hesitating? Images of Lillia's dejected gaze plagued Ayela. Her turning away, leaving Ayela in the street, abandoning her because she abused dark magic. What if Lillia turned her over to the city guard? What if she accused Ayela of being a necromancer?

Ayela turned over. Lillia wouldn't do that. Regardless, she needed to be rid of the bow. Pain caught in her throat at the thought of parting with the weapon. It'd served her so well. Saved her life, and possibly Lillia's. How could this be a bad thing? She needed the bow, that bow. Ayela's thoughts dwindled as fatigue overtook her, pushing out all sense of concern.

Ayela's back ached when she stirred awake on the cold cellar floor. The torchless room was dark, lit only by a faint orange light peeking through the bottom of the door.

"No dreams, thank the gods," Ayela moaned. She stretched, smiling as she imagined the breakfast Nikul might have ready. Ayela eased open the storage room door, careful not to wake Lillia, who lay sleeping on the floor. Ayela shook her head when she saw the extra burlap sack Lillia had found. One labeled flour. Ayela smiled at her peaceful, elegant form before sneaking out and closing the door.

"Beautiful," Ayela gasped when she turned toward the tavern windows. The brilliant rising sun filled the street outside, centered between the cobbled-together Southtown buildings.

Silhouetted against the sun in the center of the street stood the oppressive Citadel Tower. Ayela stepped forward, basking in the light.

"It is a marvelous view," Bahn's gruff voice resonated behind Ayela.

"I didn't notice you sitting there." Ayela ran her fingers through her knotted hair to fix what she could only imagine was the worst case of bed hair ever seen. "Any idea what we are having for breakfast?"

"Not sure," Bahn yawned. He stretched his back before rising from a barstool and walking toward Ayela. "I plan to find a magic tutor for you today, as well as an archery master, to help with your training."

"Before that, though, want to get some more training in," Ayela asked.

"Sure." Bahn moved to a more open part of the bar, past the stacked chairs and clean tables. "Do you remember the defense drills I taught you?" He asked.

"Yes."

"Then I think we should pick up the speed." Bahn struck without warning.

Ayela clumsily sidestepped, barely avoiding his strike before punching his side, causing Bahn to stumble backward.

"You're stronger than you look." Bahn smiled after catching his breath. "Again, but try to control your blows. Save your strength for enemies."

Bahn and Ayela exchanged blows with the two drills he had taught her for several minutes before Bahn stepped away, slightly winded.

"Alright, let's break for a minute and try something new." Bahn motioned for Ayela to rest before continuing. "The third drill is slightly different. I'm going to kick you. You are going to dodge. Just like with the punches, don't block my kick. You'll sidestep away from whatever side I kick with and toward me, then hit me several times in the back, side, or stomach. I'll show you, kick me."

Ayela aimed a clumsy kick toward Bahn's stomach, only to have him sidestep and lightly tap her side with his fists three times before stepping away from her.

"Does that make sense?" Bahn asked.

"Yeah, let's start." Ayela and Bahn exchanged kicks and punches back and forth for several rounds before Nikul came out from the back of the bar.

"What are you two up to?" Nikul was dressed in a plain-white overshirt and gray wool trousers. "Having a bit of a sparring match?"

"Training," Ayela mustered a reply, dodging a kick from Bahn before sliding behind him for a strike to his side.

"What did I say about control?" Bahn groaned, massaging his rib cage.

"I am in control." Ayela dropped her guard and stepped away from Bahn. "Nikul, what would you charge for some breakfast?"

"Your meals are paid for, remember? Some bread is in the oven. It'll be ready soon, then we'll all dine on fresh bread and honey with some eggs."

"I guess we're done training for now." Bahn stepped away and took a seat at the bar.

"Eggs and honey." Ayela marveled quietly to herself, recalling the honey biscuits her mother used to make for dinner. She slipped onto a bar stool some distance from Bahn.

"Morning, Ayela," Lillia yawned as she stepped out of the storeroom.

"Pft," Ayela giggled when she turned to see Lillia's hair. Clumps of flour speckled her matted hair, which now looked near solid white.

"What?" Lillia tilted her head to Ayela in confusion.

"Come on." Ayela motioned for Lillia to return to the storeroom.

"I don't think the flour sack was a good idea as a pillow," Ayela said when they were out of sight of the others. "You look like you just came in from a snowstorm." Ayela gestured to the splotches of flour coating her hair.

Lillia's white cheeks turned rose red while Ayela ran her hands through her blond curls to remove the flour.

"At least it was soft, like a pillow. Is it really that bad?"

"How did you manage this? You were just sleeping on a sack of flour." Ayela looked down to see that the tie on the sack of flour had come undone in the night, spilling the white powder onto the floor of the storeroom. "Hmm. You know what, I think you'd look good with white hair," Ayela mumbled.

"Shut up." Lillia brushed Ayela's hand away and set her lips in a pout.

"I got most of the flour out," Ayela laughed. "But your hair is about two shades lighter now. We'll need to visit a bathhouse."

"Maybe the others won't notice?"

"Please, they're guys. They'll never notice. Besides, it's just Bahn and Nikul here. The others left," Ayela laughed. "So. The markets today. I want to get some armor and supplies. We need new tents as well."

"You don't want to spend all your money." Lillia smiled while Ayela and she began cleaning up the flour. "Armor and weapons are expensive. We may need to save enough for later, also don't forget about your bow."

Ayela's breath again caught, she closed her eyes, setting her nerves before continuing.

"What's with you, every time I mention that bow, you tense up."

"I won't spend it all. I just want enough to get set up. Four or five-hundred should do it. We could get you a staff or something, too."

"True enough," Lillia sighed at Ayela's obvious evasion. "As long as we hit the enchanter before the shops close tonight." Lillia eyed the bow propped against the storeroom wall. More than a little suspicion apparent in her eyes. "We'll get your bow identified and get you tested." Lillia kneeled and began cleaning the mess of flour on the floor. "That bow has me too worried about you."

Ayela held the dustpan for her until the mess was clear. "I," she started to say something, her gaze glancing toward the bow. Her knuckles ached against the broom. She wanted to say something, needed to say something. But why couldn't she? "Okay." Was all she could manage.

Lillia placed the full dustpan beside the broom they propped against the wall and headed out into the bar.

"Morning all," Lillia called while Nikul brought out the fresh bread and hot honey. Lillia took a seat beside Bahn, thanking Nikul for the breakfast. "Ayela and I are going to go to the Midtown markets today. We'll try to find some decent gear."

"Sounds like a good idea," Bahn nodded.

"And we'll have an enchanter look at my bow," Ayela cringed, nauseous at the mere thought of it. As terrifying as it was, it was concerning just how attached she was to the bow. That, and the thoughts she'd been having ever since firing it. Lillia was right. But she needed to tell Lillia before the enchanter. Lillia deserved to know what she'd done. She shouldn't be hiding it from her. Not when she was about to find out.

"If you're looking for weapons and armor, I'd try The Iron Thimble. Good, mid-quality armorer in Southtown, about ten minutes' walk down that road." Nikul pointed down the street toward the Citadel Tower.

"Thanks, but we'll be hitting the midtown markets instead. I suspect we'll be able to find some higher-quality gear there." Lillia smiled while she ate. "Nikul, this bread is amazing."

"Thank you. It's my father's recipe." Nikul beamed. "I'd better set up for the day. You lot are welcome to stay as long as you need."

"Alright." Bahn stood, his plate finished. "Logane and the others said to meet back tonight to look over potential contracts. That gives us today to find new gear. There should be enough time. See you tonight, and may Musar be with you." Bahn bowed farewell before leaving the tavern on his own.

"Where's he off to," Lillia asked.

"He said he was going to find me a tutor for magic," Ayela said.

"But why? Didn't the others say their friend would train you," Lillia asked.

"Come to think of it, yeah." Ayela looked after Bahn. She recalled the first time they'd met in the city and the frightening visage she'd seen in him. No, he'd been so helpful and seemed so genuine. But then again, so had Adina. "What do you think he's up to?"

"Who knows. I don't think it's anything to worry about, though," Lillia chimed. "Off to the enchanter?"

"This armor's going to take some getting used to." Ayela stretched her arms, testing the limitations of the hard leather pauldrons covering her shoulders and the tight cuirass over her torso. "I know the armorer said it would be, but do you think this leather will be enough to stop a blade or an arrow?" Ayela adjusted the bundled tent slung over her shoulder, jostling the gold marks stashed in a secure leather backpack.

"It is better than not wearing anything," Lillia laughed. "And you look nice in armor."

"I'm just glad we could find some that matched my quiver." Ayela admired the detailed floral designs etched into the surface of her hardened leather bracers. "We've got about 3 hours before sunset. I think we have time for one more stop. Is there anything else you wanted to do?" Ayela rested her hand on the hilt of a newly purchased short sword.

"No. I think you've procrastinated enough. We're going to the enchanter. It's just a few streets away." Lillia skipped subtly beside Ayela as they fished their way through the crowded, yet organized midtown street. "Hopefully, Bradus will have a staff that'll work for me."

"Yea." Ayela distracted herself by fidgeting with the straps of her backpack. She glanced over the crowd when the coins jostled, ringing in her bag. Forgetting they were in Midtown, where one didn't have to worry about thugs stealing all you owned. At least not to the same degree. "What kind of staff do you hope to get?"

"I'm not sure. I definitely want it to be an arcane focus, but I suppose it depends on what's available. And it'll have to be subtle. Able to pass for a walking stick. Don't want just anyone seeing it as a focus."

"Should I have waited to buy the armor?" Ayela mumbled. "Maybe I should have gotten an enchanted weapon instead."

"No. Even the sword you got is dangerous enough, since you don't know how to use it." Lillia pointed to the sword clanking against Ayela's side.

"I can learn." Ayela shrugged in defense. "It can't be that hard. Can it?"

"Besides, enchanted weapons are extremely expensive. It would have taken all you had to buy one." Lillia pointed out. "How much do you have left, anyway?"

"We cashed out seven hundred gold marks. Between the armor and the short sword, we have three hundred left. Probably not enough to do much at a magic shop after you get a staff."

"A few more missions and you'll have enough to get your new sword enchanted." Lillia said. "At least by then, hopefully, you'll have a little training with it."

"You're right." Ayela followed Lillia through a group of commoners huddled around a market stall.

"Thought you said the enchanter was close," Ayela asked.

"We're almost there, see." Lillia pointed through the thinning crowd toward a drab gray building on the far side of the road. Its front was near featureless and extremely small when compared to the neighboring buildings. Unlike the other shops in Midtown, it had no fancy paint or carved designs. Only flat gray walls and a small black sign with white lettering that hung unevenly over the door. Notably, a tall figure in a blue robe stood at attention by the door. He carried an ornately carved white-wood staff that ended with an inset of purple stone. A guard from The Citadel.

"Enchanter's Bits," Ayela asked, reading the sign. The skinny windows on either side were old and fogged, blurring the contents of the store into a collection of lights and sparkling shapes.

"Quality enchantments for your everyday magical needs." Lillia smiled, reading the inscription perfectly carved above the door when they passed the shop, and turned a corner, having successfully avoided the attention of the guard.

They wound through a few back alleys until they were behind the shop. Lillia lightly knocked on the door. A few moments later, a lock twisted, and the door cracked open. The man behind it was old, with wrinkled skin and a long, neatly groomed white beard. He wore a long red robe with runes embroidered in the fabric. His eyes rested on the two women for a time before lighting into a smile upon recognizing Lillia.

"Lillia! Thank Mahtsar you're alright! Your father is worried sick. He's already visited me twice, looking for you." He opened the door wider to reveal a small but cluttered space with various magical trinkets hanging from the walls. There was a large workbench on the far side with wood-shavings spilling over the side. "Come on in! And you must be Ayela." The man's smile lingered on Ayela before migrating to the bow on her back with eyes that gleamed with questions unasked.

The old man looked down both ends of the alley before closing and locking the door behind the two of them. "So, besides giving your father a heart attack and sparking the ire of one of the most powerful noble houses, what have you been up to? Practicing what I've taught you?" Bradus eyed Lillia before taking a seat at the workbench.

"I have," Lillia beamed. "Even successfully used the shield spell you taught me. Good thing too, otherwise Ayela here would have taken an arrow."

"An arrow! Gods, what type of trouble have you two gotten yourselves into?" Bradus lowered his gaze.

"Mercenary work. We're apprenticing with The King's Guild," Ayela said.

Bradus sighed before returning to Lillia. "Just like your mother. I could have guessed. But why are you here? You signed up with the guild, surely their connections could get you less filtered access to spell books."

"Because I trust you, and you've always done right by me," Lillia said with a nod. "I need a focus in the form of a staff. We'll pay you your usual rate, plus the personal commission we've agreed on."

"Sure," Bradus mumbled, eying her bag with hungry eyes. "Your coin is always welcome." Bradus scowled. "Why not go with a focus that is a little more your size, say, a wand or orb?"

"Because I'm trained to use a staff. And I need something that can dish out a hit or two. I also need a test kit. I want to measure how much my magic has grown since we last practiced." Lillia lied with a practiced smile, her voice unfaltering. "And some spell books that would be useful for mercenary work. Maybe an offensive spell or two."

"I've got a staff I think would work. But the spell books. You know it's illegal for me to sell any destructive spell book. Much less to unregistered magi. I have to keep an inventory of those books. If they go missing, I'll get into a lot of trouble."

"I know you, Bradus. You don't just have the books. You've made scrolls with the details for more than a few spells. And I'd wager those aren't on your inventory records."

Bradus sighed and folded his arms while he stared Lillia down.

"Fine," he relented. "Just... promise me you won't overdo it. And I expect the same courtesy of silence you ask of me."

"Pay you for," Lillia corrected with a laugh. "And of course. Our lips are sealed."

"Good. It won't be cheap, though. Three hundred marks for the lot of it." Bradus raised an eyebrow, as though expecting the amount to ward Lillia off.

"Sounds fair to me," she said while setting her bag down on the nearby table and allowing the coins to rattle.

Bradus scoffed in suppressed laughter. "Right then, I'll need to head to the front to get the staff. And retrieve the scrolls from my safe. Be back soon."

Ayela waited in silence as Lillia counted the coins. Her sweaty palms gripped the bow so hard she feared it might snap. But would that be so bad? Her mouth was dry. If she was going to say something, it had to be now. When Bradus came back, Lillia would ask about the bow. There would be no way out. There was no way out. She had to say something.

"Uh... about the bow." Ayela shrunk. She couldn't let Lillia find out on her own. "I think it used dark magic."

"What!" Lillia dropped several coins onto the table, clearly forgetting her place in counting.

"I saw it when I fired it. I... felt it."

"Ayela! Why in Mahtsar's light would you not say something?"

Ayela shrunk before Lillia, grip unwittingly tightening on the bow she held to her chest.

"Maybe you're mistaken. Maybe it was something else." Lillia resumed counting. "It changes nothing. If it's dark magic, we'll turn it in and get you a new bow."

Ayela stood behind Lillia, hugging the bow to her chest. Her knuckles whitened around the weapon's grip. Bile rose in her throat at the idea of replacing it. She clenched her teeth. Why was the idea of replacing it so revolting? Why did it matter? It shouldn't matter. She should want to get rid of it.

Lillia slammed the wood next to the coins as she finished a stack. "Shit, Ayela. Why keep this a secret? You could already be addicted!" Lillia heaved uneven breaths as she studied Ayela. Ayela stood, shoulders drooped, head down with her hair falling over her face.

"I know!" Ayela held back tears.

"I'm sorry, I," Lillia began, not knowing how to finish. She left the coins and placed a gentle hand over Ayela's clenched grip. "I should have noticed sooner," her voice quivered with fear.

Ayela followed Lillia's guidance to the bench with the coins she'd counted. Her tense arms ached. They hadn't moved from their clenched position around the bow. With a heavy breath and shaking hands, Ayela lifted the bow onto the table and allowed it to clatter free of her grip.

"It's not your fault." Lillia pulled Ayela away from the counter, spinning her so the bow was out of sight. "We'll solve this together. Now, help me count these coins." Lillia pushed a pile of coins to the side of the table opposite the bow.

Bradus returned just as Lillia and Ayela finished counting the last of the coins. In his hand was a glossy dark-wood staff with a slight crook at the top. The grain on the staff was nearly invisible, and it had a few faintly glowing runes carved in a loop around its mid-section. His other hand held a small book and several scrolls. The book had a steel spine and cover. Its spine had a steel loop protruding from each end where a thick leather strap was fastened. The second book was plain in appearance, with a simple black title written at the top. Settled atop the collection was a small rolled-up piece of leather that was bound with twine. Ayela recognized it as a mage test-kit. The same kind she'd been tested with as a child.

"I crafted this staff myself from hickory." Bradus brushed his hand over the wood. "The wood alone is one of the hardest there is, and I enchanted it to be even more durable. It can also act as a focus. Here are the books. Look through them if you like. I also threw in a spell journal for you to record any new spells you come up with. Each of the scrolls contains spells I crafted for offense and defense. Mostly studied them to defend if this shop ever got robbed. But it should come in handy for you," Bradus paused, holding his hand over the book. He studied Lillia. "If you don't already have one, I recommend getting a tutor from the guild before you try them. I don't need to remind you how dangerous magic is. And you need someone trained in combat casting. Go into a battle untrained and you'll be outclassed, if you don't burn yourself out first."

"Thank you very much," Lillia said. "There is one more thing, though. On our last mission, we happened upon this bow. We believe it uses dark magic, but we want you to identify it. If it does, we want to turn it in. Can you help us with that?"

"Sure, let me see." Bradus took the bow. He reached under the counter to pull out a magnifying glass. The enchanter intently studied the runes covering the bow's spine, turning it over several times and mouthing inaudible words.

"Interesting," he whispered before moving to another section of the bow. "Where did you say you found this?"

"Some people attacked us." Ayela adjusted her leather bracers, pulling them further up her arm to stop them from rubbing against her wrist. "One of them was carrying this."

"Well, you are most definitely right. This is a Life Seeker Bow. Meaning that it will guide your aim toward lethal strikes. But the necrotic enchantment on it allows the bow to draw energy from the wielder instead of from a power crystal like most enchanted weapons. Unfortunately, that means it causes the wielder to channel dark magic. I'm afraid I'll have to confiscate this. Weapons like this are highly illegal. And if I'm reading the runes right, this is a fairly powerful enchantment. If either of you used it, you'd be tempted to use more dark magic."

"Please do! We don't need it." Lillia studied Ayela. Concern flooded her frightened eyes. She reached for Ayela's hand, squeezing it in reassurance.

Ayela trembled not out of fear, but with disgusted longing. She needed THIS bow. "Could you fix it so it doesn't use dark magic?"

Lillia's jaw slacked. She closed her eyes, shaking her head in disbelief. "No! Are you insane! We have more than enough to buy another that doesn't use evil magic."

"You didn't use the bow, did you?" Bradus' voice trickled toward concern. "Ayela, if you used it…"

"No!" Ayela overacted.

"Because that would mean you've developed a connection with Erithia's magic."

"Exactly! Which is why she didn't use it." Lillia grabbed Ayela's shoulder, turning her around, so they were eye to eye. "Why are you even considering this? There's no need to keep it."

Ayela lowered her gaze to the floor. "I," Ayela began. Her breath quivered, her words unwilling to leave her mouth.

"Turn the bow in, do whatever with it. I don't care." Lillia shoved the books and test-kit into her bag. She pulled out another fist full of gold marks and placed them on the counter. "You never saw us. Don't tell my father. She then snatched Ayela's wrist and drug her out of the shop. Lillia pulled the door closed with the hooked end of her staff.

Ayela was silent, following thoughtlessly behind Lillia while she dragged them through the streets toward The Headless Snake and away from the Life Seeker bow. "I think I'm going to be sick," Ayela said. With every step away, her thoughts became clearer. Her stomach revolted, burning in her throat. Her hands quivered, her legs fought against her with every street they passed. Ayela closed her eyes, picturing the bow and the magic that had flown through it. She sighed, feeling unwelcome tears of longing fall from her eyes.

"Ayela," Lillia's voice was soft. They'd stopped in a midtown alley. The gate to Southtown was ahead of them. Ayela half-smirked at the irony. Was this the same alley Adina and her had stopped in? The sky was already turning amber with the sunset's approach. Lillia placed a single hand on Ayela's cheek, drawing their gazes together. She wiped Ayela's tear away with her thumb. "Are you okay?" Her voice was soft and even. Her gentle hazel eyes gleamed in the setting sun, casting her face with a golden glow.

A twinge of guilt tugged at Ayela's heart. She opened her mouth to speak, but her throat clenched shut. She shook her head no. Her shoulders rose and fell with uneven breaths. Ayela pictured herself pushing Lillia against the wall and breaking free from her grasp. She'd dash to the enchanter's shop, pound on the closed door and demand he return her bow. "Damit!" Ayela screamed, backing away from Lillia and falling against a wall behind her. Tears streamed from her eyes. The feeling of the bow's magic flowed through her arms, bringing images of the black smoke to her mind accompanied by words in shadow speech. The words Adina had used to cast her disguise spell. Ayela buried her head in her hands.

Lillia sat next to Ayela, pulling her close with arms wrapped around her. She didn't say a word, only held Ayela tight.

"Thank you," Ayela's voice was nearly inaudible. Her sobs lessened, broken by Lillia's hands stroking through her hair. "Do you think it's too late? Do you think Erithia's corrupted me?"

"I think the fact that you can still ask that question means you aren't corrupted." Lillia smiled reassuringly, tugging apart a knot in Ayela's hair.

"How can you be sure?" Ayela brushed a tear from her cheek. She sat up slightly, looking Lillia in the eye.

"Erithia is all about selfish desire, and that's not you." Lillia smiled. Her hands dropped from Ayela's hair to grasp Ayela's hands. "You've always put others first, and you've got the strongest will of anyone I know. If anyone can say no to that monster, you can. You already did once."

Ayela looked at the even stone beneath them, at their tightly clasped hands. Her mind flashed back to the magnificent mansion Erithia had tempted her with. Eyes closed, she imagined what her life would have been if she had accepted their offer. Then she remembered why she'd said no. It had been Lillia's friendship that had allowed her to resist. Maybe this was enough.

"I wanted to keep it." Tears again surfaced as she sobbed. "I knew it used dark magic since I first fired it at the other archer. It felt…" Ayela's words choked in her throat. "It felt good. Great, actually. I've wanted more ever since. I'm so weak. I was worried you'd leave."

"Oh, Ayela," Lillia was tearing up now, her grasp tightening on Ayela's hands. "Listen to me." Ayela again lifted her sight to meet Lillia's. "You are not weak. If you were, you would not have been able to walk away. You wouldn't be feeling what you feel now. You wouldn't feel guilty about having wanted it, and I could never leave you."

"I don't know what to do, Lillia." Ayela leaned back against the building they were sitting against. Her head slapped against the brick, bringing sharp pain and clarity. "I can't help but relive the way their magic felt, and I can't stop wanting it."

"I think we should speak to someone about this," Lillia muttered. "A priest from the Mahtsarian church, perhaps. They could help."

"No!" Ayela's heart lurched. She recalled how the guards had treated her when they thought she'd used dark magic. How the priest, who'd been her counsel, had seen her before her innocence was proven. Now she had used dark magic. She was guilty. A paladin of Naqam would execute her for what she'd done. How would a priest treat her? "I'm just a worthless Southtowner." Tears fell down her cheeks at the repetition of Eema's rhetoric. "The guards, gods, the church. They don't care about me. No one will care. No one will understand. At best, they'll lock me up and throw away the key. At worst… and maybe I'd deserve it."

"Ayela, I care. And you know you've never been just some Southtowner." Lillia's grip on Ayela's hand tightened. "Not to me. But you're right about the priests. We'll figure this out, okay? I don't care how much you want it. It doesn't make you a monster. I love you, Ayela, and I always will." Lillia's cheeks burned crimson. "We'll get through this."

"What did I ever do to deserve a friend like you?" Ayela leaned back again, missing Lillia's dejected gaze.

A painful pause lingered between the two. "Your magic tutor," Lillia's voice faltered. "They'll need to be someone with experience resisting dark magic." She stood, discreetly wiping her eyes before helping Ayela to her feet. "They mentioned their friend Raesra was a cleric. Let's hope she's a cleric of Mahtsar."

"Maybe." Ayela's heart ached with fear. She looked at Lillia with tired eyes and leaned into her. "For now, it is late, and the others will be waiting for us."

"Ayela."

"Best not to think about it." Ayela pulled Lillia into a hug, squeezing her shoulders and resting her head on Lillia's neck. Lillia's heart was racing as she returned the hug.

"Thank you, Lillia." Ayela breathed, unwilling to let go. "We're rid of the bow now and thus rid of its temptation." Ayela forced a smile, pulling away from Lillia. She hoped it was true, but thanks to Adina, she knew the words to a dark magic spell.

"I know," Lillia replied, wiping away a tear of her own. "We'll withdraw some money and get you a better bow. Something perfectly fit to you, maybe a custom job." Lillia's eyes sparkled, free of the judgement Ayela had expected her to harbor. "I'll even pitch in if we need to."

"You don't have to do that."

"But I will."

"It's late. We should probably head back," Lillia muttered after a moment of silence between them. "At least if we hope to meet the others before dark."

"Yeah," Ayela agreed, loathing the long walk through a dusk-shrouded Southtown.

Together they left for The Headless Snake in silence. Thanks to Lillia's writ of passage, there were no questions from the guards as they passed the Midtown gate. The streets of Southtown were thinning, with only a few citizens still roaming. Given Ayela's armor and Lillia's staff, it was a fair assumption that they would face little threat of robbery. They no longer looked the part of an easy target.

As with other nights, The Headless Snake was the liveliest on the block. Warm music flitted from the windows, where the shadows of patrons danced in the firelight. Inside would be Bahn and the others. Would Raesra be there? Shit, would she have to explain the bow to everyone? She sighed, hoping beyond hope that the desire would fade with time.

"I'm not ready to tell the others," Ayela admitted as they neared the door.

"And you won't have to," Lillia said. "So long as you can keep resisting Erithia's magic. It can be our secret. Study with Raesra. Learn as much light magic as you can. It will keep Erithia's temptations at bay."

"Thank you," Ayela breathed a sigh of relief before they entered the lively tavern. That is what she would do. She would learn as much of Mahtsar's magic as she could. That would keep the darkness at bay.

16

Shadow Magic

The inside of the tavern was nearly the same as the first day they'd entered. Lively music radiated from the trio of dancing bards on stage. They sang in a language foreign to Ayela, yet their notes carried a pleasant warmth that nearly erased the temptation at the edges of her mind.

A quick scan of the tavern found their group sitting at a round table near the bar. Logane and Zaktan wore fur cloaks over colored tunics, notably missing their usual armor. Logane beckoned them over with a full tankard in his hand.

"Took y'all long enough," Zaktan said as they approached. "Where's your bow?"

"I didn't like the enchantment," Ayela cringed at the obvious lie. She could have at least come up with something more believable.

"It had some features that made it hard to control." Lillia stepped between Ayela and the group when Zaktan looked questioningly at Ayela. "Dangerous even. Going to find a new one tomorrow."

"Smart move, then," Logane said.

"Any luck finding a magic tutor?" Ayela took a seat at the table opposite Bahn.

"None, sadly," Bahn replied.

"Magic tutor?" Zaktan scoffed. "What? Raesra not good enough for you?"

"I'm sure Raesra will be more than," Ayela stopped

All sound faded as her sight fell upon an individual wearing lavish purple and white robes. She was sitting at a table in the opposite corner of the bar, her arms propped on the table to support her chin. She wore a hood that draped far over her face, and a layer of cloth wrappings covered every inch of skin. Ayela shuttered. A chill fell down her spine. Despite the lack of detail visible under her hood, she was sure the woman was looking at her.

The woman bent down, reaching under the table to pick up an ornately carved black and gold box. Ayela flinched when the woman opened the box and the corner behind her darkened. A pair of shimmering gold eyes flashed in the shadow before disappearing all together. A few wisps of black mist floated into the air from the open box. Dark magic. Ayela's breath stopped. Her vision focused on the smoke. Ayela's body ached for the familiar sensation of Erithia's euphoric magic. She needed it. Just one last time; to feel their dark energy flooding her senses.

The woman reached in and grabbed a stack of cards, placing them on her table. She closed the box and returned it to its place under her table. Dark magic trailed behind the box. Ayela forced herself to breathe. Sweat beaded on her forehead as she imagined what sensations would flow through her from the box or the cards. What spells would a simple deck of cards carry? What purpose could they serve?

"Ayela," Bahn asked, waving a hand before Ayela to grab her attention.

"What?" Ayela muttered, her attention to the woman's stare broken.

"She wasn't even listening," Zaktan grumbled.

Ayela directed her attention to the group.

"I said we put in your petition with the guild," Logane's voice carried a hint of annoyance. "In a few weeks, you'll officially be a mercenary in training."

"Really?" Ayela chimed, her voice carrying more than a hint of surprise. "I didn't expect it to be that fast. Or that easy."

Ayela's gaze again shifted to the robed woman at the back of the bar. She was leaning back in her chair, watching Ayela with what felt like a knowing smirk under her hood. One of her legs folded confidently atop the other. Her arms spread over the back of her booth.

"Stop worrying about that old witch and listen!" Zaktan slammed his mug on the table. "We were clear about your inexperience."

"Yes, had to be." Logane rested a hand on Zaktan's shoulder to calm him down. "A condition of your joining is that we handle your training. As I was saying before, the surviving member of our group who was injured; Raesra. She is a cleric. Worships Mahtsar but is skilled in all forms of magic. She will return from The Citadel in a few days. Raesra'll train you in magic. We just need to find someone skilled in archery. Bahn and Zaktan will continue training you in combat," Logane said.

Zaktan grinned, lowering his gaze at the last bit. "We're gonna have so much fun." He growled, cracking his knuckles in a clenched fist.

"Who is that?" Ayela nodded toward the woman in the corner. "You seem to know her," she asked Zaktan.

"Still?" Zaktan grumbled. "That's old Hada." Zaktan turned in his seat, raising his mug toward the woman. He turned back to Ayela with a smirk. "You know what? I'll introduce you."

"Zaktan," Logane groaned. "Be careful. She's more dangerous than she lets on." Logane shook his head when Zaktan stood and motioned for Ayela to do the same.

"Lighten up. Even you've used her services. She's the one Moonborn that isn't a threat." He pulled Bahn up by the shoulder. "You too, tree boy." He continued toward the witch. "All three of you, you'll wanna see this. She does great work."

"She's a charlatan," Logane muttered, with an air of apprehension in his voice. He stood, following behind Bahn. "Just don't put too much faith in what she says. She is using dark magic, after all."

"No." Zaktan shook his head. "Shadow magic, remember?"

"You think there's really a difference?" Logane muttered as they all followed Zaktan.

"The guards you reported her to seemed to think so."

"Clueless fucks," Logane grumbled.

"I've never heard of shadow magic." Ayela frowned, perhaps a little too eager to learn.

"The principal forms of magic come from the gods, right? Fire, water, storms, earth, light, dark. Each from their respective gods." Zaktan weaved through the crowds near the stage on their way to the witch. "There are lesser forms of magic that pull from smaller deities. Shadow magic pulls from a lessor deity within the shadow realm. Not Erithia, so it's not dark magic. It doesn't have the same corrupting potential that dark magic has. Not addictive."

"Why isn't it more well known," Lillia asked.

"Because warlocks like me are so rare." The woman's smooth voice wormed into their conversation. "Unlike necromancers, us warlocks are beholden to lesser, more neutral, otherworldly beings of power. Loraxa, keeper of prophecy, is my patron. These lesser beings are much harder to broker deals with."

"And Loraxa is beholden to Erithia." Logane stood stiff, arms crossed.

"You're talking about divination magic. That's dark magic," Lillia confirmed.

"Oh, stop scaring them with your propaganda." The woman leaned forward and motioned for Ayela to take a seat. "Divination is no more dark magic than a volcano is fire magic. I am Hada, a pleasure to meet you, Ayela."

"How do you know my name?" Ayela stared, hesitating to follow her request.

"My patron tells me a great many things. Now sit, please."

Ayela wondered what might lurk beyond the wraps concealing Hada's face. Their gazes locked intently. Hada reached up, removing her hood. Her mask covered everything but one of her gray eyes and a side of her face where no hair grew. Hada reached behind her head, unwinding the silk fabric.

Ayela stifled a gasp when the silk wrappings fell. Where her left eye should be was only a caved-in patch of scarred skin. Hada's upper lip was partially missing, as was part of her left cheek. Her scalp was hairless and covered in a patchy web of scar tissue.

"Ih ohay, ah he raction ost ethol et." Hada's melodic voice was distorted and gargled. She struggled to speak through her gaping, healed injuries. She smiled, her cheek stretching back far enough to reveal the back of her throat, her sporadically missing teeth, scarred gums, and distinct lack of a tongue.

Hada lifted the wraps, replacing them around her head, before looking back to Ayela. "The wraps are a gift from my patron. So I may speak and feel as if it never happened."

"What happened?" Ayela struggled to lose the imagery of Hada's disfigured form.

"I'm a Moonborn. I used to live in the Mahtsarian Republic. Certain people of their church falsely accused me of using dark magic. So, they tortured me, cut out my tongue, placed a coal in my eye, scalped me, that sort of thing." Hada held her left hand over the wraps on her face, revealing two missing fingers and a complete lack of fingernails. "Erithia offered to get me out. I resisted for a time. And when I was about to give in, another voice called to me. My patron, Loraxa, found me. She and I struck an accord. So, here I am, free to use what little shadow magic she can give me in exchange for my services to her cause. Without her, I'd have died in The Republic's Cages."

"You mean you spoke with Erithia?" Ayela said.

"Gods no." Hada laughed. "Not in person, for sure. Erithia's temptations are more like thoughts that aren't yours or shadows that whisper promises, apparitions of his minions, the Eribi. He never tempts people in person. Not sure he even has a human form."

"So, you do use dark magic?" Lillia looked at Ayela, her knowing gaze pleading for them to leave. To escape this danger, "just not Erithia's."

"No, shadow magic. I understand the confusion. It looks similar. But my magic cannot corrupt you. It can't raise the dead or heal injuries. It can cast illusions and tell fortunes. That's all. The only reason I escaped was that Loraxa herself got me out. Opened a portal to the shadow world and pulled me through, carried me to safety and dumped me in Hatave with enough gold to get to work."

"What's it matter, dark magic in itself ain't illegal anyhow." Zaktan sat at the table beside Hada.

"Yes, dark magic's not illegal in The Union unless you become a necromancer or turn it into a weapon. I am no necromancer. My rags are no weapon. My magic is harmless." Hada's eye squinted in a smile. She placed her uninjured hand over the deck of cards she'd pulled from the box under the table. They were thick cards, longer and wider than Hada's hand. The backs were a dark purple hue with gold floral designs that shimmered in the candlelight. "It's not as... intense as Erithia's magic. But it's enough to stave off the need to return to him, usually."

"Don't let ol' scar-face fool you. She's got some power and some serious problems," Zaktan laughed before tossing a silver mark onto the table. "I'll cover their fortunes, make it something spooky if you can. Gotta scare the rookies."

"Why don't you go fetch me a glass of wine?" Hada's iris flashed silver while her voice rang through the air.

Zaktan stood, his smile fading. He left his mead on the table and made his way to the bar. Walking oddly, as though entranced by her words.

"Now, allow me to do your reading?" Hada chimed, returning her attention to Ayela after pocketing the coin.

The hair on Ayela's neck stood on end. Hada slid her deck of cards to the center of the table. Her sole eye stared intently at Ayela, forcing her to stay still. Something about this wasn't right. Every nerve in Ayela's body told her to move. She pictured the dark magic she'd seen come from the deck. She had said it wasn't Erithia's. Could she believe her?

"Why me?"

"Because you're the one I'm supposed to do first."

"Okay," Ayela muttered, drawing back slightly in her chair.

"Loraxa has her ways, has her orders. I follow them." Hada smiled.

Ayela's heart stopped. Her eyes locked on the black smoke snaking down Hada's arm. Her nerves tingled in anticipation, in hunger for the pleasure that energy had brought her before. The smoke vanished into the deck of cards.

"Ayela. Place your hand on mine."

Lillia grabbed Ayela's arm under the table, pleading for them to leave.

"You've come this far, Zaktan already paid her. Might as well get it over with," Logane relented, sitting next to Ayela.

Ayela lifted her hand above the table, hesitating partway down. Dark magic was addictive, this interest in the smoke, this desire to feel it against her skin. This wasn't right. She needed to pull away, to leave this place.

"Come now, I don't bite. And this isn't Erithia's magic. It's Loraxa's. Trust me. If anything, you won't feel it." The last part stung Ayela. Did this woman know about her use of dark magic?

Ayela's hand fell, resting on Hada's cold wrist. Surely it wasn't that bad. Surely, she'd get a small twinge of the sensations that she'd felt with the bow. And it wasn't like she was casting the magic. There was no need to worry.

"I know what you're worried about, Lillia." Hada nodded to Lillia. "Don't worry. She cannot become addicted to my magic. First off, it's shadow magic. Second, I am casting it, not her. Even you know Erithia's temptations only affect the caster."

"It'll be fine." Ayela smiled, hiding the disappointment of knowing she would feel nothing.

"This is a bad idea." Lillia squeezed Ayela's hand under the table.

"As much as I don't like it," Logane grumbled. "Hada's right here. Morally questionable, but not dangerous and not illegal."

"Do what you want, Ayela." Lillia relinquished Ayela's hand. "But I won't be part of it."

"Lillia." Ayela's chest ached at Lillia's retreat. She should leave, follow her example. Then, why wasn't she? Ayela closed her eyes and nodded to Hada. The black smoke rose from the deck. Ayela's shoulders sagged when she felt nothing from the magic. Her chest ached with an alien emptiness; the smoke encircled their hands before condensing into rings around her and Hada's wrists.

Ayela's breath quickened. The white of Hada's eye turned black. But unlike Adina's, hers maintained its gray iris. Now, against the black, it seemed almost silver. Almost like Erithia's eyes.

"Now, remove your hand and place both of your hands palm down on the table in front of the cards." Ayela did as Hada instructed. "Do not move them. Removing either hand from the table will cause the spell to fail. This is important. Do not move them." No sooner had Hada finished than a slight itch formed under Ayela's eye. "I mean it," Hada's voice adopted a serious tone. "You don't want this spell to fail. Failed spells of this magnitude are very dangerous." Ayela nodded in response, a half-smile spreading across her face. She was a fortune teller. How dangerous could her spell really be? The smile quickly faded to guilt. She tried to look over her shoulder to find Lillia. But it was no use. She couldn't turn far enough without lifting a hand. What if Lillia was right?

"Loraxa, lady in shadow, lord of The Nali. Answer us this prayer," Hada softly sung, her gaze unmoving. The wall behind Hada darkened once more. Faintly glowing gold eyes pierced through the darkness some distance away.

Words spoken in shadow speech echoed from the darkness behind Hada, who repeated them. "Kachakh Nali'roet"

"We thank them for thy gift, that we may see with your sight," Hada's voice rose and fell with melodic notes that drew all thought from Ayela's mind. "That we may see as you do. That we may peer into the great tapestry that is our past, present, and futures. Show us this one's optimal path. Lead her to whatever destiny will serve her most." Hada removed her hand from the deck of cards. The black smoke spinning over her and Ayela's wrists dissipated. As did the apparition behind her. Ayela looked at the others, expecting horror or surprise.

"You okay," Bahn asked.

"Yea." Ayela struggled to conceal the disappointment dripping from her voice. "Didn't feel a thing."

"Like I said." Hada smiled. "Now, keep your attention on me. We want an accurate reading after all. Don't worry about what you might have seen. It is a side effect of Loraxa's gaze. Only you and I can see it. Only you and I can read the cards."

Hada's inhuman eye never left Ayela while she drew the first card. She placed it face down beside Ayela's hand.

"The first will show your past. It will establish the truthfulness of Loraxa's sight and strengthen our connection to her." Hada drew a second card. She positioned it in front of Ayela's hand, then a third atop the second. "These will show your present, both known and unknown." Next, she placed a fourth to the right of Ayela's hand. "Then, you're near future. Something that will happen and is likely unavoidable." She placed the final card in the center of the table, away from Ayela. "Lastly, your distant future. The result of your optimal path."

Ayela forcefully blinked, striving to remove the itch. Hada tilted her head, glaring at Ayela. She grabbed the remaining cards, turning them over and spreading them out. Each of the cards' face side had nothing but a solid black surface, void of any design.

"The cards are blank until Loraxa paints them. Only you and I will see their etching. She paints them in reaction to what she sees in The Nali about you."

"What is The Nali," Ayela asked.

"It is the primordial force of fate. A sentient energy stronger than any magic that is the tapestry of past, present and futures. Loraxa can read this tapestry, and the possible futures ahead of you." Hada re-stacked, then turned over the cards. She looked at the first of the cards in front of Ayela before slowly turning it to reveal its painted side.

The illustration on the card bloomed as starlight against its black background. It depicted two swords stabbed into the back of a warrior who huddled on the ground, sparkling tears streamed from his eyes. The lines on the man's back trembled.

"Someone hurt you, betrayed you." Hada began. "You believe it was the painful end of a relationship? But this one isn't over. You need to watch for this person's return. It may bring further heartache."

Ayela's breath caught in her chest at the possibility of Adina's return. She was unsure of how to feel. Would Adina return, penitent of what she'd done? Or would she return as something else? No, she was reading more into this than it was. She glanced at Logane. He was convinced this wasn't real. She hadn't felt any dark magic. This was all an illusion. Everyone has been hurt before; it was a safe guess. Ayela smiled, waiting to see what the next cards would bring.

Hada moved to the second set of cards and flipped them over. One was a single chalice with six stars hanging over it. The stars spun and pulsed to the rhythm of a heart. They moved closer together, joining to form one brilliant star. The other was a single malformed stick that grew in thickness as it neared the top of the card before forking in two directions.

"You have gained allies. If allowed to, these relationships will grow into lasting bonds of friendship and even family." The card Hada had flipped darkened. The lines returned in the shape of a snake coiled around a heart.

"Oh." Hada paused, her eyes saddening. "It's rare for the cards to change. A viper has worked its way into your life. Something or someone new. Its grip tightens, strangling you."

Ayela turned to Bahn. Once again recalling the sight she'd seen when he first found her in Hatave and the odd claim that he'd find her a tutor. Exactly where had he gone? No, more likely it was the bow. The desire for dark magic it seeded in her. Hada couldn't have guessed that. Could she?

"With these allies and the viper," resumed Hada. "Comes a split in the road. The opportunity for growth and greatness lies before you. With hard work, you will reach potential before unimagined. But as you grow, you will face a critical decision. One that will shape your future. You will need to choose, the viper or your newfound family."

Hada sighed when she turned the fourth card over. It was a depiction of The Citadel Tower, with its multiple levels ablaze with fire.

"A grand tragedy awaits you in your future. All paths lead there. It will bring great turmoil, but you will emerge forever transformed. There will be no going back. What was before will be lost forever."

Ayela's heart sank. Her breath quickened. She wanted to believe this was a mere trick. Hada moved toward the last card. Lillia had been right. She'd already used dark magic with the bow, and she wanted to keep it. She'd wanted more than anything for this fortune to bring her the same feeling. And she wanted to continue using dark magic.

Ayela's cheeks flushed. She grew dizzy. That was her future. Adina would return, and Ayela would accept Erithia and join her. And that would mean she'd lose Lillia and the others. If all choices lead here, if this was unavoidable, she had no desire to hear the last card. If this was her destiny, she didn't want to hear it. The itch under Ayela's eye grew in intensity. Tears welled in her eyes. This was too much. She had to decide now. She'd choose Lillia.

"No!" Hada yelled. Ayela lifted her hand from the table to wipe her eye.

Streams of dark magic poured from the remaining card. A void formed on the table. Ayela felt herself pulled into the void. The faint sound of shattering glass reached her ears, accompanied by Lillia's distant scream. Then, all was black.

17

Fallout

"Do what you want, Ayela." Lillia relinquished Ayela's hand. "But I won't be part of it." Lillia threw up her hands, turning away from Ayela's impending decision. No matter how harmless they said Hada was, she didn't trust her. There was no such thing as shadow magic, she'd have heard of it. "Please reconsider." She muttered, unsure Ayela even heard her.

Hada's shadow speech chanting drowned Lillia's voice. But no tendrils of smoke appeared. No impending sense of unease like she had felt with Adina. So maybe this was as harmless as they said.

Lillia released a defeated breath at seeing her friend's gaze locked with Hada's, eyes practically glazed over. She headed to the bar.

Lillia waved Nikul over while she listened to Hada speak in Erithia's tongue. Ayela was tense, barely breathing. Her arms twitched on the table. Worse still, it looked as though Ayela understood what was being said. Like she was feeling the effects of dark magic.

"Water, please," Lillia asked Nikul when he approached.

"Don't be too worried about Hada. She's told fortunes to just about every merc in here." He gestured to the half-full bar. "She's odd, but not dangerous. No necromancer."

Lillia didn't respond. She wished she trusted Nikul, but she couldn't help but wonder if Ayela's dabbling in dark magic made this dangerous. It wasn't like she could ask. She watched Ayela carefully before looking away with a heavy sigh. At least she was vouched for by more than just Zaktan.

"So, her shadow…" Hada's shrill screech cut Lillia off. Lillia watched as black ooze seeped through Hada's wraps. Shadows in the tavern darkened, swelling beyond their natural forms.

Tendrils of black spewed forth from the table and wrapped around Ayela.

No. Lillia dropped her glass, not noticing as it shattered at her feet. "Mamana shehl'ore" she took aim for the tendrils with an open, glowing palm. The spell she intended shouldn't hurt Ayela.

Then, all was black. Darkness blanketed Lillia's vision. It was so palpably thick it felt as though Lillia was moving through liquid. Unable to even see her hands in front of her face, Lillia thrust her hand to the ceiling. "Laruthah!" She grabbed hold of Mahtsar's energy and channeled it through her tingling palm.

A ray of light, brilliant as the moon, shot from her palm into the ceiling, lightly scorching the wood. Shadows retreated from her light, falling back to their rightful places. Lillia stumbled over a fallen chair, making her way to Ayela.

She saw similar spells being cast by various patrons, creating pockets of light in the darkness. Armed mercenaries grouped into their party structures, barking various commands.

Eventually, Lillia's light reached Hada's corner. The wood where she had been was splintered, and the bench broken in two. Black sludge was splattered on the wall behind her and on the table, along with the shredded remains of Hada's wrappings.

"Ayela!" Lillia cried, seeing Ayela on her back, eyes closed and not moving, the dam of her control ruptured. White-hot sunlight poured from her glowing arm, scorching the ceiling. Her knees trembled before falling out from under her. Lillia fought through labored breaths; eyes locked on Ayela's motionless form. Shadows over the entire bar retreated, battered back as though running from the noon sun.

Her muscles ached and rebelled, but Lillia closed her hand, clamped her eyes shut and took a deep breath. Lillia wouldn't be able to help anyone if she overcast. She took another shaky breath, and her heart slowed as she braced herself on the floor.

The earthy scent of burning wood reached her before the pain she knew was coming. "Dai." Her arm was no longer glowing. She'd stopped the magic. But her fingers and wrists were numb. The world spun. She'd lost control and nearly overcast. Lillia heaved, her stomach expelling the meager contents of her last meal.

Lillia crawled over to Ayela, careful to avoid the mess. "Ayela!" Lillia cried out, lifting Ayela's limp head onto her folded knees. "No. No." Her arm muscles cramped and seized as her fingers stiffened.

"Get that fire out!" She heard someone yell from behind her. But she didn't look.

Lillia pushed the pain in her arm aside. She held the fingers of her left hand to Ayela's neck. Her skin was cold as ice and pale. Lillia swallowed. This couldn't be.

Lillia closed her eyes, hanging her head as her shoulders dropped. There was a pulse. Faint, but it was there. And Ayela's chest rose and fell in shallow breaths. She was alive.

Lillia scanned her for visible injuries, not that she could do anything about them in her state.

"Is she," Bahn asked, gently touching Lillia's arm.

"She won't wake up!" Lillia's voice cracked. Her chest tightened. Tears welled.

Bahn knelt beside Ayela as Logane and Zaktan crawled to their feet from behind the bench they'd been flung over.

By now, a small crowd of mercenaries was gathering around their corner. Each was in varying states of upset, annoyance, and morbid curiosity.

"Well, shit. There goes our fortune teller," one spoke.

But Lillia paid them no mind.

Logane knelt beside Lillia. "Is anyone here a healer?" he yelled to the crowd.

A woman stepped forward. She wore blue and white robes. Her brown hair was tied in two small pigtails. At her waist was a small wand fastened to her belt.

The woman palpated Ayela's chest, feeling for injuries or broken bones. She felt Ayela's neck and rolled it gently. Then she checked Ayela's head for any signs of injury. "I don't see anything wrong. She needs someone better than me."

Zaktan approached, his fist clenched around a strip of fabric. "She needs Raesra."

"Raesra's mourning period..." Logane started.

"Fuck that. You and I both know she'll help." Zaktan let the strip of fabric fall and stood at Ayela's feet. He bent her knees, then reached for her hands and swung Ayela onto his back in a fluid, practiced motion. "Don't you all have contracts to talk about!" He growled and hurried toward the door.

Lillia followed, closely trailed by Logane and Bahn. Outside was calm, with a menacing sunset casting blood-orange hues over the buildings. They walked for an eternity, through thinning crowds and alleyways. Lillia's eyes never left Ayela's limp form, held tightly over Zaktan's shoulders.

They turned onto a wide street, and a temple came into view. Lillia recognized the architecture and motifs along the front as a Mahtsarian temple. It had pillars that ended in ornate spirals and carvings of the sun bathing the world in light along the walls. From within the building, solemn choirs sang to a low organ. Zaktan didn't knock, just pushed his way in.

"Raesra," Zaktan yelled, looking over the surprised faces of clergy and pedestrians alike. The priest at the pulpit glared toward them, stepping down with flowing white and gold robes trailing behind. The organist stopped playing, missing a note as the choir fizzled out. A woman in a white and gold dress with a black veil stood from the front row.

The woman didn't say a word. Her shoes thudded against the tile of the silent cathedral with each painstaking step toward the party.

She looked over Ayela, then to Zaktan and Logane and finally Lillia and Bahn. "This way." Was her eventual reply before turning and leading Zaktan out of the main hall, to a side door and narrow hallway. Lillia noticed the priest following them, abandoning whatever sermon he was giving.

They passed several rooms filled with the sick and dying, some too far gone to help. Is this what Ayela was to become? Lillia's hands trembled as they walked. She needed Mahtsar to be with Ayela, to not allow her only friend to be too far gone.

"Set her down in here." The woman opened the door to a plain room with a single tall bed in the center. Zaktan gently laid Ayela on the bed and Lillia rushed to her side.

"She was caught in a dark magic spell that backfired," Lillia said. "We can't wake her."

"Doesn't appear injured." The woman felt Ayela's head and neck before holding two fingers over Ayela's wrist, "Her heart is steady."

A young man in a gray robe stepped in the doorway. "Lady Alebahl."

"Get me the head priest. This woman needs healing," the woman examining Ayela said without looking up.

"Mamana shehl'lahee," the woman said, holding two closed fists over Ayela. Lillia couldn't help but notice the burn scars on her left arm and the side of her neck. "Nehfesh roee." She opened her palm, and a pillar of golden light fell over Ayela. Lillia recognized the words. Mahtsar's magic, soul sight. It was a spell Lillia had never heard of.

The light faded, and the woman lowered her hands. "Her soul..." the woman hesitated.

"What is it?" Lillia begged.

"Ayela's soul isn't here. Her body is fine, but her soul..." A shimmering gold thread appeared above Ayela's chest, reaching into the air before fading. "Her soul is tethered? She isn't dead. But her soul is absent from her body."

"What does that mean?" Lillia held her breath, fist clenched over her chest. How was it even possible that her soul wasn't in her body? And how could that mean she wasn't dead?

"It means her soul wanders the land of the dead," an old man said from the doorway. He wore elaborate white and red robes. A neatly combed white beard fell over his chest in stark contrast to his bald head, spotted with aging skin. "There is little we can do for her." His sad eyes turned to Lillia, passing between the two in understanding.

"What do you mean there's nothing you can do?" Lillia dropped her hands into clenched fists. "There must be something! Surely you've seen this thing before."

"We have," the woman sighed beneath her black veil.

"Raesra, this is my fault. There has to be something you can do." Zaktan stepped toward the robed woman.

"I'll be honest with you," Raesra breathed, and the priest bowed his head. "It is entirely up to her." She gestured to Ayela. "She has to find her way back. We will keep her body alive, keep the door open as long as we can. But the human body can only survive so long without a soul."

"How long," Lillia asked.

"A month. The longest I've seen someone last is a month."

"And how many make their way back," Logane asked solemnly.

"In all my years, I've only seen a handful of cases like this," the old man said. "And only one ever came back."

"And she had promise too" Logane rubbed the back of his neck with his palm, his expression one of resignation.

"You're just going to write her off," Bahn asked. "You convinced her to trust Hada," his voice rose as he turned to Zaktan.

"No. I am being realistic. Housing her at the temple is going to be expensive. If she's gone for a month. We can't afford that." Logane clenched his teeth.

"I can cover it," Lillia affirmed. "Whatever the cost, I will cover it."

"Me as well," Bahn said, resting a hand on Lillia's shoulder.

"Can I talk to you two for a moment?" Raesra's tone was sharp. She motioned for Logane and Zaktan to leave the room and followed them out. She closed the door, leaving Bahn and Lillia with Ayela's body.

Her muffled voice rose from outside. Angry about something, scolding the two of them. But Lillia couldn't make out the words, and she didn't care to pay attention. She just pulled a simple stool from beside the wall and sat next to Ayela. "Why didn't you listen?" Lillia breathed unevenly. Bahn remained silent, looking at Ayela as though worlds away.

Neither of them talked.

The door opened, and Raesra walked in. "She will stay, free of charge," she said before again checking Ayela's pulse. "And you are welcome to visit as much as you like. But the temple doors lock an hour after sunset."

"Thank you." Lillia wiped at her eyes and looked back at Ayela, unsure of what to say.

"How do you know them," Bahn asked. "Logane and Zaktan."

"We're part of the same mercenary band. The one I'm assuming you have joined."

"Then why weren't you with us when we guarded the caravan?" Lillia asked.

"The mission before they hired you. My brother was killed, and I was injured. I've been observing the mourning period."

"I'm sorry," Lillia whispered and grasped Ayela's hand.

"Me too." Raesra stepped out of the room. "The temple will do what we can. But try not to get your hopes up. Make yourselves ready to say goodbye. It makes things easier."

Lillia collapsed when Raesra left, her breath quaked and chest throbbed. She squeezed Ayela's icy hand. She refused to let go. Ayela would come back. She had to. Lillia couldn't lose Ayela. Not again.

18

Moving Forward

Lillia woke with a stiff back, lying across Ayela's legs. There was a knock at the door, and a woman in a white tunic walked in. She held a bucket of water. Neither of them said a word as the woman wiped Ayela's arms with a sponge before turning her on her side. The woman lifted her shirt to wipe down Ayela's back, then patted it dry with a towel. She shifted and cleaned Ayela's legs in the same way before setting the bucket down. With two hands held over Ayela's stomach, the woman began a spell.

"Mamana shehl'muhvah, mezeen le'lahee."

It was another spell Lillia had never heard, but she understood the meaning. Musar's magic, nutrients for life. She guessed it was to sustain Ayela with magic. Lillia nodded to the healer, who left the room without a word.

It seemed like powerful magic, but Lillia knew it was incapable of sustaining Ayela forever. In her current state, she would simply waste away. There was no amount of magic that could stop that.

Tears resurfaced at the thought. She stood, pacing back and forth in the room as she racked her brain for any threads of hope that might help her dying friend.

There was a knock at the door.

"Lillia." It was Zaktan.

"What?" It came out harsher than she intended, or perhaps she had.

He opened the door and stepped inside. "We need to talk." Those words were never used to introduce pleasant information. "We don't know how long Ayela is going to be out. But if you are serious about joining the guild, there is still work to be done. For both of your sakes. The last mission was enough to get your foot in the door, your application was accepted, and the three of you are candidates. But if you want to remain in the guild, you must reach the rank of hunter before the end of open season fifty days from now. That means increasing your standing with the guild."

"Speak plainly," Lillia grumbled, not liking the insinuated idea of having to leave Ayela behind on her deathbed.

"You and Bahn will need to take more mercenary contracts with us. Logane thinks we can share the guild standing with Ayela, given the circumstances. At least on a probationary basis. But you and Bahn will have to come on these missions. There is no getting around that."

Lillia hung her head. Everything in her wanted to wait in this room, to be here when Ayela opened her eyes. But Zaktan was right; there was no telling when she would wake up. And Ayela wouldn't want Lillia just sitting idle.

"What do you want me to do?" Lillia's tear-parched voice cracked.

"We're discussing a contract at The Headless Snake. Come back with me. You can visit Ayela later."

Lillia rubbed sleep-deprived eyes and rolled her stiff neck.

"Better yet, you need rest in an actual bed, and Nikul has two beds ready. You and Bahn will take them," Zaktan ordered.

Lillia stood, looking back at Ayela. "If you think I'm gonna let her stay a night alone, you're delusional." She would be here every night until Ayela returned.

Zaktan didn't protest. He simply motioned for Lillia to follow.

"Lillia, I know it's hard," Zaktan said as they approached The Headless Snake.

She grimaced at what she imagined he was about to say. Lillia had no reason to listen to him. All of this, Ayela's condition, the dark magic explosion. If he hadn't pushed Ayela, hadn't convinced her it was safe. Maybe Ayela would have listened to Lillia.

Then again, if Ayela hadn't been dabbling in dark magic, maybe Hada's spell wouldn't have gone so wrong.

"We must move forward. If we stopped for everyone who fell…"

"Don't," Lillia barked. "She isn't gone; don't talk like she is." Lillia pushed ahead, entering the bar in front of Zaktan.

The tavern was as lively as ever, with upbeat music playing from a minstrel Lillia no longer cared for. Patrons talked; glasses clinked. No one so much as looked her way. And why would they? To them, nothing had changed. To them, the world wasn't ending. Lillia's gaze fell over Hada's corner. The black sludge had been cleaned, and her wraps were gone, but the wood and windows behind were still cracked. A pit formed in Lillia's stomach. She'd been so wrapped up in Ayela's condition, she hadn't realized what this had done to Hada. And Zaktan, he had seemed close with Hada.

"About Hada…" Lillia said when Zaktan entered beside her. "I'm sorry."

He stiffened, but didn't respond. "The others are waiting for us." His gruff tone was back, as though the softer side he'd shown had calloused over.

Lillia shrunk. Hada hadn't seemed so bad. She hadn't deserved that death. And now that she thought about it, it was clear she was telling the truth. By the looks of it, Hada had overcast. Something not possible with dark magic. Lillia had been mistaken.

Lillia pressed forward, eager for anything to get her mind off of Hada and Ayela's condition.

Bahn sat at the table opposite Logane, and beside Logane sat an elven woman. She wore freshly polished plate armor with white cloth bridging the gaps. Her perfectly straight, long white hair mimicked starlight. Soft eyes and a sympathetic smile accented her shrewd facial features. Propped against the table was a large steel shield, and at her waist rested a silver-plated morning star.

"Raesra will join us. She's cut her mourning short."

"Since you two can't keep out of trouble for more than a week, it seems." Raesra smirked. "Honestly, I wasn't even gone for ten days."

"I'm sorry." Lillia sat across from Raesra.

"Nothing for you to be sorry for, darling. It's these dim wits that can't leave well enough alone. And I was in the guild long before becoming a cleric. Sometimes we just have to move forward."

Logane rolled his eyes, "How's Ayela?"

"No change," Lillia muttered.

"She'll pull through." Bahn smiled with the confidence Lillia wished for.

"We have to move on, regardless." Logane's cruel words were at least spoken with a hint of sympathy. He laid a scroll on the table and rolled it out for Lillia and Bahn to see. "Should be an easy one. It's been on the job board for a month, so the client is likely desperate. I've already sent word that we'll meet them at the meeting place around noon today. The city guard is looking for someone to help gather information in a string of murders with the odd signature of black roses."

Lillia's mind wandered when she again looked at the spot where Hada had died. Her eyes glassed over. The horrid night played before her again as she studied the disheveled corner just a few seats over. She kept picturing the tendrils of shadow wrapping around Ayela, pulling her toward the table. Lillia had failed to dissuade Ayela. She'd given up. And when things really mattered, she'd been too slow.

"…torture people into telling what they know," Bahn asked.

"Torture?" Lillia snapped back to the conversation; her throat clenched. "Why would we do that?"

Logane hung his head. "We're not torturing anyone. There are far more efficient ways of getting information."

"Unless they deserve it." Zaktan smirked. "I've got some skills that I haven't been able to put to use yet." His eyes narrowed as though reliving memories of a past life.

"You will not, unless you want me returning to the temple. I won't be a part of torture." Raesra set her jaw and looked Zaktan down with a glare that made him squirm in his seat.

"Relax princess. I was only joking." Zaktan retreated, sinking into his chair. But Lillia kept watching his distant, dreamy gaze.

Silence dropped around them for a moment before Logane stood. "So, we're headed to the meeting point. It's an hour's walk away."

Lillia thought of asking for the details she missed but decided against it. She needed to prove she could be relied on, for Ayela's sake. This was their dream, after all.

"Doesn't give us long to get there," Raesra said.

"Have you eaten," Bahn asked Lillia.

"No," Lillia breathed at the admission. She vaguely remembered a temple servant offering her a tray of food. But she wasn't hungry. Still wasn't. How could she be?

"Get something from Nikul before we leave." Zaktan tossed her a few silver coins. "You need your strength."

"Okay," Lillia whispered before standing with the group. Wherever they were going, it was far from where she wanted to be. Far from where she was. She wondered just how useless she'd be in a fight, unable to even focus on a conversation, much less a spell.

The five of them ambled through street after chaotic street, making their way to the meeting point. Lillia hadn't imagined Southtown could get worse than she saw, but every step was further into the warrens. Buildings fell further into disrepair, and any semblance of common craftsmanship long vanished. Trash littered every gutter. Foul-smelling piles of matter dominated some corners, and it seemed everyone they passed eyed the party as potential victims. Still, they continued.

"It's just up ahead." Logane motioned to a building with a sign that read Axe Brothers Winery. "The alley just before that building."

"If you can call it that," Lillia whispered. The structure stank of fermentation, and the piecemeal wooden walls were littered with broken and rotting boards. The thatched roof even looked partially caved in from what Lillia could see.

They rounded the corner and froze. Kneeling over the corpse of a city guard was a man Lillia recognized. Gold pauldrons adorned his shoulders, and a mantle of crow feathers was draped around his neck. He wore extravagant red and black clothes. The man was turned away from the party. He hadn't noticed them.

Blood stained the mud beneath the assassin. "Where are you, girl?" He growled under his breath.

Logan drew his sword, the piercing sound of it rang over the still street. The man looked over his shoulder, black hair, short and wild, danced over a pearl-white countenance. His gray eyes scanned the party before turning back to the corpse, unthreatened. He whispered a spell, and a gust of wind blew dust toward the party as the assassin floated to the rooftops.

Logane's wings unfurled from beneath his cloak. He ran, sword drawn, toward the alley before leaping onto the rooftop with a powerful swoop. Bahn followed, jumping from wall to wall in the narrow space between buildings. The two disappeared, giving pursuit. Lillia examined every way up the wall, cursing herself for not learning or studying any of the jump or flight spells in the spell-book she purchased. There was a haphazardly stacked pile of crates and barrels, but she didn't trust herself to climb them without falling. Sure, she could craft a spell, but there was no way of knowing how much energy it would take without trying it. And no way of knowing what fight awaited on the rooftop.

Zaktan seemed to puzzle similarly. "No way we'll get up there after them. Really wish the fool would think before running off," Zaktan grumbled. "Raesra, help me with this?" Zaktan stepped forward, kneeling before the guard's body.

An officer's chain rested over his breastplate. Not just any guard, a guard captain.

But what caught Lillia's attention was a flower caught between his teeth. She walked over, looking away as she picked it up off the corpse. Her stomach rebelled at feeling the tug of the man's teeth on the thorns. The thorns were angular and curved downward along a stem that was twisted and patterned with black veins. The base of the petals was white. No doubt, a mountain rose from the northern border of The Dragon Fang Mountains, where the corruption of The Erithian Empire leached into the land. A rare rose, difficult to come by.

"What is it," Zaktan asked.

"The rose. It's odd. This type only grows north of The Dragon Fang Mountains. They're very hard to grow here unless you use dark magic." Lillia examined the rose, testing the sharpness of a thorn. She made the mistake of looking at the many stab wounds in the guard's chest. Her vision locked, bile churned in her stomach, her eyes narrowed before Raesra stepped between them.

"A crime of passion, clearly." Raesra said. "What's that?" She pointed to the guard captain's hand, where a crumpled-up slip of blood-stained paper was held.

Zaktan pried the paper from the dead guard's hand and unfolded it. "It's hastily written. It says, if I don't make it, speak to Lieutenant Markus at Southern Barracks number three."

"He got away." Bahn dropped from the rooftop, breathing heavy clouds of fog in the chilled winter air.

"Lillia, you looked like you recognized him," Logane said with a grunt, folding his wings and landing at the entrance to the alley. "Who was he to you?"

"A man my father knew. Some noble he said not to trust. His name started with Z. Maybe Zed… something. I can't remember. There was a lot going on." Lillia smelled the rose, enjoying its sweet, earthy aroma. "The rose is a good lead, though. It's rare, I can't imagine many florists selling it. So, either our killer grows them, or they'd buy them from one of a handful of people."

"This note is as well. It tells us to talk to someone else if the guard captain dies." Zaktan handed the blood-stained parchment to Logane.

"Sounds like a good place to start," Logane said.

"We aren't going to take a minute to investigate the body," Bahn asked.

"No need. Unless you're secretly a necromancer and can make the dead talk?" Zaktan shrugged. "Nothing more to learn from the corpse. A crime of passion and the two leads, it's all we have."

"We don't know which shops sell the flowers." Raesra rolled her wrist. "So maybe the lieutenant? We can have Nikul dig up some info on local flower shops later."

"The barracks then, they're not far," Logane sighed. "This is turning into a more complex mission than it's worth."

It took them fifteen minutes to make their way to the barracks, where a young guard stood watch. He studied the party nervously. His hands fidgeted with his cloak. Logane spoke first.

"We're mercenaries hired by Captain Noah, looking for Markus." Logane held the contract and the note out to the guard.

The guard relaxed at seeing the contract. "Shit," the guard breathed. "I warned the captain this was a bad idea. Now I have to tell his wife." The guard cradled the bridge of his nose in his hands. "I'm Markus. Look, these murders, someone powerful doesn't want them investigated." He looked over the group's shoulder before pulling a small pouch of gold out from under his robes. "The captain wanted me to continue the investigation if something happened to him. I'd really rather keep my head down. And you'd best stay out of it too." Markus tossed the coin-bag to Logane. "For your trouble. I'll clean the captain's notes out of his office, tomorrow." Markus emphasized the last word, as though trying to communicate something unsaid. "The captain's quarters in the back of the barracks will be heavily guarded, tomorrow, once they learn what happened. And I'd rather not be exposed. I believe your payment is adequate." The lieutenant walked off, not waiting for an answer or affirmation from the group.

"I think he wants us to investigate," Bahn whispered once he was out of earshot.

"You think?" Zaktan smirked.

"But I don't think we should," Logane muttered. "That bag looks too light to investigate a murder the city guard doesn't want solved."

"Murder is murder, the old you would have wanted it stopped." Raesra held out a hand for the bag, opening it once Logane handed it over. She rummaged through for a bit before pulling out a single iron key.

Logan closed his eyes, turning his nose to the sky. "Raesra," he groaned. "Do you always have to take the high ground?"

"We investigate," Raesra affirmed, walking off toward the guardhouse.

Lillia lagged behind the party while they snuck to the barracks. She twirled the rose she still held and looked at the sun overhead. Ayela was lying on a straw bed, in a temple she'd never been in, dedicated to a god she had never worshiped. She sighed. Would Mahtsar even extend a hand? Would she help someone who had never worshiped her? And if she woke up, she'd be confused and afraid. Would she think Lillia had abandoned her? Would she remember wandering the world of the dead? Would it change her? Lillia hoped she would simply not remember.

The group approached the rear guardhouse to find it oddly vacant. "Anyone else feel like this may be a trap," Bahn questioned.

Logane regarded him. "It's possible, but unlikely. What do you propose?"

"Out here, we're exposed." Bahn scanned the rooftops surrounding the small porch that led to the captain's quarters. "So, anyone staying out here isn't the best idea. Raesra should enter first with her shield raised, closely followed by Logane, Lillia and I. Zaktan will enter last and wait by the door as a lookout.

"Seems fair." Logane nodded, and everyone got into position without complaint. Raesra lifted her shield and pushed the door open with her mace before easing her way inside.

All was quiet within the dimly lit strewn office. There were piles of papers on the desk and a board on the rear wall with lines of red thread that hung between nails and parchment. There were some books on the mostly sparse bookshelf by the door. A chest sat along the far wall beneath the investigation board.

"Quaint," Bahn said. "I guess we search?"

Lillia ignored the urge to see what books were lined up on the captain's shelf and instead moved to the stacks of papers on the desk. There were reports, guard movements, requisition orders and many other documents that held no bearing on their investigation. Lillia looked through each of the drawers, briefly rummaging through the quills and scrolls within. None looked useful until she reached the last drawer. She noticed the sides were shorter than the other drawers she'd pulled out. Curious, she knelt down.

"Ha!" Lillia grinned when she spied the hidden drawer. She pulled, tugging it free with a slight click. Inside was a single leather-bound journal. "I think I found something," Lillia said.

Logane was beside her in a moment, looking over her shoulder at the book. She opened the well-worn journal to find surprisingly neat handwriting detailing various investigations: the captain's journal. She thumbed through the pages until she found the mention and drawing of a black rose.

"It starts with a list of victims, thirty of them, it looks like. And," Lillia hesitated. Not wanting to be wrong in her assumption, "I think I recognize some of these names from news bulletins my father used to bring home from the palace."

"Just who was your father that he was regularly attending the palace?" Zaktan scoffed from the door. "What are you, some kind of princess?"

"No," Lillia scoffed. "Even if I had been, I have forsaken my title to join Ayela." Lillia's throat clenched. If Ayela didn't make it, she would have done it for nothing. She'll have doomed herself to a hard life, never to find happiness. Lillia may as well have stayed with her father and agreed to the loveless marriage. She took a sharp breath, forcing that dreadful thought as far down as it would go. "My father is the librarian at The King's Library."

"Cushy life, can't imagine why you'd want to leave it." Raesra smirked, side-eyeing Lillia with a look that said she knew all too well.

"Over here," Bahn said. He was standing by the bulletin board. "Looks like a woman witnessed one of the murders, but she refused to talk to the city guard. Said she couldn't remember. There's a note that says to hire mercenaries to question her. Maybe that's what the captain wanted us to do."

"There's one more thing." Lillia said, turning the page to see a single line that made the hair on her neck rise. "It says The Nighthawks are involved."

"Shit," Logane's exasperated tone and defeated expression mimicked that of the rest of the group.

"Someone's coming," Zaktan whispered from the door.

Logane snatched the book from Lillia and tucked it into a pocket of his tunic. "Get back from the door." He pushed Lillia out of the way and slunk to the wall, hand resting over a dagger at his belt.

Lillia crouched behind the desk, only just able to see into the courtyard from between the legs of the chair.

A lone city guardsman, an initiate by the looks of him, entered the courtyard. He stopped when he saw the open door and started toward it, craning his head in curiosity.

"No!" Bahn whispered as he knocked into a tall vase in the far corner. It fell before he could catch it, shattering on the ground with a crash that could've woken the dead.

The guard jumped, then turned and ran, presumably to get reinforcements.

"Nice going, tree boy," Zaktan growled.

"We need to leave, now!" Logane rushed toward the door, leading the group out and around the corner.

The sounds of rustling armor and yelling buzzed from within the barracks. Images of what the guards would do if they were caught played through Lillia's mind in rapid succession. They rounded another corner toward the street.

"Mamana shehl'ore!" Raesra shouted and held a hand forward. "Close your eyes!" She said to the group, holding one hand over her face. "bakwa shehl'alua."

A flash of white erupted from the street ahead, bathing everything in warm white light bright as the sun. The party rushed into the street, passing two sets of guards dazed by her spell.

Lillia smirked, noting the spell. Burst of Light, not dissimilar to what she'd used to fight Adina. But stunning, not damaging.

They rushed past the guards, turning down several streets. Lillia's lungs burned, but she kept pace. Sure, the others would not stop for her. Eventually, their pace slowed. Logane turned around. Not seeing any pursuers, he burst into laughter.

"What are you laughing about? We almost got arrested." Lillia bent over, grasping her knees in exhaustion as the air stabbed her throbbing lungs.

"Haven't had a rush like that since we faced a dragon." Logane's face drained of color, his laughter ceasing.

"Asshole." Zaktan grunted before punching Logane with enough force to send him stumbling back. Zaktan breathed through clenched teeth. "Think before you speak."

Logane cradled the side of his face, gaze down turned.

"It's… fine." Raesra's whisper was uneven. Clearly not fine. She walked past Logane, patting him on the shoulder before breaking away from the group.

"Sorry," Logane muttered. "I didn't…"

"Too soon." Zaktan pushed Logane aside and followed Raesra toward The Headless Snake.

Their group walked in silence, with Logane periodically stretching his bruised jaw.

"You fought a dragon?" Lillia hoped her whisper didn't reach the others as she walked beside Logane.

"Yea," Logane's heavy reply closed any prospect of further questions as they neared The Headless Snake. "Get yourself something to drink. Maybe it's a story you'll hear sometime. But not today."

MOVING FORWARD

Lillia sat curled in her chair while she listened to the group argue about whether to continue the mission. They'd been going in circles for nearly an hour at this point.

"Guild law prohibits interfering with Nighthawks' business. They already warded us off once. They won't take our interfering again so kindly." Logane argued.

"We don't know they're responsible," Bahn retorted.

"And it isn't their MO," Lillia added. "Crow feathers dipped in blood. That's the Nighthawk signature. Not black roses." Lillia waved to Nikul to bring a glass of water.

"But there are guardsmen and city officials being murdered. And the guard isn't trying to stop them," Raesra said.

"I agree. That's what bothers me. Whoever it is, is above the law," Zaktan said. "We need to find out who they are and put a stop to it."

"I know there's a connection between the names. The captain couldn't put it together, and I can't put my finger on it." Lilia accepted the glass from Nikul and folded the journal she'd read for the third time. "I just wish I had those old news scrolls. But I really don't want to go ask my father for them."

"You may have to," Bahn said.

"Not tonight."

"Going to visit Ayela," Raesra asked.

"Yea."

"Then you'd better get going. It'll be dark soon, and the priests won't let you in after the guard puts the city lights out." Raesra smiled as though to apologize.

"We'll have the next steps figured out tomorrow. Don't you worry." Zaktan nodded to Lillia. "And try to get some actual sleep tonight. Please. See if they'll let you use an empty bed."

"Thank you." Lillia stood and left the tavern. She crossed street after street without so much as checking the alleys she passed. She needed to get to the temple. Had to know if Ayela was awake, despite the odds.

She reached the temple and reverently opened the doors. Inside, the priest was closing a sermon with a small audience. She slowed her pace, taking a moment to listen to his closing remarks about embracing the changes life brings. Lillia traced the intricately designed architecture of the interior. Despite its construction in Southtown, this building was held to the standards that most Midtown structures adhered to. White stone walls, tall ceilings with coffers, fluted pillars and ornately carved footboards.

Lillia's boots clacked on the stone floor. She nodded to the priest before slipping away and into the healer's corridors. Lillia had the path memorized by now, not needing to look at the other beds and rooms.

She reached Ayela's room and, with a held breath, pushed open the door. "Ayela?"

Silence. Ayela lay exactly where Lillia had left her. Lillia sighed before stepping into the room. She noted a folded pile of thick bedding tucked in a corner and was grateful that someone at least respected her choice to stay.

"Started a new mission today," Lillia said before closing the door.

"Investigating some murders in Southtown. The city guard doesn't want them solved. And surprise, The Nighthawks are involved somehow." Lillia pulled the rose out of her pocket and laid it down next to Ayela.

"Raesra is nice. I can tell there is a lot of history between her, Logane and Zaktan. We're going to feel like outsiders for a while, I'm afraid," Lillia giggled before kneeling next to Ayela.

"We searched the guard captain's quarters for information on the murders. Probably not the smartest idea, seeing as it almost got us arrested."

"You would have liked this mission. I know how much you love mysteries." Lillia thought back to the numerous novels Ayela had snuck out of the library. Mystery and adventure. Those were Ayela's favorite things to read.

Lillia brushed a strand of hair out of Ayela's face and straightened her shirt ever so slightly. "You'll get past this, you hear." Lillia bit back tears. "Find your way back to me."

Lillia shuffled back, then clasped her hands together and bent her head.

Then, after a moment of silence, "Mahtsar, bringer of life. Thank you for every moment you have given me, every smile and memory we share. But Mahtsar, please. Do not take her from me. Have mercy on Ayela, let your light burn in her, purify the darkness that was planted through Erithia's trickery." She paused, as though waiting for an answer. "Amen."

Lillia lifted her head, tears welled as she studied Ayela's unchanging face. There was truly nothing more she could do but pray. Pray to the gods she only hoped were real. To gods that had allowed such a tragedy, allowed Ayela to suffer so much, to be tricked into using dark magic.

Lillia stood, wiped her eyes, and yawned. She spread out the quilts and made herself some semblance of a bed, allowing just enough room for someone to walk between her and Ayela. "Goodnight." She whispered and closed her eyes, begging for a peaceful sleep.

19

Whispering Shadows

Lillia smiled, enjoying the music of Ayela's laughter. Candlelight flickered around them, as did the myriad of voices that melded into the silence. A meal was before them, savory and sweet. They talked about missions gone by and days passed in happiness, about riding whales through storms and across seas. Lillia's heart swelled, and tears flooded her vision.

They walked over the battlements of a city in the clouds. Hand in hand, they watched birds fly by. The summer air was pleasantly warm and smelled of fresh mortar used in preparing the walls. Someone called Lillia's name, soft, distant.

Lillia jolted awake at a knock at the door. Her back ached from sleeping on the stone floor of the temple with only the blankets beneath her.

"Ms. Kote," the voice from the other side of the door was young.

"Come in." Lillia rubbed sleep from her crusty eyes. She choked back tears as her heart dropped. The realization that it had been just another dream dawned too quickly. Ayela still lay on the bed beside her, barely breathing, unmoving, skin clammy and cold as ice. Ayela's eyes looked bruised and recessed into her skull. She looked more like a corpse than a person.

It was the third morning Lillia had woken up here, and if the bags under her eyes were any indication. Lillia desperately needed a bed.

A small boy carrying a satchel opened the door. "A delivery for you." The boy held the satchel for Lillia. Visible at the top were several scrolls and a letter.

Curious, she took the bag and opened the letter. The boy just waited expectantly.

"To my daughter, Lillia." She started aloud, her eyes widening. A letter! She'd been gone for more than a week and his first attempt to reach her was a letter? She'd expected him to come in person or to have his private militia drag her back to the library by now. Maybe send private physicians for Ayela. But a letter.

I wish for you to know that I am not angry with you. Perhaps I should be, but I understand why you did what you did. I am more sick with myself for not seeing it sooner. I regret that it came to the extreme that it did.

Lillia took a breath. She hadn't even thought about her father since the group decided to abandon the quest and stay out of The Nighthawk's way. Now she felt she could hear his detached tone in every word. The tone he got when he was trying too hard to conceal something or hold back his emotions.

Over the past week, I have given you the space you needed, but I felt it was time to extend a hand. You are my daughter, and Ayela, like my daughter. It grieves me to learn of the injury she has sustained. In the satchel I have included every tome within The Library on soul separation. I hope you can find more than I could. I have also included the news articles you desired to aid in your investigation. Your leaders may have been hasty in their move to dismiss the contract.

How could he know that?

I know you have questions. And I would love to answer them over dinner or tea should you decide to return, if only for a visit. For now, know that I have not stopped looking after you. Tell the courier, rats win where mice fail.

Lillia read the line again in confusion, noting its odd placement before continuing.

I have faith that you will easily find the solution to the murders. It will not take you long to come to the same conclusion I have. Everything is in the satchel.

The Library, our home, is always open to you if you wish to visit or return. I love you, Lillia Kote, and I am proud of you. You really are your mother's daughter.

"How did he…" Lillia asked, looking through the heavy satchel.

"You don't question The Shadow." The boy interrupted her.

Lillia blinked in silence. Shadow? Surely, he wasn't referring to her father. The two exchanged expectant glances before Ayela rattled off the phrase. "Rats win where mice fail?"

The boy nodded and left without a word. Lillia sat back in silence. Was her father watching her the whole time? If so, how? Was it someone in The Headless Snake? But he knew about Ayela too, so it had to be someone close. And what sort of message did she pass to the courier? And the courier… was her father working with someone to spy on her and Ayela?

"You know, Ayela," she mumbled before standing and stretching her back. She groaned with pleasure when several ribs popped back into place. "I think I would have preferred him angry. I was ready for angry."

Lillia swallowed, resting a hand on Ayela's shoulder. "I'll be back tonight. I'm going to take these to The Headless Snake and pour over them with the others."

Lillia stepped out of the room, and into the hallway that comprised the temple's infirmary. Concern played at the back of her mind of catching some illness. Certainly, being in this place posed its risks. But it didn't matter. Not when Ayela was still here.

Lillia adjusted the satchel on her shoulder. She took a breath, imagining how she would tell the group she had come to possess her father's satchel. If she told the truth, there would be all kinds of questions as to her father's true identity. Questions Lillia wasn't sure she knew the answers too, questions she wasn't sure she wanted answered. She wasn't returning there any time soon, but every part of her wanted to hold onto the image she held of her father. Just the same old dad. The man who'd been there when Lillia's mom died. The one who'd raised her, had her trained in magic privately, sheltered her from The Citadel's inquiries. The strong, confident, loving and virtuous man she knew him to be. She refused to question further. Whatever darker imaginings her mind threatened to run with were simply fragments of the novels she poured over as a child. She was reading too much into this.

No, she would lie, tell them she went to see her father and grabbed them because the question was just nagging at her.

She took another step toward The Headless Snake's door just ahead.

It was a believable lie: a bookworm like herself not liking unanswered questions. Or maybe she went to find the books for Ayela and grabbed them on impulse? That was a better lie. But then they would ask how the meeting with her father went.

Lillia groaned, looking skyward, as though the gods would speak the answer to her. Mahtsar's teachings would lecture to always speak true. But in this case, the truth might…

"Lillia" Raesra's soft voice drew Lillia back. Raesra was standing before Lillia, her brows knitted in concern. "What's wrong?"

"My father sent me this." Lillia gritted her teeth. That wasn't what she was supposed to say. "I mean, I didn't ask…"

Raesra laughed. "There's no shame in using your connections. What did he give you?"

"Books." Lillia rattled off and bit her lip. "And the news scrolls I mentioned wanting for the murder investigation."

"Ah, I see." Raesra smirked. "Taking initiative. I like that. But you'll want to run it by Logane. He is this ragtag band's leader, after all. And don't worry. There's no harm in discussing information, at least not when you got it from a source you trust to be discrete. Be sure to mention that part when you tell him."

"Right." Lillia laughed and again adjusted the heavy pack. "What are they doing in there, anyway?"

"Same thing they do every year about this time, judging the new candidates and taking bets on who will and will not last until next year."

"New candidates?"

"Yeah, Open Season starts next week. So, the new candidates are in the various guildhalls, making nice with the mercenary bands, hoping one will sponsor them. But you don't have to worry about that. We've already sponsored you, Bahn and Ayela."

"What will happen if Ayela doesn't wake up before Open Season starts?" Lillia hated to ask. But it was a question she needed answered.

"As long as she wakes up before it ends, it will be fine." Raesra grabbed Lillia's hand. Leaving off the fact that Open Season would end long after Ayela's time was up. "Come on, you'll want to show what you brought to Logane."

Raesra led Lillia into the chaos of The Headless Snake. Prospecting adventurers of every caliber were crammed near shoulder to shoulder within. Each was dressed in varying levels of armor and clothing that denoted a variety of backgrounds. Lillia even spied some higher-end fabrics that suggested nobility was mingling amongst the candidates. Could it be that others would want to escape the trappings of noble expectations as she had? Logane and Zaktan sat with their backs against the wall in the corner opposite where Hada had died.

Lillia closed her eyes, clearing her mind as she mistakenly looked at Hada's empty, roped-off table.

"What's in the bag," Logane asked as they approached.

"News scrolls. I did some more digging." Lillia's cheeks burned at the lie.

"Digging into what?" Logane's eyes narrowed. "I thought we were dropping the murder investigation."

"I was going to leave it alone," Lillia muttered. "But it didn't work out that way. I got them from my father. He'll be discrete."

Logane shrugged. "No harm in looking at them, since you already have them. Let's see what you've got."

"Where's Bahn," Lillia asked as she dumped the heavy satchel out on the table, scattering scrolls over its surface before the books fell free. Logane pulled out the journal and turned to the page he'd dog-eared with the victim's names on it.

"Haven't seen tree boy all day." Zaktan grabbed a scroll from the pile.

"Let's get hunting," Logane sighed and glanced over the journal before picking up a scroll and looking for matching names. Lillia and the others followed.

"This is going to take a while." Raesra eyed the heaping pile of scrolls.

Lillia looked up from the fourth scroll she'd read through to observe the circus that was The Headless Snake. The mass of candidates had mostly divided into groups by now. But there were still some stragglers trying too desperately to find a new group. She even saw one set of young people in low-quality armor that had grouped up away from everyone else.

"Can candidates start their own band? Or do they have to be sponsored," Lillia asked, interrupting Logane's search.

"They can start their own. But it is much harder to get contracts and gain standing that way. Actually, that's how Raesra and I started."

"Not Zaktan," Lillia asked.

"Zaktan joined us about three years after we founded our merry band."

"Here we go!" Zaktan yelled excitedly. "I've got a name. Judge Righma was murdered days after her conviction of Maru, the... gods." Zaktan closed his eyes. "Just days after the conviction and execution of Maru, a ten-year-old, found guilty of necromancy."

Lillia's jaw dropped.

Zaktan continued. "The judgement faced public outcry because of the sister's powerful testimony and protest at the pyre. Righma was a vigorous advocate for the isolation of Moonborn and the outlawing of all forms of dark magic. The sister, a Moonborn, was held in prison to await judgement for a similar accusation but was broken out of jail by Nighthawk Assassins. Following the murder and subsequent escape, King Ashratson and The Chief Judge ordered Southtown into lockdown pending an investigation." Zaktan lowered the scroll as he finished reading.

"You think it's the sister," Lillia asked.

"Possibly. But this could be an anomaly. We need to find the other names. Or at least a few other names," Logane shrugged.

"How could they convict a ten-year-old?" Lillia imagined the boy burning at the pyre for something he surely hadn't done or hadn't known better than to do.

"It is pretty easy to tell when someone has become a necromancer. And there's no coming back from it." Raesra didn't look up from the scroll she was reading. "So, if he was one, there isn't much else to do. That said, a public execution is barbaric. The problem is that I've never heard of a child becoming a necromancer. It isn't something that happens overnight. Someone would have had to train him."

"Here's another one." Logane said, pointing to the scroll he was reading. "The arresting guard of a child executed for necromancy, found dead. His name is on the list."

"How old was the child?" Zaktan's level tone was unreadable, his expression cold.

"Mahtsar's light." Logane let the scroll fall before holding his face. "It says the boy was only eight."

"These stories are being buried," Lillia said. "Here's another. It's near the bottom of the scroll. A twelve-year-old this time. And the convicting judge was murdered just two days ago."

"I've got no love for necromancers," Zaktan growled. "But one of two things is happening here. Either some sick fuck is turning children into necromancers, or the guard is targeting Moonborn children. Each of these necromancers was a Moonborn." Zaktan crumpled the latest news scroll in an unconsciously closing fist.

"And the city guard isn't willing to investigate." Logane's face was turning several shades redder. His breath was uneven. His wings rustled.

"Calm yourself, Logane." Raesra's barely contained growl drew the attention of Logane and Zaktan. "Let's think about this." She took a deep breath. "Objectively. Different people are involved in each case. They all seem to have two things in common. They are openly racist against Moonborn and were involved in the accusation, arrest, or conviction of a Moonborn child sentenced to death for necromancy. It seems whoever is murdering the officials responsible is cleaning house. And the city guard wants to let them."

"Are you saying we don't get involved," Zaktan asked. "I, for one, want to join this murderer."

"We can't. And you know that." Logane closed his eyes.

"Still," Zaktan grumbled.

"We have two choices if we want to keep our hands clean and remain in the guild. Either we do nothing, and let it continue. Or we give this information to Markus to complete the contract and leave the rest to him."

Lillia closed her eyes and turned away. It would have been so much simpler to ignore the satchel. Do as Logane said and just wait for Ayela. Now this? She knew what Ayela would want to do. Ayela would want to stop the mistreatment of the Moonborn.

"What the city guard is doing is horrible, if it is what it seems." Lillia said. "But so many are involved. The problem is much larger than we can solve, and a string of brutal murders is only going to make it worse. We should turn the information over to Markus."

Logane nodded before resting his head on two closed fists. "I hate it. But you are right. Violence begets violence. The cycle needs to end. And there's nothing a band of low-level mercs can do against the city watch."

"But The King's Guild could do something." Zaktan said. "We should pass this to leadership. They have influence with the king and Hatave's nobility.

"Agreed. We complete the contract with Lieutenant Markus and pass the problem with the guard to guild leadership." Logane nodded. "I'll take the info to Markus personally tonight. Lillia, good work." Logane patted Lillia's shoulder before standing.

"Assuming these are for Ayela," Raesra asked, thumbing through the books. "Do you want help looking through them?"

"I was planning to look through them at the temple," Lillia said while gathering the books and unneeded scrolls into the satchel. "I won't turn down help though."

"I'll join you." Raesra smiled and placed the last book into Lillia's bag. "You two meatheads need anything from us; we'll be at the temple." She nodded to Zaktan before leaving with Lillia through the streets awash with the darkening glow of the near-setting sun.

Lillia let a cautious smile slip across her face. The answer had to be within the near dozen books her father had sent. It had to be. She would get Ayela back, no matter what the cost.

Lillia's fists clenched. She recalled the cautionary tales of those in desperation. With a bowed head, she acknowledged the shameful fact. If she had dark magic. If someone said they could bring Ayela back. She just might be desperate enough to agree. And she would forever hate herself for it.

20

King of Crows

Lillia sat, half awake, with her head laid out on the bar of The Headless Snake. The tavern was just as chaotic as the days before, but with fresh voices roaring in a sea of indistinguishable noise. Lillia turned to the side, watching Logane and the others interview a man carrying an instrument who was trying his luck at joining their party. But it didn't matter. Nothing mattered.

"Still no luck with the books?" Nikul asked, placing a steaming loaf of fresh bread beside Lillia, blocking her view.

"Two weeks," Lillia mumbled. "I've been pouring over every book over and over. Learned a lot about soul projection, which I didn't know was a thing. I've learned what happens to souls that don't choose a god when they die, or who don't find the gods."

"That one kept me up all night. I read a journal about someone who went through this and survived. But it was mostly incoherent babbling about monsters and voices that he could never stop seeing and hearing. So, that's great to know. But nothing about reaching the ones that are lost. Not in any of the books."

"You can't lose faith, Lillia," Nikul sighed. "No matter how gloomy it looks."

"I just wish," Lillia began.

"Anyone!" Lillia jumped at the familiar voice of the guard, Markus. He was standing in the doorway, drenched with sweat, panic in his eyes. The sea of voices from before was silent, all eyes were on the guard. Some with swords partially drawn. One particularly large mercenary stood and placed a hand on the guard's chest.

"City guard ain't welcome here, friend. This is a guildhall."

Markus scanned the bar, finding Logane and the others sitting by a window.

"Logane, right?" Markus struggled vainly against the bear of a man. "She's going to kill me!"

Logane stood, as did Raesra, Zaktan and Bahn. Logane led them slowly to the door, motioning for Lillia to join them. She followed, grabbing her staff from its propped location against the bar.

"If it is who I think you're talking about. We can't help you." Logane said. "Guild law prohibits us from interfering with Nighthawk affairs."

"She isn't a Nighthawk! Not anymore! She's a necromancer, and she is going to kill me!" All exhaustion left Lillia's mind at the mention of a necromancer. If this man was a target, that meant they were all in danger.

Markus again tried to get past the mercenary. But the man threw him into the street and reached for his sword. "You risk all of us by…"

"We'll handle this." Logane tapped the mercenary's shoulder before leading their party outside.

Lillia tentatively reached for Mahtsar's magic, scanning the pedestrians and rooftops.

"A necromancer," Raesra asked, "How can you be sure?"

"Black eyes, cracked skin, shrouded in dark magic." Markus paused. "I know where all this comes from, the whole reason she's doing this. And I know how to stop it. But you can't let her kill me."

"Fine," Logane said after a long breath. "One thousand gold marks. That's our price to protect you from a necromancer."

Lillia's eyes widened. They were going to have to fight this woman. It would be nothing like Adina. Adina hadn't known how to fight before becoming a necromancer. This woman was an assassin. She would be unstoppable.

"Deal." Markus didn't hesitate.

"First step is we get you out of the city," Logane ordered. "Lillia, you're the softest target, you'll be in the middle with our VIP. Bahn, you're on left, Raesra right, Zaktan front and I'll take rear. We're escorting him through the south gate."

Raesra pushed Lillia into formation. She gripped Lillia's hand for reassurance, then tightened the straps securing her shield and drew her morning star. Runes along its handle glowed the moment she touched it. Logane and Zaktan both drew their weapons as well. And they marched.

Lillia's heart roared nearly as fast as she imagined Markus's was. She was nearly sprinting to keep up with their momentum. The pleasant air still stung her fatigued lungs. She wasn't going to be able to keep this pace.

She heard Raesra chant something beside her before tapping her shoulder with the butt of her weapon. Breath surged into Lillia's lungs. Her muscles, no longer burning, sang with newfound strength.

They crossed streets and alleys, and dove through crowds that parted for the charging phalanx.

"Turn Right!" Zaktan commanded.

Lillia barely registered the command before Logane pushed her in the correct direction. Bahn almost missed the turn. Lillia looked behind to see an arrow stick into the wall of a building. They were under attack. Lillia missed Ayela even more now, wishing they had an archer to counter their attacker.

Lillia searched the rooftops. She stumbled on an uneven stone only for Bahn to catch her and pull her back into position. Lillia bit her lip, eyes darting, chasing every shadow. She was useless. Overtired, unable to react, unable to even see what was happening. But they weren't leaving her.

A city guardsman rounded a corner up ahead. His eyes bulged at seeing their armed and advancing party. He fumbled for his weapon and stumbled back, falling to the ground as they passed.

They turned again before landing on the main road. A straight shot to the city gates more than a mile away. They pushed their way through crowds, avoided carts, and stopped for nothing.

Lightning cracked the sky in a blinding white flash. Ahead of them, a horse drawing a cargo wagon collapsed, the contents spilled over the road. Screams echoed from behind them.

"About Face!" Logane ordered.

Zaktan spun on his heels and pushed past Lillia, taking position beside Logane and Raesra in front of Lillia and Markus.

Walking toward the party, parting the sea of fleeing civilians, was a woman dressed entirely in black with red ribbons flowing from her shoulders. A mask covered her hooded face, and thick leather armor covered most of her skin. The little skin that was visible was deathly white. Cracks of midnight black webbed over her neck. An aura of dark mist dripped from her being, bleeding into the cobblestone beneath her.

"Give him to me, and you live," the woman's voice echoed both in Lillia's mind and ears. "Fight, and you die with him."

"The only one who will die today is you." Raesra leveled her mace at the necromancer.

"Mamana shehl'ore," Lillia muttered, reaching for Mahtsar's magic. She thrust the tip of her staff between her protectors. "Laruthah!"

But the necromancer vanished in a cloud of black smoke that parted for Lillia's beam of light. "Dai," Lillia rushed to cut off the magic, conserving her energy.

The Moonborn was gone.

A whiff of air sounded behind Lillia. Raesra spun, throwing Lillia to the ground as the strike of steel on steel rang through the air. Raesra stood where Lillia had, shield firmly held between herself and the necromancer.

Raesra swung for the necromancer, disturbing another cloud of black smoke when the Moonborn vanished.

"Back to back," Raesra shouted, and they took formation around Markus and Lillia. Tense and readying their weapons, they fell silent.

Shadow stepping, Lillia's eyes widened in realization. She'd read about this ability in the books her father had sent. This necromancer was crossing in and out of the veil.

Lillia flinched when the necromancer again appeared, this time in front of Zaktan. Her dagger deflected off his breastplate before he countered, catching only black smoke with his blade.

Lillia needed a spell that would strengthen the veil. She needed to build a stronger barrier that would stop her ability. Lillia closed her eyes, constructing the words and organizing her thoughts. She flinched at another failed attack. This was a war of attrition; they would lose if she didn't act quickly. Necromancers couldn't tire. They only grew more powerful, more erratic with each spell they cast. There was no choice, she prayed to Mahtsar that she was not about to overcast.

Lillia knelt on the ground and leaned on her staff for support. This was going to make her dizzy, the last thing she needed was to fall. Her sweaty palms slipped over the smooth wood of her staff as she gripped tighter. Lillia imagined her will projected in a sphere around the party. Her heart raced, if this worked, she'd likely be the first to attempt such a spell. If not...

"Mamana shehl'lahee," Lillia chanted under her breath, the last thing she needed was the necromancer overhearing and countering her spell. "Chizel ha'leer shehl'lahee ve'maveht."

Energy surged through Lillia, more than she'd ever held. Her hands burned as though gripping a hot iron. A shimmering, unstable sphere of light flickered above her now glowing staff.

"Chizel ha'leer shehl'lahee ve'maveht!" She again chanted and willed the sphere larger.

Numbness surged from her fingertips to her elbows, creeping up her arms. She felt herself leaning to the side, then Bahn steadied her.

With a puff of air and the assassin appeared Infront of Lillia, dagger poised to strike. Markus screamed, falling backward. Bahn kicked over Lillia's head, striking the necromancer in the chest and pushing her out of their protective circle, where she vanished in a puff of black smoke.

The orb expanded, enveloping the party and the nearby area.

The signature whiff of air revealed the necromancer in front of Raesra. But the Moonborn didn't strike. Her eyes flitted, and her weapon fell to the ground.

"Nalah!" Raesra screamed and struck the Moonborn in the chest with her glowing morning star.

There was a flash of light, and the Moonborn flew back through the air, crashing into the toppled cart. Not moving.

White light crept into the edges of Lillia's vision, and she ended the spell. Her grip loosened, and the staff clattered to the ground. She could not feel her limp arms. Her head lulled to the side to compensate for the dizziness. She'd come close. Too close. But she hadn't overcast.

Raesra approached the unconscious necromancer, ready to deliver the killing blow.

Lillia closed her eyes, head nodding to unconsciousness before she jolted awake.

Raesra was standing above the necromancer, hands up, weapon on the ground. At her throat was a floating sword, nearly as long as Raesra was tall, and broader than her thigh. A man walked into Lillia's vision. Gold pauldrons, a mantle of crow's feathers.

He spoke, but his words were distorted, distant. Lillia nodded once more when the man turned to her. She woke to his gentle hand lifting her chin. He was the Moonborn; she recognized the crow's feet tattoos under his eye.

Lillia's ears rang, unable to make out what he said. He produced a coin from his jacket pocket. It was black and had a raven's head on it. The man pressed the coin into Lillia's palm, then walked back to Raesra, who no longer stood at sword point. Her weapon was sheathed.

Lillia's vision went black. She felt firm hands lift her. Then, nothing.

Lillia was moving, being carried. Her eyes opened to see cobblestone beneath her. She could hear the casual voices of the crowd as they passed.

"She's awake," Raesra said, causing whoever was carrying her to stop.

"Can you walk," Logane asked before gently setting her down.

Surprisingly, Lillia's wobbly legs held. "I think so," Lillia muttered through the pounding in her head.

"What the hell were you thinking?" Zaktan demanded.

Lillia scowled. Confused as she was, Lillia knew she deserved better than that response. "I just saved your ass. A thank you would be nice." Lillia massaged her temples.

"And you'd have gotten all of us killed if you'd overcast," Logane lectured, stretching his neck and shoulders.

"But I didn't." Lillia stumbled, momentarily losing her balance, only for Raesra to catch her.

"You crafted that spell in the moment, didn't you?" Raesra asked with a smile. "Sleep deprived, fatigued from haste, through adrenaline, and in the middle of a fight, you crafted a spell powerful enough to stun a full-blooded necromancer, without overcasting."

"I mean..." Logane's tone shifted considerably. "It was..."

"Unbelievable." Zaktan finished Logane's thought.

"Remarkable," Raesra corrected. "You are brilliant, and lucky."

"You need rest, badly. You are staying at The Headless Snake tonight." Logane demanded.

Lillia didn't have the strength to fight. The desire to see Ayela nagged at her. But the idea of a soft bed was intoxicating. Raesra was right. She needed sleep. "Okay." She managed, leaning on Bahn, who offered her an arm as they resumed their walk home.

"Who was the guy?" Lillia's speech slurred.

"Crow. Leader of The Nighthawks." Logane stated it like it was some mundane fact. Lillia blinked and shook her head.

With each step, her mind grew a little clearer. Zethrid, that had been his name. And her father had known him. "How are you all so calm?"

"Calm?" Raesra laughed.

"Should have seen them arguing while you were out," Bahn said. "You impressed Crow so much he gave you a gift. Remember that part?"

"One favor to be cashed in by you at any point in the future," Zaktan grumbled. Lillia scrunched her eyebrows. Was that jealousy in his voice?

"Why was he even there," Lillia asked.

"Alana, the necromancer. She was his, I don't know, adopted daughter or something." Zaktan shrugged. "Apparently, he'd been trying to catch and stop her."

"So, Alana is dead then," Lillia asked.

"No." Raesra's tone soured. "Crow demanded we let him take her. He said he had a solution that would save her. And we are nowhere near capable of standing against him, so we had to let her go."

A solution for a necromancer that didn't end in their death? Lillia's head ached worse for imagining the possibilities and risks that posed. "But that doesn't make sense."

"We'll talk more about it all tomorrow. For now. You are going to sleep," Logane ordered as they reached The Headless Snake. "And I will not accept no for an answer."

Lillia drug herself up the stairs to one of the beds in an unfinished room. She didn't bother to close the door, just fell into the bed and allowed the tidal wave of sleep to overcome her.

Lillia woke from a dreamless sleep to the sun beating in through the newly furnished windows. She yawned and stretched. Glad that, for once, her body didn't ache. Lillia looked to her side, where she'd grown accustomed to seeing Ayela's body when she woke. But she was at The Headless Snake, not the temple.

Lillia stood, and her sweat-stiff clothes cracked under her. She recalled the day before. Her hand slipped into her pocket, where the large copper coin still rested. She ran a finger over the crow's head. Just how had she impressed someone so powerful? All she'd done was nearly get his daughter killed. Or perhaps he recognized her, maybe it all amounted to nepotism. Maybe if she hadn't been Lillia Kote, he'd have killed their party. She shuddered at the thought before thinking about the spell she'd cast.

"I actually did it." Lillia smiled. "I made a brand-new spell." She attempted to recite the words, experimenting with several versions. She was unsure exactly how she'd managed to phrase it before. No matter, she'd figure it out. She'd done it once; she could do it again.

Her smile faded at how irate her father would be if he learned she nearly overcast. Or maybe he already knew.

Ayela would have been proud of her... would be proud of her.

But that didn't matter right now. Right now, she needed a bath. And after the bathhouse, she would visit Ayela. Tears threatened her eyes when she realized her friend was nearing the one-month mark. Just one week left, and she showed no signs of improving. Lillia didn't want to imagine what would happen if Ayela didn't come back. She couldn't allow herself to imagine it. But it looked more and more like the harsh reality that awaited her.

"Mahtsar, please. Bring her back to me." Lillia stuffed the coin back into her pocket and headed for the door while wiping the tears she refused to let fall.

21

Death

"I'm sorry, Lillia." Raesra's voice was heavy, her words reluctant.

No, Lillia would not listen to this. Her fists clenched at her side. Lillia focused on her breathing; in, out. Her lip quivered.

"The temple has done everything they can." Raesra grabbed Lillia's hands with care, lifting them between the two. "Everyone else has said their goodbyes. Ayela isn't likely to last the night. You need…"

"Stop!" Lillia interjected, tears flowing. She couldn't accept it. Couldn't believe the month they allotted Ayela had come and gone. She was in the room behind Raesra, living, breathing. But not actually there. Ayela wouldn't leave Lillia alone. She just wouldn't

"Just…" Lillia lost her words.

"I'll give you some time, Lillia. But the head priest has already ordered us to stop support. It is time to say goodbye." Raesra pulled Lillia into a hug that Lillia didn't return.

Lillia's thoughts halted. Tears flowed, but she held back sobs. She just hung there in Raesra's arms. Limp. This wasn't happening. Couldn't be happening. If she only had a little more time, she could find a way.

Raesra released Lillia and stepped back, opening the door to Ayela's chambers. Inside, the tomb was dark and musty. Lillia's bedding had been moved out.

Lillia sniffled, set her jaw, and walked past Raesra and into the room.

"When you are ready, find me in the chapel. We'll talk about what comes next." Raesra said, her own voice quivering before she closed the door. Leaving Lillia in silence.

Lillia stood there for some time. Not moving, not thinking. Just watching the closed door.

"Damnit, Mahtsar!" Lillia cursed the goddess that had abandoned her. Lillia's shoulders trembled as tears fell anew. She didn't understand, this wasn't supposed to happen.

The others were ready for this. They had been preparing themselves for days now. But not Lillia. She'd clung onto hope, every thread she could find, and they'd been precious few. She had prayed and fasted for endless days. But every lead had run cold. There was no way for her to save Ayela. She had failed, again. She had offered prayers to all the gods but one. And none had answered. Now, part of her wished Erithia was here to extend an offer as they had done for Ayela.

She looked at the soon-to-be corpse of her friend. Ayela was hardly recognizable, little more than skin and bones with narrow, corded muscle. Her chest rose and fell with nearly imperceptible movements. Ayela's face was shrewd; the shape of her skull was visible beneath her skin. Ayela's baggy robes clung to her body, silhouetting her ribs and hips. There was practically nothing left of her.

Lillia fell back against the wall and pulled her knees into her chest. She didn't want a world without Ayela. She already had to face it once, and it had nearly broken her. Now somehow, this was so much worse. She lowered her head to her knees. Lillia's sobs came through shallow, ragged breaths as her tears soaked the fabric over her knees.

Eventually, her river of tears turned to dry sobs and the ache in her chest dulled, returning to the numbness she'd felt for days. But she didn't move. She didn't look at Ayela or any other part of the room. Maybe if she waited long enough, it would change things. Maybe Ayela would come back.

There was a knock at the door.

Lillia didn't answer, didn't move.

The door opened.

"Sister Kote." It was the high priest. The one that had been there when they first brought in Ayela.

Lillia looked up, rubbing at her puffy eyes and wiping away the tears.

"May I sit with you," the priest asked.

Lillia nodded, and the priest pulled a stool in from outside. He then grabbed another.

"I understand you follow the Mahtsarian faith," the priest said, his voice caring but calm. "So, you know what awaits Ayela?"

"I do," Lillia said.

"Do you know the final prayer?"

"Yes," Lillia answered.

"Would you like to say it?" The priest motioned for Lillia to sit on the stool he placed at the head of Ayela's bed.

Lillia's throat tightened. She drew in a long breath before standing and walking the few eternally distant steps to Ayela. She sat on the chair.

Lillia had studied the prayer, as she had many other Mahtsarian rituals. But she'd only ever heard it once: the day her father prayed for her mother. Lillia didn't know what came after this moment. But it didn't matter. Nothing did. She was saying goodbye to Ayela. Closing the door to hope, to happiness. She would never see Ayela's smile again. She was never again going to hear her laugh. They would never read another book together. Lillia was going to have to live their dream, alone. This was all she would have. The last moment, the last memory of her friend. Lillia wondered which of the gods Ayela was being ferried to. Perhaps Musar, she had always worshiped Musar.

Still more tears welled, a reprieve from her dry and burning eyes.

"When you are ready, begin. I will fill in or correct you if needed."

Lillia placed a hand on Ayela's dry, cold forehead and took a breath before closing her eyes. "Erithia," Lillia began. She imagined the room's temperature dropping several degrees. "Lord of the Dead, we beg..."

"Beseech," the priest corrected.

"We beseech thee. Before you lies Ayela. A soul soon to travel your domain. We pray, oh Lord of Desire, that your servants will ferry her soul to the god she most desires. That she may..." Lillia's throat closed, her shoulders trembled. "That she... that she..."

"That she may not be reduced but ascended." The priest continued, placing a comforting hand on Lillia's back while she sobbed. "That you will not suffer her soul to wander and whither in your eternal planes."

"Amen," Lillia whispered in harmony with the priest. Her shoulders slumped as she bent forward, placing a single kiss on Ayela's forehead. "Goodbye, Ayela." Everything in Lillia's mind fell away. Her chest ached, throat clenched. Breathing was impossible. But there were no more tears to cry. She lay there, her forehead gently resting on Ayela's.

Lillia startled, eyes wide at hearing a sharp intake of breath beneath her. Warmth surged across Ayela's forehead. Lillia jolted back, eyes wide, chest clenching. Her heart latched onto the final thread of hope and pulled.

Ayela's bloodshot eyes found Lillia's. Then her voice rasped at barely more than a dry whisper. "Lillia? Is this… they sent me back?"

To Be Continued…

The following text is a sample of book two. It is subject to change, but should remain mostly as seen.

01

The Witness

Ayela fell through darkness too palpable to be real. Below her, a dark cityscape ascended with terrible speed. She crashed against the pavement with what should have been excruciating force. Yet, Ayela felt nothing. She rose on unsteady legs. Above her, three impossibly large full moons dominated the sky and bathed the city in desaturated light. The buildings of the city closed in around her, with angles and corners that defied perspective. Despite their alien presence, a sense of familiarity purveyed across their organization. All surfaces lacked detail that should have been plain to see. The surfaces appeared smooth, like glass or dull metal.

She stood, for a time, in total stillness. No sound greeted her, not even that of her own breath. She took a step forward, and her foot clattered against the stone. A note that echoed eternally around her. Still, she felt nothing. She took another step, as the sound of the first finally faded, only for its disproportionate resonance to again envelop her.

Two more steps and she grew numb to the sound. So, she walked, wondering around corners and encroaching walls.

Shadows of buildings rested in conflicting angles that matched no available light source.

She meandered forward, following her whim at each intersection in search of a way out. As she walked, shadows followed. Their pursuit grew increasingly aggressive with each corner she turned. The distinct sounds of battle echoed as faint whispers from the insistent shadows. Metal clanged against metal, screams of dying men, the thuds of bodies hitting the ground and the squelch of blade hitting flesh. The chorus grew into a cacophony as Ayela ran through the streets, fleeing the menacing shadows.

Then she rounded the last corner in the labyrinth. Ahead of her was the body of a woman with a slashed abdomen and an arrow in her shoulder. Ayela did not recognize this woman. Yet, her knees fell out from under her and anguish bled from her sobbing throat. A scream that drowned out the symphony of war.

The woman's face featured intricate details that startlingly contrasted with the vague surroundings. The woman had

startling blue eyes under messy brown hair, a slightly curved nose and plump red lips, a pointed chin and fine jawline. Cries not her own pulled Ayela away. Lying next to the body was a baby, wrapped in swaddling clothes. Compulsion guided her as Ayela collected the baby and tried to run.

"Oh, Ayela." The familiar voice froze Ayela in her tracks. She turned, seeing Adina. Then, all was black, and she was again falling

Glossary of The Divine Language

Verbs:

    Chizel - Strengthen

    Dai - Stop

    Lahshiv - Quit

    Laruthah - Beam

    Lehlahlel - Harm

    Lehtahlen - Mend

    Loshek - Darkness

    Shafat - Judge

    Nalah - Smite

Prepositions:

    Beh - With

    Ha' - The

    Le' - For

    Shehl' - Of

    Ve' - And

Nouns:

    Aish - Fire

    Bawsawr - Flesh

    Malom - Sanctuary

    Mamanah - Gift

    Ma'avah - Desire

    Muhava - Nature

    Mishmat - Diciplined

    Mayeem - Water

    Maveht - Death

    Mezeen - Nutrient

    Nehfesh - Soul

    Nilud - Bone

    Ore - Light

    Roee - Sight

    Saeef - Veil

    Serah - Storm

    Zedecl - Justice

Afterword

Thank you for reading. I hope you enjoyed Rise of The Witnesses enough to look forward to the rest of Lillia and Ayela's story. This is First Installment of The Chronicle's of Divinity's Blight. The second book, Fall of A Witness, and the third book, Accension of The Witness, will all follow Ayela and Lillia as the protagonists.

But even these three books will not spell the end of this series. Currently, there are plans to publish at least 18 books in this series. Most of which are untitled as of now. The series will be released as multiple trilogies with each one following the journey of a separate protagonist. You will be taken through the lives of a diverse cast, from noblemen to soldiers. From wizards lusting for power to love-bound dragons and dragon riders.

This world is teaming with near limitless stories to tell. All of which are born from countless hours of Dungeons and Dragons games played with friends and family.

If you enjoyed this novel, and are a fan of Dungeons and Dragons, consider picking up the module that inspired this novel, Chronicles of Divinity's Blight - Installment 1, when it releases.

About The Author

A Texas kid with a wild imagination and a love for all things fantasy, Elias has always been a bit out of touch with reality. He always harbored a fascination with the dark, fantastical worlds created by many fiction authors, but it was dragons and the worlds they inhabited that dominated his imagination. As Elias grew older, it was no longer enough to experience the worlds created by others. He needed to create his own. So his journey to becoming an author began in 2008.

Emboldened by a discovered talent and determined to hone his craft, Elias devoured many books and whatever advice was offered. But it was the author Jenna Moreci and her YouTube channel that helped take his writing to the next level.

For over a decade now, Elias has been writing dark fantasy stories in the fantastical world of Albrene. But in 2019, Elias wrote Blight of Divinity, a Dungeons and Dragons campaign, for his college friends to play together. This campaign, set in Albrene, soon took on a life of its own, expanding far beyond what was initially written. Now, seven drafts later, Rise of The Witnesses, the first book in the Chronicles of Divinity's Blight series, is almost complete. And thanks to the campaign and the invaluable input of his players, there is a wealth of material waiting to be written in the many planned sequels and stories to come.

To stay up to date with future releases, visit eliasfenic.com/landing to sign up for my newsletter. Or look for me on social media @eliasfenic.

www.ingramcontent.com/pod-product-compliance
Lightning Source LLC
LaVergne TN
LVHW091709070526
838199LV00050B/2316